CHERUB
™

Robert Muchamore was born in 1972 and spent thirteen years working as a private investigator. *CHERUB: Mad Dogs* is his eighth novel.

The CHERUB series has won numerous awards, including the 2005 Red House Children's Book Award. For more information on Robert and his work, visit **www.muchamore.com**.

Praise for the CHERUB series:
'If you can't bear to read another story about elves, princesses or spoiled rich kids who never go to the toilet, try this. You won't regret it.' *The Ultimate Teen Book Guide*

'My sixteen-year-old son read *The Recruit* in one sitting, then went out the next day and got the sequel.' Sophie Smiley, teacher and children's author

'So good I forced my friends to read it, and they're glad I did!' Helen, age 14

'CHERUB is the first book I ever read cover to cover. It was amazing.' Scott, age 13

'The best book ever.' Madeline, age 12

'CHERUB is a must for Alex Rider lovers.' Travis, age 14

BY ROBERT MUCHAMORE

The Henderson's Boys series:

1. The Escape
2. Eagle Day
3. Secret Army
coming spring 2010

The CHERUB series:

1. The Recruit
2. Class A
3. Maximum Security
4. The Killing
5. Divine Madness
6. Man vs Beast
7. The Fall
8. Mad Dogs
9. The Sleepwalker
10. The General
11. Brigands M.C.

Look out for CHERUB: Shadow Wave
coming late 2010

MAD DOGS
Robert Muchamore

*Hodder
Children's
Books*

A division of Hachette Children's Books

A Catalogue record for this book is available
from the British Library

ISBN 978 0 340 91171 6

Typeset in Goudy by Avon DataSet Ltd,
Bidford-on-Avon, Warwickshire

Printed in the UK by CPI Bookmarque, Croydon, CR0 4TD

The paper and board used in this paperback by
Hodder Children's Books are natural recyclable products
made from wood grown in sustainable forests.
The manufacturing processes conform to the
environmental regulations of the country of origin.

Hodder Children's Books
a division of Hachette Children's Books
338 Euston Road, London NW1 3BH
An Hachette UK company
www.hachette.co.uk

WHAT IS CHERUB?

CHERUB is a branch of British Intelligence. Its agents are aged between 10 and 17 years. Cherubs are mainly orphans who have been taken out of care homes and trained to work undercover. They live on CHERUB campus, a secret facility hidden in the English countryside.

WHAT USE ARE KIDS AS INTELLIGENCE AGENTS?

Quite a lot. Nobody realises kids do undercover missions, which means they can get away with all kinds of stuff that adults can't.

WHO ARE THEY?

About three hundred children live on CHERUB campus. JAMES ADAMS is our fifteen-year-old hero. He's a well-respected CHERUB agent with several successful missions under his belt. Australian-born Dana Smith is James' girlfriend. His other close friends include BRUCE NORRIS and KYLE BLUEMAN.

James' sister, LAUREN ADAMS, is twelve and already regarded as an outstanding CHERUB agent. Her best friends are BETHANY PARKER and GREG 'RAT' RATHBONE.

CHERUB STAFF

With its large grounds, specialist training facilities and combined role as a boarding school and intelligence operation, CHERUB actually has more staff than pupils. They range from cooks and gardeners to teachers, training instructors, nurses, psychiatrists and mission specialists. CHERUB is run by its chairwoman, Zara Asker.

CHERUB T-SHIRTS

Cherubs are ranked according to the colour of the T-shirts they wear on campus. ORANGE is for visitors. RED is for kids who live on CHERUB campus but are too young to qualify as agents (the minimum age is ten). BLUE is for kids undergoing CHERUB's tough 100-day basic training regime. A GREY T-shirt means you're qualified for missions. NAVY is a reward for outstanding performance on a single mission. Lauren and James wear the BLACK T-shirt, the ultimate recognition for outstanding achievement over a number of missions. When you retire, you get the WHITE T-shirt, which is also worn by some staff.

1. HERCULES

Even by aircraft standards the toilet inside a C5 transport plane is cramped. James Adams had a shoulder touching the plastic wall on either side of him as he leaned over the steel bowl, looking at flecks of his lunch in the disinfectant-blue water.

His girlfriend Dana Smith yelled from outside. 'Are you OK?'

James had pressed the flush and didn't hear her voice over the roaring turboprop engines as his puke got sucked away. He stood up and turned to face himself in the mirror. He'd spent the last eight days camped out in the Malaysian jungle and despite regular applications of sun block, his skin was peeling.

'James,' Dana repeated, this time banging the door to make sure she got his attention.

'I'll be out in a sec.'

There were no paper cups in the dispenser, so James washed the bitter taste from his mouth by dribbling water into the palm of his hand and sucking it dry.

'Did I just hear you throwing up?'

He gargled and spat out the water before answering. 'Must have been those nasty hotdogs we had at lunchtime . . .'

But it had nothing to do with lunch and Dana knew it. 'You'll do OK, James,' she said soothingly.

James dried his hands by wiping them on his camouflage trousers and had to duck under the door frame as he stepped out into the cavernous interior of the aircraft. His hands were trembling and he couldn't help thinking he'd be visiting the toilet again soon.

'I never realised you were scared of heights,' Dana grinned, as she put a grubby hand on the back of his neck and kissed him on the cheek.

'I'm *not*,' James said defensively. 'Heights I can handle, but jumping out of an aeroplane is *slightly* different.'

'I'm surprised you've been a cherub for so long without doing a jump. I did one in basic training. Come to think of it, I did a couple before then; when I was a red-shirt.'

'I don't think I can do this,' James said warily, as they set off on an unsteady walk through the giant cargo bay. The turbulence did his stomach no favours as they clanked across the corrugated metal floor, heading away from the cockpit.

The Hercules C5 is a dual-role aircraft. For cargo operations the interior can be loaded with anything from United Nations food parcels to Challenger tanks. When the Parachute Regiment comes to town, rows of seats are bolted to the floor and the side doors can deploy a company of paratroops in ninety seconds.

This mission wouldn't stretch the aircraft's capacity: only twelve bodies would make the jump. Eight were ten- to twelve-year-olds nearing the end of CHERUB's 100-day basic training course. James and Dana were senior CHERUB agents and the final jumpers were adult instructors.

Mr Pike was the head training instructor. He was tough but fair and James respected him a great deal. He wasn't so sure about Mr Kazakov who'd been appointed less than a month earlier. He was a bully who James had got to know rather too well after sharing his tent for the past seven nights.

Like all CHERUB instructors, Kazakov was physically imposing. He was Ukrainian by birth with a dusting of cropped grey hair and a facial scar worthy of an action figure. After serving with the Spetznatz – the Russian special forces – and seeing combat during the invasion of Afghanistan, Kazakov had spent ten years training SAS soldiers in guerrilla combat techniques, before making the move to CHERUB.

'What are you lovebirds playing at?' Mr Pike roared, giving James and Dana the evil eye as he pointed at the drop clock. This bright LED display hung over the door at one side of the aircraft and indicated that there were only one hundred and eighty-six seconds until they were over the landing zone.

'He's crapping himself,' Dana explained.

Mr Pike shook his head. 'I can't believe you've never made a drop.'

'Don't you start . . .' James said, feeling even more anxious as he realised that trainees half his size already had parachutes on their backs and equipment packs strapped to their chests. Some of them were so small that they could barely see over the bed rolls on top of their packs.

Mr Kazakov was inspecting each trainee in turn: checking helmets, tightening harnesses and screaming abuse when they got something wrong. Right now he was dealing with ten-year-old Kevin Sumner. Ironically, James had helped Kevin get over his fear of heights a few months earlier.

'What's this, *Sumner?*' Kazakov spat, as he noticed a metal spork bulging through the fabric of the pack strapped to Kevin's chest. Kazakov unbuckled the pack, ripped out the metal object and wagged it in the boy's face. 'I *told* you to wrap sharp items inside something soft. Do you want to land on that? Do you want to find yourself with a spork sticking out of your chest on an island beach an hour's boat ride from the nearest emergency room?'

James hooked his parachute over his back as Kevin said, 'No sir,' guiltily.

'No time to repack,' Kazakov yelled, before sending the spork clattering across the aircraft and launching a volley of Russian swear words. 'You're not getting that back. You'll remember your lesson every time you have to eat with your fingers.'

Unlike the trainees, James didn't have equipment to contend with because the instructors' stuff was being delivered by boat.

'A hundred and twenty seconds,' Mr Pike shouted. 'Start hooking up, people.'

As Dana whispered something in Mr Pike's ear, the eight trainees formed a line and began clipping hooks – known as strops – between the back of their parachutes and a taut metal cable above their heads. The youngsters would be making a static line jump, meaning that a pull on the strop would open their chutes automatically once they were clear of the aircraft.

As the countdown dropped below one hundred seconds, Mr Kazakov and Dana both started walking towards James, who'd strapped on his helmet but was still struggling to fit his parachute harness.

'Come on,' Kazakov said, showering James with spit. 'You're *useless*; you're supposed to be helping out with the little ones.'

Kazakov grabbed the harness of James' parachute and yanked the straps so tightly that James' shoulders squeezed together. His stomach churned as the giant Russian eyeballed him.

'I can't do this,' James said weakly. 'I've psyched myself out.'

Dana interrupted. 'Mr Kazakov, I spoke to Pike about James and he's changed the drop order. I'll jump last and James second to last so that I can give him some encouragement if his nerves get to him.'

Kazakov glowered at James. 'I don't share my tent with cowards. You make that jump or tonight you sleep outside with the spiders and snakes.'

'I'm not a trainee you know,' James said indignantly. 'You can't boss me around.'

'You're jumping sixth now,' Dana said, diplomatically pointing Kazakov towards the trainees by the door. 'I'll sort James out. You'd better go hook up.'

A warning buzzer sounded as Mr Pike began opening the aircraft door, flooding the gloomy metal tube with sunlight. The numbers on the clock began to flash as the count dropped below sixty seconds.

'I feel like such a dick,' James confessed, as he looked

across at the trainees. 'Some of them are ten years old.'

'Focus,' Dana said firmly as their gloved fingers interlocked. 'You've been trained for this. Now take deep breaths and stay calm.'

'Hook up, you two,' Mr Pike shouted, from beside the door. 'Eighteen seconds.'

James fought a spasm in his gut as Dana dragged him towards the trainees lined up against the fuselage. None of them looked happy, but none had worked themselves into as much of a state as James.

'Good luck, kids,' Kazakov shouted. 'Remember: three elephants, check canopy and steer *gently* if you drift close to another jumper.'

James and Dana hooked their strops on to the cable, as an announcement loud enough to be heard in a war zone blasted out of a speaker beside them.

'This is the co-pilot speaking. Navigation confirms we are in location. Winds are nine knots north easterly, giving us a drop-zone window of fifty-eight seconds on my mark.'

James looked over the helmets of the trainees as the countdown clock flashed triple zero. There was an eleven-year-old boy less than twenty centimetres ahead and Dana right behind with a reassuring glove on his shoulder, but he felt isolated.

Part of him wanted to fling the chute off his back and go spew in the toilet, while another was acutely aware of how much abuse he'd get back on campus if he did. And if he could master his nerves, he'd be down in under two minutes.

'Mark,' the co-pilot announced.

The drop clock changed from red to green as Mr Pike began yelling, 'Go, go, go.'

To ensure that as many people as possible made the drop smoothly, the most confident trainees – mainly ones who'd jumped when they were red-shirts – were lined up first. As soon as the first trainee was out the next had to stand with their toes overhanging the door. After waiting in a crouching position for the two seconds it took the previous jumper to clear the aircraft, it was their turn to leap.

The gap of less than four seconds between jumps turned the queue into a slow walk. Every time someone lined up in the doorway, James hoped they'd mess up so that they'd be out of the drop zone before his turn came around. But each trainee had invested ninety-six gruelling days into qualifying as a CHERUB agent. Bruised, hungry and exhausted, they'd put in too much to let fear get the better of them now.

So James found himself in the doorway, buffeted by freezing air and sunlight with his strop hooked to the cable above his head. With the drop zone closing in twenty-two seconds, he crouched and felt extremely dizzy as he looked down. They were below cloud cover and the orange chute of the previous jumper was unravelling, high above seven kilometres of golden sand.

'Move your arse, James,' Mr Pike yelled impatiently. 'Seventeen seconds. Go!'

He was locked to the spot. He felt like he was going to shit and puke at the same time and made a lunge for the handle on the side of the door. But before he got a grip, Dana batted his hand away and slammed her palm into the back of his chute, tipping him forward.

'Chicken,' she sneered, exchanging smiles with Mr Pike as she took James' place in the doorway.

James found himself falling face first towards the beach. The reality of this was more than his brain could comprehend. His trousers billowed, air tore beneath his helmet, making his chin strap dig into his neck. It was awful and wonderful. Out of every moment of James' life, freefalling five hundred metres above ground was the wildest.

The shock of being pushed meant that he'd forgotten to count three elephants, but the jump training he'd received the previous day kicked in when he felt a tiny jolt as the line connecting him to the aircraft went taut and ripped open his chute before snapping away.

'Check canopy,' James shouted.

His first upward glance only earned him a face full of sunlight, but two seconds later the sun was filtered through a billowing mushroom of orange nylon. If it hadn't opened he would have had less than five seconds to deploy his reserve chute, but it seemed OK so he followed his training and shouted the next order.

'Make space.'

The brilliant sunshine turned the beach below into white glare, but he looked down and was reassured to see the previous jumper hundreds of metres away. You couldn't look up through the canopy, so the rule was that you only worried about people below you.

'Check drift,' James gasped, before looking down and realising that the ground was approaching rapidly.

The weather was calm and the landing zone huge so he didn't have to open his lift webs to correct his path. This was a huge relief, because you can't get a feel for steering a parachute while standing on the ground, and the most common cause of accidents for inexperienced jumpers is steering too violently before touchdown.

The final part of jump training had involved the landing: you're supposed to know which way the wind is blowing and get your feet in a safe position. If you get this wrong, you'll find yourself falling one way while the wind tugs your chute in another. Instead of crumpling, your body gets twisted in all directions.

So James was alarmed when he looked down and saw a crab the size of a dinner plate coming into focus. His mind was blank: he couldn't remember which way the wind was blowing, or even which way he was pointing.

All he could do was crumple and hope for the best.

2. WHITE

In the summer of 2004 a CHERUB mission was instrumental in bringing down the cocaine baron Keith Moore and his gang, known as KMG. For many years KMG imposed a kind of order on criminal activities over an area that stretched from the northern suburbs of London to Oxfordshire.

Although KMG only sold cocaine, the cash generated by this business enabled associates to diversify into other criminal activities, ranging from illegal raves to armed robbery. When more than a dozen of KMG's most senior figures were imprisoned, it created a power vacuum that gave rise to a bloody gang war.

There are at least five significant gangs operating in the territory once dominated by KMG. No single gang controls a significant area, but the most fearsome reputation belongs to the Luton-based Slasher Boys (so named because of their reputation for attacking enemies with machetes). The gang is believed to have approximately eighty members.

Slasher Boys are almost exclusively of Jamaican origin and the leaders are believed to be closely connected with Jamaican gangs who use their island as a stop-off point for illegal drugs travelling from South America . . .

. . . The mission to infiltrate and undermine the Slasher Boys will require two CHERUB agents of Afro-Caribbean appearance and has been categorised as HIGH risk . . .
(Excerpts from a mission briefing for Gabrielle O'Brien and Michael Hendry, January 2007.)

The Bedfordshire Halfway House was a residential home close to the centre of Luton, but everyone called it the Zoo. Built in the 1980s, it had been graffitied and trashed by several generations of freshly released young offenders and youths too troubled for foster homes.

To say that the Zoo had a bit of a reputation was like saying that getting run over by an eighteen-wheeled truck would give you a bit of a headache. It had seen every scandal going, from teen pregnancy to kids stabbing each other in the showers and two drunk girls almost killing a cyclist by lobbing a roof slate on to his head.

The Zoo knocked fifty thousand off the value of every house in the neighbourhood and the only reason it hadn't been shut down was the tide of objections that arose every time the council found a piece of land on which to build its replacement.

But despite two months living in the Zoo with a mattress that stank of god knows what and kids running riot 24/7, Gabrielle was happy. She'd turned fifteen at Christmas and fallen in love before New Year.

Michael Hendry was a navy-shirt CHERUB and Gabrielle's first proper boyfriend. They'd been going out for six months. At first it was kind of mechanical: going bowling, going to the cinema, going shopping and snogging in Michael's room afterwards. That's what Kerry and Gabrielle's other mates did with their boyfriends and she'd only joined them out of curiosity and the desire to fit in.

But it got more intense and they'd become one of the closest couples on CHERUB campus. Their friends felt excluded but the young lovers didn't care, and the isolation of being on mission together stoked things even further.

It was a Thursday, just gone ten. Most of the kids in the Zoo were supposed to be at school, but teachers are happy for kids like this to stay away and at least half of the dozen bedrooms on the third floor had someone who was suspended, excluded, or just couldn't be arsed to get out of bed.

Gabrielle's roommate Tisha was one of the few Zoo residents who did pack books into a bag and head for school. This suited Gabrielle, because it meant Michael could come up from the boys' floor and spend a couple of hours snuggled beneath her mauve duvet.

'Don't answer,' Michael begged, when Gabrielle's phone started ringing.

But she reached out blindly and grabbed her mobile from the vinyl floor. She expected it to be her mission controller, Chloe Blake, but was surprised by the name flashing on the display.

'It's Major Dee.'

Michael's dark torso was glazed with sweat as he sat up sharply. 'I've never known him bat an eyelid this side of lunchtime.'

'Major,' Gabrielle said, trowelling on her Jamaican twang. She'd become self-conscious and toned down her accent after joining CHERUB, but roots in the Caribbean were a big help on this mission and she'd found her old voice with surprising ease.

'Morning, sweet pea,' Major Dee said. 'Tell me what clothes you're wearing. What colour are your panties?'

Major Dee was the leader of the Slasher Boys: a big man with a line of gold teeth and a vicious reputation. In Dee's eyes, women stayed home to make food and babies. Gabrielle had to work ten times harder than Michael to prove herself and even now, Dee treated her with a lack of respect that would have earned any boy on CHERUB campus a mouthful of blood.

'My panties are *my* business,' Gabrielle said, making out like she thought his cheek was funny. 'If you're ringing me this early it better be some way to make bread.'

'I'll give you half a loaf,' the major said, which was his way of saying fifty pounds. 'Michael there?'

'In the flesh,' Gabrielle nodded.

'I've got a man who wants to buy a K bag. I want you two to dig one up in the park and bring it over.'

'You at home?'

'Yeah, but your man will be in the Green Pepper.'

Gabrielle was surprised by this instruction. The Green Pepper café was a hangout for dealers that frequently came under police surveillance. Small quantities of cocaine and marijuana got passed under tables, but high-ups like Major Dee only went there to talk trash and eat the best Jamaican food in Luton.

'You want me to take a kilo bag into the Green Pepper? Are you on a trip?'

Gabrielle heard Dee tut, then his temper snapped. 'Listen, *dumb* girl. You always trying to act like you're something and saying you want to make money. I don't want a hundred questions. You do this for me or I hang up and don't you bother showing your face no more.'

'OK, I'll pick it up,' Gabrielle said. 'I'm just saying that it's rank.'

'I know it's dodgy. That's why I want a girl for this. The cops don't have two brain cells to rub; they'll think you're somebody's bitch.'

'What's the brother look like?'

'What brother?'

Gabrielle groaned; Dee was high for sure. 'The guy I'm meeting. Unless you want me to hand a big bag of cocaine to the first random soul that comes my way.'

Major Dee didn't sound sure. 'Just get the bag to the Green Pepper. Someone will be expecting you.'

The call went dead and Gabrielle looked around at Michael.

'Pickup?' Michael asked.

Gabrielle nodded. 'But it's weird. He wants me to go into the Green Pepper with a whole K of coke.'

'Did you tell him that's insane?'

'He reckons the police won't suss me because I'm a girl . . . I mean, I know the police aren't genius IQ, but I think they can get their heads around the idea of a female drug dealer.'

'He's probably mashed,' Michael reasoned. 'Knowing Dee he's smoked about twenty joints and hasn't even been to bed yet.'

'If I get arrested it'll wreck the mission.'

Michael thought as Gabrielle pulled a T-shirt over her head. 'Here's what we do, Gab: we grab the coke from the park, but once you've got it you give Major Dee a call and say that there's a cop car circling around the Green Pepper and that you'll have to meet the dealer somewhere else. He won't want to risk losing a whole kilo of cocaine, no matter how stoned he is.'

'Sounds like a plan,' Gabrielle nodded, as she kissed Michael's shoulder and nuzzled his neck. 'But I don't like this one little bit.'

3. BEACH

James opened his eyes and saw the crab rear up and open its armoured pincers. But the bravado didn't last and it scuttled off towards a shallow pool. The ground was James' friend and he felt like hugging it, but he had to free the chute from his back before the wind caught hold.

He rolled on to his chest and was relieved to discover that nothing hurt as he looked along the plain of sand and caught a sight worthy of a soft-drink commercial: palm trees, blue sky and orange parachutes billowing in the warm breeze.

Dana had made a perfect landing three seconds after James and was jogging towards him. Parachute gear isn't exactly feminine, but she still looked good with long hair floating behind her.

'How's it going down there?' she smirked, as James pulled his chute off his shoulders and began to unbuckle his helmet.

He wasn't sure how to act. Dana was great and he didn't feel too bad now that he'd made the jump. But it's hard to ignore when your girlfriend shoves you out of an aeroplane.

'You . . .'

'Are you hurt or not?' Dana said bluntly, placing her hands on her hips.

'You should have seen the crab . . .' James smiled as he pointed towards the glistening pool.

'I saw you lying there; I thought you might be hurt.' As Dana spoke she edged in to peck James on the cheek, unsure how he'd react.

'Quite a buzz,' James shrugged, not sounding as cool as he'd hoped. 'I arsed up the landing, but I guess I wouldn't mind doing it again some time . . .'

'*Riiiiight*,' Dana smiled, as she stepped backwards. 'If you're OK I'll go pack up my chute.'

James grinned as he knelt on one knee in the sand and began gathering the waves of rustling fabric. He imagined himself fifty years in the future, an old dude surrounded by kids and grandkids, telling them about the day his wife shoved him out of an aeroplane . . .

Jumpers rolled their chutes at landing sites at hundred-metre intervals along the beach. When James' chute was half packed, the two-way radio in his trouser pocket made a double bleep.

'Yeah,' James said.

Mr Pike sounded like he was running. 'James, Dana, I'm down, but I've had a peek through my binoculars. I can see a chute a couple of hundred metres ahead of you and there's nothing going on beneath it. Leave your equipment and get over there.'

When James first looked around, all the chutes had been in a similar state. Now, one billowed conspicuously, tethered to the ground by the weight of the trainee wearing it.

As James set off, he was aware of Dana racing up behind him. She was a triathlete and by the time he was half-way towards the stricken jumper Dana had passed him in a blaze of flying sand.

The wind was light and Dana found a ten-year-old girl tangled in cords and nylon.

'Jo, sweetheart, what happened?'

James arrived as Dana peeled away the layers of fabric. At first Dana assumed that Jo McGowan was unconscious, but she was just in mild shock. James recoiled when he saw that Jo's boot was twisted at a weird angle. She'd clearly broken a bone.

'What happened?' Mr Pike puffed, as he stopped running beside James.

James kicked at a chunk of reinforced concrete lying on the sand. 'Looks like she hit this as she came down and turned over on her ankle.'

Mr Pike shook his head as he looked around at acres of level sand. 'We surveyed this beach,' he said bitterly. 'It's gotta be a million to one that you hit something.'

It looked as if Jo was fine apart from her ankle, but Dana didn't want to move the trainee until she was completely sure. She unfolded a toothed blade from her multi-tool and hacked the parachute harness away from the youngster's shoulders.

'Does it hurt anywhere else?' Dana asked.

Jo shook her head as she struggled to sit up. 'Maybe it's sprained,' she sniffed. 'Maybe I can walk it off.'

But Jo knew better when she saw the way her boot was pointing in the wrong direction. Jo was a sweet-faced girl with long black hair, but James had the misfortune to see the moment when her heart broke. After ninety-six days of training, she was devastated.

Jo was athletic, bright, a natural leader and as close as you ever get to a cert to pass basic training. But she'd been done in by debris washed up on the last tide and you're not allowed to resume basic training. When the ten-year-old recovered she'd have to restart from day one.

Dana gave Jo a tight hug and spoke comfortingly, reminding her that she was young and that nobody would blame her for failing, but Jo's future had just imploded and there was no consoling her.

Meanwhile, Mr Pike was burrowing into Jo's backpack, throwing equipment into the sand until he came across a red wallet containing a first-aid kit.

'We need to get that boot off before the ankle swells,' Mr Pike explained, as he slid out a syringe containing local anaesthetic. 'But that's gonna hurt, so I'll numb it off first.'

Although Jo's injury was serious, it was treatable. Mr Pike sounded much calmer now that he was getting a grip on things. He worked expertly, slicing a hole in the leg of Jo's padded jump suit before swabbing the patch of skin underneath with alcohol and telling her to look away before pushing the needle into her leg.

'It'll take a minute to go numb, but you'll be a lot more comfortable after that.'

Meanwhile, Mr Kazakov and the other trainees had folded their chutes up and were rushing over to see what was going on. The youngsters babbled about how bad it looked until Mr Pike lost patience with their noise.

'You all have orders and a rendezvous point for twenty-one hundred hours,' he shouted. 'Training doesn't stop just because one of you is injured. If you don't make it by twenty-two hundred you'll not be getting dinner, so I *strongly* suggest that you prepare your equipment and set off towards your first marker points.

'Mr Kazakov, organise the collection of the parachutes and jump clothing and stow it on the boat for the ride back to the mainland.'

As Dana continued to comfort Jo and Mr Pike began picking the lace out of her boot, all of the trainees except Kevin Sumner began peeling off their padded jump suits, revealing tanned skin and lightweight jungle clothing.

'Sumner, why are you standing there?' Mr Kazakov shouted, as he faced Kevin off. 'You're getting on my tits today. I can see you ending up with my boot up your backside.'

James wasn't comfortable with the way Kazakov picked on Kevin and leapt to his defence. 'Jo's his training partner,' James explained. 'Their briefings are in two languages and he can't do the mission alone because he can't understand Jo's instructions.'

Kazakov was inexperienced and looked confused, but Mr Pike quickly interrupted. 'Are you up for a jungle hike, James?'

No cherub in history had ever *wanted* to do a jungle hike, but the course had been designed for ten- to twelve-year-olds with heavy packs. James was fifteen and it would be well within his capabilities.

'I guess,' he said. 'But I'm not arsing around with some stupid briefing written in gobbledegook. I'm gonna fetch my GPS receiver off the boat and I want the coordinates.'

Mr Kazakov bristled. 'Kevin needs a challenge; it's not fair on the other trainees.'

James pointed at Jo. 'Since when was basic training ever fair? Or I tell you what, Kazakov, I'll stay here and pack up the parachute equipment and *you* can do the twenty-kilometre hike your way.'

The newly appointed instructor didn't like that suggestion one bit.

'Not keen?' James carped.

While James and Kazakov postured, Kevin stripped out his former training partner's pack. As well as grabbing all of Jo's rations, he took out some essential shared equipment and replaced his spork.

He eyed Jo guiltily as he worked. 'I feel like a vulture picking over your bones.'

Despite her pain, Jo managed an encouraging smile. 'You've got to carry on, Kev. I really hope you last out. You deserve your grey shirt.'

Kevin tried not to cry as he grabbed Jo's filthy hand and squeezed it tight. 'You don't deserve this; you've helped me out a million times. I wouldn't be here if—'

Mr Kazakov gave Kevin a shove in the back. 'Get a move on,' he growled. 'I want that jump suit before you cry all over it.'

'You'd better get ready, Kev,' Jo said. 'You'll be all right with James on the hike.'

James gave Kevin a sympathetic look. 'I've got to fill my canteen and put some equipment together for the hike,' he said. 'Finish saying your goodbyes and I'll meet you over by that sand dune in five minutes.'

As James turned away, he saw that the other three pairs of trainees were putting on sunscreen and stripping unnecessary weight from their packs in preparation for a four-hour hike in blistering heat.

His mind wandered as he jogged towards a wooden cargo boat. It had been moored at high tide and was now marooned, several hundred metres from the sea.

James hated school work and had agreed to help out the training department instead of doing extra GCSEs. The arrangement suited him, even if it didn't always make him fabulously popular with the youngsters he had to train. But he'd been working with the instructors for four months now and he'd slowly come to realise that he didn't have the ruthless streak that all good instructors needed.

As James stepped into the hull of the small motor launch and tried to find his day pack amidst cartons of equipment and tins of food, his eyes welled up as he pictured Jo and Kevin with their hands locked together and tears streaking down their cheeks.

4. PARK

Owen Campbell-Moore was a dreadlocked Jamaican who worked as a groundsman at the playing fields a couple of kilometres from the Zoo. Gabrielle and Michael found him on a deckchair inside his lock-up, with his socked feet resting on a ride-on mower. There was damp in the air, mixed up with the smell of cut grass and fumes from a Calor gas heater.

'How are me young lovers today?' Owen asked cheerfully, as he touched fists with Michael. When he stood up, his giant woolly hat brushed the corrugated roof.

'We're good,' Michael nodded, as Gabrielle smiled in agreement.

'And life in the Zoo?' Owen asked. He'd lived there himself a dozen years earlier and always made a point to ask.

'In-bloody-sane, as always,' Gabrielle smirked. 'Girl cut herself in the bathroom two nights ago and they still haven't cleaned up.'

Owen shook his head and sucked air between his teeth. 'My old home, I miss it so,' he said, before bursting into laughter. 'So you here for a K bag? You know, I almost fell on me arse when Major Dee called up so early.'

'Same here,' Michael nodded, as Owen guided his socks into a pair of muddy workman's boots and stood up without bothering to tie the laces.

He put on a pair of gardening gloves before grabbing keys from a catering-sized coffee can and strolling outside towards the men's changing block. Owen wore his jeans down low, with his boxers showing, but it was a younger man's look and it didn't seem right.

Gabrielle followed Owen and Michael into the tiled men's changing room. The floor was covered with chunks of dry mud stamped out with the shape of football studs, and she could see past the clothes hooks and benches into a toilet cubicle with damp tissue across the floor and diarrhoea sprayed up the seat.

'Do you need me in here?' she said, gagging on the combo of old sweat and blocked toilet.

'Wait outside,' Owen snorted, as he grinned at Michael. 'It's not really suited to the delicate nostrils of females in here.'

As Owen stepped on to a metal changing bench and reached up to grab a kilo of cocaine from behind a ceiling tile, Gabrielle backed into the crisp March air. She tried to wipe the foul smell from memory as she buried her fists in the front pockets of her hoodie and studied the cold breath curling in front of her face.

The playing fields were deserted, except for a dude thirty metres away, sitting on a concrete bench behind a set of goalposts. He was a little older than Gabrielle, maybe seventeen: Adidas tracksuit, with a bike flat on the pavement in front of him and a mobile phone touching a cheek covered in zits. She wouldn't have given him a second glance, but for his shocked expression when he realised she was looking his way.

He snapped his phone shut, sprang off the bench and wobbled all over the place as he began pedalling away.

'All set,' Michael said, zipping the bag of white powder into a Fila pack. He handed it over to Gabrielle as Owen locked up the changing room.

'Do you recognise that guy on the bike?' she asked, but the rider had disappeared into the glare of the low sun.

'Nice doing business, Owen,' Michael said, waving as the giant Jamaican and his trailing boot laces headed back towards his hut. 'Maybe I'll catch you in the Green Pepper.'

'Not tonight,' Owen smiled, looking back over his shoulder as he headed for his lock-up. 'My girl Erica goes to college. I got three babies to look after.'

'Sounds a blast,' Michael said, as he and Gabrielle started walking towards the gates.

'I think we're being followed,' Gabrielle whispered.

But Michael wasn't convinced. 'Are you sure? I mean, you're pretty paranoid. Remember that time we came out of the bowling alley on campus and . . .'

Gabrielle practically growled. Just one time she'd thought some guy was following them back to campus and ever since Michael had accused her of being paranoid about everything.

'It's not like that,' she snapped. 'That spotty dude can't have been expecting me to come out of the changing room straight away. You should have seen the look on his mug; and he climbed on that bike like he had a hot spud up his rear end.'

Michael glanced around. 'Well, we can't do much except keep our wits and we're doing that anyway.'

'I know,' Gabrielle nodded, as she swung the pack over her back. 'But I thought this was dodgy and now I *really* think this is dodgy.'

'Who could he be?' Michael asked.

Gabrielle shrugged. 'He had that whole chavvy thing going on; he looked like a Runt.'

Michael shook his head. The Runts were a youth gang who all came out of a couple of estates on the opposite side of town. They dealt drugs, stole cars and burgled houses, but they were mostly just tearaways. Even the leaders were barely out of their teens.

'Too sophisticated,' Michael said. 'You're suggesting that Runts are gonna send some dude into the Green Pepper to set up a sale, then keep tabs on all of Major Dee's couriers so that they can find where he keeps his stash . . .'

'OK, you're right,' Gabrielle said irritably. 'It's way too sophisticated for the Runts. But I'm telling you it's *not* me being paranoid; that dude flipped out when he saw me.'

'Could be a cop,' Michael said.

Gabrielle shrugged. 'Too young to be on the drugs squad, but I suppose it could be an informant.'

'Or some other gang . . . I mean, Major Dee's double-crossed everyone from the Russian mafia to his own uncle. Do you think we should call Chloe again?'

'What's the point?' Gabrielle asked. 'She's a mission controller, not a miracle worker. I know what she'll say: we can go ahead and deliver the drugs or pull out if we think it's too dangerous. But the second we go missing with a kilo of Major Dee's coke, he's gonna want our heads on a platter.'

By this time, Michael and Gabrielle were out of the playing fields and walking beside a breeze-block wall, with a parade of small shops across the street. The Green Pepper café was less than three minutes' walk, but they were both on edge.

'Are we gonna make this call about the police car or not?' Michael said, as he slid his mobile from his jeans.

But Michael didn't get a chance. He heard something behind him and turned to see three bikes speeding down the pavement towards them. The tracksuited riders had scarves over their faces, but Gabrielle glimpsed enough to recognise one from a police surveillance photo. He was a Runt called Aaron Reid: a twenty-two-year-old who'd done three years in youth custody after beating a schoolmate almost to death.

As the bikes closed in, Michael broke into a run whilst Gabrielle jumped off the kerb, shielding herself between two closely parked cars. Two bikes whizzed on to get Michael, but the lad she'd eyeballed in the park threw his bike down and pulled a wooden-handled kitchen knife from inside his jacket.

'Give us the pack,' he ordered.

Gabrielle stepped backwards into the road was horrified to see that the knife was smeared with fresh blood. But it was one on one. Gabrielle had passed CHERUB's advanced combat course and reckoned she could handle him.

She backed into the middle of the road as the guy closed her down. Meanwhile, Michael had disappeared around the corner with the two bikes on his tail.

'Hand over the coke and you can walk.'

'Kiss my arse, spotty,' Gabrielle scoffed, as an approaching car blasted its horn at her.

As the driver got close he realised that Gabrielle had a knife pointed at her, but he just cut into the opposite lane and kept on going.

'You're a big spotty chicken,' Gabrielle goaded. 'You haven't got the guts.'

The Runt made a clumsy lunge. Gabrielle sidestepped before snatching his wrist and twisting his arm up behind his back. The giant blade clattered to the ground as she kneed him ferociously in the balls and turned him around to smash the side of his head against the front wing of a Fiat Tipo. The first blow left him dazed. The second left a dent in the bonnet and a dead weight in her hands. She let go and the Runt slumped into the road, to the obvious surprise of a man emerging from the halal butcher's shop across the street.

Gabrielle looked around to make sure she was out of danger. She was torn about what to do next. Her heart wanted to go after Michael, but her brain knew there wasn't much chance of catching up before he reached the Green Pepper and she was all too aware of the blood smeared over the knife.

Whose blood?

A crowd was gathering across the street as she began sprinting back towards the playing fields. As she burst through the squeaky metal gate, Gabrielle noticed that the doors of both men's changing rooms had been kicked in. Her nightmare was confirmed when she rounded a corner and opened the door of the lock-up.

Owen was face-down on the concrete, with a pool of blood around his head. He was a big man, but he'd been surprised by the Runts and his throat had been slashed with the giant knife, killing him instantly.

Gabrielle realised she was in deep trouble: not only was she standing at a crime scene, but she'd been seen in the area by witnesses. CHERUB could pull her off the mission and tamper with the evidence so that she was never linked with the crime, but she'd be a suspect and the very fact that witnesses had seen her could muddy the evidence enough and make convicting the real killers impossible.

Gabrielle realised she had to leave the area fast, then call up Chloe and tell her that Michael was probably still in danger. Death is always shocking and she trembled as she backed out of the lock-up. Then she jumped with fright as a door slammed less than ten metres away, followed by a youth's voice:

'We've got two kilos and Aaron should have got the bag from the black girl by now.'

Another voice: 'Sasha's boy said there'd be a lot more than four kilos.'

'Well where is it? We've looked already.'

Gabrielle crept back inside the lock-up. It sounded like five or six Runts were stepping out of the changing rooms. She realised that her urgent desire to know if Owen was safe had made her careless. It made perfect sense that a small team of Runts would go after the K bag hooked on her back, while a larger team searched the changing rooms for Major Dee's main stash. But they were out of sight and it sounded like they were leaving.

'I'm outta here before the cops arrive,' the most dominant sounding Runt said.

'Sod that,' a younger voice said, maybe only thirteen or fourteen. 'We haven't searched the birds' changing rooms yet. There could be another twenty grand's worth of coke stashed above those ceiling tiles.'

'I tell you what, shorty, you stay here and get done for murder when the pigs turn up. I'm gonna head home and start snorting this lot.'

There were some laughs and a few jeers. The lads were egging one another on and it sounded absurdly casual; as if they were busting each other's balls over the football results rather than robbing a drug dealer and murdering his associate.

'You know what else,' another boy said. 'I need a snap of that dead Rasta man on my mobile before we get out of here.'

The lads all laughed like they thought this was a great idea. 'You'd better not let your little sister find it.'

There was a round of laughter, followed by: 'Remember that time your mum found the pictures of Brenda's boobs . . .'

Back in the lock-up, Gabrielle considered bursting out and making a run across the fields. But there were at least half a dozen boys and they had bikes which she wouldn't be able to outrun.

One of the boys started singing to the tune of *Ten Green Bottles* as they walked towards the lock-up. 'One dead Rasta, stabbed inside a shed, one dead Rasta, stabbed inside a shed . . .'

His mates laughed as Gabrielle glanced around at Owen's tools. The Runts were going to find her within a few seconds and she desperately needed a weapon.

5. PEPPER

Michael was well built and moved fast, but the two bikes were almost on his back as he rounded the corner into the main road. Knowing they'd catch up in seconds, he dodged behind a letterbox and gave the first cyclist an almighty shove as he sped past.

The bike clattered into a bush and Aaron Reid tipped off, hitting the low wall below a hedge and rolling several times before smacking head-first into a gate post.

The second guy managed to brake before Michael jumped him. But as Michael's fist slammed into his head and knocked him off the bike, he realised that five more sets of wheels were coming from the direction he'd been heading.

Even with CHERUB combat training, five against one was no good. They'd all have knives and they'd come to fight Major Dee's crew, so at least one of them would be packing a gun. Michael considered turning back, but there was no way he'd outrun five guys on bikes. He needed to get reinforcements out of the Green Pepper café, which was less than a minute's walk along the street.

Michael bundled the second cyclist and knocked him cold

with a blow to the side of the head. He spotted a small axe inside the youth's jacket and ripped it out with one hand, while sliding his mobile phone open with the other. The five bikes were now less than fifty metres away and Michael flipped through the memories until he found the number for the Green Pepper.

He crouched back behind the postbox, with the axe in one hand and his mobile at his ear. The bikes kept closing and Michael looked for a gap in the traffic that would enable him to buy a few seconds by darting across the road.

A voice sounded in his ear as he sprinted out in front of a delivery van. 'Green Pepper.'

'Clive, it's Michael Conroy here, you've got to—'

The blast of a horn drowned out his words.

'Who?' the gruff West Indian asked as Michael began running along the pavement towards the café.

'I'm making a delivery for Dee, but the Runts are all over me. I'm across the street, I need backup.'

Michael didn't hear the response, because a red traffic light had allowed three of the five cyclists to cut across the road and resume the chase. But Michael was now less than two hundred metres from the shabby frontage of the Green Pepper.

'Move,' Michael screamed, as a woman scooped a toddler into her arms to avoid getting mown down by Michael and the line of bikes on his tail.

But avoiding the toddler steered Michael into the path of a concrete bollard. His knee smacked it and his phone went flying as he twisted and fell against a parked car. As he saved himself from hitting the ground by grabbing hold of a door mirror, one of the cyclists skimmed past punching him in the back.

By the time Michael was on his feet, he was gasping for breath and penned between a car and a hedge, with the Runt who'd thrown the punch ahead of him and two more jumping off their bikes behind. He stepped away from the car and made a wild swing with the axe.

'Come on then, slags,' Michael yelled, as the axe swished through the air. 'I'm not scared of you.'

But he *was* scared. It was a huge relief to see four masked men burst through the windowless doors of the Green Pepper. There was a crack as one of them fired a shotgun blast into the air. Two of his compadres held machetes, while the other wielded a handgun and a full-sized samurai sword.

Major Dee's crew were serious gangsters. Many of them had grown up in Jamaica's most violent neighbourhoods; they'd killed rivals and served hard prison time. The Runts were just kids, deep in Major Dee's territory and suddenly out of their league.

A second blast of shotgun pellets hit one of the cyclists who hadn't crossed the road. The two guys at Michael's back grabbed their bikes to flee, but the one in front eyeballed him defiantly as he lifted up his sweatshirt, revealing the stock of an automatic pistol.

Three more tooled-up members of Major Dee's crew were emerging from the Green Pepper, making a total of seven. The guy with the shotgun was waiting for a gap in the traffic to come to Michael's aid, but Michael realised there would be a nasty – possibly deadly – stand-off if he gave the Runt time to pull his gun.

Michael lunged forward, swinging the axe. He brought it down hard into his opponent's shoulder. The kid tried aiming the gun as he collapsed backwards into the hedge, but his arm was crippled and Michael kneed him in the stomach before ripping the gun out of his hand.

Blood was pouring as Michael pocketed the handgun and levered the axe out of the Runt's shoulder. Another shotgun blast made Michael jump, but it had been aimed hopelessly at the two retreating cyclists.

'Michael, you OK?' the gunman said.

Michael was completely pumped. He hadn't recognised the gunman under his mask, but he knew Major Dee's voice.

'I thought you were home,' Michael gasped.

Major Dee shook his head. 'I listened to what your girlfriend said. She made me realise that this set-up smelled to high heaven.'

'We'd better get out of here,' Michael said.

But Major Dee looked at the bloody Runt slumped against the hedge. He pointed the shotgun at the Runt's head and pulled up his balaclava.

'Good news is, I'm gonna let you live,' Dee smiled. 'But tell all your friends that we're on your case.'

After a laugh, Dee lowered his aim and blasted the Runt's kneecap from point-blank range. Blood spattered over Michael's trainers as the Runt screamed in pain. Meantime, two saloon cars had pulled up in the road.

'Everyone outta here,' Dee shouted.

Within fifteen seconds, Michael, Major Dee and another member of the gang were inside a car and the back wheels were spinning.

As they moved away, Michael felt inside his pockets and realised that he'd lost his phone.

'Someone give us a mobile,' he begged. 'I don't know what's happened to Gabrielle.'

*

Stuart was fourteen, a lanky kid in an oversized puffa jacket. He had his mobile phone lined up to take a picture of Owen's body and he was surprised when the spade hit him in the face. Blood exploded from his nose as he stumbled backwards and collapsed to the pavement.

Gabrielle's other hand contained a small garden fork – the kind you might use to dig in flowers – and she jammed its three prongs into the belly of an older lad before ripping it out.

Two boys down. Before any of the five other lads got their heads together, she'd burst out of the lock-up and was sprinting along the paved area in front of the playing fields.

She got thirty metres before someone got a hand to her shoulder; but she stopped running and used her opponent's forward momentum to roll him over her back, slamming him hard against the concrete.

Of the remaining four lads, only two were on her tail and both were losing ground. As Gabrielle neared the gates, she noticed the Runts' bikes resting against the wall between the men's and women's changing rooms. The guys would catch her easily on bikes, giving her no choice but to grab one herself.

Gabrielle pulled up and grabbed a Muddy Fox mountain bike leaning against the wall. As she swung her leg over the saddle, one of the guys chasing kicked the back wheel. It almost knocked her off balance, but she just about kept in the saddle and started powering away.

The two boys were mounting their own bikes as she shot through the gates and out into the side street. There were now more than a dozen people standing in the road, surrounding the bloody knife and the spotty lad she'd knocked out beside the Fiat.

If she'd had time to think, Gabrielle would have turned the other way, but she couldn't do a one-eighty with two boys on her tail, so she had to cut between two parked cars and mount the pavement to get through the crowd. As she did this her back wheel slipped, knocking her into a line of wooden fruit trays on the pavement outside a greengrocer's shop.

Oranges and limes bobbling across the pavement caused an angry shout from the shopkeeper, who dashed out to gather the fruit and blocked the path of the two Runts. They slowed right down to avoid the woman and the lead rider kicked her out of the way as Gabrielle reached the junction with the main road.

As she slowed down, she could see more bikes on both sides of the road heading towards the Green Pepper. Then, as she noticed Aaron Reid lying with a serious head injury just a few metres away, she heard the unmistakable sound of a shotgun blast.

Gabrielle was worried about Michael, but with Runts coming from every direction, Major Dee's henchmen on the scene and the police sure to be arriving any second, she reckoned it best to head away and made the best of a small break in the traffic.

A car braked to let her in, but the time she'd taken to make her decision had allowed the two pursuing Runts to catch up. Gabrielle worked through the gears on the mountain bike until the parked cars were going by in a blur. But the two bikes following her were keeping up and she'd noticed two more – the bikes that had been behind Michael before the first shotgun blast – heading along the pavement.

Four against one wasn't ideal, but Gabrielle hoped her high level of fitness would soon start to count. The lights at the top of the road were red and a queue of vehicles was building up. With a narrow pavement and cement mixer blocking the channel between the parked cars, she had to cut dangerously through the oncoming traffic and mount the wider pavement on the opposite side of the road.

As she got nearer to the traffic lights, she glanced back over her shoulder and was delighted to see that one of the riders had made a mess of mounting the pavement, forcing his mate to dismount and lift his bike over him.

Two police cars with sirens blaring turned into the top of the road as Gabrielle took a right on to the bottom of a steep hill. The cops either didn't realise the significance of the chase, or didn't see it and they sped on towards the Green Pepper.

Gabrielle was getting short of breath as she stood up in her seat and powered her bike up the steep hill. Another rider had given up the chase after a couple of hundred metres and when she looked back there was only one rider after her: a stocky Asian teenager, his fingers blinged up with gold rings and a hoodie shielding his face.

One on one didn't seem too bad, but as she continued to

pedal Gabrielle's mobile phone started doing the Macarena. She took one hand off the handlebars and squeezed down her jeans to retrieve her phone. But concentrating on the phone caused her to miss a car rolling out of a narrow driveway between two houses.

She pulled the brakes and turned to swerve around the bonnet, but she overdid it and found herself going head first over the handlebars. Her skull thumped against the front wing of the car and her own bike landed on top of her as the shocked driver unbuckled and dashed out to make sure Gabrielle was OK.

But she wasn't. Gabrielle had hit the car head-on with no helmet and was now curled on the ground near the front wheel of the car. Her mouth was filling with blood and her arm felt dead, as if it had been ripped out of its socket.

'Oh my god,' the driver gasped as she crouched down beside Gabrielle. 'I'm *sorry*, but you were coming so fast I didn't . . .'

As the driver tried to help Gabrielle, the Asian lad jumped off his bike. He looked about nineteen, with beefy arms and a powerful chest. Without saying a word, he grabbed the driver by her collar and punched her in the face with his ringed hand. Then he lifted up his sweatshirt and pulled a long knife from a sheath strapped to his thigh.

Gabrielle could see the light reflecting off the blade, but the knock to the head had drained all her strength. Everything was blurred and she thought about her training. But she was stranded on the edge of consciousness and could only watch as the youth plunged the knife deep into her stomach.

The blade went into her side below her rib cage. She doubled up as he pulled it out and the driver screamed, 'Leave her alone!' as a second stab thrust the blade into her back.

The youth turned towards the driver. 'Where's your car keys?' he demanded.

'Oh Jesus,' the driver sobbed, handing over her keys as she shielded her face, fearing another punch. 'Take the car, but leave the girl alone.'

Gabrielle was losing consciousness and bleeding heavily as the youth snatched the bag of cocaine from inside her backpack. He glanced furtively down the hill, before picking up his bike and hurriedly loading it into the back of the car. After slamming the boot, he jumped into the driver's seat and started the engine.

The car's bloody-faced owner dragged Gabrielle back so that she didn't get run over as it pulled into the road. She had no idea if the skinny teenager could survive, but she had to call an ambulance as quickly as possible.

As her car pulled off in a plume of diesel smoke, the woman realised that her mobile and door keys were in her handbag on the front passenger seat. She wiped her bloody nose on her sleeve and decided to run to her next-door neighbour's and call from there. But then she heard a tinny rendition of the Macarena coming out of the gutter.

She turned sharply and picked up Gabrielle's phone. It had slid shut when it hit the ground and the woman slid it back open to answer the call.

'Gabrielle,' Michael said. 'Where are you? I'm with Major Dee and—'

'Clear the line,' the woman said urgently. 'I need to call an ambulance.'

'Gabrielle?' Michael said, as the woman cut him off. 'Gabrielle, are you all right?'

6. VENOM

They'd set up camp in a jungle clearing, with the trainees' two-man tents arranged in a semi-circle around a fire. The instructors and assistants had more luxurious tents that were tall enough to stand in, and whereas trainees had to hike with their accommodation on their backs, the instructors' equipment had been delivered by Land Cruiser and their tents erected by local guides who lived in a fishing village across the island.

It was dark now. James had washed at a nearby spring, but even at night the jungle heat was intense. He was in the tent he shared with Kazakov, sitting on an upturned crate wearing only cargo shorts and boots, while a crackly Malaysian radio station played Michael Jackson and a million insects dive bombed the outside of the tent, attracted by the glow from the electric lantern hooked to the ceiling.

Mr Kazakov lay on a metal-framed bunk, applying foul smelling glue to a pair of Russian army boots.

'You can get these from the store room on campus,' James said, as he kicked his state-of-the-art, lightweight, air-cushioned, waterproof-but-breathable boots in the air. 'They're dead comfy.'

'It makes you soft,' Kazakov spat. 'Luxury doesn't make a good soldier. All this fancy equipment you westerners use is just more things to go wrong.'

It said something about Kazakov that James had spent five nights sharing a tent with him, but still didn't know his first name. It said even more that he'd taken British citizenship and worked for various government organisations over a fifteen-year period, but still thought of British people as *you westerners*.

James smiled as he moved across to his camp bed and yawned. 'They're a lot easier on your feet than hard-soled Russian boots, that's all I know.'

Kazakov tutted, before leaning forward and wagging his finger. 'During World War Two the German soldiers had the best technology; but when the snows came the German equipment froze and supply lines broke down. The Russian soldiers didn't even have warm coats, but they were peasant stock, used to going hungry and surviving on scraps. While the Germans starved, Russian troops pulled up trees and bushes and stewed the roots until they were soft enough to eat. And if those Russians hadn't boiled up those roots, Germany would have won the war and Britain would be a German colony.'

James shook his head. 'I reckon the Americans might have had something to say about that.'

Kazakov laughed. 'The Americans don't like to fight dirty. Look at Vietnam, look at Iraq. I wear these boots because they're the same kind I used in Afghanistan and they worked just fine. I know my knife because it killed in Afghanistan. I've worked with your SAS and I've seen SA80 rifles and Glock machine pistols jam. I carry a Kalashnikov because you can walk out of a swamp or a sand storm and know that a bullet comes out when you pull the trigger.'

Kazakov only ever became animated when talking about war or weapons. James couldn't help smiling. 'You actually like all this, don't you?'

'Like what?'

'Living in the jungle, washing out your clothes by hand, patching up your kit.'

'I have no family,' Kazakov shrugged. 'The only thing I know is being a soldier – and a good soldier sticks with equipment he can trust.'

James lay back on his bed. He thought of himself as a tough guy, and compared to most fifteen-year-olds he was, but he was nothing compared to the Russian.

'It's time,' Kazakov said, cracking a rare smile as he splashed the dregs from his canteen over James' bare stomach. 'Go get the snakes; I'll prepare the rifles and simunition.'

James unzipped the tent quickly and ducked into the night, before the insects got a chance to pour in. The two-room command tent set up next door was presently empty. Dana had travelled with a local guide, taking the Land Cruiser deeper into the jungle to set up equipment for the trainees' rafting expedition for the next morning; Mr Pike had taken Jo McGowan to a hospital on the mainland.

When James was a trainee he'd assumed that CHERUB instructors had free rein to commit acts of cruelty. In fact, the 100-day training course was meticulously planned.

Every exercise took a mass of organisation and involved a complicated safety audit as well as careful consideration of what ten- to twelve-year-old trainees were capable of.

One of the guiding principles of training was that the pupils should always be uncomfortable. They were taught to expect the unexpected and to live with a little less food and sleep than they were used to. Tonight was going to be no exception.

James yawned as he walked around the back of the command tent to a pile of crates and boxes that had been unloaded from the boat. There was a glimmer of moonlight, but he needed his pocket lamp to read the laminated tags dangling from each crate.

He moved the torch beam back and forth until he found the boxes marked DAY 96 EXERCISE 7B (LIVE CARGO). The box was made from blue plastic, and as he lifted it the contents writhed around and bodies slapped against the plastic sides.

After resting his torch on the ground, James peeled off a strip of parcel tape. As he raised up the lid to peek inside, a blaze of light from a hot lamp blinded him. The lamp was set on a timer and designed to switch on and make the cold-blooded snakes inside hyperactive. The pinkish grey creatures snapped their jaws and began poking their heads into the gap beneath the lid, forcing James to slam it down in a panic.

The reptiles were Malaysian pit vipers. Although they were only babies, they would normally carry enough venom to kill a small human. However, these vipers had undergone a minor operation to remove their venom producing glands and as a result the only injury they could inflict was a nasty bite from their powerful jaws. But of course, the sleeping trainees had no idea that they were harmless.

By the time James had lugged the box around towards the trainees' tents, Mr Kazakov was standing by the fire with an M4 assault rifle over each shoulder.

'Are they loaded?' James asked, as Kazakov handed him a rifle and half a dozen ammo clips.

'Simunition rounds,' Kazakov whispered. 'The trainees won't be wearing any protective gear, so aim above their heads unless you're got a clear shot at their legs or back.'

As James crammed the clips into the pockets of his shorts and hooked the M4 over his back, he noticed that Kazakov was wearing thick gloves.

'Did you get a pair for me?' James asked.

'You should have put them on,' Kazakov said, as James turned back towards their tent. 'I'm not your mother. Where do you think you're going?'

'To get my gloves.'

'You'll be fine,' Kazakov shrugged. 'They're only babies.'

James didn't want to seem weak in front of Kazakov, so he turned back. But his confidence drained when he flipped the lid to unveil seventy-two overheated vipers.

'You undo the zips,' Kazakov said.

As James crept up to the four trainees' tents, Kazakov ripped the pin from the first of four smoke grenades hanging from a belt slung over his shoulder.

James shuffled along the ground unzipping the tents, closely followed by Kazakov who'd push his arm between the flaps of fabric and roll a smoke grenade into some far corner of each tent. None of the trainees stirred. After a parachute jump and a twenty-kilometre hike they were all dead to the world.

Once the grenades were in position, Kazakov dipped his gloves inside the box of snakes, grabbed a handful and began throwing them on the baked earth in front of the tent flaps.

'Muck in, James,' Kazakov said firmly.

Without gloves, James decided that the best strategy was to pick the box off the ground and tip the snakes out. The method was fast and effective, but one of the reptiles had already slithered on to the side of the box. It reared up, swivelled its head and snapped its jaws shut around James' bare nipple.

'JEEEEEEEESUS!' James screamed, as the first of the smoke grenades began erupting.

Within ten seconds, all four trainee tents were billowing smoke and within fifteen the seven trainees had scrambled outside, barefoot and coughing. Even at night the jungle was extremely hot and the trainees soon found the young pit vipers snapping at their toes and ankles.

As they screamed, Mr Kazakov backed up behind the fire and began shooting at them. The simulated ammunition wasn't lethal, but it was like paintballing on steroids and you knew all about it if it hit your bare skin.

Naturally, the trainees' reaction was to run away from the hail of bullets and the snakes around their tents, but Mr Kazakov began shouting orders between blasts of gunfire. 'All trainees, gather your equipment from the tents. Smoke-damaged equipment will *not* be replaced. I repeat, smoke-damaged equipment will *not* be replaced.'

As well as making everything stink, the pungent smoke would do serious damage to the trainees' navigation equipment and would stain their briefings for the following day, making maps and vital sections of text illegible. The youngsters had no option but to brave the smoke, bullets and snakes and rescue their precious equipment.

Meanwhile, James had his own problem to deal with. He should have been standing alongside Kazakov shooting simulated rounds at the trainees, but instead he was in excruciating pain, with the fangs of a baby viper embedded in the flesh around his nipple.

He twisted its surprisingly rigid body, but the jaws didn't budge. Pulling on the snake just made its fangs tear deeper into his skin, so James grabbed a section of the upper body with each hand, then did a Chinese burn; squeezing with all his might while twisting his hands in opposite directions.

It took all his strength, but eventually the viper's backbone fractured and James ripped the bottom half of its body away from its head. He'd assumed that decapitation would make the snake let go, but while its body writhed on the ground the snake's head remained latched to his nipple.

Infuriated, James looked around and saw that the barefoot trainees had come up with a method for clearing the snakes from around their tents: they'd ducked to the opposite side of the fire from where Mr Kazakov was shooting at them and pulled glowing sticks out of the embers.

While snakes are surprisingly blasé about being ripped in half, they don't like fire and sprang away as the trainees swept their flaming sticks across the ground.

As James moved in to grab his own stick, Kevin Sumner became the first trainee to get back inside his tent. As he reached into the billowing smoke, feeling blindly for the chunky canister, one of Mr Kazakov's simulated rounds hit him up the arse.

Powdery yellow paint spattered up Kevin's back as he found his hand wrapped around the hot smoke canister and – with a move he would later swear was accidental – ripped it out of the tent and threw it with all his ten-year-old might towards his tormentor.

'I'm sick of you picking on me, dickwad,' Kevin shouted.

James didn't hear this because he'd grabbed a dried-out palm frond from the fire and he could feel its heat as he brought the flame towards the snake's head. As soon as the flame licked the snake's eyeball, its mouth sprang open and the head briefly joined the body on the floor, before James booted it into the flames.

After a glance at the blood streaking down his torso, James looked up and realised that the shooting had stopped. The trainees had all thrown their smoke canisters out of their tents and now stood over Mr Kazakov, who lay unconscious on his back with a cut the shape of a smoke canister on his forehead.

'What happened?' James yelled.

'I think one of the smoke canisters hit him on the head,' a twelve-year-old recruit called Ellie said.

'Accidentally,' Kevin added. 'Because there's no *way* I could have seen where he was through all the smoke . . .'

James realised he was in charge. 'OK,' he said firmly. 'If a couple of you help me to drag Kazakov into the command tent, the rest of you had better go back and vent the smoke out of your tents and equipment.'

'Where's Pike and Dana?' Kevin asked. 'Can't they move him?'

James shook his head. 'Pike's still on the mainland. Dana's off with the guide, setting up your equipment for tomorrow morning.'

'So you're the *only* instructor,' a tough-looking Irish lad called Ronan smirked. 'There's seven of us and only one of you . . .'

'Grab him,' Kevin yelled, and before James had a chance to go for his gun, he had a trainee latched on to each arm while another knocked him down from behind with a Karate kick to the back of his knee.

'Tie him up,' Ellie squealed. 'He's third dan black belt, you can't let him get loose.'

The seven trainees were a lot smaller than James, but they'd all done combat training and they worked together to pin him to the ground. Within seconds, several trainees had run into the command tent.

'There's tons of grub in there,' Kevin shouted, as he emerged holding a length of climbing rope.

'You're all gonna get punished for this,' James screamed. 'You'll all fail training.'

'We're showing initiative,' Ronan giggled, digging his knee into James' back as he tightened the rope around his wrists. 'Isn't that what we're supposed to do?'

'It's true, James,' Kevin nodded. 'And besides, CHERUB is always short of agents. There's no way they'd fail all seven of us.'

'We'll see,' James said, trying to sound cocky even though he knew the youngsters were right. Physically, basic training was as tough as when James had done it three years earlier, but Mr Pike wasn't especially scary and the trainees got away with stuff you wouldn't have dared even think about when Mr Large ran the show.

There were a couple of boys who weren't involved in tying James up and they were clearly worried about getting in trouble. 'Help me out,' James begged. 'I'll make sure that you get off easy.'

But the two trainees were indecisive: they weren't the strongest characters within the group and they were outnumbered five to two. Then a shout came up from inside the command tent. 'I've found a cooler box full of chocolate and Coke!'

The trainees' evening meal had been an evil-smelling bowl of fish-head soup and the thought of chocolate made up the waverers' minds. James was now lying face-down with grit coating his bloody chest. He tried wriggling, but the trainees had made a decent job of trussing his arms and legs and there was no chance of escape.

'I can't believe you're doing this to me,' James yelled, as the sounds of a kids' party erupted from inside the command tent. 'I'm always looking out for you guys. Don't expect any favours out of me from now on.'

James heard Ronan's grubby feet scuffing through the dirt behind him. The boy crouched down and waved the chewed up end of a Snickers bar under his nose.

'Fancy a bite?' he chirped.

'You bloody wait,' James growled.

'Temper temper,' Ronan grinned as he stuffed the remainder of the Snickers bar into his own mouth, before rolling the wrapper into a ball and flicking it in James' face.

7. POLITICS

It had been twenty-five years since a CHERUB agent had died on a mission. Zara Asker had only been the organisation's chairwoman for ten months and she'd learned about the worst crisis of her career while sitting in a hospital ward, comforting her three-year-old son Joshua, who'd broken his arm after deciding to jump from the top of the slide at his nursery school.

It was a complex break and Joshua had been kept in overnight, following a minor operation to insert a metal pin. He was tearful and restless, and Zara felt guilty abandoning her own child to go and look after someone else's. But Joshua had his father Ewart for comfort, and while Joshua would undoubtedly cry for his mum when he got tired, his arm would heal and his cast would be off in a month or so. Gabrielle's fate was nowhere near as certain.

Zara was flashed by a dozen speed cameras as she took the family Lexus from the car park of the hospital nearest to CHERUB campus to another hospital on the outskirts of Luton. At one point she got pulled over by police while cutting through the crowded traffic, but a glimpse of her high-level security pass earned her an escort of flashing blue lights along the fast lane of the M1.

On top of being worried about Gabrielle, she was dreading the political consequences of what had happened. Only the Prime Minister and the Intelligence Minister know that CHERUB exists. Both had been reassured that cherubs are well trained, closely monitored by mission controllers and that the chances of a cherub being seriously injured or killed are slight.

Zara was going to be in for a grilling when they found out that one of her agents was on life support following a knife fight between rival drug gangs. But she was confronted with a more basic drama when she stepped past the two police officers stationed at the entrance to the intensive care unit in case of trouble between the rival gangs.

Mission controller Chloe Blake and her assistant Maureen Evans stood up and hugged Zara as she entered a waiting area between two intensive-care rooms. Chloe had been a full mission controller for less than a year and Maureen was a Trinidadian ex-cherub who'd only been appointed as Chloe's assistant after leaving university the previous October.

Zara respected them both, but knew questions would be raised about whether two of CHERUB's least experienced mission controllers should have been allowed to handle a high-risk mission.

Michael stood at the end of the room, staring out of a dirty window and trying his best not to cry. A tear broke free as Zara kissed him on the cheek and rubbed his back. Michael was much younger than his big sisters and to avoid splitting his family he'd joined CHERUB at just three years of age. Zara could remember him riding around campus on a tiny pushbike with stabilisers, back when she'd first been appointed as an assistant mission controller.

'What's the medical situation?' Zara asked, as she let Michael go.

Chloe answered. 'Gabrielle's in a sterile room to prevent infection. She's under sedation and her breathing is being supported mechanically. They've given her clotting agents to stem the bleeding.'

'How are they describing her condition?'

'Critical but stable. The doctor has been checking in every half an hour and the surgeon came by forty minutes ago. She said they've stemmed most of the external bleeding, but that the knife went in deep and is still lodged in Gabrielle's back.

'Five Runts were also seriously injured. At the moment a boy who took a shotgun blast in the back is in surgery, but as soon as he's out of theatre they're going to wheel in Gabrielle and try removing the knife. The trauma surgeon said they won't know how severe her injuries are until they open her up.'

'Sounds grim,' Zara said, as she swept her hand through her hair and looked around anxiously. 'Is it safe to speak here?'

'As long as you're quiet,' Chloe nodded. 'There's tight security around the hospital. The police think that some of Major Dee's men could come by the hospital and try to finish the job.'

'Major Dee has previous on that score,' Maureen

explained. 'In 2005 a witness who'd agreed to testify against him on an attempted murder beef was shot in her hospital bed.'

Zara shook her head in disbelief. 'The ethics committee can't have realised that this gang war was so hot when they authorised the mission.'

Chloe twisted her trainer awkwardly as she addressed her boss. 'I wrote the risk assessment, Zara. I'll tender my resignation if you ask me to.'

'Chloe, you're an excellent mission controller,' Zara said reassuringly. 'I'm sure it won't come to that.'

Michael turned away from the window and spoke. He was only fifteen, but he was taller than the three women and his voice carried a certain authority. 'The Runts have declared war on the Slasher Boys, which nobody could have predicted. You can't blame Chloe.'

'I appreciate that, Michael,' Zara said. 'I'm not blaming anyone.'

'You're not going to pull the plug on the mission, are you?' he asked.

Zara seemed uncertain. 'The circumstances make it very difficult—'

'You *can't*,' Michael interrupted. 'We've been at this for two months and Major Dee is really starting to put faith in us. Besides, after today there's no way I'm going back to campus before these gangs are *hammered*.'

'Keep your voice *down*, Michael,' Chloe said anxiously, as the policeman at the entrance poked his head between the doors.

'Sorry,' Michael whispered. 'I'm messed up right now.'

'I know,' Zara said soothingly. 'You've had a stressful day, Michael. But I can't lie to you. Gabrielle is seriously injured; she might die. I'll have to speak with the ethics committee and the Intelligence Minister and they're likely to say that the mission is too dangerous.'

Michael groaned. 'But we're *cherubs*. We go into our missions with the best training. We understand all of the risks and we accept them.'

Zara sighed. If you asked a hundred CHERUB agents they'd all say the same thing about risks being a part of their job. But adults instinctively dislike the idea of putting kids in danger, and if Gabrielle died, the government would call CHERUB's very existence into question.

8. PRIDE

The island had a ragged network of dirt roads, most of which had been carved out by illegal logging operations who'd stripped hardwood from the island's interior. After setting out the canoes and safety equipment for the trainees' morning raft trip, Dana returned the local guide to the outskirts of his village.

As she pulled away from the settlement she received a call on the satellite phone. Mr Pike had landed on the beach and didn't fancy the five-kilometre trek back to camp, so Dana set off across the island to collect him.

The Land Cruiser was designed for rough terrain, but the roads were nothing more than shrunken gaps between trees and in places tropical storms had washed the soil away, leaving a layer of volcanic rock that set the wheels spinning and sent great jolts up her spine.

The canopy of trees blocked out the moonlight, and even inside the air-conditioned Land Cruiser Dana felt uncomfortable. She was relieved when she broke on to open sand and flashed her headlights at Mr Pike, who'd dragged a large dinghy up the beach.

'How's Jo?' Dana asked, as she helped Mr Pike to lash his dinghy to the top of the car.

'Upset, obviously,' Pike said, as he threw an elasticised rope across the hull for Dana to knot around the roof bar.

'Where is she?'

'She's at the hospital, but it's not exactly state of the art. It's damp and dingy and Jo freaked when she saw a lizard climbing up the wall. But the doctor spoke good English and the nurses who did the plaster were really nice. I thought it was better to leave her there to get some sleep, rather than make her cross back to the island in the boat.'

'Is she safe?'

Pike nodded. 'She's in a children's ward. It's all families with kids.'

By this time the boat was secured and Dana pointed towards the driving seat. 'Shall I?'

'Sure,' Pike nodded. 'You drove down here, so you know the terrain better than I do.'

Dana was pleased to have a companion in the passenger seat as she fired up the big diesel engine and set off.

'God I'm knackered,' Mr Pike said, stretching into a yawn as they hit a bump in the road.

'Snap,' Dana nodded. 'I'm not sure if training is more tiring for the instructors or the trainees. James must be shattered after that twenty-K hike.'

'I think I'll be sending him home with Jo in the morning.'

Dana looked surprised. 'Can't someone from the MI5 team at the embassy pick her up?'

'Could do,' Pike nodded. 'But we've got four staff, two guides and only seven trainees left. I thought about sending you back with her, but you're our best swimmer and I want you on hand in the motor launch tomorrow in case one of those canoes gets in trouble when they hit choppy water.'

'Fair enough, I guess,' Dana said.

Dana *was* the best swimmer, but she was no fan of jungle life and envious that James would be getting back to home comforts four days early.

'Hopefully this will be the last time we have to ask agents to help out with basic training,' Pike said. 'Kazakov is rough around the edges, but he's basically sound. Miss Smoke is due back from maternity leave and we've got another new instructor starting in a fortnight.'

'Sounds good,' Dana said. 'But what about Mr Large? I heard he's recovered from his heart attack.'

'I believe so,' Pike said awkwardly.

'Do you have a problem with Mr Large?'

Pike shrugged. 'I've got no personal grudge, but he was my boss. Then he got demoted – partly because I stood up to him and made a complaint – and now I'm *his* boss, which makes our relationship pretty awkward.'

'Suppose it must do.'

Branches lashed the car as Dana flung the steering wheel around sharply to make a tight turn. 'But he's got that disciplinary hearing for being drunk on duty. Maybe Zara won't reinstate him . . .'

'Maybe,' Pike yawned. 'Maybe, maybe, maybe. Right now all I care about is getting back to camp and dreaming some dreams.'

Dana nodded, as she caught on to his yawn. 'We're only a few minutes out.'

Despite the jarring surface, Mr Pike had somehow dozed off by the time they reached camp. Dana considered leaving him, but he'd wake up stiff, and even at night the interior of the Land Cruiser would become stifling once the air conditioning was switched off.

'Wakey wakey,' Dana said, as she gave Mr Pike a nudge.

Dana led the way from the Land Cruiser and through a steep patch of undergrowth towards the clearing where they'd made camp. The fire was smouldering and all seemed peaceful until she stepped into the command tent and saw Kazakov asleep on the floor with a pillow under his head and James lying face-down, covered in grit with his arms and legs tied together.

'MUFF-MUF!' James yelled, which only served to prove that it's impossible to say anything when you've got a rag crammed in your mouth.

'What happened?' Dana gasped, as she crouched in front of James and started pulling out the sock. 'Was it bandits? Did they rob us? Where are the trainees?'

'It was *those* little sods who did this,' James shouted, as Dana began untying his wrists.

By this time Mr Pike had stepped in and pinched Mr Kazakov's cheek to bring him around. As Kazakov sat up, rubbing his aching head, Dana fetched some bottled water and James did his best to explain what had happened.

Dana couldn't help seeing the funny side. 'Well I guess we've spent ninety-six days training them to work as a team and seize the initiative.'

'Don't laugh,' James spluttered, as he swished the dryness

out of his mouth. 'It's a total breakdown of authority. They've got to be punished . . .'

Mr Kazakov nodded. 'They should all be sent home in disgrace.'

Mr Pike still looked like a man who wanted his bed more than anything else. 'Don't be daft, Kazakov. If I get back to campus and tell the chairwoman and mission control staff that every single recruit failed training I'll get my head chewed off.'

'And they *were* showing initiative,' Dana added.

'Stop taking their side,' James said angrily. 'I bet you wouldn't be talking like that if you'd just spent an hour and a half tied up on the ground with cockroaches trying to crawl up your nose.'

'I wouldn't have been stupid enough to let myself get outwitted by a bunch of ten- and eleven-year-olds,' Dana grinned.

James gritted his teeth. 'I think the canister hitting Kazakov was an accident, and they took *me* by surprise.'

'Everyone, calm down,' Mr Pike said irritably. 'We can't have trainees assaulting instructors with smoke canisters and tying them up. It sets a dangerous precedent.'

'It's not like they planned it,' Dana interrupted. 'They acted on the spur of the moment.'

'They've got to be given a clear warning,' Pike continued. 'Who were the ringleaders?'

'Kevin Sumner and Ronan Walsh,' James said.

'Snitch,' Dana tutted.

'Right,' Mr Pike said. 'If you two want to get your own back, go and drag them out of their tents. You can punish them, but I want them in a fit state to continue training in the morning.'

'Loud and clear, boss,' Kazakov said. 'Come on James, bring the rifles.'

Dana scowled at James as he followed Kazakov out of the command tent and across to the trainees.

'And no bloody yelling,' Pike yelled after them. 'I want my sleep.'

'What are we doing to them?' James asked, as he strode briskly around the smouldering fire behind Kazakov.

'Follow my lead,' Kazakov ordered as he unzipped Kevin's tent. 'You get Ronan.'

The smell of feet and musty kit invaded James' nose as he crawled inside Ronan and Ellie's tent and shook the stocky eleven-year-old awake.

'All right mate?' James said cockily. 'Guess who just got untied!'

'Bring your kit,' Kazakov yelled, as he dragged Kevin from his tent by his ankle.

It took a couple of minutes for the two trainees to put on their boots and cram all of their kit inside their packs.

'Stand to attention,' Mr Kazakov whispered, eyeballing the trainees menacingly.

Kevin and Ronan stood in the dirt with their boots together, stomachs in, chests out and arms rigid at their sides.

'I only hit you by accident,' Kevin said sleepily.

'Really?' Kazakov nodded. 'And I suppose you tied James up by accident too?'

'You're idiots,' James added. 'Why risk getting punished

or flung out of training when you're so close to getting your grey T-shirts?'

'Just because,' Ronan said defiantly.

Kevin's expression was more rueful. 'We got carried away . . . I'm sorry James, especially after you helped me out on the hike.'

The boys were young and this was probably the point where James would have accepted an apology and sent them back to bed with a dire warning and a kick up the arse; but Kazakov had other plans.

'Rifles, James,' he ordered.

James handed each of the trainees one of the M4s they'd used to fire the simunitions earlier on.

'Now,' Kazakov grinned. 'Hold them up above your heads and commence running on the spot, raising your knees high, thusly.'

Kazakov did a little demonstration. It looked easy enough, but the trainees were half asleep and the heavy packs, rifles and heat made it hard work.

Within a minute, both lads had sweat streaking out of their hair. Then Kazakov walked behind Kevin and kicked his feet from beneath him. The boy crashed forward, with the weight of his pack pinning him to the floor and the heavy rifle digging into his chest.

'Did I give you permission to stop running?' Kazakov grinned, as he kicked dust into Kevin's gaping eyes and mouth. 'On your feet, prom queen.'

Kazakov turned towards James as Kevin began running on the spot again. 'Kick Ronan.'

This only served to remind James that he'd never make a

good training instructor. Ronan had acted pretty nasty when he'd tied James up; he was also a bully who didn't hesitate to drop the weaker trainees in it when an exercise went wrong. But he was still just a kid and James didn't want to hurt him.

Mr Kazakov wasn't impressed. He shoved James aside before slamming his dilapidated boot into the soft flesh between Ronan's hip bone and rib cage. It knocked the boy sideways with such force that he clattered into Kevin and both lads ended up back on the ground, with their limbs tangled and coughing as they breathed the dust kicked up by running on the spot.

'Get up, stand still, rifles held high.'

It took the two gasping boys half a minute to stop coughing and stand in line with their rifles above their heads.

'OK,' Kazakov grinned, as he looked at his watch. 'It's now sixteen minutes until one. Sunrise is at six-thirty. You will stand to attention with your rifles held high until then. If I see you move off the spot or stop or if the rifle drops I'll come out and make both of you run till you either puke or pass out.'

'Can I go to the toilet first?' Kevin asked.

Mr Kazakov shook his head. 'You can hold it in, or piss your pants. I don't care which, but if you move off that spot before morning you'll be sorry.'

Kevin glanced at James as if to say *can you help us out*, but James didn't like appearing weak in front of Kazakov and he didn't have the authority to help even if he tried.

'A soldier is only as tough as the person who trains them,' Kazakov said, as he and James started the short walk back to their tent.

James tried to explain as he unzipped the tent and stepped inside. 'It's just – they're not perfect but . . . They're nice little kids. You know?'

Kazakov grunted. 'I've seen a lot of men die, James. Some of them weren't much older than you and a lot of them would still be around if they'd been trained by someone like *me* instead of someone like *you*.'

As Kazakov sat on the edge of his fold-up bed and began unlacing his boots, James realised that he needed to pee before going to bed and stepped back out of the tent.

He couldn't bear to look at the moonlit silhouettes of Kevin and Ronan, with their arms struggling to hold the rifles in the air. He cut through the gap between the command tent and his own as Dana's torch suddenly lit up his face.

'All right big man?' she sneered. 'Proud of yourself?'

James tutted and shook his head. 'You should have been there when they tied me up, Dana. It was basically high spirits with Kevin, but Ronan's a nasty piece of work.'

'Two wrongs never make a right,' Dana said.

'I hate helping out with training,' James moaned. 'I know why CHERUB does it, I know they have to, but I'm not cut out for it. Pushing little kids around is depressing. I'm starting to think about seeing Meryl and asking to take extra exams instead.'

'At least you're flying home in the morning.'

James looked surprised. 'You what?'

'I guess Pike didn't get a chance to tell you. There are only seven trainees now and Jo's got a broken ankle so she needs someone to fly back to Britain with her.'

'Sweet,' James grinned. 'I could kill for a proper shower and a dossy night in front of the telly.'

Dana grinned back reluctantly. 'Anyway, I'm shattered and we've all got to be up in five hours.'

'Do I get a goodnight kiss?'

Dana was almost as tall as James and she gave him a gentle peck. 'Not that you deserve it after you snitched on little Kev.'

'I reckon he'll survive,' James shrugged. 'Pike clearly doesn't want another trainee to fail.'

James pecked Dana back then tried going for a full-on snog, but she wouldn't have it.

'I'm too tired.'

'But we might not get another chance until we're back on campus.'

'Whatever,' Dana shrugged. 'All I want is sleep.'

'Night then,' James said, sounding a touch wounded.

As they backed away from each other, Dana whispered a warning. 'And don't go anywhere near the third bush on the left beside the big tree. I just did something that you wouldn't want to put your boot in.'

9. WOOF

Meatball was an eleven-month-old beagle. Bred for experimentation, the little dog had been rescued by James Adams' sister Lauren when they'd infiltrated an animal rights group the previous summer.

CHERUB agents aren't allowed to keep pets, so when the mission was over Meatball ended up living with chairwoman Zara Asker and her family in their detached house half a kilometre from CHERUB campus.

Although Zara's kids got rough at times, Meatball had settled into a comfortable routine, with a cosy dog basket beside the sofa, a big garden to run around and visitors from campus who made a fuss and took him for walks.

But on this particular Thursday, Meatball had worked out that something was wrong. Zara or Ewart always brought the kids home from nursery before it got dark. None of the house lights were on, his water bowl was dry and he ended up huddled under the telephone table, where he usually went to sulk after getting yelled at for chewing something.

Meatball sprang up when he heard a key in the front door

and started barking when he recognised Lauren's smell through the letterbox.

'Hello, Meatball,' Lauren said fondly, as she ran her hands through his bristly coat and felt his tongue lap at her bare ankle. 'Is you a lonely doggykins? Did they all go out and leave you on your own?'

Meatball had reached adult size, but he was still a young dog and he liked to play. Lauren hadn't visited for over a week and was pleased to see him, but she couldn't get Gabrielle's fight for life out of her mind. The whole of CHERUB campus was on tenterhooks.

Meatball scratched at the door, wanting a walk, then realised it was feeding time as Lauren headed for the kitchen. She flicked on the light and reached into the cupboard above the oven. Lauren was vegetarian, and it pleased her that the Askers had stuck to their promise to feed the animal she'd given them with vegetarian food.

After refilling the water bowl, Lauren snipped open the plastic food packet and smiled when she found Meatball standing with his tail wagging and a set of legs on either side of his food dish. He'd never sussed out that you can't put the food into a bowl if you stand on top of it.

'Dozy dog,' Lauren complained, as she lifted up his back legs and squeezed the packet of food into the bowl.

The result looked uncannily like a turd, but Meatball stuck his head in the bowl and began wolfing his dinner as the phone in Lauren's jeans started to vibrate. It was her friend, Rat. He'd been Lauren's boyfriend for a while, but they were both only twelve and after a couple of months the novelty of snogging had worn off and they'd gone back to being mates.

'Hey,' Lauren said urgently. 'What's happened?'

Rat was under strict instructions to ring Lauren with news about Gabrielle, on pain of an arse-kicking if he forgot.

'Still in surgery the last we heard,' Rat said, in his Australian accent. 'We thought you might know something, seeing as Ewart asked you to check on the dog.'

Lauren tutted. 'Maybe Meatball will open up on the matter after his sachet of VeggyPet, but I wouldn't put money on it.'

'OK, don't bite my head off. We just thought there was a chance you might have heard something.'

'So what's going on up there?'

'They've turned on the heating in the chapel. The vicar is coming in from the village and everyone who wants to can go and light a candle.'

Rat had spent the first eleven years of his life living in a strict religious commune, and tended to freak out at the slightest mention of religion.

'Are you going?' Lauren asked.

'I guess . . . I don't think there's anyone on campus who won't be there.'

'It's so sad,' Lauren said, as she felt a lump in her throat. 'Listen, I've got to take Meatball for his walk, but I'll be back on campus within an hour. Maybe we can go and do the candle thing together.'

'So will Meatball be on his own all night?'

Lauren shook her head as she sniffed slightly. 'Ewart should be home with Joshua and Tiffany by the time I get back from walkies.'

'Try not to worry,' Rat said. 'She's in surgery now; they're doing all they can.'

'I'll see you later,' Lauren said, then shut the call off because she felt tears coming on for the third time that day. She hadn't been this sad since her mum died. She looked enviously down at Meatball as he licked up the last of his food. She reckoned it would be nice to have nothing do but play, sleep and eat VeggyPet.

'You greedy pig,' Lauren said, managing a smile as she slid her hand along Meatball's back. 'How could a little dog like you eat that so fast?'

Meatball jumped up on Lauren's leg as she picked up his lead. When he was a puppy Meatball used to make a big fuss about having his lead hooked on, but now he knew that it meant he was going for a walk and he sat to attention while she hooked it to his collar.

As Lauren slammed the front door and started walking down the patio, she noticed an oversized figure moving through the shadows on the other side of the wall. She froze when she realised it was the hulking figure of the legendary training instructor, Norman Large.

'Oh it's *you*,' Large said.

Following his heart attack seven months earlier, Mr Large had run off a lot of weight and slowly brought himself back to peak fitness. He lived with his partner and daughter in the house next door to the Askers' and had spent the last hour pumping weights in his garage. His sweatshirt was darkened with sweat.

'Hello, sir,' Lauren said awkwardly. She'd once knocked Mr Large out after losing her temper during a training exercise and their relationship hadn't improved since.

'Where are you off to?' Large said, trying to sound friendly.

'Come over here for a minute. I've been hoping to bump into you at some stage.'

Although Mr Large had been on sick leave for half a year, he was still a member of the CHERUB staff and Lauren had to treat him with respect. But she hated the man's guts and certainly didn't want a full-blown conversation.

'I've got to take Meatball for his walk and then I've got to get back to campus and do my homework.'

'It'll only take a minute,' Large grinned, as Lauren reluctantly stepped across the dark patio, setting off the motion-sensitive light over the Askers' garage door. 'As you know, I've got to face a disciplinary panel before I can have my job back, because of the erm . . . *unfortunate* incident leading up to my heart attack last year.'

Lauren smiled acidly. 'You mean the fact that you went to the pub and got hammered when you were supposed to be in charge of a bunch of kids.'

Large smiled awkwardly back. 'Well that's not really fair . . .'

'Well you *certainly* didn't look sober from where I was sitting.'

'OK, I was drunk on duty,' Large admitted. 'I know that you and I have never really gotten along, but you were the only senior agent who saw the state I was in before my heart attack that night. Your evidence could be the deciding factor in whether I get my job back after the hearing on Friday next week.'

Lauren enjoyed having some power over Mr Large. After all the times he'd bullied her and made her suffer, he was now reduced to begging her to lie on his behalf.

'I won't exaggerate,' Lauren said firmly. 'But I am going to tell the truth, which is that you'd had a skinful of beer and you could hardly walk.'

Mr Large changed the subject. 'He's a nice little dog, Meatball, isn't he?'

'Yeah,' Lauren nodded.

'You seem especially fond of him.'

'He's really cool; I just wish I'd been able to keep him in my room on campus.'

'Mmm,' Large said. 'But he's tiny. I mean, *very* fragile. And I was thinking, if you tell that inquiry that I was drunk, they'll never reinstate me as an instructor. I could be pottering around this house all day with little Meatball right next door and it would be *so* easy for an accident to occur.'

'*What?*' Lauren choked.

'Oh, you know. Maybe I could step on his little spine and crush him. Or he could get tangled under my lawnmower, or Saddam and Thatcher could accidentally get over the garden fence and maul him . . .'

Lauren was stunned. 'You're blackmailing me? How can you? He's an innocent little dog!'

Mr Large nodded. 'And if I get my job back, he'll *stay* an innocent little dog.'

'You . . . you *bastard*,' Lauren shouted. 'Only a scumbag like you could come out with a scheme as low as this.'

Mr Large broke into one of his most satanic grins. 'Temper, temper, little lady.'

'Zara won't stand for it if you kill Meatball. She's the chairwoman; she's connected to some of the most powerful people in the country.'

Large shrugged. 'I'll say it was an accident and nobody will ever prove that it wasn't.'

'I can't believe you,' Lauren said, as she stepped backwards. 'You're barely even human, do you know that?'

'I'm only asking for one little favour,' Mr Large coaxed. 'And you know, Meatball's pelt would be just the right size for a nice winter hat.'

'Come on, Meatball,' Lauren said, tugging on the lead as she started walking towards the road.

She tried not to let the fear show in her voice, but she was shaking all over.

10. CANDLES

The chapel was one of the few buildings on campus that had existed before CHERUB was founded. The humble stone church had served a rural parish from the 1780s until the entire area was commandeered by the government during World War Two.

With pews for fewer than eighty, it was too small for major occasions like Christmas carol services, and the various faith groups on campus preferred using more comfortable meeting rooms in the main building. But the drafty chapel remained the spiritual heart of campus and when lit by candles the uneven walls and cobwebbed roof beams were as emotive as the grandest cathedral.

More than a hundred candles had been placed around the framed photograph of Gabrielle on a long table. James' best mate Kyle Blueman and his ex-girlfriend Kerry Chang stood at the entrance, handing candles to the procession of cherubs and staff. They each took a turn, stepping up to the table and lighting their candle before standing it with the others.

Kyle stood in the chapel entrance facing CHERUB's

death-in-service memorial. The names of four agents were carved on its stone surface:

Johan Urminski	*1940–1954*
Jason Lennox	*1944–1954*
Katherine Field	*1951–1968*
Thomas Webb	*1967–1982*

There was space for more names and everyone hoped Gabrielle O'Brien wouldn't be the next.

'We'll need more candles in a minute,' Kerry whispered, as she looked under the fold-out table in front of them and realised that she was on the last box.

Kyle nodded. 'There's a load more in the vestry. I'll go and fetch them.'

But as Kyle turned away, his mobile phone chimed into life. Evil eyes came at him from all directions.

'Turn that thing off,' Dennis King – one of the senior mission controllers – said stiffly, as several kids tutted.

'Sorry,' Kyle grimaced, but as he pulled the phone out of his top he saw the name *Michael Hendry* on the display. He dived around the table and into the graveyard outside as he flipped the phone open.

'Michael, how's it going?'

'I can think of better days,' Michael said, as Kyle realised he'd sounded too flippant. 'Just wanted to call someone for a chat, you know?'

Kyle had recently turned seventeen. Despite a reputation as a con-merchant, he was well liked and a lot of people came to him for advice.

'I'm here whenever,' Kyle said. The wind blew through the darkness as he crouched beside the headstone of a long-dead farmer to stop the buffeting in his ear. 'Are you still at the hospital?'

'Nah, I'm back at the Zoo – that's the care home we've been living in. They're talking about pulling our mission, but I put up a fight so they're letting me carry on for now.'

'Are you sure it's safe?'

'I'm sure it's *not* safe,' Michael said bluntly. 'Another gang just declared war, but me and Gab have put two months into this. I want to carry on and I know she'd be the same if I'd taken the knife.'

'Maybe you *would* be better off back at campus,' Kyle said tactfully. 'It sounds like you got into a serious row and the cops will be after you, won't they?'

'We've got a liaison with the head of the anti-gang taskforce, but he's the only cop who knows about our mission,' Michael said. 'There's going to be a full-scale murder investigation and I dropped my phone at the scene, so they're bound to haul me in. But the gang members will want to sort their own business and it's not the kind of neighbourhood where eyewitnesses are gonna pour out of the woodwork.'

'Wall of silence,' Kyle said.

'Exactly.'

'So have you seen Gabrielle?'

'She was in a sterile room,' Michael explained. 'All I got was a two-second glimpse as they wheeled her into theatre. The doctor explained that your guts are a whole maze of organs and tubes. She could be in surgery all night and it all depends where she was stabbed. A couple of centimetres can make the difference between being OK and bleeding to death.'

'Any news on who stabbed her?'

'The cops are looking at CCTV from some of the buildings around there. Hopefully Gab can identify him when she comes round – if she comes round . . . Or at least give a description.'

'Let's hope, eh?'

'So what's going on back there, does everyone on campus know what went down?'

'Yeah,' Kyle said. 'We're all totally depressed. There's a candlelit vigil in the chapel.'

Michael managed a dry laugh. 'You *know* you're in trouble when they put on a vigil. Anyhow, I gotta go. I'm heading into town to see if anyone knows what's happening – but don't tell any of the staff that. Zara gave me instructions to stay out of the way until she'd spoken to the ethics committee.'

'Michael, you be careful out there.'

'I can't sit around here with my thoughts, Kyle. I'm going nuts.'

'Well good luck,' Kyle said uncertainly. 'I'm gonna keep my phone on, so call us any time you feel like it.'

'Will do,' Michael said, as he ended the call.

Kyle looked around the graveyard and felt sad. He was at the end of his CHERUB career and everywhere on campus was suddenly full of memories.

In less solemn times, the graveyard around the chapel was used as a play area by red-shirts, and Kyle had spent many summer nights chasing around with torches and water pistols and wandering nervously amidst the headstones, looking for ghosts the older kids had warned them about.

'Hey, Kyle,' Lauren said, sounding a touch out of breath.

She'd crept up behind and made him jump.

'Sorry,' Lauren said. 'Kerry told me you were out here and . . . I know you're busy with Gabrielle and candles and everything, but James isn't here and I *really* need to talk to someone.'

'What about?'

Lauren explained that she was giving evidence at Mr Large's disciplinary hearing and how he'd threatened to kill Meatball if she didn't cover for him.

'So what do you think?' Lauren asked. 'I suppose the *right* thing to do is report it straight to my handler, but Meryl might not believe me. And you know how gossip spreads around campus. Large might find out that I snitched and whack Meatball . . .'

Kyle thought for a second. 'I'm sure you can trust Meryl, but all the senior staff are having an emergency meeting about Gabrielle at the moment. I don't think they'd appreciate it if you knocked on the door because you're worried about a dog.'

Lauren nodded. 'I know my problem isn't the biggest in the world right now, but I can't ignore it.'

Kyle put a reassuring hand on her shoulder. 'If the worst comes to the worst, we'll walk down to Zara's house and kidnap Meatball ourselves. But I'm sure it won't come to that. We'll speak to Meryl tomorrow and sort something out, so don't go losing any sleep.'

'Thanks, Kyle,' Lauren smiled. 'I'm gonna go inside and see if there's any candles left. And let's be honest: I can't see anyone on campus sleeping too soundly tonight.'

11. AIR

James had to get up after less than five hours' sleep so that a local fisherman could sail him to the mainland. When he arrived at the hospital all the kids on Jo's ward were asleep and James had to throw a small stack of Malaysian notes at a porter to secure a pair of crutches.

It was supposed to be an hour's taxi ride to the international airport, but it was morning rush hour and they eventually reached the business-class check-in less than forty minutes before take-off. After a row – and mainly because they were kids who didn't have bags to check – the desk manager reluctantly reopened the flight to issue boarding passes and arranged for a beeping electric cart to speed them through a kilometre of airport corridors to the departure gate.

James had a set of clean clothes in his backpack and had hoped to shower in the lounge before boarding, but their late arrival forced him to board the aeroplane in a sweaty T-shirt and combat trousers stiffened by dirt. Still, he was too tired to care about the businessmen staring over their laptop screens as they boarded, or even Jo's complaints that his feet stank when he pulled off his boots.

As soon as the seatbelt light went out, James pushed his seat back until it became a bed, slapped a hot towel over his face and indulged in twelve glorious hours of teenage idleness, interrupted only by meals and toilet breaks.

The time difference meant they reached London at two in the afternoon. James wanted to freshen up and get a free lunch in the Heathrow arrivals lounge, but Jo was all excited about returning to campus and seeing her friends and he was too chilled to argue with the exuberant ten-year-old.

He thought Jo would be more upset after coming so close to passing basic training, but like most kids who'd grown up on CHERUB campus from an early age, she had a sense of her own self-worth that bordered on cockiness. Jo wouldn't recover in time for the next session of basic training in a month, but when she did restart she'd be close to her eleventh birthday and only another freak accident would keep her out of a grey shirt.

To speed things up, Jo sat on a luggage trolley with her crutches held aloft and James steered her through customs and the arrivals gate. They expected to see a member of CHERUB staff waiting for them, or a driver holding up a card with their names on, but there was no sign. James spent a few minutes wandering around to make sure someone wasn't at waiting at another exit.

'Not a soul,' he said irritably.

'You'd better call campus,' Jo said. 'I reckon they've forgotten us.'

James patted his pockets. His mobile battery was dead

after a week in the jungle and he didn't have any British money. 'You haven't got twenty pence for a payphone have you?'

Jo shook her head.

'Great,' James sighed.

Eventually they found a help desk and the attendant let them use a phone to call up the CHERUB emergency number. The assistant mission controller on the end of the line put James through to Meryl Spencer, who apologised and said that she'd forgotten all about them.

'You can't get shot of me that easily,' James grinned.

Meryl usually had a good sense of humour and James was surprised when she just grunted. 'I haven't even been to bed yet. Everyone's been up all night worrying about Gabrielle and—'

'Eh?' James gasped. 'What's happened to Gabrielle?'

'Right, James I'm sorry,' Meryl said. 'My head is all mixed up. You haven't heard, have you?'

*

Meryl Spencer had only grabbed two hours' sleep, and at thirty-nine the former Olympic athlete was past the age where you can get away with that sort of thing. She was exhausted and had a thumping headache, but mainly she was scared for Gabrielle.

As a CHERUB handler, Meryl was a substitute parent to many of Gabrielle's closest friends and she had to be strong for them. She'd cried in the washroom attached to her office, but had to put on a brave face when the kids were around.

'Come in,' Meryl said, as she looked up from her cluttered

desk and recognised Lauren and Kyle through the frosted glass.

'Any news?' Kyle said hopefully, as they stepped inside.

Meryl was sick of constantly being asked the same question and sounded narked. 'If that's all you're here for, I don't know *anything* that wasn't pinned up on the noticeboard at eight this morning. Gabrielle was in surgery for eleven hours and came out of theatre just after 6 a.m. . . . She's suffered severe internal haemorrhaging but there's no sign of serious organ damage—'

'I read the notice,' Kyle said. 'I'm sorry; I guess you've been asked a million times. But if you're not too busy, we're actually here to talk about a little problem that Lauren's got.'

Meryl smiled. 'You know, the odd thing is that I'm not part of the mission staff. I *don't* actually have much to do except sit around waiting for news like everyone else. But I've got to be here if information comes through and I don't think I'd sleep if I tried.'

Lauren and Kyle sat down.

'Last night was *so* weird,' Lauren said. 'I didn't get to bed until midnight, but I couldn't sleep and four of us spent half the night cuddled up in Rat's room watching MTV. People were just wandering the corridors in their night clothes and everyone was out of it in lessons this morning.'

'I had a call from your brother, by the way,' Meryl said. 'He's coming back early with an injured trainee; landed at Heathrow an hour ago and I forgot to send anyone to pick him up.'

Lauren smiled. 'You won't get rid of him that easily.'

Meryl wagged her finger. 'That's *exactly* what he said. So what's your problem, anyway?'

Lauren explained what had happened on the Askers' driveway the night before.

'And I know I've had run-ins with Mr Large in the past,' Lauren said. 'But I'm *not* lying or exaggerating about this, I swear.'

Meryl nodded. 'Of course I believe you. Norman Large is one of the most obnoxious people I've ever met. It's rumoured that Zara doesn't have a lot of time for him and wants him booted out for good.'

'Really?' Lauren grinned.

Meryl realised that she'd said more than she should and had to cover herself. 'When Mac was chairman, he often gave Mr Large the benefit of the doubt. Zara's thirty years younger and our generation has different opinions about how kids are treated. As far as she's concerned, there's fine line between tough training and child abuse and Mr Large has overstepped it. But I've only told you two that, so I *don't* want it repeated outside this room.'

Kyle and Lauren both nodded.

'I did have one idea,' Kyle said. 'What if Lauren put her evidence in writing, but Mr Large was shown a different version of what she'd said?'

Meryl shook her head. 'It wouldn't wash. It's a formal misconduct hearing before the ethics committee. Mr Large has the right to see all the evidence against him and refute it.'

Kyle nodded.

'I guess we could speak to Zara and tell her to move Meatball on to campus until this blows over,' Meryl said.

'We thought about that,' Lauren said. 'But Zara's kids would get upset and I don't want the red-shirts getting their mitts on him. I mean, most red-shirts are OK, but some of the boys are right sadists.'

'It's true,' Kyle said. 'Remember when they had to mount video surveillance to catch the little sod who kept shaving the guinea pigs?'

Meryl drummed her pointing finger on her cheek, 'You know, I'd always understood that Large was quite fond of dogs. It might be an empty threat.'

'Maybe,' Lauren said anxiously, 'but we can't be sure.'

'What about entrapment?' Meryl said. 'You could wear a microphone and try getting him to repeat the threat. If the evidence was incontrovertible, he'd be out on his arse for sure.'

'Wouldn't work,' Kyle said. 'First off, Large wouldn't be stupid enough to repeat the threat. Second, even if we got the evidence, there's nothing to stop him going after Meatball.'

Meryl rubbed her eyes as she thought. 'You know, Lauren, the one thing I admire in all this is that you haven't even mentioned the possibility of giving in to his blackmail.'

'I'd *never* do that,' Lauren said.

'But our options *are* limited,' Meryl said. 'You don't officially exist so you can hardly report the threat to the police, and if you make an official complaint here on campus, it'll just boil down to your word against Large's. The only sensible thing to do is speak to Ewart or Zara and suggest that Meatball be moved into safe-keeping here on campus. No red-shirt will dare to harm the chairwoman's dog.'

'But Joshua—' Lauren interrupted.

'He's a three-year-old boy,' Meryl shrugged. 'He'll get over it.'

'Bloody Large,' Lauren spluttered.

'Right now Zara's stressed out with all that's going on around Gabrielle,' Meryl said. 'But I'll speak to Ewart straight away and suggest that we move Meatball on to campus before next week's hearing so that Mr Large can't get hold of him.'

Neither Kyle nor Lauren were completely satisfied, but at least Lauren would be able to give her evidence and Meatball would be safe.

12. REVIVAL

Dr Shah was a slender Indian with a bald head. He stepped out of Gabrielle's room and pulled down his surgical mask as Chloe, Zara and Michael crowded around him.

'How's it going?' Michael asked. 'Can we still go in to see her?'

The doctor nodded. 'Fortunately she's young and in excellent health. She's responding well. We've reduced the level of sedation and she's steadily regaining consciousness.'

'Can she speak?' Chloe asked.

'A little,' the doctor nodded. 'She has eighty stitches in her stomach and thirty in her back. Those are very large wounds and if they become infected the complications will be serious.'

'Is her condition still life-threatening?' Michael asked.

'The surgeon worked for more than five hours, repairing damage to her stomach and cauterising areas where the bleeding was most severe. Because Gabrielle is young and seems to have escaped serious organ damage, I'd say that her situation is now stable rather than critical. She's maintaining blood pressure without transfusions, which indicates that the operation has stemmed most of the internal bleeding.

Having said that, her injuries *are* grave and it's too early to rule out complications.'

Dr Shah pointed Chloe, Michael and Zara towards a dressing room where a nurse made them wash their hands with alcohol gel and put on gowns and disposable gloves.

'I know that you need to ask her about the attack,' the nurse said, 'but she's just come around and you *absolutely* mustn't excite her. If something upsets her, leave her be.'

'We understand,' Zara nodded, as they walked back into the corridor. The nurse entered a security code to open Gabrielle's room.

Michael led the way and recoiled at what he saw. With stab wounds front and back and a badly swollen face, Gabrielle lay awkwardly on her side. Blood had seeped into the dressings and an oxygen tube ran under her nose. Electrodes stuck to her skin monitored blood pressure and heart rate.

Gabrielle found it hard to express emotion with pillows piled around her head, but she managed to smile and brought her arm forward for Michael to hold her hand.

'We can't touch,' Michael said, shaking his head as a tear streaked down behind his mask. 'But the doc says you're doing great.'

Gabrielle rocked her head. 'Doesn't feel great,' she said. Her voice was weak and slightly nasal because of the oxygen tube. 'What's the time?'

'Just after three.'

Chloe spoke next. 'Gabrielle, it's me. I don't know if you feel like talking, or even how much you can remember, but I'd like to ask you some questions.'

'Are you recording?'

'Yes,' Chloe said. 'If that's OK?'

'Who else?' Gabrielle asked, as she struggled to recognise masked people with blurry eyes.

'It's me, Zara.'

'The boys who killed Owen, we're . . .' Gabrielle's throat was raw and she gagged every time she attempted more than half a sentence.

'Take your time,' Zara said.

'We know you were chased from the football pitches,' Michael said. 'The police got witness statements from people in the street. They've identified some of the Runts and made arrests in connection with the murder of Owen Campbell-Moore.'

'Listen,' Gabrielle croaked impatiently, sensing that she might pass out at any second. 'I was in the shed with Owen's body. They didn't know I was there.'

Gab seemed helpless as she paused to catch her breath. Michael badly wanted to hug her.

'All talking, the Runts – and one goes: *Sasha's boy said . . . there'd be a lot more than f . . . than four kilos.*'

'What does that mean?' Zara asked.

Chloe raised her palm to silence her boss and leaned in close to Gabrielle. 'Are you *completely* sure?'

'Sure,' Gabrielle said, rocking her head on the pillow to nod.

'What about the man who stabbed you?' Chloe asked. 'The police have a description from the lady who had her car stolen and a CCTV image from a car park where he abandoned it, but did you recognise him?'

'Not seen before . . . Just one of the Runts.'

As Gabrielle said this, an alarm sounded from the monitoring unit beside her bed. By the time Michael had turned around to look at the display, Dr Shah was coming through the door.

'Low oxygen,' Shah explained. 'Her lungs are fine, but she gets pain when she inhales and as a result she's not breathing deeply enough. We're going to have to increase her pain medication, but that will knock her out for another few hours.'

'We'd better go,' Chloe said, as she stepped away from the bed.

'I love you Gabrielle,' Michael said. 'Everyone's praying for you.'

As they backed out of the room, Dr Shah stripped the cellophane away from a needle pack and prepared to give Gabrielle her shot.

'Love you,' Gabrielle said, her voice weaker than before.

Zara put her arm around Michael's back once they'd returned to the changing area and stripped off their masks.

'You did great,' Zara said. 'But I didn't understand what was so significant about what she said. Who's Sasha?'

Chloe explained as she dropped her latex gloves into a medical waste unit. 'It never made sense that a teenage gang like the Runts would take on a hardcore crew like the Slasher Boys. But the Slasher Boys' biggest rival is a group known as the Mad Dogs. Sasha Thompson is their main man.

'The Mad Dogs are led by old-timers; people who worked for or had close ties to KMG. Armed robbers and big-time dealers. Rather than smuggling drugs themselves, they let other gangs take the risks, and then they steal their money, drugs or ideally both.'

Zara nodded. 'So *Sasha's boy said there'd be a lot more than four kilos* indicates that the Runts were tipped off by the Mad Dogs about Major Dee keeping his cocaine stashed above the roof tiles?'

'Seems that way,' Chloe said.

'Why wouldn't Sasha take the cocaine himself?' Zara asked.

'The Slasher Boys and Mad Dogs have been squaring up for the best part of a year. But it looks like Sasha's worked out that it's easier to have the Runts do his dirty work for him.'

Michael nodded. 'And once the Runts and Slashers have spent six months stabbing and shooting one another, the Mad Dogs can move in and clean up.'

'Our biggest problem with this mission has always been that we don't have enough manpower,' Chloe explained. 'There are several large gangs and the balance of power shifts regularly. The only way we can really get a full picture of what's happening is by putting agents into another major gang.'

Zara smiled uneasily. 'That's a tough ask, Chloe. I'm facing a grilling about whether the mission was too dangerous in the first place and you're talking about expanding it.'

Michael liked Chloe's suggestion and nodded enthusiastically. 'Which gang would you target? The Runts accept anyone who can throw a punch. They'd be dead easy to infiltrate.'

'It would be easy,' Chloe said, 'but the Runts aren't much more than random teenage thugs. We really need to get someone inside the Mad Dogs. They're the ones pulling all the strings.'

'I take your point,' Zara said. 'But didn't you consider infiltrating the Mad Dogs before and decide that they were too tight-knit?'

'We did,' Chloe nodded. 'But we've learned a lot over the past couple of months. Maureen and I talked it over and we think there might be a way.'

Zara couldn't help laughing. 'You're not joking, are you? You *really* want me to go to the ethics committee and suggest that we put another agent on to the mission where Gabrielle almost died!'

'Two agents, actually,' Chloe said sheepishly, wondering if her boss was about to bite her head off. 'This mission has progressed slowly from the start and now that Michael is working alone it's not going to get any faster. It's pointless going on with one agent. We've either got to expand and go after the Mad Dogs, or pull the plug and head back to campus.'

Michael hated the idea of pulling the plug, but kept his trap shut because he could see that Chloe was fighting to save the mission.

'OK,' Zara nodded, 'I'll consider your plan. How long will it take you to make a written proposal and e-mail it to me?'

Chloe shrugged. 'We've already done most of the work. I could get it to you in two or three hours.'

'Right,' Zara said. 'Gabrielle's not going to benefit from us hanging around here while she's unconscious. I'm going to drive back to campus. I need your proposal by the time I arrive. Once I've read it through, I'll set up an emergency meeting with the ethics committee. If I like what I see and if the committee isn't too pent-up over what happened to Gabrielle, I'll raise the plan and see if it floats.'

'There's one other thing,' Chloe said. 'The mission we're proposing relies on an established relationship with an associate of the Mad Dogs. There's only one agent who'd be able to do it.'

'And who's that?' Zara asked.

'James Adams.'

13. REVENGE

The sun was setting as a Toyota saloon dropped James and Jo at the main campus gate. A few of Jo's red-shirt friends ran out of the reception area and gave her consoling hugs as James headed off to the lift, slightly put out that none of his mates had shown their faces.

'Brucey!' James yelled, as he pounded his fist on his fourteen-year-old mate's door. 'You in there?'

'Wait a sec,' Bruce yelled shakily. 'Just . . . I'm getting dressed.'

But it was Kerry that James saw pulling a T-shirt over her head as he burst into the room.

'Sorry,' James gasped, averting his eyes. 'I didn't know you were in here. I was trying to catch Bruce in the nuddy.'

'We were just . . . You know,' Bruce spluttered awkwardly.

'Making out like randy dogs,' James grinned.

'Not that it's any of your business if we were,' Kerry said sourly.

James and Kerry were just about on speaking terms, but she was still sore after he'd dumped her for Dana.

'How was Malaysia?' Bruce asked.

James shrugged. 'Hot, wet and too many bugs. Any breaking news on Gabrielle?'

'Nothing new since breakfast,' Kerry said.

James gave her a smile. 'Have you been OK? Gab's pretty much your best mate?'

'I'm no worse off than a lot of other people.'

'So is anyone else around?'

'Lauren's in Kyle's room,' Bruce said. 'They've got a problem with Mr Large and they wanted to ask us about it. We said we'd head up there after we'd had some time to ourselves . . .'

Kerry raised an eyebrow. 'We might as well go *now*, seeing as James disturbed us.'

James had dated a few girls on missions but he'd never had to live with them after the break-up. Kerry was part of his crowd and over the past few months he'd learned that no matter how much you pretend it doesn't matter, it's still uncomfortable having an ex-girlfriend around.

The trio headed along the sixth-floor corridor and found Kyle's door open. Lauren lay face-down on Kyle's bed flipping through a copy of *Heat* magazine, with the man himself sprawled over a leather beanbag.

'Good news everyone, it's me!' James said exuberantly.

'We noticed,' Lauren said, as she faked a yawn.

James tutted. 'Don't die of over-enthusiasm, will you?'

'You've only been away for ten days,' Kyle said. 'What do you expect, a ticker-tape parade?'

'And nobody's exactly in a laughing mood at the moment,' Lauren added.

'So what's this problem?' Kerry asked, as she slid her arm around Bruce's back.

Kyle explained about Large threatening Meatball and that Meryl was going to speak to Ewart and arrange to have the dog taken into campus.

'So it's not ideal, but Meatball's safe,' James said. 'What's the big problem?'

'Rod Nilsson,' Kyle said.

James was fuzzy-headed after the long flight and wondered if he'd missed something. 'Who?'

'You know, James,' Lauren said. 'Remember that night we were in your room and everyone started getting out photos from when they were little?'

'Gotcha,' James nodded. 'Rod was Kyle's best friend; the one who never made it through basic training.'

'That's the man,' Kyle said. 'Rod took basic training with me and he got to day eighty-three. He's asthmatic and we were in the desert. Large had decided that it was Rod's day to be picked on. The air was really dusty and I carried most of Rod's kit because he was fighting for breath. Not long after we set camp for the night this massive sandstorm blew up. It snuffed our fire before we could cook any food and all we could do was huddle inside our tents and hope they didn't get blown away.

'After about an hour, the winds died off, but the air was still thick with dust. Large dragged Rod out of his tent because of his *bad attitude* and started making him do push-ups and squats. There was no way he could do it and he started coughing really badly. Large ran off to get a canteen, but Rod ended up having a full-scale asthma attack and passing out. Luckily we were in America and there was a medical chopper on the scene within fifteen minutes.

'Rod ended up in hospital for three days. The asthma attack was really bad and he started getting nightmares about being unable to breathe. He went back to campus and built himself up to full fitness, but when it came to restarting basic training, he couldn't face Mr Large putting him in that kind of position again, so he quit.'

James nodded. 'You told me this story before. You still send him letters and stuff, don't you?'

'Mostly e-mails,' Kyle said. 'We usually meet up every year around Christmas time and he's going travelling with me after he's sat his A-levels.'

'Maybe it was for the best though,' James said. 'I mean, if he was a severe asthmatic . . .'

'He wasn't,' Kerry said angrily. 'Rod had an inhaler and he got short of breath sometimes, but he only collapsed because Mr Large was bullying him.'

'Didn't Large get a reprimand or anything?'

Kyle shook his head. 'Large wrote up a report saying that Rod hadn't experienced any previous problems with his asthma that day and all the other instructors backed him up.'

'Did you say anything?' James asked.

Kyle shook his head. 'Maybe I should have, but I was ten years old. In those days, Mr Large had the other instructors in his pocket and it would have been our word against theirs. And you can imagine the misery Large would have put Rod through if he'd made a formal complaint and then restarted basic training.'

'So Large is a buttwipe,' James said. 'It's hardly earth-shattering news. And *what* does any of this have to do with Lauren and Meatball?'

'Nothing,' Kyle said. 'Except for the fact that seven years on, Large is up to the same dirty tricks: trying to blackmail Lauren and weasel his way back into a job as a training instructor. I'm leaving CHERUB in two months and I've decided that before I go, I'm gonna get Large back for all the nasty stuff he's done.'

'Cool,' James grinned. 'I'm in. What's the plan?'

'That's our problem,' Lauren said. 'We haven't got one.'

'Maybe we should leave it to the staff,' Kerry said. 'He's probably going to be kicked out anyway and we could get in trouble.'

James shook his head and Bruce tutted.

'Come on Kerry,' Lauren said. 'You're always *so* straight. You've got as much reason to hate Large as anyone else.'

'I'm leaving in two months so I'll take the rap,' Kyle said. 'They can't punish me because I'll just walk out early.'

'I've got it,' Bruce announced. 'Why don't we go to his house in the dead of night carrying baseball bats and dressed in masks and stuff, then drag him out of bed and beat the crap out of him?'

'Subtle,' James laughed.

'Brilliant,' Lauren said. 'Unless he has another heart attack and dies and we all end up getting done for murder. And even if he's just battered we'd all get expelled.'

Bruce snapped his fingers. 'Large is smart: he threatened Lauren by getting to Meatball. We've got to find a way of winding him up by getting at something close to him. Maybe we could do over his Rottweilers, Thatcher and Saddam.'

'No way,' Lauren said. 'We're not hurting those poor defenceless animals.'

James smirked. 'They didn't seem defenceless when they were trying to bite chunks out of my arse.'

'Kidnapping and poisoning are too extreme,' Kyle said. 'I like Bruce's idea of getting to him, but it's got to be subtle.'

'Well,' Kerry said. 'I don't really want any part of this, but he's got a fourteen-year-old daughter. I think she's called Hayley and fathers tend to be *very* protective towards teenage daughters.'

'Yes,' Kyle said triumphantly. 'Kerry, that's it. I could *kiss* you.'

'You wanting to kiss a girl,' James grinned, 'there's a first.'

It was a cheap shot and everybody groaned.

James tutted. 'Sorry I spoke. So what can we do to Large's daughter?'

'We've got to do something that upsets Large, but isn't actually too harmful to his daughter,' Lauren said.

'Exactly,' Kyle agreed. 'I've seen Hayley Large at the bowling alley in town a few times and I don't think she has a boyfriend.'

James nodded. 'I highly doubt it, she's a complete heifer.'

Kerry punched James on the arm. 'Don't be so sexist.'

'Hey,' James yelled. 'You're not my bird any more so if you go around hitting me I might just hit you back.'

Kerry laughed. 'Try it and see where it gets you.'

Kerry had a point. She was miles smaller than James, but she could still kick his arse.

'Here we go again. . .' Lauren sighed. 'I definitely preferred it when you two weren't talking to each other.'

'Getting back to the subject in hand,' Kyle said firmly, 'what we need is a boyfriend for Hayley Large. A good-looking guy who's comfortable around girls, but who would also make Mr Large throw a fit if he thought the lad was trying to get his hands on his daughter's goodies.'

'That's a *sweet* idea,' Lauren grinned.

James nodded until he realised that four sets of eyes were staring at him.

'Oh no,' James said. 'Not me . . .'

'Totally you,' Lauren said, as she bounced on Kyle's bed with excitement. 'You're always mouthing off about what a stud you are and how girls find you irresistible. Now you've got a chance to prove it.'

14. ETHICS

James had slept on the plane and his body clock was stuck on mid-afternoon when everyone started going to bed. He had a restless night and when it got to 5:30 a.m. he gave up on sleep and headed for the fitness centre in the recently refurbished gym.

It was a Saturday. Following a lonely walk across campus, James found the gym deserted and drew childish delight from running his hand over banks of light switches, setting off hundreds of fluorescent tubes.

After warming up with stretches and shuttle runs, James started pumping weights. He wasn't big on team sports, but he found pushing himself in the gym or on the athletics track satisfying, and working out was always better when the gym was empty and you didn't have to fight over the equipment.

Fifty minutes later, James was soaked in sweat, his veins were all pumped and the exertion had kick-started his brain. A couple of staff members were on the treadmills as he headed off to soothe himself in the plunge pool, but the dining room was virtually empty when he arrived for breakfast.

James knew he needed protein to replenish his aching muscles and the chef obliged by cooking up thin strips of steak with scrambled eggs and mushrooms. Zara came up behind and tapped his shoulder while he sat at a table reading the Premiership preview in the Saturday paper.

'You're up early,' Zara said.

'Jet lag,' James explained. 'Couldn't sleep so I hit the weights.'

Zara nodded. 'You want to be careful. If you start looking too much like a bodybuilder, it restricts the kinds of missions we can send you on.'

James slapped his belly. 'There's not much chance I'll ever look like a bodybuilder. I'm too fond of my food.'

To prove the point, the chef put a plate stacked up with steak and eggs on the table, along with his side of toasted muffins and jam.

'Cheers,' James grinned, as the chef looked towards Zara.

'I'm afraid the buffet won't be ready for another twenty minutes or so, but I'd be happy to cook anything you fancy.'

'Well I wouldn't normally...' Zara said guiltily, as she watched James tuck into his food. 'But I quite fancy what he's having. I'll have my steak well done and a pot of strong coffee.'

'No worries. It'll take seven minutes to fry the steak.'

'Thanks,' Zara nodded. Then she looked at James. 'I need a proper meal. I've been back and forth between campus and Luton for the last two days and it seems like all I've eaten is Burger King and hospital sandwiches.'

James noticed that three little red-shirts had gathered

around a notice by the door. 'Is that an update on Gabrielle?' he asked.

'I just pinned it up,' Zara nodded. 'She's been *incredibly* lucky. The knife went into her back this much' – Zara held her hands twenty centimetres apart – 'but despite that, it missed all of her major organs, and it's the same with the injury to her side. The surgeon described it as a minor miracle.'

'So she's going to be OK?'

'It's not a hundred per cent, but it looks good. She's lucid now and they've moved her out of intensive care. She could be out of hospital within five days, although she might need another operation if her tubes don't heal properly.'

'That's *quick*,' James said, as he gulped a lump of steak that he hadn't chewed enough and almost choked himself.

'There are a lot of antibiotic-resistant bacteria around in hospitals these days,' Zara explained, as James hacked chewed-up steak into a serviette. 'She's got less chance of picking up an infection on campus, so they want her off the ward as soon as possible. I'm going to have her placed in a room in the medical unit.'

'Fantastic,' James grinned. 'Everyone will be able to see her and that.'

'It certainly is,' Zara smiled. 'I actually need to talk something over with you regarding Gabrielle and Michael's mission. Do you mind if I sit down?'

James shrugged. 'I'll probably get called *Chairwoman's pet* if I'm seen sitting with you, but I'll just thump 'em.'

'Well don't thump 'em too hard,' Zara said as she sat opposite James, her smile turning into a huge yawn. 'I was up until one-thirty this morning with the ethics committee.'

'That *does* sound like fun,' James said, as one of the kitchen staff placed Zara's coffee on the table.

'I've barely slept,' Zara continued. 'And when I did get home, Joshua was playing up and insisted on sleeping in our bed. He's got his arm in plaster and he gets really frustrated when he can't do something.'

'Poor kid,' James said. 'If I get a chance I'll pay him a visit.'

'Oh *please* do,' Zara grinned. 'You're still his hero.'

'I'm due a week off after helping out with training, so I've got loads of spare time. And what's this you said about the mission?'

'Last night's meeting was to determine the future of Gabrielle and Michael's mission. We had all six ethics-committee members there, and to start with they were split down the middle: three in favour of pulling the plug because the gang war had gotten too hot; three who accepted my argument that all CHERUB missions are inherently dangerous and that you shouldn't give up because one bad thing happens.

'We also had the Intelligence Minister on a conference call from London. Surprisingly he sided with me, and after a couple of hours we got a five-to-one vote in favour of continuing the mission. And that's where you come in.'

James was taken aback. 'I've just got back from Malaysia.'

'Don't worry about your week off,' Zara smiled. 'It'll take time to set everything up. But we're trying to infiltrate a gang known as the Mad Dogs and you're uniquely placed to pull it off.'

'How come?' said James, confused.

Zara pulled a black-and-white mug shot out of a cardboard file and slid it across the table. The head-and-shoulders shot showed a lad of about fifteen. He was a touch smaller than James with a stocky build and a daft goatee beard. The boy had matured since James had known him and he took a couple of seconds to catch on.

'Is that Junior Moore?' James gasped.

Zara nodded. 'Son of drug baron, Keith Moore. You two got pretty friendly when we were in Luton two years back.'

'Yeah,' James nodded. 'We went to Florida together and we had a total laugh – well, at least until the drug dealers started shooting at us.'

'Junior's had a rough couple of years. His mother sent him to boarding school, but he kept running away and was eventually expelled for smoking cannabis. He moved back in with his mother and siblings near Luton, and despite her attempts to keep him under control, he's been in and out of trouble ever since. Last October he was caught behind the wheel of a stolen car. He was over the alcohol limit and there were two kilos of cocaine under the front passenger seat.

'Junior got off on the more serious drugs charge because the police couldn't disprove his claim that the drugs had been in the car when he stole it, but he still got six months' youth custody. He was sentenced before Christmas and released on a good behaviour bond two weeks ago.'

James sucked air between his teeth. 'Sounds like he's turning into his old man.'

'Anything but,' Zara said pointedly. 'Keith Moore was a professional criminal who ran KMG like a business. Junior

Moore has drug and alcohol problems and is going the right way about spending serious time in prison.'

'Junior's dad stashed millions in a trust fund though,' James said. 'Why's he risking his neck for a few grand's worth of cocaine?'

'Junior can't access any of his dad's money until he's twenty-one. And like a lot of teenagers, I suppose he's testing the limits and trying to make a name for himself by associating with the Mad Dogs.'

'So the plan is that I go undercover, link up with Junior again and use him to get all the information I can on the Mad Dogs?'

'If you're willing to accept the mission,' Zara nodded. 'It would all be routine but for the gang war and the risk of further violence. Michael will be on the same mission, but he'll be inside a rival gang so you'll have to keep apart. And to be on the safe side, we want you accompanied by another agent who can cover your back.'

James nodded. 'If anyone's going to be covering my back, I'd ask for Bruce Norris.'

Zara hummed uncertainly. 'We're careful about the missions we use Bruce on. He isn't the most mature fourteen-year-old.'

'No disrespect,' James said warily, 'I know you're the boss, but I think Bruce gets a bum rap. He used to act babyish sometimes, but he's really changed over the last year or so. He's filled out, he's less moody and I think going out with Kerry has really made him grow up.'

'And there's no friction because he's seeing your ex-girlfriend?'

'Me and Kerry fancied each other like mad, but it never really worked between us. She's still upset because I dumped her, but she seems happier with Bruce than she ever was with me and I'm a million times happier with Dana.'

'Your self-defence skills aren't bad,' Zara said thoughtfully. 'But I can see the benefits of having someone with Bruce's combat ability on a mission where some kind of physical confrontation is likely. And despite a few people saying he's immature, he earned his navy shirt and I don't ever recall him doing much wrong on any of his missions.'

James grinned. 'So, do you want me to tell him, or what?'

'Not yet,' Zara said. 'I'd better run it by Chloe and Maureen to make sure they're happy, but I'm inclined to agree that Bruce is a good choice.'

15. SNEAKS

James wasn't the only one who'd got up early. Lauren crept into Rat's room and leaned over his bed until her lips almost touched his ear.

'COCK-A-DOODLE-DOO!'

Rat jolted so hard that he thumped his skull on the headboard. He rubbed the injury as he sat up and glowered at Lauren.

'What was that in aid of?'

Lauren was killing herself laughing. 'I wish I'd videoed that on my mobile. The look on your face . . .'

'What time is it?'

'Almost seven,' Lauren said. 'You'd better start getting ready. I've got a lesson at eight-thirty and we've got to have breakfast.'

'I hate getting up,' Rat groaned, picking a lump of sleep off his eyelid as he swung out of bed dressed in boxers and socks. It took him thirty seconds to pull on his trousers and a grey CHERUB T-shirt and slide his feet into his boots.

'Ready,' he announced, slapping his thighs as he stood up.

Lauren was stunned. She'd spent longer than that

doing her hair. 'Don't you want to comb your hair, or clean your teeth?'

'Can't be arsed at this time,' Rat said, as he grabbed a watch off the window ledge and slid it over his hand. 'Let's go.'

'Is that all you ever do when you get up in the morning?' Lauren said, as they set off down the corridor towards the lift.

'Sometimes I'll take a shower, but I've got combat training at half nine. I'll be all sweaty afterwards so what's the point?'

'Mr Hygiene rides again. You're *such* a boy.'

Rat tutted. 'Do you want me to help you? If I'm not clean enough for you, I'd be happy to crawl back under my doona.'

'You were all in favour of getting Large back last night,' Lauren pointed out, as the lift doors parted.

'Still am,' Rat yawned. 'But you know I hate getting up early.'

Two other kids made a dash along the corridor and stepped into the car behind them, so they couldn't say any more as they rode from the eighth floor all the way down to the basement archives.

Agents rarely used the archives and this was the first time Rat had seen them. The main building on campus was thirty years old, and while the offices and accommodation above had been refurbished, the basement was still decked out in its original 1970s furniture, with avocado-green fittings and threadbare carpet tiles.

The lift opened into a corridor with double doors at either end. To the left was the library, but Rat was attracted to the large space on the right which contained a mainframe computer the size of two dozen fridge-freezers. It was surrounded by racks of giant data tapes and looked like something out of an old sci-fi movie.

'Old skool,' Rat grinned, giving a double thumbs-up as he peered through the glass door. 'Do you reckon they still use it?'

'Doubt it,' Lauren said as she pulled a plastic pass out of her trousers. 'Now stop lusting after the big computer, you geek. I need you to keep your eyes open.'

She swiped the pass through a magnetic reader and the door clicked open.

'Nice one,' Rat nodded, as Lauren held the door open for him. 'I wonder where Kyle got the pass.'

Lauren shrugged. 'Knowing Kyle he traded it for a stack of pirate DVDs.'

The archive smelled of dust and furniture polish. It was only staffed during regular office hours so the reception desk was unmanned.

As Rat peered down the fifty-metre-long lines of metal shelves and filing cabinets to make sure they were alone, Lauren sat in front of an old PC with a glowing green screen. She looked for a mouse, but after a few seconds she realised there wasn't one and used the cursor keys to navigate down the screen to a field marked SEARCH.

Lauren typed NORMAN LARGE and after twenty seconds a list of files and reference numbers scrolled up from the bottom of the screen.

After moving through the list, she spotted the *Personnel Record 1996 – present* and jotted the shelf reference on to a Post-It, before pressing the escape button several times to clear the evidence of her search.

'There's nobody around,' Rat confirmed, as Lauren stood up from the desk. 'What's down here? How come this place is so huge?'

'There's records on every CHERUB mission before 1992, after which they're all computerised,' Lauren explained. 'Then there's paper records for everyone who has ever visited campus and required security clearance, from the chairwoman all the way down to some bloke who popped in twenty-five years ago to replace the filter on a swimming pool. There's also other stuff like contracts, building plans, accounts . . .'

Rat's face lit up with mischief. 'Are *our* personal files down here?'

Lauren shook her head. 'Files on current agents and recent missions are in the mission preparation building, but they all get scanned and digitised after five years.'

'Pity; a peek at our own files might have been a laugh.'

'FGS-271C,' Lauren said as she peered down one of the long lines of shelves. 'Now where's that gonna be . . .'

'Tell you what,' Rat said. 'We'll need to make photocopies. You start looking for the file; I'll go over and make sure the copiers are switched on and warmed up.'

'Good thinking,' Lauren said, as she set off between the lines of shelving, trying to figure out the filing system.

It started out at AAA-000A, so she guessed that her reference starting with F would be in the second or third aisle. She found the Fs in less than a minute, but had to locate a sliding ladder and push it along the front of the shelving units to retrieve the chunky box file from its slot on the top shelf.

As Lauren opened the file for a quick peek the mound of papers inside spewed over the carpet.

'Balls,' she cursed.

Rat heard the noise and came jogging between the shelves to help her pick up. They were both tense, but couldn't help laughing when they spotted a picture of a university-age Norman Large dressed in bleached jeans, sporting an extraordinary mullet hairstyle and holding a placard that said *LSE Student Union boycotts South African goods*.

Once the papers were back in order, Lauren took the file to a small table that lay between the ends of two storage racks and sifted through cream-coloured wallets until she came to the one marked *Descendants*.

'It's spooky to think that CHERUB will keep files on us for years after we leave,' Rat said. 'And not just on us, but our kids and our wives and stuff.'

'It's a big job making sure CHERUB stays a secret,' Lauren nodded. 'I've heard that there's an enforcement unit of some of the toughest ex-cherubs. They go around making sure *nothing* ever leaks out.'

'Like how?'

'Whatever it takes, I guess.'

'Cool,' Rat grinned. 'Do you reckon they kill people? Like, imagine if someone threatened to publish a book about CHERUB and there was no other way to stop them.'

Lauren shrugged impatiently. 'I don't know Rat, it's just a rumour. At *this* moment, we have to look at this file and get out of here before we're busted.'

She opened the Descendants file and quickly read the title page:

NORMAN LARGE

Descendants – 1

Name – Hayley June Large-Brooks

Born – 16.05.1991

Parents – N/A

NOTE – Hayley is the adopted daughter of Norman Large and his long-term partner Gareth Brooks.

'It's all here,' Lauren said excitedly as she flipped through the pages. 'Hayley's school photos, dental records, DNA records, details of her birth parents and of where she goes to school. It's even got what clubs she belongs to and details of her closest school friends.'

'The copier should be warmed up by now.'

Lauren nodded as she followed Rat towards the copiers. The pages weren't bound, so Rat pushed the entire stack into the document feeder and pressed the button to start copying.

It only took one person to watch the copier. Lauren backed gingerly towards the reception desk. She'd covered her tracks, but she was paranoid and wanted to make absolutely sure. As she turned away from the desk, she heard the lift doors opening.

'Rat, someone's coming,' Lauren gasped, as she dived beneath the desk.

Rat looked around anxiously. He considered making a run and hiding amongst the shelves, but there wasn't time and he ended up squeezing into a gap between the copier and the wall as a man stepped into the room.

Lauren peeked through a tiny crack of light between the back panel of the desk and the drawer unit. She recognised the brown suit and bald head of mission controller John Jones. John had worked with Lauren on two of her missions and they'd always got along; but that didn't mean he'd let her off if he caught her rummaging through secret archives without permission.

John stopped walking and turned his head towards the noise coming out of the copying area, as the machine continued to swallow and spit pages from Hayley Large-Brooks' file. John was about to head over and investigate, but Rat managed to squeeze his arm behind the copier and rip the plug out of the wall.

This turned the heat on to Lauren. As John decided that the noise must have been a gurgle from the ventilation system, he turned back towards reception to look up a shelf reference in the computerised catalogue.

There wasn't much space under the desk. Lauren squeezed herself against the backboard as John's shoe landed on the carpet, centimetres from her right boot. She'd be caught right away if John sat down and pulled the chair into the desk, but mercifully he was in a rush and he tapped at the keyboard while standing up.

'Dammit,' John said, as he thumped the keyboard and lowered himself into the chair.

Lauren shuddered as John sat down. She put her hand over her face, because if John moved forward quickly his knee would smash her in the mouth.

Please god don't let him pull the chair in, she thought, crossing her fingers as the mission controller stared curiously at a sheet of paper. After fifteen seconds – which felt more like fifteen years – John suddenly kicked the chair backwards and reached across to grab the telephone from the desk return.

The phone was as dated as all the other fittings in the archive. The metal bell inside dinged as John lifted the receiver and Lauren agonised as he entered the number using an old-fashioned dial.

'Chris,' John said, addressing his assistant. 'I'm down in the archive, but I think I left the piece of paper with the list of documents I needed on my desk. I was wondering if you could remember the date of . . .'

John paused as his assistant said something on the other end of the line. When John opened his mouth again, he sounded a lot more cheerful.

'So you came down and collected the documents last night . . .? Chris, you're an *absolute* star! I was just on the way over to my office and I came down here to save on leg work . . . So they're all waiting on my desk? Thanks very much and I'll see you at the meeting this afternoon.'

John put the phone down and let the chair shoot backwards into a metal cabinet as he sprang cheerfully to his feet.

'You're a good man, Chris,' John muttered to himself, as he picked his briefcase off the floor and headed out towards the lift.

Lauren crawled out and poked her eyes above the desk, then waited until she saw John's legs disappear up the fire stairs before running over to Rat.

'That was *too* close,' Lauren huffed, as Rat plugged the copier back in. 'He was practically touching me. I was already counting my punishment laps.'

'Well we're not out of the woods yet,' Rat shrugged.

The machine had been in mid-copy when Rat pulled the plug, and the result was jammed paper and a control panel ablaze with warning lights.

'Can you fix it?' Lauren asked, as Rat crouched in front of the machine and opened a plastic flap.

'I guess all those years working in the office at the Survivor's Ark did teach me something,' Rat said, as he expertly released a lever, then twisted a green wheel until two jammed sheets of paper rolled into the output tray.

He closed the flap and Lauren was relieved to see the red lights disappear and the words *ready to copy* appear on the touch screen.

'Go and keep look-out,' Rat said. 'There's only about six pages left. Then we'll put the file back and get the hell out of here.'

16. STING

Hayley Large-Brooks was a Year Ten student at St Aloysius girls' school, which was six kilometres from campus. Cherubs often saw Aloysius girls when they went into town, so everyone knew the uniform.

Lauren cobbled together a copy from the stock of school uniform kept on campus, and when she dressed on Monday morning, the only way to distinguish her from a genuine St Aloysius pupil was the lack of a school crest on her green blazer.

'Don't worry,' Kyle said as they headed down the back stairs towards the car park, 'nobody will ever notice if you keep your coat zipped.'

Like all cherubs, Kyle had learned to drive as soon as he was tall enough, but now he'd turned seventeen he'd been issued with a driving licence and was allowed to use the pool cars, provided he drove sensibly and mucked in with shuttling younger kids around.

When they reached the fire exit at the bottom of the staircase, Kyle stepped into the crisp morning air and glanced around, making sure there was nobody about.

Lauren was nervous as they walked briskly across the tarmac. She was supposed to be at an 8 a.m. combat-training session in the dojo, but she'd sent Miss Takada an instant message saying that she'd twisted her ankle. Takada was strict, and if she found out that Lauren had bunked off, her punishment would be two gruelling weeks scrubbing the dojo floor, cleaning the changing rooms and laundering the mountain of sweaty combat suits and damp towels used by the hundred-plus cherubs who trained there every day.

Kyle slid a plipper from inside his tracksuit top and pressed the button to unlock an anonymous Mazda estate. As he buckled up in the front, Lauren clambered in the back and squeezed herself into the footwell behind the front seats so that she wasn't seen as they drove out. Unfortunately, CHERUB pool cars were unloved and the carpet was covered in mud and biscuit crumbs.

Once Kyle had rolled over the speed bumps and pushed his card into the security gate to leave campus, Lauren climbed up on to the seat and brushed the filth off her jacket and uniform before pulling her mobile out of her pocket. She dialled James.

'Any sign?' Lauren asked.

James was camped out in the trees around the back of Norman Large's house, with binoculars around his neck.

'Hayley's got her uniform on,' James said. 'Gareth Brooks headed off for work about an hour ago, so it looks like Large is gonna drive her to school.'

Lauren looked at her watch. 'They're cutting it fine aren't they?'

'Don't blame *me*, I'm only watching,' James said. 'And I think Meatball has picked up my scent. He's running around in the Askers' garden and yapping like crazy.'

'Clever dog,' Lauren grinned, before remembering that she was in a tight spot. 'This is such a pain. I've *got* to head back to campus and get into CHERUB uniform before first lesson.'

'Stop worrying,' James said. 'We timed it all out and Takada is the only person you have to worry about.'

'It's OK for *you*,' Lauren moaned. 'You've got the week off and Kyle's only got one A-level to revise for—'

'Here we go,' James interrupted. 'Hayley and Large have just opened the front door. You'll be following a dark blue Renault Megane.'

Lauren banged on the headrest behind Kyle. 'Slow down, they're about to leave.'

But the road leading out of campus was lined with cameras which the CHERUB security staff monitored for any suspicious activity.

'I can't,' Kyle said. 'It'll be too obvious that we're following them.'

But Kyle did slow down slightly, and he rolled past the isolated parade of houses where Mr Large and the Askers lived as Hayley was climbing into the front passenger seat of the Renault.

'She's a *big* girl,' Kyle grinned. 'Even bigger than in the pictures.'

Lauren giggled. 'I know, James is really pissed off.'

Apart from the odd tractor, there were never hold-ups on the country roads around campus and the drive to the school took less than ten minutes. Along the way, Kyle deliberately took a wrong turn on to a housing estate and reversed out once Mr Large's car was ahead of them.

St Aloysius was an old building set amidst hockey fields and an athletics track. At this time of the day – less than ten minutes before morning registration – the narrow hill leading up to the school was crammed with parents, parking in the middle of the road to drop off their daughters.

Kyle found himself snarled in traffic a few hundred metres from the school gates, with Mr Large's Renault four vehicles ahead of them. After standing still for several minutes, Kyle noticed Hayley step out of the Renault and throw a pack over her shoulder.

'Looks like she's walking the last couple of hundred metres,' Kyle said. 'Hopefully Large won't be looking in your direction, but keep your collar up and your hair over your face until you've gone past.'

'No worries,' Lauren said, as she scooted across the back seat and stepped into the cold air. 'Don't drive too far away, I've got to make my History lesson or I'm dead meat.'

Lauren's confidence plunged as she jogged uphill, trying to catch Hayley. With James going on a mission inside a week they had to act fast, and there was no plausible reason for James to be hanging around a girls' school on a Monday morning. This left Lauren with the awkward task of setting up a date, and while she'd felt OK about the idea the previous night, the whole plan now seemed rickety.

'Excuse me,' Lauren said, as she tapped Hayley on the arm.

Hayley was three years older than Lauren and she turned

around with *who the hell are you kid* all over her face.

Lauren's head was spinning. So many things could go wrong: Hayley might be grounded, she could already have a boyfriend, James might not be her type.

'Hi, I'm Susan,' Lauren lied nervously.

'And why should I give a shit?' Hayley growled.

Lauren smiled uneasily and put Hayley's mood down to Monday morning blues.

'This is going to sound *so* stupid,' Lauren said. 'You don't know me, but I've seen you with your mates at the bowling alley. And my older brother, well, he *kind of* says that he likes you.'

Hayley suspected a prank and looked around suspiciously. 'Why don't you stroll on back to your giggly little chums before I slap you into next week?'

'Please listen,' Lauren begged. 'This isn't a wind-up, I swear. You've seen my brother at the bowling alley. He's called James. He's blond, muscley, I guess you *could* say he's good-looking, but he's dead shy around girls . . .'

Hayley stopped walking. 'I think I know who you mean. He looks a bit like you, but he seemed more like a big mouth to me.'

Lauren grimaced. 'Well . . . I mean, he is a bit loud but that's just front. I mean, I think he's liked you for a while, but he's never had the bottle to go up to you.'

'Since when did you go to St Aloysius?' Hayley said suspiciously. 'I've never seen you around.'

'Just over a week. I mean, I was at Edgeton Comprehensive, over on the other side of campu— umm, the other side of the military firing range.'

Lauren realised her nerves were showing and that she was saying *I mean* too much.

'He's fit,' Hayley said as she raised one eyebrow. 'Fit enough to do better than a fat bird like me. So why's he interested?'

'Umm . . . Well, I think he likes fat . . . I mean *prefers* larger girls. I've seen him looking at magazines with big girls in.'

Hayley screwed up her face. 'You mean he looks at pornos?'

'No,' Lauren gasped, realising that she'd said completely the wrong thing. 'Look, we're going to the bowling alley tonight. My brother will be there, but there's gonna be a big group of us, so it won't be like a date. Maybe you could bring a couple of your friends so it's less awkward . . . And it's half price on Mondays.'

'Maybe,' Hayley said. 'But it's short notice. I'd have to clear it with my parents.'

Lauren shrugged. 'We could postpone. Tuesday or Wednesday if that suits you better.'

'Roll up your sleeve,' Hayley said, as she took her pack off her shoulder and began unzipping.

Lauren was confused until she saw Hayley pull out a black marker. She grabbed Lauren's wrist and wrote a mobile number on her skin.

'I'll be home at about half four,' Hayley said. 'Tell James that I said he's fit, but I'm *not* going on any date unless I've spoken to him first.'

'Fair enough,' Lauren smiled, taking care not to smudge the number as she pulled the sleeve of her blazer back down. 'So, do you reckon you'll make it to the bowling alley?'

Hayley tutted. 'I don't bloody know, just tell him to ring me later and I'll see what he sounds like.'

'Thanks,' Lauren smiled. 'He'll be dead chuffed.'

17. WAFFLES

James flipped his mobile shut and stepped out of the hallway into Kyle's bedroom. Kyle, Bruce, Kerry, Rat, Lauren, the twins Callum and Connor and Rat's mate Andy all stared at James, but he teased them by keeping his mouth zipped.

'So?' Lauren said anxiously.

James shrugged. 'So I spoke to Hayley. She'll be at the bowling alley with two of her mates at around seven tonight. I told her I'd buy her a hot dog and we'll talk it over.'

Bruce slapped his thighs. 'Good stuff.'

'Remember, James, we need good photos,' Lauren said. 'So even if you're not getting anywhere, at least try putting your hand on her knee or something.'

James tutted. 'I've chatted up loads of girls, Lauren. I know what I'm doing.'

Kerry shook her head. 'How many when you were supposed to be going out with me?'

James hated the way that Kerry kept having digs at him, even though their relationship had been over for months. He usually ignored it, but he was getting fed up.

'I had to cheat on you, Kerry,' James said bitterly. 'I needed to get some action from somewhere instead of sitting in your room getting lectured on what I wasn't allowed to do.'

Rat and the twins made *oooh* sounds which were followed by a tense silence and a look on Kerry's face that could have melted a steel bar.

'It's finished between you and me,' James said. 'Get over yourself.'

Kerry stood up. 'I *know* it's over, James,' she spat. 'I just don't want everyone to forget what a two-faced pile of dog—'

'Hey,' Kyle interrupted. 'Ding ding, end of round three!'

'I'm outta here,' Kerry said, as she headed for the door. 'This is a stupid plan and I don't want anything to do with it.'

Kyle's door slammed as Kerry stormed back to her room.

'She's a bitter little lemon,' Rat said, which earned him a punch from Lauren. Lauren then nudged Bruce between the shoulder blades.

'You'd better go after her and check that she's OK.'

Bruce climbed reluctantly off the carpet. 'What am I supposed to say? I'm no good at stuff like this.'

'I don't know,' Kyle said, 'but Lauren's right. Go give her a cuddle or something.'

James waited until Bruce was out of the room before spreading his hands out wide and groaning. 'What *is* Kerry's problem?'

Lauren rested a finger on her lips. 'Oooh let me see,' she said sarcastically. 'You went out with Kerry on and off for two years, during which time you constantly cheated on her. Finally, you dumped her for someone else and broke her heart. Do you think it might be that?'

James' instinct was to throw something equally sarcastic back at his sister, but he knew he'd treated Kerry badly and ended up backing silently on to the spot of carpet where Bruce had been sitting.

'And before anyone asks,' James said, 'I'm gonna chat Hayley up, maybe a peck on the cheek, but that's *it*. Dana's my girlfriend and I don't want to do anything that might upset her when she gets back from Malaysia.'

'You're a gentleman and a scholar,' Connor said, putting on a ridiculously posh accent.

'Absolutely, old bean,' Callum added, sounding even posher. 'But will young Master Adams' resolve stand up to scrutiny when the prospective beau is a female of a more attractive persuasion than Hayley Large-Brooks?'

'For god's sake!' James groaned. 'I hate it when you two speak in those stupid accents. It's so immature.'

'Face it, James,' Rat said. 'Everyone knows what you're like. You'd cheat on Dana in the blink of an eye if you fancied the girl and thought you could get away with it.'

James was annoyed when he looked around and saw everyone nodding. 'I'm not that bad,' he spluttered. 'You make me sound like some kind of complete pig.'

Lauren burst out laughing. 'You made your bed, brother.'

*

Gossip had a way of exploding around campus and a lot of kids were in the mood for some light relief after the trauma of Gabrielle's stabbing. Unfortunately for James, the two big rumours currently spreading around campus concerned him.

Rumour number one was that he was going to try and get off with Mr Large's daughter. Rumour number two was that

Hayley Large-Brooks was overweight. As is the way with rumours, the truth had become exaggerated and there was at least one group of red-shirts who'd heard that Hayley weighed over two hundred kilos and that James had to have sex with her in order to win a £50 bet.

The carers were used to fads on campus: nobody went fishing for two years then suddenly twenty boys started going every day. Scoubidous, Furbys, Beyblade and Pokemon had all done the rounds; but the staff were still surprised to discover a sudden appetite for bowling.

The queue for the minibus that typically took a dozen kids to the local bowling alley stretched back more than twenty metres and contained close to a quarter of the kids on campus.

James was embarrassed and Kyle was fuming. Someone had leaked the plan and if any of the staff found out they'd get in trouble. Worst of all, Mr Large still had friends on campus and if word of their revenge got back to him, Meatball would be in serious danger.

'It's a disaster,' Lauren said, as she stood by the fountain outside the main building looking at the queue of cherubs. James, Kyle, Bruce and Rat were with her. 'What *idiot* opened their big mouth?'

But Lauren herself hadn't been able to resist telling her friend Tiffany; Rat and Andy had told a couple of mates in confidence; Callum and Connor *might* have mentioned something and Kerry had been overheard whilst badmouthing James in the dining-room.

And of course, some of those people had gone on to tell *their* friends in the strictest confidence, and by the time everyone had eaten dinner, most of campus had some idea of what was about to go down.

'There's no way we can go to the bowling alley with all that lot,' James said. 'I'll have twenty idiots gawping at me the whole time and Hayley will suspect in ten seconds flat.'

'We need a change of venue,' Kyle said. 'What about Alien World?'

Alien World was one of those places where you put on plastic vests and shoot laser beams at one another, whilst running between chipboard partitions with spaceships and three-eyed monsters painted on them. As campus had a live-ammunition shooting range and a paintballing arena that was fifty times cooler, nobody from CHERUB ever went there.

'Sounds perfect,' James nodded. 'But do you reckon Hayley will go for it?'

Kyle shrugged. 'I can get a people carrier out of the car pool and drive you there. But what excuse are we gonna use?'

Rat was a master of excuses. 'Tell them that you called the bowling alley to book a couple of lanes, but that it's all booked up,' he said.

'But it's Monday night,' Lauren noted. 'It's always empty on a Monday.'

Rat shrugged. 'Then say that there's a special event on: a works outing or something.'

James liked Rat's idea. He pulled his phone out of his jacket and hit the last number button to call Hayley.

'Hi, it's me again. Have you left home yet . . .? Great. Listen, you're not gonna believe this but I called the bowling alley to reserve a couple of lanes and the whole joint has been booked out to some big party of computer salesmen. I was wondering if you fancied going to Alien World instead?'

Hayley burst out laughing. 'How old am I, nine? Besides, I get completely shagged out running around in those places.'

James looked up from the phone and mouthed: '*She's not buying it.*' Lauren and the others all looked disappointed.

'Well is there anywhere else you can think of?'

'Are your mates going to Alien World?' Hayley asked.

'Yeah,' James said uncertainly. 'At least I think they are.'

'Tell you what then,' Hayley said. 'There's a steakhouse on the other side of the lot to Alien World, next to KFC. We can go there while your mates are in Alien World. They do an all-you-can-eat buffet for six-ninety-nine on a Monday, but you'll have to pay my share, 'cos I'm broke.'

'Cool,' James said enthusiastically. 'That sounds perfect, just you and me.'

'Well it'll probably be my mate Rosie and her boyfriend Dean as well, but we can always ditch 'em if things get interesting.'

James got carried away for a moment. 'Yeah,' he grinned. 'Maybe they'll get interesting.'

He was ecstatic as he ended the call and looked at his friends. 'It's going down at the steakhouse opposite Alien World. And the way she was talking . . . Well, let's just say that she sounded like the kind of girl who's going to provide us with some good photo opportunities.'

'But if we're all in Alien World, who'll be there to take photos?' Kyle asked.

'Oh . . .' James said. 'We'll need another couple to go in with us.'

'Me and Rat could do it,' Lauren said.

James shook his head. 'No offence, but I can hardly turn up on a date with my little sister and her pee-wee boyfriend.'

Rat scowled at James. He didn't appreciate the description.

'Kerry's only sitting in her room sulking,' Bruce said. 'I could try persuading her.'

'That's gonna make my life awkward,' James said. 'Isn't there anyone else?'

Kyle looked at his watch and shook his head. 'We haven't got much time. Bruce, you'd better run upstairs and invite Kerry to dinner.'

'Beg if you have to,' Lauren added.

*

The steakhouse was busy for a Monday night, but James was underwhelmed by the crushed velvet seating and carpet dotted with shiny black patches. He was even less impressed when he found out that the £6.99 buffet didn't include drinks. It might have been Kyle and Lauren's plan, but he doubted they'd be queuing up to refund his twenty quid.

Bruce wore chinos and a smart black shirt, while Kerry had made a quick change into a denim micro-skirt and a figure-hugging top. James could hardly stand being in the same room with Kerry these days, but she was still sexy and he couldn't help feeling jealous when Bruce felt up her bum while they waited for Hayley, Dean and Rosie to arrive.

Rosie was cute, with rows of straight teeth and big red hair. Dean was older, maybe seventeen, and he held a carrier bag containing a McDonald's uniform. He said that he'd have to leave early because his shift started at nine and he had to get two buses across town to reach work.

Hayley herself looked surprisingly good. Not eyes-out-on-stalks beautiful, but she wore a green flower-print dress that suited her curvy figure and white pumps. She was too bulky for James to fancy her, but he reckoned she was only a couple of hours a week on the Stairmaster away from being quite attractive.

Everyone exchanged hellos while the waitress found a table for six and the three girls commented on how much they liked each other's outfits. They all headed off to the buffet and Bruce sneaked a tiny low-light camera out of his trousers and snapped a couple of pictures as James and Hayley bantered in the queue.

Kerry, Bruce, Dean and Rosie were all relaxed as they ate their roast meat, shrimp and salads. But James felt awkward facing Hayley across the table. Her plate was stacked with slices of roast lamb and she'd built a dam out of batter pudding and rice to hold up the teetering mound of veg and pickles in the middle.

'You're not eating much,' Hayley noted gruffly, as she crunched on a large pickled onion.

'It was all a bit last-minute,' James explained. 'I ate already.'

Hayley burst out laughing. 'So did I, but that doesn't stop me.'

As everyone around the table laughed, James reached across the table and slid his fingers over Hayley's chunky wrist. 'I'm really glad we got together and I *completely* dig the way you look.'

'That's nice, James,' Hayley smiled. 'I always say that I'm fat and proud of it. And you know what? I never have any problem getting boys.'

James nodded and smiled. He remembered that when his mum was alive she was always on diets and got depressed about her weight. He was glad that Hayley was confident about herself, but it didn't alter the fact that she wasn't his type.

Rosie nodded as she bit on a slice of garlic bread. 'You've been out with way more boys than me, haven't you Hayley?'

Hayley wagged her fork at her friend. 'Don't say that, Rosie. You're making me sound like a slapper.'

Kerry spoke when the laughter calmed down. 'I'm just so glad that James has met you, Hayley. He's always a disaster around girls . . .'

Hayley nodded. 'You know James, getting your little sister to ask me out was dead creepy. I thought she was on a wind-up. I almost battered her.'

As Hayley said this, James felt her foot sliding up his calf. He leaned across the table and smiled to show that he liked it.

'Kerry's right though,' James said. 'There's only one girl I've gone out with for a long time and she was dead boring. It was like, *take the rod out of your arse and have some fun, girl!* I just *had* to dump her in the end.'

James was delighted by the scowl on Kerry's face as everyone else laughed.

The conversation ticked over as food disappeared from plates. Hayley and James kept playing footsie until eventually she had her painted toenails resting in his lap and he had a socked foot up her long skirt and resting against her thigh. He couldn't help being flattered by the fact that she obviously fancied him, and like most teenage boys, it only took a foot on his leg to get his hormones racing.

'I'm going to the lav,' Hayley said, as she swabbed the last traces of mayonnaise off her plate with a chunk of bread and crammed it into her mouth. As she stood up, she made a gesture with her thumb, indicating that James should come with her.

James glanced at Bruce as he stood up, desperate to convey that something was about to happen and that he wanted Bruce close by with the camera. This part of the operation would have been much easier at the bowling alley, where couples just snogged in the open while they were waiting to take their shot.

It was a large restaurant and Hayley and James had to cut between a dozen tables and pass a kids' play area before they came to a corridor with a couple of payphones and a cash machine that led towards the toilets.

'Where are we going?' James asked, as Hayley grabbed his hand and led him past the doors of the ladies, gents and disabled toilets. He turned back briefly and was reassured to see Bruce walking behind them, doing his best to look innocent.

'You'll see where,' Hayley said, as she leaned on the bar of a fire door.

It opened with a shudder on to a deserted stretch of tarmac behind the restaurant.

'I *want* you, James,' Hayley said, as she grabbed his bum and shoved him against the wall.

It was dark, cold and James only had a polo shirt on, but this wasn't a problem because Hayley engulfed him. The foot play and the sexual tension had been slightly exciting, but now James faced the reality of being kissed by someone he didn't fancy.

Even worse, James hated the taste and smell of mayonnaise. As he opened his mouth to kiss, he could smell it on her breath.

'You're really fit, James,' Hayley said, taking a deep breath as she slid a sticky hand up the back of his shirt. 'I can feel all your big strong muscles.'

James' head was pinned to the wall as Hayley thrust her vinegary tongue into his mouth. He moved his eyes around. He hoped Bruce had sneaked out through another exit to take some pictures, but there was no sign of him.

James didn't want to make out with Hayley for any longer than he had to, but after all the effort they'd put in, he couldn't stop until he knew Bruce had a picture.

'You've got the best arse,' James lied, as he gave Hayley a squeeze. 'Can I touch your tits?'

'Course you can,' she slathered, as she kissed his neck. 'Nobody ever comes back here, you know. We can do *anything*.'

James was consumed with guilt for leading Hayley on and hairs-standing-on-the-back-of-his-neck revulsion at the thought of a second snog.

'Hadn't we better go inside?' he gasped. 'The others will wonder where we've got to.'

'So?' Hayley said. 'Who gives a shit?'

'I guess,' James said weakly, as her hand went down the back of his trousers.

Mercifully, as Hayley sank her fingernails into his bum James spotted Bruce moving in the shadows. He tried to see what his friend was up to without making Hayley suspicious, and after about twenty seconds, Bruce gave a thumbs-up sign and scurried back into the darkness.

As soon as Bruce was out of sight, James tried to gently prise Hayley's shoulders away, but her beefy arms were locked around his back and her tongue moved in for another attack.

'Stop it . . .' James begged, when he finally managed to push her head away.

Hayley stumbled as she stepped backwards, clearly not happy. 'What's your sodding problem?'

'Nothing . . . Just, I'm not in the mood.'

Hayley put one hand on her hip and shook her head. 'You asked *me* out, James. I got all tarted up, I arranged for Dean and Rosie to come along and now you tell me you're not in the mood.'

'Look . . .' James muttered, 'I tell you what, I saw you looking at the dessert menu. Why don't we go back inside and I'll buy you some of those Belgian waffles you said you fancied.'

'Waffles,' Hayley spat, as she smacked James hard across the face. 'What is this? I'm a fat bird, so you think you can push me away and then buy me off with waffles?'

The slap really stung. 'Jesus,' James moaned, as he backed up towards the fire door. 'I haven't said one word about you being fat. The only person who's even mentioned it is *you*.'

'I put off my science coursework for this,' Hayley said. 'I had to beg Rosie to come out at short notice. So next time you call me up and ask for a date, you'd *better* be in the mood.'

James found the combination of a slap followed by the offer of another date confusing.

'I'm really sorry,' James said. 'I'm just—'

'I never thought I'd meet a boy who wasn't in the mood,' Hayley said, shaking her head as she straightened her dress and walked back inside.

'Are you leaving?' James asked, as he followed her back down the corridor towards the restaurant.

'Yeah, I'm leaving, as soon as you've bought me some waffles.'

18. SHOOTING

The team for the Luton mission was due on campus for a Tuesday-morning meeting, but the police investigating the street fight and the murder of Owen Campbell-Moore had picked Michael up for questioning the previous afternoon. They kept him in overnight, hoping the fifteen-year-old would be easier to crack than the older members of Major Dee's gang. But like everyone else the cops interrogated, Michael kept his mouth shut.

Gabrielle was discharged from hospital at 5:30 in the morning. Assistant mission controller Maureen Evans collected her in a big Mercedes. With a five-day-old wound in her back, Gabrielle found it difficult to sit still for any length of time. The big car and pre-rush-hour start were designed to make her journey as short and comfortable as possible.

Gabrielle could walk a few steps, but she found breathing painful and Maureen used a wheelchair to push her through reception to a rapturous breakfast-time welcome in the dining-room. Kerry and some of Gabrielle's other close friends gave her kisses and the gentlest of hugs, after which a crowd lined up to exchange high fives.

Touched by waves of positive feeling, Gabrielle began to sob. She was surprised by how many others had tears on their faces: boys, and girls, many of them people she hardly knew. Every cherub knows that missions are dangerous, and Gabrielle's breathless presence in the wheelchair was a powerful symbol of survival, but also a reminder of those dangers.

The crowd drifted away once the pips went for first lesson and Maureen immediately pulled a sterile wipe from her handbag and told Gabrielle to wipe her face and hands. She'd been desperate to see all of her friends, but Gabrielle was weak and even catching a cold would affect her recovery.

*

Michael caught a train as soon as the cops let him go. He arrived at the station nearest campus shortly after eleven and took a cab the rest of the way. The police work under strict rules about questioning suspects – especially suspects aged under eighteen – but they also know a million tricks, and one way to intimidate a suspect is to make them wait in a dirty cell for as long as possible.

Michael had spent eight hours in a tiny space with a blocked toilet and a rubber mattress that a drunk had peed on. As soon as he arrived on campus, Michael raced up to his room, knotted his filthy clothes in a bin liner because he couldn't even stand the thought of washing them and scrubbed himself under a scalding hot shower.

This made him late for the 11:30 mission briefing and everyone stared as he raced into the conference room. Zara sat at the head of a long table, with mission controller

Chloe and her assistant Maureen next to her. James and Bruce were there, along with a man called Terry from the technical department. But Michael only had eyes for Gabrielle, and he crossed the room before leaning forward and giving her a kiss.

'You're looking stronger every time I see you,' Michael smiled at Gabrielle, before turning to Chloe. 'Sorry I'm late, but I didn't get a wink of sleep and CHERUB owes me one Nike tracksuit and a pair of trainers.'

Chloe looked surprised. 'Can't they be washed?'

Michael wasn't in a good mood. 'Those cops were animals. They pushed me around, called me every racist name under the sun and then threw me in a cell with piss everywhere and the smell . . .'

James and Bruce eyed each other across the table and started to giggle.

'Yeah it's *really* funny, boys,' Michael snarled, but his look turned to a smile when Gabrielle started laughing too, wincing with the effort.

'OK,' Zara said impatiently. 'We're already late and I'm sure everyone in this room has seen enough police cells in their time not to need *too* graphic a description. Chloe, under the circumstances, I'm sure we can stretch the mission budget to providing Michael with some replacement clothing. Michael, have you had a chance to see the mission update that Chloe prepared overnight?'

'I've only just got here,' Michael said, shaking his head as Maureen slid a document across the table.

MISSION UPDATE FOR: JAMES ADAMS,
MICHAEL HENDRY, BRUCE NORRIS
& GABRIELLE O'BRIEN
THIS DOCUMENT IS PROTECTED WITH A RADIO
FREQUENCY IDENTIFICATION TAG
DO NOT PHOTOCOPY OR MAKE NOTES

THE FIRST PHASE

In January 2007 CHERUB agents Gabrielle O'Brien and
Michael Hendry (under the names Gabrielle Smith and Michael
Conroy) were sent to live in the Bedfordshire Halfway House,
known locally as the Zoo.

Their mission objectives were:
(1) To infiltrate the gang known as the Slasher Boys and collect
information on their criminal activities. In particular, to try and
uncover the methods they use for smuggling cocaine and other
illegal drugs into the country.
(2) To gather information about rival gangs, with the aim of
giving the police a better understanding of the rivalries
between them.

Progress was slow but Michael and Gabrielle successfully
infiltrated the Slasher Boys and began associating with known
members, gaining knowledge and slowly winning the trust of the
group's leader DeShawn Andrews, more commonly known as
Major Dee.

Unfortunately, the mission suffered a major setback on
15 March, when the two agents became entangled in a violent

robbery that led to two members of a rival gang known as the Runts being shot, another Runt suffering a fractured skull, the stabbing of Gabrielle O'Brien and the murder of Owen Campbell-Moore.

While it first appeared that the Runts had attacked the Slasher Boys, it has now become clear that the attack was orchestrated by a third gang known as the Mad Dogs. Agents should note that the Slasher Boys are not yet aware that the Mad Dogs set up the robbery.

The Revised Mission

Following a meeting of the ethics committee and the news that Gabrielle's injuries were not as serious as first feared, a decision was made to press ahead with the mission using two separate teams.

Team one will consist of Michael Hendry working with assistant mission controller Maureen Evans. Michael will continue with his existing mission to infiltrate the Slasher Boys. Gabrielle O'Brien has stated that she would also like to return to the mission. It is unlikely she will recover sufficiently before the mission ends, but a cover story involving her recuperating at an aunt's house in London will be put in place to allow for her return.

Team two will consist of James Adams and Bruce Norris. James will reprise his role as James Beckett from his 2004 anti-drugs mission. Bruce will take on the identity of James Beckett's cousin. They will work with mission controller Chloe Blake.

Their task will be to infiltrate the Mad Dogs, initially by rekindling James' past relationship with Junior Moore. They will live in the Bedfordshire Halfway House along with Michael, *but for the purposes of the mission they must pretend not to know one another.*

Due to the high risk of this mission, overall control for the operation will be handled directly by chairwoman Zara Asker, with Chloe Blake in charge of day-to-day operations.

TRAINING AND PRECAUTIONS

When the ethics committee approved the expansion of this mission they imposed strict conditions:

(1) Before being redeployed, all agents will be issued with protective equipment including body armour, easy-to-conceal knives, miniature stun guns and a small handgun for use in situations of extreme danger.

(2) The ethics committee has placed the mission on seven-day review status. This means that three members of the committee will review the progress of the mission every week. If they feel the situation has become too dangerous they will cancel the operation and order the agents back to campus.

(3) All agents are reminded of their right to refuse this mission or to withdraw at any time.

'Here's what I don't get,' James said, as he waggled his copy of the briefing in the air. 'How can we go around with guns and body armour? We're hardly going to blend in, are we?'

'Actually, there's been that many stabbings and assaults going down that most gang members are wearing protection,' Michael said. 'I'm not so sure about kids our age packing guns though.'

Terry Campbell cleared his throat. He was an old bloke with a bristly white beard. His job with the technical department mainly involved communications equipment, such as adapting the mobile phones CHERUB agents used to work on any network, or manufacturing listening devices that looked like personal items belonging to a target. He also dealt with weapons, physical protection and all the other equipment agents used on their missions.

'I'm looking at issuing all three of you with sub-compact handguns that will fit under your clothing,' Terry began. 'I'll get three new weapons, each one a slightly different model, then I'll rough up the exteriors to make it look like they're the kind of piece that you might have picked up on the street. But internally, they'll be in excellent shape. As you're using them primarily for deterrence, I'd suggest that you load a blank into the chamber then fill the rest of the clip with real ammunition.'

'Small handguns aren't the easiest to use accurately,' Chloe added. 'So we'll be taking the three of you down to the firing range for a couple of refresher lessons before you head off to Luton.'

'What about the protective equipment?' Zara asked.

'First off, all three of you will be issued with standard sets of body armour,' Terry said. 'It's too bulky to wear all the time, but if you're heading into a potentially dangerous situation it's both bullet and stab proof. I've also got an experimental batch of this stuff.' He pulled a small square of silvery fabric out of his jacket.

'What's that, a magic hanky?' James grinned.

Terry raised an eyebrow to indicate that he didn't find James funny, before continuing his speech. 'This fabric is interwoven with something called carbon nanotube fibres.

It's very new, very high tech. Diamonds are pure carbon and one of the hardest substances known to man. You can think of a carbon nanotube as a thread made from diamond. The material is as light as polyester, but it will protect you from stabbing. If you get shot, the bullet is unlikely to pass through the fabric and kill, but because a bullet travels at enormous speed and the material isn't rigid, you'll still be absorbing a massive amount of energy and I'd expect internal bleeding and broken bones.'

Gabrielle sounded a little bit annoyed. 'How come we're only getting this *now?*' she asked. 'I might not be sitting in this wheelchair if I'd had clothes made out of that stuff.'

Terry swept the back of his hand across his face. 'Unfortunately it's a matter of cost,' he admitted. 'One square metre of carbon nanotube fabric currently costs around six thousand pounds. I'm proposing that James, Bruce and Michael each select two garments such as a hoodie and a lightweight jacket. I'll then get our seamstress to pull the clothes apart and stitch in a layer of the nanotube fabric.

'We'll need around one and a half metres of fabric for each piece. That's nine thousand pounds each, fifty-four thousand for the six and another eighteen thousand pounds on top if Gabrielle returns to the mission.'

'That's a *lot* of dough,' Bruce said.

Zara nodded. 'We do everything we can to protect agents on missions, but we don't have unlimited resources. The only way we can afford this is by paying for it out of the research and development budget, rather than the mission budget.'

'We're hoping that nanotube fabric will be much cheaper

once it goes into mass production,' Terry said. 'In five or six years, clothes reinforced with this stuff could be as much a part of a CHERUB agent's standard kit as a lock gun or multitool is today, but right now it's too expensive.'

Maureen smiled. 'And whatever you do, don't go using your nine-thousand-pound sweatshirt as a goalpost and then leave it on the grass.'

19. SHOWDOWN

Kyle was only studying for the one A-level he needed to secure his place at university and Lauren had a free period after lunch. They met up by the main campus gates and began the ten-minute journey to Mr Large's house.

'Nervous?' Kyle asked, as they walked briskly, with gloves on and breath curling in front of them.

'A bit,' Lauren nodded. 'But I've dealt with FBI sharp shooters and paedos, so I reckon I can survive an encounter with Large.'

'He might not even be home,' Kyle said.

But Mr Large came to his front door in a pair of baggy jogging pants and an England rugby shirt, scratching his moustache as he stood in the doorway.

'What?'

Lauren spoke politely. 'We'd like to come in and talk. You know that *thing* you mentioned the other night?'

Large was smart enough to realise that they might be recording the conversation. 'It was just a friendly chat, Lauren.'

'We know you're a busy man,' Kyle said, trowelling on the irony because he knew that Large was suspended from his job and had nothing to do. 'We'll try not to take up too much of your *valuable* time.'

Large leaned out of the doorway and glanced left and right suspiciously before waving the pair inside.

'Nice and warm in here,' Lauren said, pulling off her gloves as she walked down a neatly furnished hallway.

Mr Large's morning was spread across the living-room for all to see: a copy of the *Times* with the crossword half done, a breakfast bowl with a splash of milk in the bottom, a Crunchie bar wrapper and an American chat show blaring out of the TV.

Lauren smiled. 'Mind if we sit down?'

Mr Large was clearly uneasy, but he scooped the newspaper off the sofa to make space for Lauren. Kyle sat in an armchair facing her.

'What's this all about?' Large asked.

'My old mate Rod Nilsson sends his regards,' Kyle said. 'Remember him?'

Large looked uncertain. 'Red-headed lad,' he nodded finally. 'Nice boy, but he didn't have the stomach for a second go at training.'

'He still gets nightmares,' Kyle said pointedly. 'Nightmares about choking on sand and suffocating.'

'Look,' Large said firmly. 'I don't know what this is – sour grapes or whatever – but I had a job to do and I was damned good at it.'

Lauren raised an eyebrow. 'I guess that's *one* way of looking at it . . .'

'And you're going to tell the truth and stick up for me at my hearing on Friday, *aren't* you?'

Lauren smiled. 'The *truth* is exactly what I'm going to be telling.'

'I just hope that everyone will be *safe* and happy afterwards,' Large threatened.

'Lauren tells me that you tried to blackmail her,' Kyle said bluntly.

Mr Large suddenly looked uncomfortable. 'Is this some kind of joke?' he said, scowling at Lauren. 'I haven't met either of you in months, except for a few nights back when Lauren and I exchanged hellos on my doorstep.'

'We're *not* recording you,' Lauren said. 'I knew you wouldn't be stupid enough to repeat what you said. But I'm not the only one who has vulnerabilities.'

As Lauren spoke, Kyle pulled a small stack of photos out of his jacket. He held up the top one, which was a flattering head-and-shoulders enlargement of Hayley.

'Quite a nice-looking girl, your daughter,' Kyle said casually, as he switched the picture to the back of the pile, revealing the next shot of Hayley and James kissing, with James' fingers clutching her bum.

'My brother certainly seems to be getting along with her, doesn't he?' Lauren grinned.

Mr Large gasped.

Kyle flipped to another picture, an extreme close-up of James and Hayley kissing.

'And that was just their first date,' Lauren added. 'Imagine what they'll get up to next time.'

'I can hear something,' Kyle said, cupping a hand to his ear. 'Could it be the patter of tiny feet?'

'Nah,' Lauren shook her head. 'Knowing my brother,

he'll just dump her and break her heart.'

'But don't worry,' Kyle said. 'You've trained a lot of boys on campus. They're all fit guys and I bet that once James ditches her, they'll all be queuing up to take a shot at your daughter . . .'

Mr Large didn't know what to say or where to look.

'Dozens of big strapping teenagers throwing themselves at Hayley,' Lauren sighed. 'And you know what teenagers are like. If you stand between Hayley and some boy she fancies, she'll only end up hating your guts.'

Lauren and Kyle weren't proud that they'd manipulated Hayley and had no intention of taking things further. But people judge others by their own standards. Hopefully Large would believe their threats, because it was the sort of dastardly scheme he might have concocted himself.

'But of course none of this *has* to go any further,' Lauren emphasised. 'We're prepared to back off, as long as you guarantee that Meatball stays safe.'

Mr Large was turning extremely red. 'Why bring my daughter into this?" he screamed. 'She's innocent.'

'Innocent?' Lauren snapped. 'Is she really? And I suppose Meatball is a little doggie serial killer. Or maybe he sneaks on to campus and sells crack to the red-shirts.'

'We have it on good authority that Zara Asker doesn't like you, Norman,' Kyle said. 'Mac kept saving your bacon, but his days are over. When Lauren tells that disciplinary panel the truth, you know you're going to be out on your arse.'

'Especially now you've upset me,' Lauren added. 'I might even be tempted to exaggerate.'

'You can't do this!' Large spluttered, sending his breakfast bowl and a couple of remote controls flying as he booted the coffee table up in the air.

The noise made Lauren jump, but she kept herself together and faked a grin. 'Oh dear, now you've gone and spilled milk on the carpet.'

'And just to make sure that you're not reinstated, we're going to send a petition around campus. Agents will refuse to go on missions if you are,' Kyle added.

This was news to Lauren, mainly because Kyle had only thought up the idea two seconds earlier.

'And we've already told Meryl Spencer that you tried to blackmail me,' Lauren said. 'Zara doesn't know yet, but I wouldn't expect a Christmas card from the Askers this year.'

Mr Large was going so red that Lauren was frightened he'd keel over with another heart attack.

'CHERUB has been my whole life,' Large bellowed. 'I'm a training instructor, that's what I *am*.'

'No,' Lauren corrected. 'What you are is an arsehole.'

Kyle couldn't help giggling as Mr Large stepped towards Lauren. She was a quarter of his age and a third of his size, but she didn't flinch.

'You've wrecked my life, Lauren Adams,' Large shouted. 'You put my back out when you hit me with the spade and knocked me into that ditch. I hardly ever drank until I found out that it helped relieve the pain. And it was the drink that made me put on weight, which gave me the heart attack, and to top it all off you now want to hammer the nail into my career—'

'Don't blame *me*,' Lauren screamed back. 'I only hit you

because you were making Bethany dig a grave when she was in agony with *her* back. It all sounds a lot like poetic justice to me.'

'Come on Lauren,' Kyle said, as he stepped out of the armchair. 'We've said everything we came here to say. It's up to him whether he resigns now or lets himself and his daughter be humiliated.'

But as Lauren tried to step around Mr Large and leave, he placed a hand on her shoulder and pushed her backwards across the sofa.

Lauren tried knocking him away with a two-footed kick, but Large was enormous and his stomach felt like concrete. Her legs buckled under his weight as he leaned forward and grabbed her cheeks, squishing her lips out of shape.

Kyle wrapped his arms around Large's waist and tried dragging him off, but Large launched a powerful kick that sent him clattering backwards into a drinks cabinet.

'Your fancy moves won't work on me,' Large grinned, as he pushed down hard, squeezing Lauren's head against the sofa cushion. 'Remember, I'm the guy that taught 'em to you.'

Lauren looked towards Kyle, hoping that he'd be able to find a weapon or something, but the kick had winded him and he was crumpled against the wall, clutching his stomach.

'You won't get away with this,' Lauren croaked.

'I guess I won't,' Mr Large agreed. 'I guess I'll have to resign. We'll move somewhere near where my partner works and I'll make sure it's far enough from campus that your perverted brother can't touch Hayley. But here's the good part: just so that you never forget me, I'm gonna head next door and wring Meatball's neck.'

Lauren broke into a coughing fit as Large let go and stormed out of the room, slamming the door behind him.

'We've got to stop him, Kyle,' Lauren screamed. 'He's gonna kill Meatball.'

As the two injured cherubs stumbled into the hallway, Large ran across the driveway and made the Asker's front door shudder as he shoulder-charged it.

Kyle reached the inside of Large's front door a second later, but it didn't move when he turned the handle.

'He must have put the deadlock on. We'll have to go out the back.'

As they scrambled towards the rear of the unfamiliar house, Large's second kick knocked the Askers' front door off its hinges. He shouted, 'I'll show you Lauren Adams,' as the burglar alarm erupted.

Kyle made it out of the back door and sprinted across Large's garden towards the driveway.

'You've *got* to bite him, Meatball,' Lauren shouted desperately as she charged after Kyle. 'Don't let him get hold of you.'

As the chairwoman of CHERUB, Zara Asker was one of the highest ranking officials in the British Intelligence Service. This made her a potential hostage target and her home was fitted with a state-of-the-art alarm. When Meatball heard the claxon, he went into a frenzy, running around the living-room couch and barking like mad.

Mr Large had looked after Meatball when the Askers were on holiday and the little dog padded curiously towards a man who'd fed him on many occasions. But as Mr Large reached down to grab Meatball off the carpet, the dog picked up the scent of Lauren racing up the driveway.

While Mr Large had fed him, Lauren not only fed Meatball but also played with him, took him for really long walks and never shouted at him. As a result, Meatball vaulted over Mr Large's hands, cut between his legs and charged on through the splintered front door.

But Kyle was running ahead of Lauren and before Meatball knew it, he'd put a hand under the dog's belly and plucked him off the ground. Meatball hadn't seen Kyle since he was a puppy, but the dog remembered Kyle's smell and seemed happy enough, until he looked back and noticed that Mr Large was charging down the hallway towards them and yelling noisily.

With Meatball in his arms, Kyle scrambled out on to the driveway. But Large had a good turn of speed for a man in his forties. He'd built up momentum while Kyle turned, and soon got his arms around Kyle's waist.

As Kyle tumbled forward on to the patio, Meatball spilled out, yapping frantically as he ran towards Lauren.

Down on the patio, Kyle had wriggled on to his back and put Mr Large in a headlock, while Large was using his trunk-like arms to crush Kyle's ribs.

Lauren considered grabbing Meatball and making a dash back towards campus, but the fight was horribly uneven. Large was powerful and completely out of control, and she could see Kyle getting seriously hurt. To emphasise this, Large freed himself from the headlock and pressed his elbow against Kyle's windpipe.

'You'll kill him,' Lauren screamed, as she searched desperately for a weapon.

As Meatball wagged his tail, excited by the running around and the blaring alarm, Lauren raced towards the Askers' front door. She was greatly relieved to see a muddy implement leaning against the inside of the front porch.

Mr Large saw Lauren charging towards him, but he had Kyle's legs locked around his waist and only one free arm to fend her off. Kyle used all his strength to keep Large still as Lauren swung at him, hitting him square in the back of the head.

The blow made a huge clang and sent a wave of vibration up the handle. Large groaned, as Kyle felt his opponent's strength evaporate. He wound up with Large's dead weight slumped on top of him.

'Are you OK?' Lauren asked, as she threw down the spade and pushed Large's unconscious body off Kyle.

Kyle was bright red, with sweat pouring down his face. 'Just about,' he coughed.

As he stood up and brushed off his trousers, a white BMW came to an abrupt halt in the road. Two men slid handguns from under their jackets as they opened the doors and ran up the driveway. Lauren recognised them as campus security officers and realised that the Askers' alarm was linked up to the campus security room.

'What's going on here?' one of the guards shouted, glancing between the unconscious Large and the busted front door as his colleague used a plipper to shut off the alarm.

20. RECKONING

Zara Asker had never liked Mr Large, and she had to hide her smile when Lauren admitted that she'd battered him with a spade for the second time.

Large had only been stunned and he'd regained consciousness shortly after being lifted on to a bed in the medical unit on campus. When Zara arrived ten minutes later, he sat on the edge of his mattress sipping water out of a plastic cup.

'Ahh, here she is,' Large grinned sarcastically. 'Her Royal Highness, gracing me with her presence.'

'Funny,' Zara said, her manner making it clear she thought it anything but. 'I was just speaking to my husband. Is it true that you threatened to kill my son's dog?'

Large shrugged, acting like he couldn't have cared less. 'That fancy security rig on your house must have CCTV. Why don't you work it out for yourself?'

'I haven't had a chance to look, but I'll take your answer as a yes,' Zara said.

Large smiled. 'You can take it as whatever you like and then you can shove it up your big fat arse.'

'Listen, *Norman*,' Zara snapped. 'Nothing would make me happier than to kick you out of here and never see you and that ridiculous moustache again. But you know about CHERUB, you've worked here most of your life and that means we're obliged to help you out.'

'Only so you can keep tabs on me,' he snorted.

'You've known that we'll keep tabs on you since you were ten years old,' Zara said. 'What's the saying? Once you know, we can't let go. Now the question is, are we going to have to go through the charade of a disciplinary hearing, or can I expect a resignation letter?'

'You write the letter and I'll sign it.'

'Good,' Zara said. 'You own your house jointly with Gareth, don't you?'

Large nodded. 'He's doing a fifty-mile commute every day so he's after moving anyway.'

'CHERUB has steadily been buying up that row of houses to use as staff quarters,' Zara said. 'We'll pay you twenty per cent over market value which should cover your moving costs. You can have three months' severance pay and I'll guarantee to write you a good job reference if you want to work elsewhere within the security or intelligence business. But *don't* expect any kind of help if you apply for a job that involves kids. I won't have that on my conscience.'

Large grunted.

Zara put her hands on her hips and stiffened her voice. 'Considering that you've attempted to blackmail a twelve-year-old girl and strangle Kyle, I think we're being *very* generous. And this isn't a negotiating position. You can take my offer right now, or we'll go through the disciplinary process and you'll come out with diddly squat.'

'Whatever.' Large sounded like a spoilt kid as he crumpled his plastic cup and threw it at a waste bin. 'Just give me something to sign.'

'Excellent,' Zara said. 'The nurse said it's probably best if you stay here and rest for an hour or so. They've taken a head X-ray, but they doubt there's any lasting damage. If you have any belongings over in the instructors' building I can send someone to collect them.'

Large shook his head. 'There's a few pairs of muddy boots, but you're welcome to 'em.'

'Like all ex-cherubs you'll be welcome to return to campus for reunions and anniversary events, but your regular access will be revoked as soon as you step off the grounds.'

Zara reached out to shake hands, but Large kept his arms at his side.

'Maybe you don't believe me when I say this, Norman,' Zara said after a pause, 'but I'm truly sorry that your career had to end like this. I wish you luck with whatever you choose to do and you're welcome to call me at any time if you think I can help you.'

Large didn't respond and Zara thought he was being rude. But as soon as she left the room, Norman Large tipped his head and started to cry.

*

The photographs had dropped from Kyle's pocket when he ran from Mr Large's living-room. They'd been picked up by the security team and handed to Zara as evidence. Most pictures were of James and Hayley, but Bruce and Kerry were identifiable on some shots taken inside the steakhouse and there was even a pic Bruce had snapped while testing the camera inside the mini-bus which revealed Callum, Connor and Rat. Andy was the only one who got off.

The chairman's office had recently been redecorated. Zara's glass desk, iMac and Herman Miller chairs made the room feel less intimidating than the leather and oak of her predecessor. There weren't enough seats, so major perps Lauren, Kyle and James were told to sit down, while Kerry, Bruce, Callum, Connor and Rat stood in line behind them.

Strict discipline was important because cherubs have to perform to the highest standards when they're out on mission. But Zara didn't enjoy punishing kids and when she'd first become chairwoman some staff had accused her of being soft. She'd reluctantly accepted the criticism and become stricter, but she wasn't consistent about it.

When Mac was chairman, a cherub could be certain of their punishment for most routine offences. An agent returning to campus after curfew could always expect twenty punishment laps for every quarter hour they were late. With Zara, you might get anything from ten to a hundred, depending upon her mood.

This randomness made kids who were about to be punished nervous, and cherubs could no longer do something wrong because they could *take the punishment* if they got caught. Oddly, while Zara generally punished kids less severely than Mac had done, it was tales of the harshest penalties that circulated around campus and she'd gained a fearsome reputation.

'I'm very much torn about how to punish all of you,' Zara

began. 'The whole affair was instigated because Mr Large tried to blackmail Lauren, but that doesn't excuse the way you acted.'

Kyle spoke boldly. 'I'm the oldest and it was my idea to get revenge. I'm prepared to accept full responsibility.'

Zara smiled. 'And how much longer are you with us, Kyle?'

'Just over seven weeks.'

'So if I punish you and you don't fancy it, you'll just quit a few weeks early,' Zara said.

Kyle realised he'd been rumbled and looked down at his lap.

'I know I haven't been chairwoman for long, Kyle, but I'm not a *complete* idiot. It's Hayley I feel really sorry for in all this. As she doesn't know that CHERUB exists there's no way I can have you make it up to her. I just hope that her feelings weren't *too* badly hurt.'

James shrugged. 'She didn't seem all that impressed, so I don't think she'll be upset if she never hears from me again.'

'Sensible girl,' Zara said. 'First of all I'm going to deal with you five standing along the back. I'm giving each of you two hundred punishment laps, to be run over a three-week interval along with eighty hours' gardening duty—'

'But that's not fair,' Kerry shouted, 'I was barely involved.'

All the other agents turned to give Kerry dirty looks, even Bruce.

'You were in the restaurant, which means you were more involved than me or the twins,' Rat pointed out.

'Quiet,' Zara yelled. 'If you'll *just* let me finish. The laps and the gardening duty will be suspended for six months. If you break any other rules before the end of September, you'll serve this punishment, plus the punishment for whatever else you did wrong.'

Kerry was pleased by this. She hardly ever got in trouble and reckoned a suspended was as good as no punishment at all. The four boys were also relieved, but didn't relish having to tiptoe around on their best behaviour with a big punishment hanging over them.

Zara continued. 'James, you played a major role, but you *weren't* an instigator. I'm giving you two hundred laps and a hundred hours' decorating duty, but I'm suspending everything except fifty laps, which I want you to run before you go off on your mission.'

James was fairly happy with this. He liked to run a couple of times a week and twenty-five laps was a ten-kilometre run, which took him less than fifty minutes.

'Now I want those of you who've received their punishments to leave the room. I need to talk with Kyle and Lauren in private.'

Bruce spoke as they headed out of the room. 'Can I just ask: has Mr Large been kicked out?'

Zara nodded and everyone started to smile.

'You'd *better* wipe those grins,' Zara said sternly as the six kids headed out. 'If I see *any* of you gloating about this, I might just decide to unsuspend some of those laps. Mr Large would almost certainly have been dismissed at his disciplinary hearing, so all you've really done is brought a lot of trouble upon yourselves.'

James was the last one out of the room. As he closed the door, Lauren and Kyle looked anxiously towards Zara.

'Kyle,' Zara said, breaking into a friendly smile. 'I think we've reached the end of the line, don't you?'

Kyle was confused. 'Pardon me?'

'This was mainly your idea and you're the most senior agent involved. But I can't punish you effectively because you'll just leave. You passed the bulk of our exams last year and you're only studying maths. I've spoken to Meryl Spencer. She's just bought a sizeable house off campus and says she'd be happy to have you as a lodger for a couple of months until you set off on your travels.'

Kyle gasped. 'But—'

Zara raised her hand. 'There's not enough time for you to prepare for another mission. I think the only reasonable solution is for you to pack your things up and leave campus a few weeks earlier than planned.'

'But what about my lessons and stuff?'

'You can come back on to campus to attend the revision sessions for your maths A-level. And I believe James has been tutoring you, so you can come back for that, but only in the campus library, not up in his room. Obviously, you're welcome to socialise with your friends off campus, but the leisure facilities on campus will be out of bounds and I don't want you hanging around anywhere else on campus either.'

Kyle had been preparing to leave for a while, but seemed choked by this sudden end to ten years as a cherub. 'I knew the risk I was taking,' he said, nodding weakly. 'Can I please have a few days to say goodbye to everyone and stuff?'

'I can live with that,' Zara nodded. 'It'll take that long to sort out the details of your new identity and set you up financially anyway.'

'Right,' Kyle nodded.

'And I think that's it for you,' Zara said. 'I'll speak to Meryl and she can start making arrangements for your departure.'

As Kyle left the room, it occurred to Lauren that she'd been left till last because she was in the biggest trouble of all. Her heart was banging.

'And then there was one,' Zara said dramatically as she reached behind and took Lauren's personal file from a glass shelf. 'I never realised that we had a serious problem with you until I looked into your file.'

Lauren gulped when she heard *serious problem*. 'I don't *exactly* know what you mean,' she said meekly.

'Don't you indeed?' Zara smiled. 'You're one of the best agents we've got and you're *still* the youngest black-shirt on campus, but your disciplinary record *on* campus is wretched.'

Zara opened Lauren's file and began to read. 'In late 2004, you assaulted Mr Large with a shovel. Mac put you on six months' ditch-digging and gave you a final warning. In summer 2006, you were caught and punished after blackmailing James and breaking into the basic training compound to assist the trainees. Now you're back in this office because of a second scheme you've concoted, this time to get revenge on Mr Large and force him to resign.'

'But he blackmailed *me*,' Lauren said. 'I was just—'

'I *know* what Mr Large did. And you did the correct thing by approaching Meryl Spencer and reporting the incident, which was resolved. What you did afterwards with Hayley and James was *utterly* unacceptable. And the thing I really don't like is that you invented a scheme in a similar fashion just over a year ago.'

'A lot of that one was Bethany's idea though,' Lauren protested.

Zara didn't appreciate Lauren's squirming. 'Well, Bethany is away on a mission, so it certainly wasn't her fault this time, was it?'

'No, Miss.'

'Your four-hundred-lap punishment seems to have had no effect, which has left me in a tricky position. My conclusion is that you need to spend a period of time demonstrating exemplary behaviour on campus before you can continue your career as an agent.'

'You mean I'm suspended from missions?' Lauren gasped.

'You're suspended for three months. Then, for three months after that I'm going to have you restricted to smaller scale missions: security checks, recruitment missions, things like that.'

'OK,' Lauren nodded miserably.

'I also want you to make a bigger contribution to campus life and to take part in some activities that will give you responsibility and hopefully make you grow up. We've been recruiting aggressively over the last couple of years and we've currently got more than a dozen red-shirts aged under seven. The staff over in the junior block could do with a hand looking after them, so I want you to help out four nights a week for the next six months.

'It's all fairly simple: helping with their reading, making sure they take baths and showers, putting them to bed and maybe occasional activities such as swimming lessons, or trips out. Some of them are also going through a difficult time adjusting to campus life after losing parents or loved ones, so they can be demanding and they need plenty of emotional support.'

Lauren nodded, but she wasn't happy. Maybe the punishment wasn't as physically demanding as running laps, but six months was a long stretch and she'd never been shy about rubbing her elevated status into the faces of friends who were still mostly grey-shirts. They were going to *love* it when they found out she'd been suspended from missions.

21. GUNS

It was Friday lunchtime and although it was supposed to be the last day of his week off, James' morning had been hectic: another briefing on the Luton gang situation with Chloe, the last third of his fifty punishment laps and a practice session with his specially prepared handgun on the shooting range. Through all of this, James worried about Kyle, who hadn't been himself since Zara had ordered him to leave.

'You there, mate?' James shouted, as he knocked on Kyle's door.

He didn't get an answer so he stepped inside. Kyle's room was always neat, but now it was also bare, with just a few cardboard boxes stacked up by the window. James noticed that the bed had been stripped and the mattress flipped over. He couldn't see his best friend, but he could hear the shower running in the bathroom and he pulled a sub-compact pistol out of his tracksuit top as he approached the bathroom door.

James quietly pushed down the handle and was pleased to find the door unlocked. It was hard to see through the steam swirling out of the shower cubicle as he crept inside, gun in hand.

'Stick 'em up,' James shouted, as he ripped back the shower curtain.

But it wasn't Kyle that yelped.

'What the hell?' Kevin Sumner shouted, as he dropped his shampoo bottle and covered his privates with his hands.

'Sorry,' James said, almost as shocked as Kevin. 'I thought you were Kyle. What are you doing in here?'

'We all got back from training this morning,' Kevin explained. 'Everyone wanted one of the newer rooms up on the eighth floor, but I had to go in the loo and by the time I got upstairs they'd all been snaffled. But Kyle's so neat that this room is almost as good.'

James saw Kevin's grey T-shirt hanging on the towel rail and reached out to shake his hand. 'Congrats,' James said. 'I guess we're neighbours then. I'm directly across the hall.'

Kevin was dripping and he shivered as he shook James' hand.

'I hope there's no hard feelings about what happened in the jungle the other night,' Kevin said.

James waved his hand across his face. 'It's not like I would have acted any different in your shoes. How was Kazakov after I left?'

'Brutal, exactly like you'd expect,' Kevin shrugged. 'But now it's over I hardly care. I want a mission. And then there's the absolute best thing about being a grey-shirt.'

James was curious. 'What's that?'

Kevin smiled. 'You were never a red-shirt, were you?'

'Nope. I was twelve when I joined CHERUB so I went straight into basic training.'

'I've *finally* got my own bath and shower,' Kevin explained. 'It's communal over in the junior block and you always end up with some six-year-old trying to climb into your bath, or some joker lobbing cups of cold water at you.'

'I can see that would get on your tits,' James nodded. 'Though you might want to consider bolting the door next time.'

'Yeah,' Kevin nodded.

'So, do you know where Kyle is? He's been miserable and I'm worried about him.'

'I think he's driving the last of his clothes over to Meryl's house. He said he'd help me to move my stuff out of the junior block when he got back.'

'Right,' James said, as he put the gun back in his pocket. 'And sorry about this . . .'

As James backed out of the bathroom he realised that if Kevin was home then Dana must be too. But as he headed towards Dana's room, Kyle emerged from the lift holding a cardboard box loaded with Kevin's stuff.

'Hey,' James said. 'What's with your room?'

'I gave it to Kevin.'

'I saw *that*. But Zara said you can stay until Sunday.'

Kyle looked sad as he shook his head. 'I'm moving out today.'

'No,' James gasped. 'Saturday night's your big leaving party. Everyone on campus is gonna be there and I know for a fact that Kerry and some of the others are getting you a prezzie.'

'I'm not coming,' Kyle said. 'I told you I don't want a big fuss.'

'Give over, *everyone* has a leaving party.'

'Well, I've got nowhere to sleep now I've let Kevin have my room.'

'Bunk on my floor,' James shrugged. 'Hell, you can have my bed if it means you stick around for the party.'

But Kyle turned angry. 'Stop going on, James. I just want to get out of here.'

And then Kyle sniffed, which made James feel sad and awkward at the same time. 'I'd give you a hug if you weren't holding that box,' James said, as a tear welled up in his own eye. 'The sixth floor's not gonna be the same when you're gone.'

Kyle took the hint and put the box down so that James could embrace him.

'I'll miss you,' James said, pulling Kyle in close and slapping him on the back.

'Miss you too,' Kyle said, as a tear streaked down his face. 'Ten years just whizzed by, you know? When I drive off campus it scares me.'

'It's shitty,' James nodded. 'But you've got your whole life. You're seventeen, you're going off travelling which is gonna be totally amazing. Then you've got university which is gonna be a blast. Give it a year and I bet you'll be wondering what was ever cool about living in a corridor with a bunch of noisy yobs like me.'

'You're a good friend, James,' Kyle said, as he rubbed an eye with the back of his hand. 'I thought you were such a spoiled brat when I first met you. I never told you this before, but when CHERUB recruited you from Nebraska House I recommended that they didn't accept you. I got overruled by that shrink, Jennifer Mitchum. She thought you had potential.'

'You git!' James laughed. 'Why am I still hugging you?'

'Guess I was wrong,' Kyle said, sounding more like his usual self as the boys separated. 'And I spoke to Meryl. She says I'll be able to come back to campus for holidays like Christmas and stuff once I start university. She's also gonna ask about getting me some paid work in the summer, helping out at the CHERUB hostel or something; but she said it's best to leave it a while before speaking to Zara because I'm not exactly flavour of the month after her front door got kicked down.'

'We'll see each other loads,' James smiled.

'I'd better get on,' Kyle said, as he bent down to pick Kevin's box off the floor. 'And by the way, I think Dana's looking for you. She was getting lunch downstairs when I saw her.'

'When was that?'

'Ten minutes, you'll catch her easily.'

'My mission starts on Monday, so I've got to cram months of red-hot love action into three days,' James said as he started moving towards the lift. But after three paces he turned back and yelled at Kyle: 'Hey.'

'What?' Kyle asked.

'You've *got* to be here Saturday night. You've only got two days left to hang here and a whole lifetime afterwards.'

Kyle smiled. 'Kevin did say that him and all the other new grey-shirts were planning to have a party. I guess I *could* stick around. I wouldn't want anyone's last memory to be that I'm an unsociable git, would I?'

*

The party started at eight and fizzled out by three on Sunday morning. Kyle spent his last night in James' bed while James crashed on the sofa in Dana's room. James woke with a crick in his neck and a touch of hangover. There was also a text on his mobile, telling him to call Chloe as soon as he got the message.

James called her as he sat on Dana's toilet.

'Good morning, James,' Chloe said brightly. 'How's your head?'

'I've survived worse,' James yawned.

'Listen, we've had a couple of plain-clothes cops looking into Junior Moore's movements. It seems he's scheduled for a meeting with his probation officer tomorrow morning. His school is oversubscribed and we've had no luck getting you a place there. But he's only just been released from youth custody and he has to visit his parole officer every Monday. We think that's going to be your best opportunity to bump into him.'

'I can do that,' James nodded. 'It might be a bit of a rush if we're moving into the halfway house in the morning but—'

Chloe interrupted. 'That's the thing: Junior's parole meeting is at ten, which means I really need you and Bruce to move into the halfway house today.'

James baulked. 'But it's Kyle's last day. He's gonna have Sunday lunch with everyone . . .'

'I know,' Chloe said sympathetically. 'If it's really that important, I guess we can find another opportunity.'

'No,' James said. 'I guess the party was the main thing. The meal's gonna be depressing anyway.'

'If you're sure,' Chloe said. 'I appreciate your commitment.'

'Have you spoken to Bruce yet?'

'Yes. He said he'd go, as long as you were OK about it.'

'Cool. So what time do we need to get on the road?'

'Well it's almost noon, so I reckon we should set off as soon as you've both had some brekky and packed your bags.'

Dana was awake when James stepped out of her bathroom. She sat on the corner of her bed, still dressed in her party clothes, with black eyeliner smudged over her face.

'And how's my beautiful baby?' James grinned sarcastically.

'Delicate,' Dana groaned. 'I can't remember anything. Did you put me to bed?'

James nodded. 'Me and the twins had to lift you. You were completely wasted.'

'Tequila slammers. Never *ever* again.'

James got a whiff of stale booze and sweat as he kissed Dana. 'I'm afraid I've gotta go, they've brought my mission forward.'

Normally they would have had a proper snog before parting, but Dana was in no fit state. All she could do was mumble, 'Keep safe,' as James headed out.

James stepped into his room and found that Kyle was already up. He'd showered, eaten some cereal, remade James' bed with clean sheets and even taken all the dirty clothes and linen downstairs to the laundry.

'I'm not gonna make it to Sunday lunch,' James explained as he grabbed a holdall out of his wardrobe and began stuffing it with clothes.

'I'm dead jealous,' Kyle smiled. 'It's weird to think that it's all over. No more campus, no more missions, no more summer hostel. I'm just an ordinary student.'

James tried not to start blubbing again. 'I'm gonna miss the shit out of you, Kyle.'

Kyle started to grin. 'You know what I was thinking?'

'What?'

'Whenever you get stuck with your school work or you want to copy someone, it's always me or Kerry. But I'm leaving and you're not *exactly* on homework-copying terms with Kerry these days.'

'You're not wrong,' James nodded, as he broke into a wry smile. 'I'm basically screwed.'

Kyle crouched down and ripped a big carrier bag stuffed with exercise books and folders out of his overnight pack.

'That's my parting gift,' he said, as the heavy bag bounced on James' mattress. 'All my revision notes, essays, cheat sheets.'

'Sweet,' James grinned. 'That's *so* cool. We all chipped in and got you a present, but they're giving it to you after dinner so I guess I'll miss it. Do you fancy coming down and having breakfast with me?'

Kyle shook his head. 'I'd love to, but I woke up late and I want to make the rounds and say goodbye to a few people. Especially some of the junior-block staff who looked after me when I was little. Besides, you're still gonna be tutoring me for my maths.'

James shrugged. '*If* I get back from my mission before your exam. It's only six weeks away and this could be a long one.'

'I guess it's goodbye then,' Kyle said as he backed up towards the door. 'I'd say good luck with the mission, but you're such a jammy sod that I know you won't need it.'

22. CONTACT

Bedfordshire Halfway House (AKA the Zoo) was meant to be a refuge for troubled teens and freshly released young offenders. The reality was a dumping ground for kids who'd been failed by the care system. Eighty per cent were either permanently excluded from school or didn't bother going. Half the boys and a quarter of the girls had already served time and plenty would be going back.

James and Bruce shared a small room with a vinyl floor, beds that smelled like other people and walls carrying a million lines of graffiti. Both boys had been inside care homes before, but neither had encountered anywhere as desperate as the Zoo.

They'd arrived late afternoon and eaten greasy chicken burgers and chips for tea. An Asian girl offered to sell them cannabis on the staircase up to the boys' floor, where a skinny kid was being shaken down at the end of the hallway.

James and Bruce both felt delicate after Kyle's party and they were in bed by ten. But it was impossible to sleep with all kinds of craziness occurring in the rooms and corridors around them. There were fights, chases and the dude in the next room had his music going full blast. He turned it down after James banged on his door and threatened to rip his head off, but that only exposed them to another layer of noise from the girls downstairs. Their music wasn't as loud, but their singing made up for it.

It was midnight when James finally got to sleep with a pillow stretched over his head to shield the noise. Shortly afterwards, two huge guys burst into their room. They were both aged about seventeen and they filled the air around them with the smell of cigarettes as they kicked the end of James and Bruce's beds.

'Twenty pounds now or we batter you,' a long-haired kid shouted. They'd find out later that he was called Mark.

His mate Karl flipped on the lights. 'Wakey wakey, the taxman's here!'

James and Bruce sprang up in their beds, but by the time their eyes had adjusted to the light they each had a giant looming over them.

'Give us your cash,' Karl ordered, showering James with spit as he spoke.

'I've got a better idea,' James sneered. 'Why don't you suck my balls?'

Karl tried swinging his knee across James' body to pin him, but whatever he'd been smoking made him slow and James knocked him off with a double blow: one knee in the stomach and an elbow in the jaw.

As Karl stumbled, James drove him back until he clattered into a locker. Once he was trapped, James smashed a palm into his nose, and the back of his head slammed the metal door as James swept his feet from beneath him. Across the room, Bruce had gone for a more clinical approach, taking out Mark with a single punch to the side of the head.

'You wanna tax me now?' James shouted, as the teenager at his feet wrapped his arms over his face, fearing another punch. 'Empty your pockets.'

While Karl handed James a mobile, lighter, cigarettes and wallet, Bruce knelt down and went through the unconscious Mark's pockets. His haul was the same as James', except for a small bag of cannabis resin and a plastic-handled flick-knife.

James and Bruce stripped the money from the wallets and Bruce put the knife in his locker. Other lads had heard the rumble and stood out in the hallway trying to see what was going on.

'One Nokia, one Samsung,' Bruce said casually, as he lobbed the phones, cigarettes and lighters into the crowd. 'Compliments of Bruce Beckett.'

James grabbed his multitool from the jeans crumpled on the floor and held the saw-toothed blade under his opponent's bloody nose.

'You'd better drag your mate out of here,' James snarled.

Karl nodded, but James' brutal punches had torn his stomach muscles and he could barely stand straight, let alone haul his friend. In the end, James and Bruce had to drag Mark down the hallway to his room, where they dumped him on the floor between the beds.

The two agents were pumped after the fight and James stared at his bloody fist as they walked back to their room.

'It's all spattered over your chest as well,' Bruce noted. 'You'd better take a shower.'

Onlookers shrank away as James passed them in the hallway with his shower gel in hand and a towel slung over his back. He'd done nothing to be proud of, but he couldn't help feeling big when he saw how they all backed off.

*

'Bloody hell,' James gasped, as he scrambled into his jeans and slid his trainers on without socks.

Bruce propped an elbow on his pillow and did a big yawn. 'What's up?'

'It's nine-forty,' James said. 'I'm supposed to be at the parole office already. Chloe's gonna go bananas.'

'Didn't you set an alarm?'

James shook his head as he grabbed his jacket and checked his money was still in his pocket. 'I didn't bother, I'm usually awake by nine, but I haven't gotten to sleep until really late the last two nights.'

'Oh well,' Bruce said nonchalantly. 'Nothing I can do. I'm going back to sleep.'

'Get off your arse and move the locker,' James yelled, as he pulled his jacket up his arms.

There was a chance of a revenge attack after the fight with Karl and Mark. The room didn't have a lock, so they'd barricaded the door with Bruce's metal locker. It wouldn't stop anyone getting in, but the metal scraping across the floor would give them plenty of warning.

As soon as there was a big enough gap for James to squeeze through, he bolted into the corridor. He'd just woken up, so he sprinted into the toilet and started to pee without realising that Mark was standing right beside him. He had two swollen eyes and a massive egg on his forehead.

'You ain't heard the last of this,' Mark said menacingly.

James was tempted to smack Mark's head against the wall to remind him who was boss, but he was in a state of panic and he didn't even stop to wash his hands before hurtling down the four flights of stairs to the ground floor.

He charged down the main hallway and out on to the street, before crossing the road and sprinting four hundred metres to the bus stop. Luckily, he had to wait less than two minutes for the bus, but he still didn't reach the parole office until 10:07.

The single-storey building was situated between a petrol station and a place that did car valeting. The central heating was set way too high and a bunch of teenage boys and young men sat on foam chairs. Some had newspapers or forms mounted on clipboards, but most stared into space.

'Can I help you?' the overweight receptionist asked politely, as James glanced around and saw no sign of Junior Moore.

'My name's James Beckett,' he said breathlessly. 'I got out of young offenders last week and they said I've got to register here within seven days.'

'OK,' the woman nodded, as she tapped something into her computer. 'Is that Beckett with one T or two?'

'Two,' James said, as he wiped the sweat off his forehead on to the sleeve of his jacket.

'I'm not getting anything under that name. Which institution were you released from?'

'Peterwalk, near Glasgow,' James said.

This detail of James' background story had been devised so that he'd be unlikely to bump into anyone he was supposed to have been locked up with.

'Scottish institutions aren't on our computer,' the receptionist explained as she reached around and grabbed an eight-page form and a clipboard. 'You'll need to fill out one of these. If you have difficulty reading and writing, I'll get one of the support staff to help out.'

James stepped over outstretched legs until he reached an empty chair on the far side of the room. He was sweating because it was so hot and he unzipped his jacket as he sat down.

His best chance of bumping into Junior and making a connection would have been in the waiting room before his appointment, but he'd missed that opportunity by oversleeping and now he'd have to scramble after Junior as he left. If Junior was in a rush, he might leave before they got a proper chance to talk and the mission would be down the toilet – or at least severely delayed – before it had even started.

James decided to fill the form in quickly, so that he could hand it in and leave with Junior if the opportunity arose.

'Junior Moore,' a man shouted firmly.

James looked up at a skinny man in a brown suit who had to be Junior's parole officer. The officer headed over towards the receptionist and after a brief conversation she put an announcement over the tannoy.

'If Junior Moore is still in the building, please report to office D immediately. That's Junior Moore, office D immediately.'

After a few seconds, the parole officer shook his head and began walking away from the desk, but James was startled by a crashing noise just a few metres behind him. He looked up to see Junior standing in the doorway, with his head buried inside the furry hood of a black parka.

'Mr Ormondroyd,' Junior shouted, as he pointed into the toilet and began stepping between the chairs and legs. 'Sorry, mate. I was sitting on the bog and I nodded off.'

This caused a great deal of mirth amongst the other offenders, but the parole officer looked furiously at his watch.

'I can have you back inside like that, Moore,' the parole officer said, as he snapped his fingers. 'In my office *now*.'

But as Junior stumbled across the room, he recognised James' face. 'James Beckett,' Junior giggled, spreading his arms out wide. 'James bloody Beckett!'

James looked up and gave Junior a smile. 'I should have known that there couldn't be two people of that name,' he said, 'but I thought they sent you off to some nobby boarding school. What the *hell* are you doing here?'

'It's a parole office,' Junior said. 'I came here to buy postage stamps, obviously.'

'Same here.'

'This is *so* cool,' Junior grinned, but then he caught the angry stare from his parole officer. 'But . . . I've got this appointment,' he continued edgily. 'We've got to catch up. Can you wait around?'

'Sure,' James said, trying not to sound relieved. 'I've only got to fill in this form, but I can stick around till you're out of your meeting.'

23. SMOKE

'You got much going on?' Junior asked when he came out. 'There's nobody around, so you can come over mine and catch up if you like.'

'Whatever,' James nodded, zipping up his coat as they headed out of the parole office into a bitterly cold wind. 'How'd it go in there?'

Junior shrugged. 'You know, same as always: straighten up, fly right, tuck in your shirt, go to school, be home by eight, don't smoke, don't drink, don't do drugs and if you do get caught *little boy* we're locking you up again. How's about you?'

'I got busted up in Scotland,' James lied. 'I served my time and I don't have to see the parole officer any more, but I had to register to say that I've moved back down here.'

'Taxi!' Junior shouted, waving his arm and making a battered Nissan pull up to the curve.

'You must be loaded,' James said, as they clambered on to the tartan seat cover in the back.

'Buses are for peasants,' Junior grinned. 'You wait half an hour and it turns up full of old biddies and screaming kids.'

James shook his head as they pulled away inside the car. 'I guess your rich daddy left you with a few bucks.'

Junior shook his head. 'Ma gives me pocket money. But I've gotta duck and weave to make anything real, you know?'

'What's your scam?'

'Anything I think I can get away with,' Junior grinned. 'Buy a bit of this, sell a bit of that and then snort the profit!'

James shook his head. 'You still doing coke?'

'What do you think I was up to in that toilet?' Junior smirked. 'There's no way I could get through forty-five minutes with that egghead parole officer without putting a couple of lines up my sniffer.'

James noticed that the driver seemed shocked by their conversation. Junior banged on the headrest.

'Concentrate on the road and mind your own business,' he yelled arrogantly, before turning back to James. 'I can't believe I've caught up to you. Where have you been? What happened to your foster parents and all that?'

'Ewart and Zara kicked me out in the end,' James said. 'I was bunking off and stuff. Ended up running away to Scotland with my cousin Bruce and getting nicked trying to rob a cigarette machine.'

'Cigarette machine,' Junior tutted. 'That's so low rent! And you're living at the Zoo? What's that place like?'

'Major shithole,' James shrugged. 'Only got there last night and we've already got a war with two tossers who tried to rob us.'

'What were they, girl guides or brownies?' Junior snickered.

'They were huge, as a matter of fact,' James said. 'So what about you? Are you still boxing?'

'Nah. I went to this kickboxing place for a while, but then I got sent down.'

'What about your folks? Is your dad OK in prison?'

'I go visit every month, but he's miserable. I mean, you're locked up twenty-four seven so what can you expect?'

'And your brother and sisters?' James asked.

'Ringo's at university, giving our mum an orgasm every time he gets top grades. April's at school. She's no fun any more; all she's interested in is GCSEs and straight-laced boyfriends. And my little sister Erin got a scholarship to some fancy boarding school. Turns out she's a genius.'

'So is April still shaggable?' James teased.

'You'd better keep your hands *off* my twin this time,' Junior grinned. 'Not that she'll go anywhere near you. She was completely pissed off when you blanked her letters.'

'You never know with birds though,' James grinned back. 'I might take another shot.'

'No chance,' Junior said. 'So anyway, I've got some beers, a little bit of coke and a big bag of weed. So how about we catch up on old times, while ingesting massive quantities of booze and drugs?'

James had read Junior's file and knew that he had a drug problem, but the reality was still a shock.

'I'll take you up on a few beers,' James said, 'but the other stuff's not really my cup of tea.'

Junior looked offended. 'Oh well, more for me then.'

'Haven't you got to go to school?'

'Nah,' Junior said. 'Well, yeah actually, but I hate it. I'll just tell 'em I was sick or something. GCSEs are such toss anyway. I messed up all my coursework and . . . Oh, who gives a shit?'

James wanted to get Bruce involved in the mission as quickly as possible. 'Listen,' he said, as the cab took a corner slightly too fast. 'We just moved into the Zoo and my cousin's all on his lonesome. Do you mind if I call up and invite him over?'

'Course not,' Junior said. 'The more the merrier.'

*

Keith Moore had been in prison for more than two years, but his ex-wife Julie lived comfortably off the carefully laundered proceeds of his extinct drug empire. She'd recently moved into a seven-bedroom detached house with three acres and an indoor pool. She drove a convertible Mercedes and her life revolved around hair, nails, tanning and the gym.

'Junior!' she screamed, as she dumped her car keys and tennis racket on the kitchen cabinet and caught a nose full of burnt plastic. 'Junior, get your arse down here *right* now.'

Julie looked in horror at orange juice spilled over the floor and dirty plates piled up in the sink. The worst of the smell came from an oven dish with a pizza welded to it. It would have been the boys' lunch if Junior had been sober enough to strip off the polystyrene base before putting it in the oven.

Julie headed out of the kitchen and yelled again as she ran up the stairs. Junior's bedroom door was open. Radiohead pounded at full blast and marijuana smoke curled into the corridor. The music was so loud that James and Bruce didn't hear her storming up the stairs.

'Who the hell are you two?' Julie screamed, as she

grabbed the remote for Junior's hi-fi and turned off the music.

James had downed three beers and felt light-headed. 'Hey Mrs Moore,' he said, smiling dopily. 'Long time no see.'

'Yo,' Bruce giggled as he rolled off the bed. 'Junior never told us that his mum was so fit.'

'I'll give you fit in a minute,' Julie growled. 'Where's my son?'

James pointed drunkenly towards the en-suite bathroom. 'Shitting,' he explained.

'Junior, get the hell out of there,' Julie shouted, as she stepped over dirty clothes, dirty books and beer cans before opening the window as wide as it would go. 'What have I told you about smoking in the new house?'

It was a couple of minutes before Junior emerged, looking completely out of it with his hair tangled and his T-shirt on back to front.

'Hello, Mum,' Junior said, trying to sound sensible. 'How was your charity lunch thingy?'

'Whatthebloodyhellisthis?' Julie squealed, as she grabbed her son by his shoulder and cracked him around the back of the head.

'Oww,' Junior moaned. 'Mind your rings.'

'How was the parole office?' she demanded.

'Cool,' Junior said, pointing at James. 'Remember James from before Dad got busted? He was there too.'

'Do you really think I care about *that*, Junior? You've ruined that oven dish. The whole house stinks and you clearly haven't been to school.'

'I couldn't go to school,' Junior slurred. 'I met James. It was like . . . like *historical* or something.'

'Going to school is a condition of your release. Do you want to get locked up again?'

'Might as well,' Junior grinned. 'At least I wouldn't be getting all this earache off you.'

Julie cracked her son around the head again before turning towards James and Bruce. 'And I don't know what gutter he dragged you in from, but I want you out.'

James and Bruce stumbled up and started looking around for their coats.

'I'll see you tonight at the football club,' Junior mumbled. 'You can meet some of my muckers.'

'What about your curfew?' Julie interrupted. 'You might be too big for me to stop you getting out of the house, Junior, but I can call the parole office.'

'Play a different record, Mum. That one's so boring . . .'

'Don't you think I'm bluffing. I'll ring that parole office and tell them *everything*.'

But Junior shook his head, knowing that his mum would never grass him up. 'I'm fifteen years old,' he shouted. 'Get out of my face, you dumb bitch.'

James was shocked. If he'd called his mum a bitch when she was alive she'd have bounced him off every wall in the house.

'Oh that's nice,' Julie said, looking hurt. 'I'm the one who feeds you and puts clothes on your back. I'm the one who bails you out. The one who visits you in prison and—'

'Yeah you work *so* hard,' Junior sneered. 'You haven't had a job since you married Dad twenty years ago.'

'I've raised four kids,' Julie screamed, close to tears. 'Three of 'em are just fine, so how's it my fault that your life's messed up?'

James was embarrassed and he pointed a thumb towards the door. 'We'll be going then.'

Julie continued yelling at her son as James and Bruce headed down the stairs.

'Did you see the way Junior was smoking that joint?' Bruce whispered.

James nodded. 'Just breathing the smoke was making my eyes water, but he was sucking it down like lemonade.'

'Seems like a nice guy though.'

'Yeah,' James nodded. 'I really got on with him last time and he was always a bit crazy, but now he's gone *completely* off the rails . . .'

24. TALENT

'I play sometimes,' Junior explained as he led James and Bruce along a damp path towards a floodlit football pitch. 'But to be honest, I'm a bit out of shape.'

It was seven at night and James had sobered up, but the beers had left him with a headache.

'I'm not surprised you're out of shape,' James grinned. 'The amount you smoked and drank today, it's a miracle you can walk.'

'These are nice guys you're gonna be meeting,' Junior explained. 'They put a lot of money my way, but don't mess with them. Especially Sasha.'

'Who's Sasha?' Bruce asked innocently.

'Serious gangster,' Junior said. 'I'm OK with him because he goes back to my dad and the old days, but he's ruthless. He was in a country pub one time and this dude he bumped into called him a *clumsy wanker*. Sasha had two of his boys drag him outside. They tied him to the bumper of a transit van and drove five miles before cutting what was left of him loose.'

'Shit,' James gasped. He'd read many similar stories about

Sasha Thompson and the Mad Dogs, but this particular anecdote hadn't appeared in the mission briefing.

As they got closer, James saw that five teams were training in yellow kits. They ranged from under-elevens through to adults, all with *Thompson Exhaust Centres* as their shirt sponsors. Sasha Thompson himself sat on a bench wearing football boots and a tight fitting tracksuit tucked into yellow socks. Every so often he'd cup his hands around his mouth and yell at one of the players.

'Jonesy you tit, you're supposed to be marking him!'

Sasha was forty-six years old. He'd given up playing football a couple of years earlier because of a dodgy knee, but he kept in shape by running and lifting weights and he looked hard. His eyes lit up when he saw Junior.

'Mr Moore, how nice of you to join us,' Sasha said fruitily. 'Can I have a word?'

Junior looked anxiously at James and Bruce. 'You'd better stay back.'

But as Junior started jogging, Sasha yelled out: 'And bring your two little friends.'

So Junior arrived first and a couple of Sasha's flunkies shifted over to make space on the bench. James and Bruce stopped a couple of metres in front of Sasha, their trainers sinking into the mud along the touchline.

'I had a call from your mum,' Sasha said seriously. 'She's really upset. Are these two little yobbos the ones who were round your house causing mayhem earlier?'

'Yeah,' Junior nodded, with a touch of fear in his voice.

'Your ma was crying when she spoke to me,' Sasha said. '*What* did you call her?'

'Um . . .'

'She says that you messed up at the parole office. She says you missed school and called her a bitch. Is all that true?'

Junior shrugged. 'Pretty much.'

'Did you smoke a joint in the house?'

James could see that Junior was scared of Sasha. 'Yeah,' he admitted meekly.

Sasha grabbed Junior by the back of his neck and squeezed tight, making his head tilt back in spasm.

'When he got sent down, your dad said you were trouble and asked me to keep an eye on you,' Sasha growled. 'I asked him how far I could go and he said, *slap the piss out of him if you have to.* But that's not a place you want to go with me, is it Junior?'

'No, boss,' Junior croaked.

'Buy your mother a bunch of flowers and count yourself lucky that Mr Ormondroyd at the parole office is an old friend of mine. He won't be writing you up for bunking school.'

'Thanks, Sasha,' Junior said, half smiling as the hand slipped from around his neck.

Sasha looked up at James and Bruce. 'And which hole in the ground did you two crawl out of?' he asked nastily.

'James is an old mate,' Junior explained.

'Did I ask *you?*' Sasha snapped.

'Junior brought us here,' James explained. 'We got moved back round this way after a spell living with our aunt in Scotland.'

'All right,' Sasha said, waving a hand in front of his face. 'I didn't ask for your bleedin' life story. You upset Julie

Moore who *happens* to be one of my oldest friends, so you'd better stay away from her, away from Junior and out of my face.'

James could feel the mission falling apart before his eyes. Sasha had taken an instant dislike to him and Bruce, which put his chances of infiltrating the Mad Dogs on a par with his chances of winning the lottery two weeks running.

'Why are you still here?' Sasha said, as he made a walking motion with his fingers. 'Scoot before I get my boys to rearrange your heads with a crowbar.'

'Come *on*, Sasha,' Junior grovelled. 'They're mates of mine. They haven't done nothing.'

'Did I ask you, Junior?' Sasha said again. 'Maybe you'd be a better judge of character if you didn't put so much shit up your nose.'

But Junior gave it one more shot as James and Bruce turned away. 'Remember when Crazy Joe's Ford Mustang got burned out?' Junior asked. 'That was James and his stepsister.'

This was like flipping a switch. Sasha's face lit up and he even got off the bench. 'Hey kid, where you going?'

James turned around and was surprised to see Sasha coming forward and reaching out to shake his hand. 'You're the dude that burned out Crazy Joe's Mustang? That was the funniest goddamned thing that *ever* happened. I laughed so hard I almost pissed my pants. We all did, didn't we?'

Sasha turned to look back at the hard men sitting on or standing around his bench. They all started nodding and laughing, and before James knew it, the most notorious members of Sasha's crew were lining up to shake his hand.

'Keith Moore took a bit of a shine to you, didn't he?' Sasha asked.

'James was with me in Miami when Dad got busted,' Junior said. 'We might have got killed if James hadn't broken out and called the cops.'

'Sorry kid,' Sasha said. 'I didn't realise you knew Keith. I just thought you were some dickhead Junior met at the parole office this morning.'

As the big men laughed and squeezed James' hand, he remembered Kyle's comment that he wouldn't wish him luck because he was so jammy that he wouldn't need it.

'So are you football men?' Sasha asked.

James shrugged. 'I can kick a ball, but I'm pretty crap. My cousin here's not bad.'

Sasha turned to Bruce. 'What age are you?'

'Fourteen,' Bruce said.

'What position?'

'Midfield, or on the wing, but I'll play anywhere except in goal.'

Sasha looked at his watch before pointing across the pitches. 'The under-fifteens are over there. There's about forty minutes of the session left if you want to take a shot. It's slippery, so you'd better grab some spare boots from the clubhouse.'

Bruce preferred kicking people to kicking balls, but he reckoned getting into one of Sasha's teams would be a big boost for the mission. 'I don't mind giving it a go,' he shrugged. 'I've got nothing else going on.'

'What about you, James?' Sasha asked as Bruce headed into the clubhouse to find some boots. 'You look like a strong lad.'

'I've seen him play and I wouldn't get too excited,' Junior said. 'Besides, these are the proper teams, James. You should play in the Sunday league side with me, it's total carnage and way more of a laugh.'

'Sunday sounds good,' James nodded. 'I could handle that.'

Sasha looked disappointed. 'It's not serious football, but if your heart's not in it . . .'

A few minutes later Bruce was over on the far side, trying out with the under-fifteens, Sasha was back on the bench yelling at the Mad Dogs' first team, whilst James and Junior had moved twenty metres along the touchline to chat with a couple of Sasha's associates. One was a twenty-eight-year-old named Savvas, the other a nineteen-year-old who was called David but everyone knew him as Wheels.

James had read their police files while he was preparing for the mission. Savvas came from a poor Turkish background. He'd trained as an accountant, but his career nosedived when he got a four-year stretch for heroin smuggling.

Wheels had been a teenage go-kart champion, but his parents weren't rich enough to pay his way into single-seat racing, so he'd turned his talents into a career driving getaway vehicles. Despite a reputation as a drug user, gambler and complete head case, the only thing the cops had ever pinned on Wheels was a speeding ticket and a £75 fine for peeing in the street.

'Can one of you boys put an earner my way?' Junior asked. 'I'm flat broke.'

Wheels and Savvas both sucked air through their teeth. Savvas pointed at Sasha. 'I've got plenty of ways for you to make money, but not unless the big man gives the OK.'

194

'Same here,' Wheels said.

'Come *on*,' Junior begged. 'Just give me a couple of grams of coke to sell or a bag of weed. There's tons of little rich kids at my school who I can sell it to and they're dickheads, so I can charge way over the odds.'

'Speak to the man,' Savvas said firmly. 'He's let you do stuff before.'

'I know,' Junior nodded. 'But only little stuff and if I ask Sasha now he's gonna rip my head off.'

'What about me?' James asked. 'You got something for me?'

Savvas shook his head. 'I don't know you from Adam.'

'Yes you do,' Junior said. 'He's the guy who did Crazy Joe's car.'

'Yeah, two years ago,' Savvas sneered. 'No offence, James, but for all we know you grassed on half of Scotland while you were up there.'

In contrast, Wheels seemed keen to work with James. 'I'll take you out and show you a few tricks,' he said. 'I could do with a dogsbody and you look as if you can handle yourself.'

'Seriously?' James grinned.

'What about me?' Junior whined. 'I need money *so* bad.'

'Yeah right,' Savvas snorted. 'With your mum driving a seventy-grand Mercedes and a two-million trust fund.'

'I don't need money when I'm twenty-one,' Junior spluttered. 'I need money for this weekend.'

Junior's argument was going around in circles and Savvas was losing patience. 'So go and speak to Sasha. Nobody's gonna go against what he says.'

'You're all tossers,' Junior moaned, as a football sailed

over their heads. 'You all want me wrapped in cotton wool. I'm not a baby.'

Despite his claims to maturity, Junior flounced off like a five-year-old who'd had his sweets taken away. Then he turned back, annoyed that James hadn't followed.

'Are you coming or not?' Junior asked.

This was an awkward moment. James had to balance his friendship with Junior with the fact that Wheels was offering him some action.

'Coming where?' James said.

Junior pointed towards a row of terraced houses at the far side of the playing fields. 'I might as well go over to Sasha's house and get warm.'

James looked eagerly at Wheels. 'Were you serious about putting some money my way?'

'If you're up for it,' Wheels grinned. 'But there's no rush. You go over to Sasha's with the spoiled brat and I'll catch up later.'

James was slightly mystified. 'Does everyone go over there?'

Wheels nodded. 'Sasha's got a big ol' basement and the crew always hangs out there after football.'

'Right,' James said. 'Guess I'll see you over there.'

But as he started walking towards Junior he heard Sasha shout Bruce's name.

'Jesus Harold Christ,' Sasha yelled. 'Will you look at that little fella run?'

James turned towards the pitch, where a practice game had started between the under-fifteens and under-seventeens. Bruce was the smallest kid on the pitch and wore boots two sizes too big for him, but he was running on goal with a beanpole defender and the keeper to beat.

On campus Bruce rarely played football, but the speed and co-ordination he showed fighting in the dojo translated beautifully on to the floodlit pitch. The ball seemed glued to his foot as he spun around and delicately chipped the ball into the air, then vaulted the defender's clumsy tackle.

The keeper closed down the angle, but Bruce kept his cool. He tapped the ball on to his knee and then volleyed into the right-hand corner of the net.

Junior had seen the whole thing and came running back to James on the touchline. 'Holy shit,' Junior yelled. 'Did you see that? Your cousin walked the entire defence.'

James had heard kids on campus begging Bruce to join their team, but it was only now that he actually saw why. Bruce stopped running and gave a casual shrug as his muddy team-mates steamed down the pitch to hug him.

'Genius,' Sasha was yelling, as he jumped in the air. 'That kid is pure genius.'

25. HOUSE

Most members of the Mad Dogs Football Club were regular guys who showered in the clubhouse after training and went home to their families. But the club was also the core of Sasha's criminal gang, and the crew that went on to his basement consisted of a dozen hardcore criminals aged from their late twenties up to around fifty and a similar number of hangers-on: youngsters like Wheels and Junior who saw the gang as a way of having fun and making easy money.

Sasha had lived in the same row of four-storey houses his whole life. His elderly mother owned number forty-three, while Sasha lived next door with his wife and daughter. The basements of the two houses had been knocked together to make a gloomy hang-out with a nicotine-stained ceiling.

Whilst Junior and the younger lads held pool cues and drank supermarket-brand lager, Sasha, Wheels and the older gang members downed spirits and battled over the green felt of a poker table. To begin with it was low stakes, with the players coming and going and everyone talking, puffing cigars and telling stories as bottles of spirits drained away. But by eleven the casual players had drifted home and things started getting serious.

Sasha lost a couple of hundred pounds when Wheels beat him with three queens and he yelled at the kids around the pool tables to shut up and stop distracting him. Most of the youngsters took this as a cue to leave, including Junior.

'You don't wanna be here when one of those guys starts losing big,' Junior explained. 'I've seen Sasha stick a guy's head through a wall just for looking at him funny.'

Bruce was tired and wanted to go back to the Zoo, but James couldn't leave until he'd spoken to Wheels.

'Scuse me,' James said nervously, as he approached the big shots at the table and crouched down beside Wheels. 'I'm gonna get going, but you said about putting some business my way; so maybe I could give you my mobile number or something?'

Wheels was a pup compared to the others around the table, but he had the biggest pile of cash. 'I'm out,' Wheels said dramatically as he pushed back his chair, stood up and began gathering his money.

'Yeah, best to quit while you're ahead,' Sasha said. 'Go back to playing with the little kiddies.'

Wheels smiled as he straightened his pile of money so that it would fit in his pocket. 'I'll be back on Friday,' he said casually. 'I want to win all your money a bit at a time, 'cos I know how upset you gents would get if I won it all in one go.'

James smiled as the men around the table laughed. But Sasha looked at Wheels seriously. 'Are you taking James out for a ride?'

Wheels nodded. 'If that's OK with you, boss.'

'He worked for Keith so I guess we can trust him,' Sasha shrugged; then he pointed at Junior and Bruce. 'But you're not planning on bringing these two along, are you?'

The way Sasha said *are you* made it clear that he meant *don't even think about it*. James knew that Sasha was looking out for Junior, but he couldn't understand the concern for Bruce.

'Here,' Sasha said, grabbing a £20 note off the poker table and waving it at Junior. 'It's late, so grab a car from the mini-cab office on the corner, and you can drop my man Bruce off at the Zoo along the way.'

Bruce looked towards Wheels. 'Can't I go with them?'

Sasha shook his head. 'You're the new star of Mad Dogs' under-fifteens. I want those nimble feet tucked up in bed and fit for the match on Thursday night.'

Bruce was pissed off. He'd put on a show on the football pitch to attract Sasha's attention, but he was supposed to get involved in the criminal side of the gang and it seemed footballing talent was no help on that score.

'Here,' Sasha said, reaching out to hand Bruce three tenners. 'I expect you could do with a bit of pocket money.'

'Cheers,' Bruce smiled.

Junior and Bruce said their goodbyes and James followed Wheels up the basement steps a few minutes later. At the top they passed Sasha's sixteen-year-old daughter Lois, her curvy figure clad in a towelling gown.

'Hey, Wheels,' Lois said warmly, before turning towards James. 'I haven't seen you before.'

'This is James Beckett,' Wheels said uneasily. 'He's a mate of Junior's.'

'How's it going?' Lois asked.

'Not bad,' James said, as he studied her freshly painted nails and unfeasibly perfect teeth. It seemed Sasha had forked out for some expensive dental work.

'We've really gotta split, Lois,' Wheels said. 'See you around, yeah?'

Wheels sighed with relief as they stepped out on to the front doorstep.

'You got a problem with her?' James asked.

'Let's just say that a psychotic gangster and a hot teenage daughter is a dangerous combination.'

'She's got a great rack though,' James smirked, as they headed towards Wheels' car.

'Don't even think about her,' Wheels said, shaking his head. 'She's been around with a few guys from sixth-form college, but Sasha's made it clear that she's not for the likes of us.'

James was disappointed as Wheels stopped walking beside an anonymous Vauxhall hatchback. He'd been expecting a hot rod.

'Flash cars attract attention,' Wheels explained as they climbed inside. 'Besides, it's what you do behind the wheel that counts. So where do you want to go?'

James was confused. 'I thought you had a plan or something.'

Wheels looked over his shoulder into the oncoming traffic before pulling away from the kerb. It was less than thirty metres to the junction with a main road.

'I was about your age when Sasha took me under his wing,' Wheels explained, as they cruised past a line of shops.

It was midnight and everywhere except the convenience stores and take-aways had their shutters down. 'Sasha taught me that the streets are paved with money.'

James smiled.

'It's true,' Wheels grinned, as he pointed at a shopfront. 'Fried chicken joint, even on a Monday you can bet that there's two hundred quid sitting behind the counter. Maybe three times that on a Friday or Saturday . . . That's a nice BMW over there, roll it on to a low-loader and drive off and you can sell it to a used-parts dealer for a couple of grand. What's more, if you dress up like a wheel clamper you can haul it away in broad daylight and nobody will bat an eyelid.

'British Telecom,' Wheels smiled, pointing at a grey van as they turned another corner. 'If you try robbing a van, never go for some anonymous white number. Chances are the owner's self-employed and he takes all of his gear out at night. But the guys who work for telephone, electric and gas companies are employees. Nothing belongs to them so they don't care what gets nicked: copper pipe, electrical equipment, tools, even laptops sometimes.'

'So that's all you do,' James said, obviously disappointed. 'You rob gear out of vans?'

Wheels tutted. 'No you dickhead, I'm trying to make a point, which is that money is lying around everywhere if you look for it.'

James shrugged. 'Point taken.'

Wheels continued, 'The second thing Sasha taught me is that you have to mix it up. You know on the TV news when you read about a spate of robberies, or a spate of muggings?'

James nodded.

'No smart criminal ever gets involved in a spate of anything. Cops can't catch everyone, so they go for the crooks who make their lives easy. When you do the same thing ten times, chances are the civilians are gonna be behind their net curtains looking for you and the police will be on your tail.'

'So you pull lots of different scams?' James asked.

'Exactly,' Wheels said. 'That's why Sasha Thompson's been so good for so long. One week he's selling cocaine, the next week he's robbing a bank or stealing air-conditioning units off a building site and shipping them to Dubai.

'And Sasha's third golden rule is to never get too big for your boots. You know in the movies how crooks always talk about doing one big score and then retiring?'

'Yeah, always,' James nodded.

'That's the last thing you should ever do. If you steal a hundred grand, it'll get in the local paper and you'll have the local CID on your back for a day or two. But if you steal ten million, you're gonna be in the papers, on the TV news and they'll put the best cops in the country on your back.'

'What about drugs?' James asked. 'Sasha's an old mate of Junior's dad so I assumed he was mainly into dealing.'

'Sure he's into drugs,' Wheels nodded. 'Making 'em, selling 'em or ripping off dealers. No crook can ignore drugs because that's where all the money is. But first and foremost, Sasha and the whole Mad Dogs crew are old-school thieves.

'Your chum Keith Moore's the *classic* example of someone who got too big for his boots. In the end he had everyone from the local cops to M15 and the FBI on his back. When you're drawing that much heat, sooner or later you're going to slip up and get nailed.'

James nodded. He'd read the police files on Sasha Thompson and the thing that stood out over a thirty-year criminal career was his ability to stay out of trouble while those around him got busted. When Keith Moore was sent to prison, many had expected Sasha to step into his shoes and take control of the drug trade. Now James understood why he hadn't.

But James knew Sasha had two weaknesses. Firstly, staying small makes it hard to stop ambitious upstarts like Major Dee from taking away your business. Second, Wheels' delight in showing how clever he was would surely be a big help with the mission.

'So are we just gonna drive around all night?' James asked.

Wheels smiled. 'I've had a little scam on the cards for a few weeks now, but I need an extra body to pull it off. Take a look in the glove box.'

James flipped it open and looked suitably impressed when he saw a large Glock handgun. 'Nice piece.'

'Cheers,' Wheels said, 'but I was actually talking about the plastic card.'

James picked the card out of the glove box. It was silver, with a picture of a revolving door and the words *Ambassador Suites* written at the top.

'Hotel room key,' James said, as he turned it over in his hands. 'So what?'

'It's a brand-new hotel down in the city,' Wheels explained. 'The cheapest rooms are four hundred a night and the suites are nearer to two grand. That card you're holding is a duplicate of the hotel manager's key. It lets you into every single room.'

'Cool,' James said, glancing at his watch. 'But won't everyone be in their rooms at this time of night?'

'Absolutely,' Wheels smiled. 'That's the whole point.'

26. CONCIERGE

The traffic was light but it still took an hour to drive from Bedfordshire to the Ambassador Hotel, built amidst the office towers in the City of London.

'Just be confident,' Wheels said, as they headed towards the revolving doors with baseball caps pulled over their heads. 'Place like this is gonna have security cameras everywhere, so move fast and keep your head pointing towards your feet.'

A blast of warm air hit the pair as they passed into the lobby. An elderly couple stood around a mound of designer luggage waiting for a car to pick them up. The gent wore a Rolex and the lady had diamonds the size of marbles over her wrinkled fingers.

'You can smell the money in this joint,' Wheels said happily as they waited for the lift.

The reception was at ground level, but most of the tower block was office space and the hotel rooms didn't start until the 33rd floor. Wheels pressed the button marked *Suites 38*, but the light wouldn't come on and the doors stayed open.

James felt edgy as a hotel employee in a black suit walked towards them. 'Can I help you gentlemen?' he asked.

'I need the thirty-eighth floor,' Wheels said.

The employee nodded. 'May I see your room key?'

Wheels handed the plastic card over and the hotel employee pushed it into a slot above the lift buttons.

'There you go, sir.'

'Ahh,' Wheels said innocently. 'I didn't realise. The bell boy must have done that when we went up with our luggage earlier.'

'Not a problem sir,' the employee replied politely. 'I hope you have a relaxing night.'

The high-speed lift made James queasy as it belted up to the thirty-eighth floor. He felt a bit scared as he saw the Glock bulging beneath the waistband of Wheels' jeans. His own gun was back in his room at the Zoo.

They stepped out of the lift and Wheels handed James disposable gloves as they moved briskly over deep carpet. It was more than ten paces between each door, meaning the suites behind them had to be huge. But Wheels had an even grander ambition and kept going until they came to some double doors at the end of the hallway. The brass plaque on the door said *Room 38020: Winston Churchill Suite.*

'Rich scum, here I come,' Wheels chanted, as he pushed the plastic card inside the lock. It took a couple of seconds for the mechanism to work and Wheels ripped the gun out of his waistband as he stormed into the huge suite. But the bed was pristine and there was no sign of any luggage or personal items spread about.

'Empty room,' James said.

Wheels swore under his breath as he tucked the gun back inside his jeans and almost trod on James' foot as spun around. 'Look where you're going, *kid*.'

James didn't fuss over getting blamed as Wheels stepped back into the hallway and slotted the key card into the door of the nearest suite. This time he pushed the door and got hit by green light from a TV screen. As James stepped in, he noticed a woman standing in the bathroom wearing only knickers and a woolly mammoth on the bed in polka-dot boxers.

'Where are you going, honey?' the man asked, in an American accent; clearly thinking that the sound of the door was caused by his wife leaving. But he knew something was wrong when she screamed.

'Get on the bed,' Wheels ordered, as he pointed the gun in the woman's face. 'Now.'

'Keep cool, boys,' the man said, raising both hands in surrender as Wheels bundled the woman across the bed. 'We don't want any trouble.'

'Nor do we,' Wheels said as he opened up a large mirrored door and spotted the small electronic safe in the bottom of the wardrobe. 'What's the code?' he demanded.

As Wheels unlocked the safe and retrieved a laptop and the lady's diamond necklace, James walked around to the bedside table where he found a mobile phone, a wallet and the keys to a Lexus. James flipped the wallet open and showed Wheels the rack of bank cards inside.

'He's loaded,' James said, as Wheels crammed the laptop and jewellery inside a Nike backpack, then aimed the gun at the lady.

'I don't see your purse,' Wheels yelled. 'Where is it?'

The woman sat with a luxurious satin pillow in her lap to shield her breasts. 'Find it yourself,' she spat, her body language indicating that she wasn't too impressed by her husband's meek surrender.

'This says Patek Philippe,' James said, as he picked up the man's watch. 'Never heard of it.'

Wheels laughed. 'That's because you can't afford it. They're dearer and more exclusive than a Rolex. Trouble is that makes 'em buggers to fence.'

James reached over and dropped the watch into a backpack as Wheels searched around for the purse. Finally, he lost patience and smashed the barrel of his gun into the woman's face.

As she howled and sobbed, her husband pointed towards a yellow handbag resting in the gap between the mattress and the bedside table.

'No,' the woman gasped. 'My grandmother's brooch is in there. Please don't take it.'

'Your granny's brooch,' Wheels sneered. 'Quite frankly, I don't give a damn.'

The woman sniffled as Wheels ripped her purse from the bag and began inspecting her collection of plastic cards.

'Very impressive,' Wheels snorted. 'Do you know, this card comes with a twenty-four-hour concierge service? That's gonna come in handy for replacing all this stuff we're stealing.'

'You've got what you came for,' the man said firmly. 'Now why don't you leave?'

Wheels broke into a nasty laugh as he ripped the hotel

telephone out of the wall socket. 'I'm afraid that we're only just starting. What's the registration of your car?'

'Why do you need it?' he asked.

Wheels looked at the woman. 'Do you want me to smash her one?'

'Seven one, D E F, two five nine.'

'Right,' Wheels said. 'And is it parked down in the basement?'

The man nodded.

'Valet or self-park?'

'Self-park, basement level three outside the elevator.'

Wheels snapped the cord from the base of the handset and threw the length of telephone cord at James before pointing at the woman. 'Tie her up.'

'What are you doing?' the man demanded.

'It's *very* simple,' Wheels grinned. 'You're going to tell me the PIN numbers for all of your lovely cards. Once we've tied you up, I'm going downstairs to take your car. Then I'm gonna drive around London, stopping off at cash machines and drawing two-fifty or five hundred quid on every one of them. It should only take an hour or so, and my little pal will wait here pointing this gun at you. If you make a fuss or try to escape, or if it turns out that you told fibs when you gave me your PIN numbers, he's gonna put bullets through both of your heads.'

James felt bad about tying the woman's wrists together as Wheels made the man write a list of his own and his wife's PIN numbers on Ambassador Hotel stationery.

'Turn on to your stomach,' James ordered, as the woman sobbed desperately.

James knotted flex around her ankles before trussing the wrists and ankles together and cramming one of her husband's handkerchiefs in her mouth. The man scowled at James when he moved in to repeat the exercise, but gave in when Wheels squished the tip of his nose with the gun.

'Any noise, any lies, any fuss and you're both *dead*,' Wheels grunted while James finished tying the couple up. Then he handed the gun to James. 'You feeling OK?'

The Glock was heavy and James felt awful about the sobbing woman. But he nodded.

'Don't sweat it, I'll call in about an hour and meet you back where we parked,' Wheels said.

As Wheels walked out of the room James settled into an armchair and kept one eye on the couple as he tried to work out how much they'd stolen: the laptop was worth a few hundred, the watches, the woman's jewellery, cufflinks plus the money Wheels was collecting from the cash machines and whatever the new Lexus was worth to a stolen car syndicate. All told it had to be the best part of ten grand and Wheels had promised James a share.

But crime didn't look so good from the perspective of the woman trussed up on the bed with tears streaking down her face. James grabbed the remote and flicked the television from 24-hour news to VH1, but even when he turned the sound up he couldn't not think about the two desperate humans less than three metres away from him.

Getting involved with Sasha's crew was an essential part of the mission and there was no way to do that without getting involved in some bad stuff. But he did rummage through the backpack and drop the antique brooch on to the carpet.

*

James drove the Vauxhall to the outskirts of London and met up with Wheels, who'd dumped the Lexus in a side street. Apparently a friend in the motor trade was already on his way to collect it and it would be resprayed and shipped off to Eastern Europe within days.

Wheels had taken over two grand out of the cash machines and he gave James half, with a promise of more money when he'd been paid for the car and fenced the stolen gear.

'You did good,' Wheels said.

'So can we do some more jobs together?'

Wheels nodded. 'But not straight away. You're only fifteen and I reckon that grand is going to burn a hole on your pocket. The Zoo is full of snitches, so take your time spending it and *don't* go mouthing off.'

'I'm not a *complete* idiot,' James said.

'Sasha's short of bodies right now, so I'll put in a word and see if he can find something more permanent for you.'

'Cheers, and goodnight,' James said as he popped the door of the car. But when he looked up at the sky he could see the sun coming up behind a line of houses. 'Or maybe that's good morning.'

James had left all the stolen stuff with Wheels for him to sell, but he patted the back pocket of his jeans to make sure that he had his wedge of money. It might have been half five in the morning, but the care worker stationed on the entrance didn't bat an eye as James sauntered in. A couple who looked about thirteen were making out in the non-smoking lounge and a bunch of kids were watching a DVD and smoking in the other one.

But most people were asleep and James crept into the room to avoid waking Bruce. Unfortunately, his trainers made a racket as they crackled on the filthy vinyl floor.

'What happened?' Bruce whispered, as James pulled his shirt over his head.

'Hotel robbery,' James said, pulling the money out of his jeans and fanning it.

Bruce grinned. 'I might just know why Wheels was so keen to take you out, even though he barely knows you.'

'You reckon?' James said.

'I was speaking to Junior and there's a rumour going around that Wheels isn't exactly what you'd call a ladies' man.'

'You mean he's gay?'

Bruce nodded. 'It would certainly explain why he took a shine to your pretty blond head within about five minutes of meeting you.'

The idea that Wheels was attracted to him made James uneasy. 'Well,' he said. 'If it's true it's kind of worked to our advantage, but he'd better not try anything. And speaking of people who keep things under their hat, what was going on out on that football pitch?'

'I've always been good at football, but I'm not really into it.'

James shook his head in disbelief. Most boys would give *anything* to be that good at football. 'You never practise or anything,' he said. 'If you did you'd be awesome.'

'I'm a talented guy,' Bruce said immodestly. 'By the way, you might want to be careful when you climb into bed; there's a couple of teeth around somewhere.'

James raised an eyebrow. 'Teeth?'

'Mark and Kurt came by again,' Bruce explained. 'They must have realised you were out and thought they'd stand a better chance if it was two against one. They were wrong, *obviously . . .*'

27. EXTORTION

It was now Thursday, two weeks from the day Gabrielle had been stabbed. Michael Hendry sat in the Green Pepper café, his plate loaded with spiced chicken and macaroni. The place had been empty in the days after the murder of Owen Campbell-Moore, but custom had drifted back once the cops took down their cordons and stopped hassling everyone who came within a hundred metres.

The customers shot pool, dealt drugs and fattened the owner's bank balance by stuffing coins into the fruit machines, while the radio was tuned to an internet station bringing news and music out of Kingston, Jamaica.

Michael might have had the same colour skin as the rest of the customers, but he was a middle-class English boy and he'd never have been able to infiltrate the Slasher Boys without Gabrielle's authentic Jamaican heritage.

Michael glanced at his watch – a gold-strapped Bulgari which he'd bought off one of the Slasher Boys for less than a tenth of its legitimate value. Major Dee was forty minutes late, but that was normal. Making people wait around was Dee's way of showing that his time was more important than yours and you showed respect by not complaining about it.

Michael was chewing the last piece of chicken off a drumstick when Dee finally pulled up outside in a Ford Mondeo. He had a mean-looking sidekick called Colin Wragg in the back. Dee owned some fancy cars, but the discreet wheels meant he was on serious business.

As he stepped into the passenger seat, Michael had his gun strapped around his waist and ten grand's worth of nanotube-reinforced fabric sewn into the lining of his grey top.

'What's occurring?' Michael asked, as he slammed the door and pulled a seatbelt across his chest.

'We tracked down a Runt,' Major Dee grinned. 'I thought you'd like to ride along after what they did to your girl.'

Over the past two weeks, the Slasher Boys had been devoted to finding Runts; but the Runts knew Dee's crew was after them and they'd stuck to their home turf on the opposite side of town.

'Which one?' Michael asked.

'Aaron Reid,' Colin said, as he cracked his knuckles.

'Sweet as,' Michael said, but he felt queasy as he remembered the noise Aaron's head made when he'd pushed him into a concrete post.

'My girl went out to buy some stuff for the garden,' Colin explained. 'Recognised him straight away. Apparently he's still got a bandage round his head.'

Michael joined Dee and Colin's laughter, but he was worried. If Major Dee did get his hands on Aaron Reid, it wasn't going to be for a friendly chat.

'We knew you'd want to come,' Dee grinned.

'Definitely,' Michael said, faking enthusiasm. 'I want those pricks to suffer.'

'How's Gabrielle doing, anyway?' Colin asked.

'Not too bad,' Michael said. 'I want to go up and see her, but her aunt won't let me near.'

'She's a good girl,' Dee purred. 'There's real fire in her belly.'

Michael thought about Gabrielle as they turned on to a stretch of dual carriageway. He missed her every second she wasn't around.

*

James spent most of Tuesday in bed and a quiet Wednesday hanging around the Zoo and going to the multiplex with Bruce and Junior in the evening. Wheels called James on Thursday morning and offered him sixty quid to help sort out a problem with a money-lending racket run by the Mad Dogs.

Wheels' Vauxhall pulled up in a parking bay outside a little supermarket. James sat in the passenger seat next to him.

'Traffic wardens round here are psychos,' Wheels said, as he pointed to a stack of twenty-pence pieces in a compartment on top of the dashboard. 'Stick some money in the pay-and-display; we shouldn't be more than ten minutes.'

The first pay-and-display machine James came to was busted, so he had to jog fifty metres to the next one as Wheels pulled up the hood of his tracksuit top and walked into the supermarket. A teenager dressed in a veil stood behind the counter and Wheels told her to get her father.

'All right Mr Patel?' Wheels said brashly. The bell over

the door jangled as James stepped in with his hoodie covering his face.

'My name's not Patel,' the man said angrily. 'Do I look like a Hindu to you?'

'You look brown,' Wheels shrugged. 'You owe us three weeks' money, now open the register or there's gonna be some shit.'

The shopkeeper furiously shook his bald head. 'I borrowed five hundred pounds from you people. I've paid that back ten times over.'

'You owe three weeks at one-twenty-five a week. That makes three hundred and seventy-five pounds.'

The shopkeeper pounded his fist on his counter. 'I've paid enough,' he insisted. 'You won't get another penny from me.'

Wheels turned and winked at James, who swept his arm along a shelf sending tins of baby food and hotdogs clattering to the floor.

'Oh *dear* me,' Wheels grinned. 'Accidents will happen.'

The shopkeeper's jowls swelled as he pointed towards the door. 'Leave my shop or I'll call the police.'

James grabbed a carousel stacked with greetings cards and upended it into a freezer stacked with frozen veg as an elderly woman stepped into the doorway.

'We're closed,' Wheels snarled.

To make sure no more customers came in, James slid a bolt across the door.

'I *will* call the police,' the shopkeeper shouted as he grabbed a phone from behind the counter.

Wheels flipped open a spring-loaded cosh and smashed the handset out of the shopkeeper's hand.

'Bad things *will* happen, Mr Patel,' Wheels warned. 'Your shop could burn to the ground. Two big men could come in here, drag you out on to the street and beat you senseless. Or maybe we could pick up one of your pretty little daughters.'

The shopkeeper scowled at Wheels as he clutched his agonised knuckles to his chest.

'How much is in the till?' Wheels asked.

'I can give you two hundred,' the shopkeeper said reluctantly, as he pressed the button to open the cash drawer under the register.

James noticed a sudden change in the light as the door from the stock room burst open. The shopkeeper's daughter charged out, brandishing a cricket bat.

'Don't give in to 'em, Dad,' the teenager cried, as she swung at Wheels' head.

The blow missed Wheels' skull, but cracked viciously on the elbow he raised to defend himself. He screamed in pain as his cosh clattered to the ground.

James was impressed by the girl's courage, but he had to stick by Wheels if he was going to win Sasha Thompson's trust. He grabbed the girl under her armpit and snatched the bat out of her hands as he dragged her over a counter top covered in newspapers.

'Smash that bitch's skull,' Wheels ordered.

But there was no way James was going to do that. He threw the bat down and twisted the girl's arm up behind her back, then glowered at the shopkeeper.

'Put the paper money out of that cash drawer into a bag or I'll break her arm.'

The shopkeeper gritted his teeth as he ripped a carrier bag

from a hook and began stuffing it with notes. James was too tense to count, but it looked close to the three-seventy-five they'd come looking for.

James snatched the bag, shoved the girl back across the counter and looked at Wheels. 'You OK?'

'Do I look OK, you *dick*?' Wheels snapped, as he grasped his elbow. 'I can barely move my arm. There's no way I can drive.'

'You'd better give us the keys then,' James said, as he took the bolt off the door and stepped out into the street.

Unfortunately, the old dear Wheels brushed off had gone into the launderette next door and told everyone who'd listen that the supermarket was being robbed. A nervous crowd gathered in the launderette doorway. Someone must have called the cops and a couple of people looked as if they were thinking about wading in. Meanwhile, Wheels still had the car keys.

'For god's sake,' James yelled, watching in horror as Wheels struggled to pull the keys out of his jeans with a dead arm.

James pushed Wheels' hand aside and grabbed the keys himself, then pressed the button to unlock the doors and walked into the road to take the driver's seat.

Wheels couldn't do anything fast because of his arm. By the time he was in the passenger seat, James had the engine running and the clutch poised. Once the passenger door slammed he took a quick look behind before pulling out and working quickly through the gearbox.

'You drive well,' Wheels said admiringly, pulling down his hood as James squealed around a corner.

'I try my best,' James grinned.

But once he'd got over James' proficiency, Wheels turned angry. 'This is such *shit*,' he moaned. 'My elbow's in agony, I'm gonna have to ditch this car and Sasha's gonna go mental when he hears that half the street watched us leave. Why didn't you lock the shop door?'

James knew he should have locked the door, but he didn't appreciate Wheels trying to lay all the blame on him. 'It was my first time,' he said bitterly. 'If you wanted something done you should have told me.'

'Christ,' Wheels screamed, as he kicked down hard in the footwell. 'That shopkeeper's gonna pay for this.'

*

For every rich and clever criminal like Sasha Thompson, there are armies of poor, stupid criminals like Aaron Reid. Not only had Sasha arranged for the Runts to rob Major Dee's cocaine store, he'd also set up some of his associates to buy the cocaine off them at rock-bottom prices.

Aaron was twenty-two and his role in the murder of Owen Campbell-Moore might land him with a life sentence if someone talked; but all it had earned him was three nights in hospital, twenty hours in a police cell and a four-hundred-pound share from selling the cocaine. He would have earned more if he'd spent the last two weeks stacking shelves in a supermarket.

But with his card marked by the Slasher Boys, Aaron couldn't ply his usual trade selling ecstasy and marijuana in pubs and he'd been forced into a straight job. He could have got work in a burger joint or the cinema in town, but he'd picked the garden centre because he didn't think he'd encounter too many Jamaican gangsters on the prowl for potting compost and spider plants. He hadn't counted upon Colin Wragg having a green-fingered girlfriend who'd been in the year below him at secondary school.

'*Aaron to reception please. Aaron to reception please.*'

Aaron wasn't surprised to hear his name over the tannoy. The manageress was always on his back, complaining about everything from over-watering plants to spilling soil in the car park. He sauntered out of the open-air section, but picked up speed when he got inside the store where his boss might have an eye on him.

As he came towards the counter, Aaron saw a large black man standing at the customer service desk with a police badge in his hand. The manageress looked annoyed and Aaron seethed: it was out of order for the police to come after him at work, although it was exactly the kind of sly stunt they liked to pull when they were trying to break you.

'George Peck, Bedfordshire CID,' Colin Wragg lied, as he flashed the badge again.

If this had been on the street, Aaron would have told the cop to either arrest him or piss off, but he'd lied about his criminal record on his job application and he didn't want his new boss seeing him act cocky with the police.

'I've got work to do,' Aaron said. 'Is this gonna take long?'

'Ten minutes,' Colin smiled. 'Fifteen max.'

'Make sure you clock out,' the manageress said firmly.

Colin led Aaron past the checkouts and through the two sets of automatic doors into the car park.

'I'm just parked up over there.'

But Colin didn't put as much work into covering his Jamaican accent as he'd done in store and Aaron's heart vaulted into his mouth. He glanced around and considered running, but Colin realised Aaron was suspicious and he ripped a pistol out of his jacket.

'One move and I'll blow a hole in your back.'

Aaron was terrified when he saw the gun, but more terrified to realise that he'd fallen into the hands of a gang that used machetes and electric shocks to get the truth.

'What is it you want?' Aaron asked.

'Just shut your mouth. We're going for a little ride.'

28. WAR

James parked up in a quiet road leading to an industrial estate. Wheels was fond of his Vauxhall and he'd already spoken to a mate who'd give it a respray and fit another set of false plates.

It took twenty minutes for James to get back to the Zoo and he worried as he walked. Sasha had a violent temper. He wouldn't be impressed that the cops had been called during the collection of a loan payment and Wheels struck him as the type who'd try passing off as much blame as he could.

*

Aaron Reid felt sick. Sweat patches grew on his *Discount Garden Centre* polo shirt as Major Dee, Colin Wragg and Michael stared at the passing streets, giving him the silent treatment. He could handle the idea of dying – so long as he blocked out the prospect of never seeing his girlfriend and eight-month-old daughter again – but Major Dee had a reputation for making his enemies suffer. Aaron's train of thought kept arriving at the same question: *how bad will the pain get?*

After a few miles of A-roads and roundabouts, they pulled on to the driveway of a detached house. With the gun at his back, Aaron was led down the hallway into a living room. It was a standard deal, with sofas, nested tables and a TV, but everything was covered in heavy-duty plastic sheets.

'Have a seat,' Major Dee said, as Colin shoved Aaron towards the sofa.

Michael wasn't facing death, but he was still scared as he sank on to a plastic-covered armchair. He'd decided that he couldn't watch Aaron die; but even with a gun strapped around his waist, taking out Major Dee and Colin would be tricky. He'd probably have to kill them both and he wasn't certain he'd be able to pull the trigger.

'As you can see, Aaron, we're all set up to make you talk without spoiling the carpets.' Dee smiled, as he reached under a plastic sheet and took a hammer drill from a cocktail cabinet. He pulled the trigger, sending the bit into a high-pitched spin.

'I find the cordless model gives me enough freedom to work,' Dee explained. 'Top of the range. Eighteen-volt, variable speed, sixty-nine ninety-nine from the Argos catalogue.'

Aaron flinched as Dee sat next to him on the sofa. 'I know what you thinking, Aaron,' Dee continued. 'You're wondering if there's any way you can get out of this room alive.'

Aaron was too scared to respond. The tendons in his hand stood out as his fingers clutched the arm of the sofa.

'You *can* get out of here,' Dee said soothingly. 'As a matter of fact you can get out without a scratch by telling me everything I want to know. And you might as well tell me, because you'll talk one way or another.'

Dee gave the drill another spin to make his point.

'What is it you want to know?' Aaron asked, managing a timid smile.

Dee placed a hand on Aaron's shoulder. 'I've never had a beef with the Runts before,' he said. 'You're street dealers, muggers, hustlers, small-timers. But now you're suddenly organised: you've got information, you know where all my dealers are and you're smart enough to uncover my stash. Who's the traitor in my organisation?'

Michael was surprised that Dee thought the Runts had learned about the cocaine from one of his own men; but actually it *was* the most logical explanation.

'Listen,' Aaron said, so scared that his whole head twitched when he moved his jaw. 'I don't mean you no disrespect Major Dee, but I'm not exactly on the top rung of the ladder. I can only tell you what I know.'

Dee shrugged. 'Then tell me what you know and pray it makes me happy.'

'We got the information about the cocaine off this guy. He's black, but I don't think he works for you.'

'What's his name?'

'Kelvin Holmes.'

Major Dee looked towards Colin. 'I don't know that name. You ever hear it?'

'From my boxing days,' Colin nodded. 'Kelvin used to coach in the old gym on the Thornton Estate. Had a shot as a pro-fighter, but got busted for dealing.'

Dee raised an eyebrow. 'You talking about Keith Moore's old gym?'

Colin nodded. 'Which means Kelvin's probably mixing with the Mad Dogs now.'

Major Dee turned back to Aaron. 'You hear this Kelvin say anything about Sasha Thompson, or the Mad Dogs?'

Aaron nodded. 'Well . . . not *exactly* about the Mad Dogs, but Kelvin put us in touch with this brother who said he'd give us a good price for whatever coke we stole.'

'And what was his name?' Dee asked.

'That I don't know, I *swear*. But everyone seemed to think that he worked with the Mad Dogs – and come to think of it, I heard one or two others say that Kelvin was one of Sasha Thompson's boys too.'

Dee's eyes bulged like ping-pong balls. 'I knew Runts weren't capable of this,' he hissed, as he threw down the drill and pounded a fist into his palm. 'Sasha hasn't got enough manpower to take me on, so he sets up a war with the Runts . . .'

'Makes sense,' Colin said.

Michael was relieved that Aaron wasn't getting tortured, but in every other way this was the worst thing that could have happened. Major Dee knowing that Sasha had robbed him could only lead to an all-out war.

Dee smiled at Aaron as he pulled a money clip out of his pocket and began peeling twenties. 'You know the Mad Dogs created a lot of trouble for you? I'll need a man on the inside. Here's a hundred pounds. I'll pay you more every time you tell me what you hear about the Runts and Mad Dogs.'

Aaron was in no position to refuse Dee's offer. He'd been expecting a drill through the back of his head and his smile was pathetically grateful as he grabbed the banknotes fluttering into his lap.

'But don't deceive me,' Dee warned. 'Colin's been through your wallet. We have your address and a picture of your family. Any slips and you be back here with the Black and Decker.'

'I understand,' Aaron stammered. 'I completely understand.'

'Glad you do,' Dee nodded. 'Now you better prove where your loyalty lies.'

'I won't mess you about, Dee. I'm not a smart guy like you or Sasha. All I've ever wanted was a bit of extra money to make things good for my girl and my baby.'

'How *nice*,' Dee grinned. 'But Owen Campbell-Moore was a long-standing friend and I bet you know details of the other boys that were around when he got done in.'

Aaron looked edgy. 'Not addresses and everything, but I know all their names.'

'That'll do,' Dee nodded, as his eyes turned to Michael. 'Mickey boy, have a look around. There's gotta be a pen and paper in this house.'

As Michael began lifting back the plastic sheeting to look in cupboards around the room, Dee continued to explain. 'You going to write down the names and everything you know about the men who killed Owen. Then at the bottom, I want your signature.'

Aaron looked worried as Michael found an airmail pad and a pen inside a bureau and passed them to Major Dee.

'If that got out I'd be a dead man,' Aaron whispered.

'As long as you're loyal to me, you have no problem,' Dee said, but nobody believed that for a second.

29. VENGEANCE

Major Dee hadn't become boss of the Slasher Boys without some guile and cunning. But his defining characteristic – some said his Achilles heel – was his capacity for swift and completely ruthless violence.

Most people starting a war with a man regarded as one of the cleverest criminals in the country might have sat down and put some thought in. But Dee was angry that Sasha had made him look foolish, and while the Mad Dogs were a small crew, Dee was all too aware that they had informants everywhere. He reckoned the only way to ensure complete surprise was to attack immediately.

Once they'd ditched Aaron, Michael and Colin took part in a mass ring-round of Major Dee's most trusted associates. Within an hour a meeting was taking place in a private room above the Green Pepper, and by the time the sun had dropped, Michael was part of a posse, with four vehicles gathered in an empty lot behind a fried chicken shop and a car wash.

The lead car was a dilapidated Range Rover with huge bull bars over the headlamps. The eighteen-man crew was tooled up with everything from baseball bats to machetes and the pride of Major Dee's gun collection, a Skorpion ultra-compact machine gun.

Dee was paranoid about traitors and made it clear that he didn't want anyone ringing out on their mobile phones. Michael managed to sneak into the filthy bathroom at the chicken joint and text Maureen Evans to say that something big was going down, but Dee had given no clue about the target. The only sure thing was that people would get seriously hurt.

*

The Mad Dogs' first team were three-nil up, which made Sasha Thompson happy enough to embrace sweaty players as they headed into the clubhouse at half-time. Bruce was playing away with the under-fifteens, but James and Junior had turned out to train for the Sunday league side.

The first team and the various Mad Dogs youth teams took their football seriously, playing in competitive leagues with proper kits, three paid officials and an FA qualified coach. In contrast, the two Sunday sides played in a local pub league. Their yellow kit was shabby because the first team got a couple of years' wear out of it first, and Thursday night training was usually nothing more than a couple of warm-up laps and a kick-about.

The youngest Sunday players were James' age, whilst the oldest were flabby-legged men with rose-tinted memories of the first team behind them. James was no fan of playing in the cold, but once he'd accepted that he was going to end up muddy, he had a pretty good time of it. He was fit enough to side-step all but one of the crazy tackles and fast enough –

at least in such mediocre company – to look like a half-decent footballer.

On the other hand, Junior was a disgrace. James had sparred in the ring with Junior when they were both twelve. He'd been shorter than James, but Junior had been lightning quick and even with gloves on you knew all about it when he hit you. But the intervening three years had seen James continue combat training while regularly running and lifting weights. Junior had developed a taste for cigs and a tidy cocaine habit, and the only time he ran anywhere was when the cops were on his back. Junior was still young enough to look OK, but he struggled to keep up with the ball and a sixty-metre run down the wing left him doubled over, hacking phlegm on to the ground between his boots.

As the Sunday team headed into the changing room for their half-time break, James was called inside the clubhouse to speak with Sasha. This meant he didn't get a chance to check his mobile in his kit bag, where he would have picked up a voicemail telling him to call Maureen urgently.

*

James felt edgy as he ditched his muddy boots in the doorway and walked to the small bar in his socks. The Mad Dogs had the smartest clubhouse in their league and Sasha acted like lord of the manor, propping up the bar with a brandy in hand and the Mad Dogs FC's trophy cabinet at his back. Nobody else was in earshot.

'Drink?' Sasha asked, as James got close.

James was out of breath and Sasha reached behind the bar to grab him a bottle of Coke. As he pulled the lid with a bottle opener, James propped himself on a stool.

'For god's sake,' Sasha yelled. 'Get off there.'

James shot up and saw that his muddy shorts had left a brown mark on the stool.

'Sorry,' he gasped.

'Haven't you got *any* sense?' Sasha snarled, as he tried brushing the mud away with a bar towel. The towel was damp and made everything worse. 'Kids these days . . . If this doesn't brush off when it dries, *you're* paying for a new stool.'

James didn't know where to look or what to say, but he knew it wasn't a good sign when the three other men in the clubhouse headed for the exit.

'What happened out there with you and Wheels today?'

'Things got untidy,' James shrugged. 'We didn't lock the shop door and this old dear—'

'Who's *we?*' Sasha snapped. 'Who was responsible for locking the door?'

'Well, I was the last one in so I guess it was me.'

Sasha grunted. 'So Wheels *told* you to lock the door?'

'No, but I guess it was obvious.'

'Not if you're nervous and you've never done something like that before,' Sasha said. 'He definitely *didn't* tell you to lock the door?'

'No way.'

'I had Wheels round my house earlier. He's trying to say that you messed up and the little piss-taker even tried getting me to pay towards having his car resprayed.'

James grinned slightly, unsure if he'd get his head ripped off if he laughed.

'Wheels is a good lad if you keep him on a leash,' Sasha

said. 'But he's too casual about details and he likes to lay the blame. As far as I'm concerned, you're the new kid while he's been around for a few years. If something goes wrong the only thing I want Wheels to do is doff his cap and say *sorry boss*.'

'I'm not a baby though,' James said. 'We messed up and I'll take my share of the blame.'

This seemed to be what Sasha wanted to hear. As James placed his empty Coke bottle on the bar, Sasha reached around and grabbed him another.

'Cheers.'

'I've been asking around,' Sasha said. 'Ormondroyd down at the parole office pulled your file. Apparently you never cooperated with the cops and you never gave the screws an inch while you were in young offenders. A couple of Keith Moore's old mates also told me you're solid.'

James didn't know what this was leading up to, but he couldn't help smiling. The mission required him to feed the cops information on who the Mad Dogs were and how they operated. Winning Sasha's trust made that a lot easier.

'What are you like with electronics, computers and stuff like that?' Sasha asked.

'I can use 'em, but I'm no boffin,' James said.

'Do you think you could handle it if I asked you to rig up some CCTV equipment and keep tabs on who's coming and going at a certain address?'

'I suppose,' James said. 'As long as I've got all the instructions and that.'

'Yeah, course you will. I'll pay you thirty quid a day. Once you've set up the cameras I want you to go in every day and skim through the recordings. I want a written log of who's coming in, who's going out and how many people are putting money through the letterbox to buy drugs.'

'Drugs?' James nodded casually.

'It's a hard front,' Sasha said. 'You know what a hard front is?'

James did, but he wouldn't have known if he wasn't a cherub, so he asked Sasha to explain.

'A hard front is a place where people deal drugs. Sometimes it's a house, but usually it's a flat in a multi-storey block. The dealers put steel reinforcement up behind the front door, bars over the windows and keep the curtains shut twenty-four seven. There will always be two or three people inside. Business is arranged over the telephone and people turn up at the door, push money through the letterbox and get handed drugs.

'A hard front is a dealer's dream and a policeman's nightmare. If the cops find the place and start picking up the individuals buying drugs outside, the dealers just buy another lump of steel and move to another flat. The cops can *try* taking the place by storm, but by the time they batter their way through all that steel you can guarantee that anything illegal will have been flushed down the toilet or thrown over the balcony.

'The cops' third option is to video the dealers, but all you can ever film is hands passing stuff back and forward through a letterbox. As long as there's always two or three dealers inside, it's impossible for the cops to prove who was actually selling the drugs. The dealers all blame each other and the case gets laughed out of court.'

'Sounds neat,' James nodded.

'It's tried and tested,' Sasha said. 'Hard fronts are used everywhere, from Brazilian slums to Siberian ghettos.'

'So what use is this surveillance to you?' James asked.

Sasha smiled. 'A dickie bird tells me the joint is also being used for some major heroin deals. If I'm gonna get my mitts on that gear, I need to know what makes them open the front door.'

'Gotcha,' James said. 'Every dealer's got to bring the groceries home once in a while.'

'Or carry a big pile of cash out.' Sasha grinned. 'You're a smart boy, James.'

But James didn't want to seem too eager. 'You know, thirty a day isn't a lot if you're planning to rip off a major drug dealer.'

Sasha bristled. 'I look after my crew, James old son. If you do a good job I'll see you get a cut, but don't go expecting fortunes in week one.'

James nodded, but Sasha had jumped off his stool and was dashing towards the French windows along the front of the clubhouse.

'What the hell's that noise?' Sasha asked, as he stared out into the dark.

30. YELLOW

Michael thumped his masked head on the roof of the Range Rover as it veered off-road and ploughed through a low hedge. With a Slasher Boy squished up on either side, machetes resting in their laps, it was a scary moment.

This was as wrong as something could get and Michael was shitting himself. He looked behind and saw two more cars ploughing through the hedge. The fourth was a little Nissan laden with five thugs, and it ended up wedged on a split tree trunk with its front wheels spinning helplessly in mid air.

Colin Wragg accelerated over the grass towards an under-twelves game, as Major Dee pointed his Skorpion out of the passenger side window. The compact machine gun was a short-range weapon, designed for close-quarter work like spraying bullets up a staircase when you're clearing a building. But people don't know that kind of stuff. All anyone knew was the sound of gunfire and the orange flashes around the muzzle.

The under-twelves scattered; mums on the touchline screamed. Only the referee stood still, hands on hips and whistle in mouth, until he figured that blowing wasn't going to stop the four-tonne Range Rover ploughing towards him and he began to run.

Whilst the big 4x4 had been used to batter its way on to the pitches, the Mitsubishi Evo behind it had better acceleration. As the ref scrambled away, the yellow car swerved and went after him. The ref looked desperately back over his shoulder as the powerful car closed down and smashed into his legs.

'Did you see *that*,' the man sitting next to Michael in the Range Rover shouted jubilantly, as the referee flew over the bonnet of the Evo and did a full 360-degree flip before slamming down in the mud. The Evo made a slight course correction before the driver floored the accelerator, aiming for boys in shorts and mums heading for the protection of a wooded area nearby.

Meantime the Range Rover and the Jeep Cherokee running behind it threw up mud as Colin ploughed on towards the first team.

'We're going for the clubhouse,' Dee said. 'Victor, get the stuff outta the back.'

Glass chinked as the dude sitting beside Michael grabbed bottles from behind the rear seat. They were filled with petrol and had pieces of rag stuffed in the necks.

'Line me up for a shot at the clubhouse,' Dee ordered, as the first-team players scattered.

Most of the first-teamers turned a blind eye to their club chairman being a major villain. But turning a blind eye becomes hard when six guys with knives and bats jump out of a Jeep and start chasing after you.

Fortunately, most of the first-teamers were fitter than their masked pursuants and their studs gave them better traction in the mud. But the opposition goalie got cornered near the perimeter wall, whilst another player who'd run towards the under-twelves pitch to make sure that his kid brother was safe lost his footing and found three men surrounding him.

The player put his hands up to defend himself, but before he knew it he was taking a savage beating.

Major Dee fired his machine gun into the front windows of the clubhouse, splintering the bar and sending a cascade of glass on to the polished wooden floor.

'Spread out and look for Sasha,' Dee ordered, broken glass crunching under his Nikes as he stepped into the clubhouse.

Michael had been sandwiched in the middle so he was last out of the car. The opposition goalkeeper screamed fewer than ten metres away from him, and Michael was horrified to see a streak of blood where he'd been dragged across the floodlit grass by his hair.

He felt sick as he looked to the poorly lit pitches where the Sunday team played, and watched the players scrambling over a wall as one of guys from the Jeep fired a shotgun at them.

'Michael, check the changing rooms,' Dee shouted furiously. 'He must have got away.'

Michael put his hand on the gun strapped to his waist as he stepped gingerly into the changing rooms. Everyone had scarpered, and a breeze blew through open fire doors at the back of the tiled room.

As he leaned into the deserted shower area, Michael realised that Major Dee had put all of his effort into the speed of the operation and none into tactics. If he'd sent the two cars in from each side of the playing field, the Mad Dogs would have been caught in a pincer and the raid probably would have turned into the bloodbath he'd been hoping for.

'Get outta there,' Colin shouted. 'It's going up.'

Dee and a couple of others had already lit petrol bombs and Michael heard a whoosh of fire in the adjoining clubhouse. As he ducked out through the back doors, a flaming bottle spun wildly across the muddy floor, turning into a fireball as it shattered beneath the changing bench and set light to a nylon backpack.

By the time Michael had run around the flaming building and back towards the Range Rover, the entire back wall of the Mad Dogs clubhouse was ablaze and the metal roof struts were buckling from the heat.

'We did good,' Colin said, blasting the horn of the Range Rover as Michael became the last man squeezed back inside the car.

'I wanted Thompson,' Dee snarled, ripping off his balaclava as the big car pulled away. 'Tonight was our chance to win this before it even started.'

And you messed it up, Michael thought, as the 4x4 dropped off a kerb into the Mad Dogs FC parking lot and powered on through the main gates.

*

James made it out of the door behind the bar and ran for his life, with his socked feet skidding hopelessly on the mud.

His football boots were in the clubhouse doorway and the rest of his stuff hung from a hook in the burning changing room, including his trainers, his mobile and nine-grand's worth of carbon-nanotube-reinforced sweatshirt.

The first port of call was Sasha's house, but Sasha didn't want the heat and ordered everyone to clear out, including crying kids and a hysterical mother who'd seen her eleven-year-old chased into the trees by an armed man.

There was no sign of Junior, so James did what he was told and headed down a side street. There were plenty of people with cars, but most of the owners were dressed in their football kits and their keys were inside the blazing clubhouse.

It was a frosty night, and within a few hundred metres James' soles were numb with cold. He was dressed for football and didn't even have change for a bus fare, but he knew it was best to keep moving. There was a chance some of the Slasher Boys would still be on the prowl and his mud-caked socks and yellow football shirt would tell them exactly who he was.

After jogging for a couple of minutes, James heard a car pull up alongside and blast its horn. He ducked instinctively, but when he bobbed up he saw a woman sitting in the front, three young lads in their Mad Dogs kit in the back and another on the front passenger seat.

'Would you like a lift home?' the woman asked, as her electric window purred down. James could see she was shaken, with black streaks of eyeliner down her face.

'I'm really muddy,' James said apologetically, as he walked towards the car.

'All the boys are muddy,' she said. 'You'll freeze out there in this cold.'

The spooked eleven-year-old on the front passenger seat had to climb out and squeeze in the back with his three friends.

'I appreciate this,' James smiled, pulling open the door and enjoying his first breath of heated air.

'I've got quite a route dropping all these home,' the woman said, as she pulled away. 'Where do you need to go?'

'The halfway house,' James said. His socks were absolutely sodden and he peeled them off so that he didn't trash the footwell. He was pleased to be in the warm, but the four lads behind him were eerily quiet and at least two of them had been crying.

The driver slammed the brakes as she pulled out of the turning without looking, almost flattening a motorbike parked at the opposite kerb.

'Are you OK?' James asked. 'Maybe you should pull over until you've calmed down.'

'I've got to get all the boys home,' the woman said with determination. 'If the parents hear what happened before I drop them back they'll go out of their minds.'

'But drive careful,' James said gently. 'It won't do much good if you crash before you get there, will it?'

The woman nodded and gave James a tiny smile. But her hands were shaking and her eyes were blurred with tears.

'I yelled at that referee,' she sniffed. 'He kept having a go at my Samuel and I called him a *pompous tit*. Two minutes later he went up over that car. I don't know if he was killed or what . . .'

'It's over now, Mum,' one of the kids said, trying to sound grown up as he pushed his muddy face between the front seats.

'How can that happen?' the woman sobbed. 'How can you do something like that to another human being?'

31. BUGS

'. . . There is some speculation that the savage assault was launched as part of a vendetta against notorious underworld figure and Mad Dogs FC chairman Sasha Thompson.

However, Detective Inspector Robert Hunt who is heading up the investigation has emphasised that none of the people attacked had criminal records or any association with Mr Thompson beyond the football club.

The victim, twenty-year-old Julian Pogue, was a first-year law student at the University of East Anglia. He'd recently returned home for the Easter holidays and had only been called back into the Mad Dogs team following an injury to a colleague. It is believed that Pogue became separated from his team-mates whilst trying to locate his twelve-year-old brother.

Pogue's family issued a statement asking for privacy and describing their son as a 'wonderful, caring boy who loved playing football and had a bright future ahead of him.'

The two other seriously injured men have been named as fifty-three-year-old referee Bert Hogg and opposition goalkeeper Leonard Goacher, thirty-one. School nurse Judith Maine was stabbed in the thigh as she tried escaping into nearby woodland with her *eighteen-month-old twins in a double buggy. She was later discharged from hospital, along with eleven others treated for minor injuries and shock.'*

BBC Radio Bedfordshire, Friday 30 March 2007

The care workers in the Zoo were supposed to be finding James and Bruce places at a local school, but they were taking their time and now the schools were about to break up for Easter anyway.

James couldn't sleep and spent most of the night with a headphone in his ear, listening to the late-night phone-in and hourly news updates on the radio. By ten on Friday morning Bruce was up and showered, but James could see no reason to get up and he hitched his duvet over his face when Bruce opened the curtains to read his latest martial arts magazine.

James' phone had melted in the blaze, so Wheels rang Bruce when he wanted to speak.

'How's it going?' James asked. 'Where were you hiding when the shit went down?'

'Sasha yelled at me twice yesterday so luckily I gave the football a wide berth.'

'Jammy git,' James said. 'So do you know anything, except for what I can hear on the radio?'

'One of the Slasher Boys' cars got stuck over the back of the playing fields. They torched it themselves before the cops arrived, but a couple of our boys caught up with one of them. The cops were swarming all over so they couldn't do anything except put a tail on him. They followed him home on the bus and woke him up at five this morning with a couple of bricks and petrol bombs.'

'Top stuff,' James said, faking enthusiasm. 'So is Sasha planning revenge?'

'Not sure,' Wheels said. 'There's talk about storming the Green Pepper.'

'You can count me out on that score,' James snorted. 'That's in the middle of their turf and there's more of them than there is of us.'

'Talk's all it is, I reckon,' Wheels said. 'Sasha's got a brain. He's not gonna go charging in like the bloody cavalry. He's gonna bide his time and then he's gonna do something that'll turn the Slasher Boys right over.'

'Exactly,' James said. 'So is this just a social call or what?'

'Two things, mate. First off, you mentioned that you had some body armour. Now I know you're not exactly one of our main guys, but Sasha says everyone should be on the look-out for ambushes. Wear your armour, carry a weapon and avoid going anywhere on your own. If you're not with me, take your little cousin with you.'

'Sounds sensible,' James said.

'And have you got money for a new phone, 'cos we might have to make some fast moves and everyone's gotta keep in touch.'

'Sure,' James said. 'I've still got a bunch of cash from the hotel robbery. I'll go into town later and grab a pay-as-you-go.'

'Great. The second thing is that Sasha says not to get bogged down in a war. We need to keep the money flowing, which means it's business as usual.'

'Have we got to go back to that supermarket?'

'Nah,' Wheels said. 'The money you got out of the

till more than covered what we're owed and Sasha says the cops were swarming all over, so we'll be leaving it alone for a while.'

'So am I still on for that bit of business with the hard front?'

'You *certainly* are,' Wheels said. 'It's miles from the nearest Slasher Boys, but things are tense so I'd bring your cousin along. Savvas has got all of the surveillance equipment you need and a set of keys for the flat. He's gonna swing by with it later.'

'What about directions?' James asked.

'Ask Savvas. He can't take you up there because he's a known face, but he'll show you on his road atlas or whatever.'

*

They missed breakfast and Savvas was late so James and Bruce stopped off for an early lunch at a Pizza Hut buffet. Chloe had arranged it so that she bumped into them. She gave James a replacement phone and said that another stab-proof sweatshirt was being made on campus and would be ready within forty-eight hours. She also told the boys that she was worried: the ethics committee weren't going to like it when they heard about the latest outbreak of violence and the death of Julian Pogue. There was a chance they'd pull the mission.

James over-ate and felt bloated as they rode the bus out of Luton and into neighbouring Dunstable. The Rudge Estate consisted of three-storey blocks. Quite a few flats had been purchased and renovated by residents complete with window boxes and neat gardens, but much of the estate was still a dump, strewn with rubbish, graffiti and the occasional abandoned car.

The hard front faced on to a second-floor balcony, but it was far from the only apartment with a reinforced door and bars up the windows, so only a nosy neighbour would have figured it was being used by drug dealers.

The blocks ran parallel to one another. James and Bruce had the keys to a second-floor flat in the next block along, with the front window directly overlooking the hard front. The previous resident's kids had drawn all over the walls, but nobody had lived there in a while and the musk of damp and dust knocked Bruce back as he pushed the door open.

'What a pen and ink,' James complained, wafting a hand in front of his face as he kicked the door shut and dumped the large sports bag that Savvas had given him on the hallway carpet. 'Better open the windows to air it out.'

It was the middle of the day, but James flipped the light switch on and off to make sure the electricity was connected as Bruce walked between rooms, opening windows.

'There's a kettle and a fridge in here,' Bruce yelled. 'Maybe we can get some tea and milk in or something.'

'If you like,' James shrugged. 'I guess it'll take a while going through the tapes, but I don't fancy spending any longer than I have to in this dump.'

'It'll be OK once it's aired and it's a bloody sight quieter than the Zoo.'

'I'm not stopping you from moving in,' James grinned. 'At least I won't have to put up with your snoring.'

'Yeah, I'm *so* obnoxious,' Bruce sneered. 'What about the other night when you kept dropping your guts? My eyes were watering.'

'It was that dodgy cheese bap Chloe got at the motorway services.'

As James said this, he unzipped the sports bag and looked at the surveillance equipment. The biggest item was a twin-tape surveillance recorder with *Property of East Midlands Health Trust* etched on top. There were also blank tapes, a bunch of tangled-up leads, a power drill for making holes and a selection of miniature cameras.

'What a bunch of crap,' Bruce said.

James shrugged. 'There's nothing here that would set the campus technical department drooling, but it's enough to get the job done.'

'Guess you're right,' Bruce said, as he pulled some of the wires out. 'You work out the best place to put the cameras and I'll start untangling this lot.'

32. BODIES

Seventeen days later

Joe Pledger and his wife had just arrived back from an Easter break at their Portuguese villa, complete with leathery tans and carrier bags of booze. Their lap pool looked unusually dark when Joe peered out through the conservatory and his heart leapt as he noticed that a section of his back fence had been knocked down.

Groggy from the flight and underdressed in short sleeves and holiday shorts, Joe slid the French door and stumbled out to the patio. The water in his pool had a brownish tint, but the shocker was the outline of a man at the bottom. The sight would have sent many souls running back to the house in shock, but Joe had been in the funeral game his whole life and his only concern was for his wife.

'Don't come out here,' he yelled, as he dashed back into the house and grabbed the phone.

Inspector Hunt from the murder squad was on the scene within ten minutes, beaten only by a female constable who'd been walking her beat half a kilometre away. Hunt was knackered and about to go off-shift, but there was no chance of that now.

The ginger-haired detective crouched on the tiles at the poolside and saw that the victim had two twenty-kilo discs strapped to his chest.

'Looks like he was alive when he was thrown in,' Hunt said, as he looked at the nervous policewoman.

Unless they suspect that the perpetrator is still in the area, regular cops are trained to stand back and protect a crime scene until detectives arrive. The young constable had her arms behind her back and her face looking up at the sunrise.

'Not seen one of these before?' Hunt asked.

'No, sir,' the constable said apologetically. 'I've only been on the force three months.'

'Do me a favour,' Hunt said, as he leaned further over the pool. 'Go into the house and ask the owner if he has a long pole, or a rake that he uses to clean leaves off the water.'

While the constable stayed inside consoling his wife, Joe ambled down the garden to unlock his shed.

'Used to hang the pole on them hooks by the poolside,' Joe explained, as he opened the shed and retrieved a long pole with a crook on the end. 'Trouble was my grandkids were too fond of whacking each other with it.'

Hunt gave a friendly nod as he took the pole from the elderly man. Joe stepped back, but kept his eyes fixed on the pool as the policeman guided the pole through the murky water. Joe was tired after the flight home and his wife was in a state, but he wasn't unhappy: retirement had proved underwhelming and a dead body in the pool was a hell of a story for the golf club.

After scraping across the floor of the pool, Hunt tucked

the hook under the dead man's arm and gave him a gentle pull so that he could see his face. The motion was enough to disturb gases in the decomposing body and a string of large bubbles rose up and broke the surface of the water.

'Maybe you should go back inside,' Hunt said.

'I dealt with bodies for forty-five years, man and boy,' Joe smiled. 'This ain't nothing much.'

Rapid identification of the body could make a difference if the crime was recent. But the face was horribly bloated and the eyes bulged.

'He's been down there a while,' Joe said knowledgably. 'Ten or twelve days at a guess.'

'I reckon you're right,' Hunt said, as he pulled the pole out of the water. 'His girlfriend reported him missing early last week.'

'So you know who he is?' Joe asked.

'Fairly certain,' Hunt nodded. 'I've only seen a passport photo and that body's in a state, but it all seems to fit together.'

*

The two mission controllers and three agents had agreed to meet up in a grotty hotel suite at a motor lodge on the edge of town. James and Bruce were the last to arrive.

'Had to wait ages for our bus,' James explained. Then he looked at Chloe, who was propped on the end of a double bed. 'How did it go with the ethics committee last night?'

'Two-hour conference call,' she groaned. 'They've given us another seven days, but all the murders are making them jittery.'

Michael looked up at James. 'Did you hear they pulled another Runt out of a swimming pool this morning?'

James shook his head. 'Anyone we know?'

'Aaron Reid,' Michael said.

'The guy who wrote the list?' Bruce gasped.

'The very same,' Michael nodded. 'He wrote seven names, plus his own on that list for Major Dee. He's the third one to turn up dead and nobody knows where the others are.'

'Either dead or in hiding,' Maureen said.

'Any news on the cars that got burned out near the Green Pepper on Saturday?' Bruce asked.

'Runts out for revenge most likely,' Chloe said. 'You and James both seemed pretty sure that it wasn't Sasha's men.'

'Breaking car windows isn't exactly his style, is it?' Bruce said. 'Major Dee might have tried starting a war, but the Mad Dogs aren't biting.'

'Sasha's sitting back while Dee does his Runt murder spree,' James explained. 'He's hoping that Dee will slip up while he concentrates on the more serious business of making money.'

Bruce nodded. 'But he's livid about what happened to the football club, so I'd bet my left nut that he's got a plan.'

'I get the impression that the ethics committee are looking for closure on this mission,' Chloe said. 'Some of us have been working this job for more than three months. We've learned a lot about the structure of the gangs and passed tons of information on to the police, but they're worried about the violence and uncomfortable with the amount of criminal activity you three are getting involved with. If we don't get a breakthrough soon they're going to pull the plug.'

'Wasn't there some plan to have a rummage inside Sasha's house?' Michael asked.

'We're on it,' James nodded. 'Now that the Mad Dogs' clubhouse is burned out, anyone who gets injured during a game is sent over the road and Sasha's missus takes a look at it – she used to be a nurse. We haven't sorted the details, but we're going training tomorrow night and if one of us fakes an injury, the other one can go over with him and take a peek in Sasha's office.'

'It's a big house,' Bruce added. 'So if we get caught, it's easy to say that we were looking for the bathroom and went through the wrong door.'

'That all sounds fair enough,' Chloe said. 'But Sasha's a dangerous man, so I want to be close by in case something goes wrong.'

'And how's the surveillance on the hard front going?' Maureen asked.

'It's OK,' Bruce said. 'It's boring going through the tapes every day, but we're getting good information on who's coming and going and what makes them open the front door. Sasha seems chuffed.'

'Good,' Chloe said. 'Have you got any indication about when Sasha's going to make his move?'

James shook his head. 'He's obviously waiting on information from one of his informants.'

'Well I hope he hurries up,' Chloe said. 'I'd say we've got another week; two if we're lucky.'

33. GLASS

James didn't realise how important Mad Dogs FC had been to Sasha Thompson until it was destroyed. The clubhouse and changing rooms could be replaced, but frightened players couldn't. Sasha had told the media that the assault on his club was unprovoked and nothing to do with a rumoured gang war between himself and a Jamaican rival, but nobody was buying it.

Sasha had always looked after his players, especially the first-teamers who were amongst the most pampered in non-league football. Everything was laid on for them: transport, clean kit, meals after games, professional coaching and even fifty quid in their pockets if they won a match.

A few remained loyal and turned up for training after the attack, some disappeared quietly; while braver souls risked Sasha's ire by asking to have their player registrations transferred to rival clubs. Either way, there weren't enough registered players to produce a side and the local branch of the Football Association suspended the Mad Dogs first team from its league after they failed to put out a team for three consecutive matches.

The death of the youth teams was even more spectacular. With rumours of more attacks, no parent would send their kid out in a Mad Dogs kit, and twenty teams – from table-topping under-seventeens to giggly under-nine girls – vanished overnight.

All that remained were the two Sunday sides: veteran players and gangsters, reinforced by the most loyal talent from the first team and the senior youth squads.

There were eight grass and two all-weather pitches in the park where the Mad Dogs trained. Tuesday-night training usually attracted fifty adults and up to a hundred kids, but tonight's meeting had an air of desperation. Fewer than two dozen men gathered around the burned-out clubhouse, and several of those were Sasha's goons dressed in suits rather than football kit.

Drizzle spiralled in the floodlit air, whilst the van that had once ferried the first team between matches was parked on the edge of the pitch with its rear doors open so that people could toss in their coats and dry kit for after training.

'Thanks for coming, son,' Sasha said, hugging Bruce with genuine affection as he stepped up to the wooden bench. 'I really appreciate you sticking by us.'

'No worries boss,' Bruce said, as he pulled a notepad from the pocket of his tracksuit bottoms and passed it over. 'We came straight from the flat. That's a list of everyone arriving and leaving at the hard front up till five this afternoon.'

'Good man,' Sasha said, then turned to James. James lacked Bruce's talent with a football, so he only got a pat on the shoulder and a thank you.

'Incoming,' Savvas shouted from a few metres away, as he spotted a man walking across one of the unlit pitches.

Although it seemed unlikely that the Slasher Boys would launch another attack with the Mad Dogs on high alert, everyone was aware of the war and Sasha had armed lookouts just in case.

'Hold still,' Savvas shouted ferociously as the man came nearer.

The man stopped walking and raised his hands in the air. 'It's me, Chris Jones.'

'Chrissie,' Sasha purred fondly as he waved the man forward.

James didn't know who it was and asked Wheels, who'd turned out dressed for football in order to win back some of the credibility he'd lost with Sasha.

'He's a local councillor,' Wheels explained in a whisper. 'He coached Mad Dogs under-fourteens and both his boys play – or at least *played* – for the club.'

'What can I do for you, councillor?' Sasha asked, as he embraced the balding man warmly. 'Any chance of seeing your boy Marcus in a Mad Dogs shirt? We could use his height at the back.'

The councillor smiled awkwardly. 'I'll come straight to the point, Sasha. Everyone has been talking: the council, some of the players' parents and the old first-team boys. We've got some of the best pitches in the country in this park. Mad Dogs was probably the biggest club in the area from under-sevens right up to county league.'

'Don't worry, we'll get it back,' Sasha grinned. 'Insurance is trying to wrangle out of paying for the clubhouse, but I've got my lawyer on it. Once the publicity dies down, the players will start coming back.'

'Maybe,' the councillor said uncertainly, 'but the council owns these pitches and we want to see them used. We don't want players drifting back in a few years' time when our kids have grown up; we want to see football on these pitches next week.'

Sasha sounded put out. 'Then tell 'em to put their kit on and come here to play.'

The councillor cleared his throat and tried not to sound nervous. 'Sasha, you've done a *magnificent* job supporting youth football in this community, but your erm ... your reputation has become a millstone. With a new chairman and committee, Mad Dogs FC could be back on its feet within—'

Sasha grabbed the councillor by his lapels and butted him in the face.

'You bloody what?' Sasha shouted, as the councillor stumbled back with blood spewing out of his nose.

'Be reasonable,' the councillor begged, shielding his face as Sasha closed him down and punched him in the face.

'This is *my* club,' Sasha screamed. 'I've lived across the street my whole life. Before I started Mad Dogs the grass was a foot high and you couldn't walk two steps without hitting a Coke can or sinking into a pile of dog shit.'

Sasha was much larger than his opponent and his next blow hit the retreating councillor in the stomach, making him crumple forward into the mud.

'Think you're smart with your council seat and your phone calls behind my back?' Sasha shouted. 'Well, let's see where it gets you.'

As James and the rest of the Mad Dogs looked on, Sasha raised his football boot out of the mud and stamped hard. Further blows rained down on the councillor's head and torso until he was balled up in the mud, with a gaping wound in the back of his head.

'Happy now, mate?' Sasha boomed, as he took a short run up and finished the councillor off with a kick in the guts. 'There's no Mad Dogs FC without me and anyone who can't live with that can piss right off.'

It was the most one-sided beating James had ever seen. Even worse, Sasha's cronies just gawped as Sasha loomed over the unconscious councillor. Half a minute passed while Sasha caught his breath, but it seemed longer.

'I reckon he'll live.' Sasha smirked as he finally backed away. 'Take him to the hospital and keep an eye on him. If he comes round and starts mouthing off, remind him that I know where his old mum lives.'

Most of the onlookers were tough guys who'd seen their share of violence. But nobody knew how to act as Savvas and a couple of other flunkies picked the councillor out of the mud and dragged his limp body towards the car park.

'What are you all standing around for?' Sasha yelled, as he waved towards the pitch. 'We're a football club, so go play some bloody football.'

Nobody was going to argue. The coach to the defunct first team blew a whistle and everyone who was dressed for football headed on to the pitch.

'Stone-cold psycho,' Junior said admiringly, as James turned around and realised that his friend had arrived and stood right behind him. 'I can think of a few people I'd like to do that to . . . My dickhead of a parole officer for starters.'

James had been trained to deal with all kinds of situations, but what Sasha had just done made him feel he'd been punched in the guts.

'Is that the worst he's ever done?' Bruce asked.

Junior shrugged. 'Worst I've seen, but I've heard much nastier stuff. Anyway, listen, I know you boys have been earning for that surveillance job. I'm *so* broke, could one of you lend us thirty quid?'

'You already owe me fifty,' James said.

'Come on,' Junior begged. 'Sasha won't put any work my way. My mum won't pay my pocket money because I'm supposed to be grounded and I've robbed everything out of April's purse.'

Bruce tutted. 'You robbed your own sister? That's low, man.'

Junior gave Bruce the finger. 'None of your business who I rob.'

'Any time today, ladies,' the coach shouted as he eyeballed the three boys from the centre circle. 'We're gonna warm up with some shuttle runs.'

Junior groaned. 'This is such crap. This is supposed to be the Sunday league side, *fun* football. But now we've got this Nazi drilling us like he's still running the first team.'

'Wimp,' James grinned. 'The only reason you can't handle it is because of all that shit you put up your nose.'

Junior looked behind and saw that Sasha was still around. 'I'd piss off now, except Sasha would bite my head off; but I swear this is the last time I'm coming down here.'

As the players lined up along the half-way line to start doing shuttle runs, James realised that Junior wasn't the only one who felt like he was in the wrong place. The quality players wanted something meatier than pub-league football, the casual Sunday players certainly didn't want shuttle runs and the youth-team players wanted to be back in a squad with their mates.

Sasha Thompson could stomp on as many people as he liked, but it wouldn't change the fact that the Slasher Boys' attack spelt the end of Mad Dogs FC.

*

After twenty minutes the coach was sick of all the moaning and gave up on serious training. He divided the players up into two nine-man teams, gave half of them red training bibs and retired to a bench next to Sasha while they played a match.

A few minutes into the game, James went into a sliding tackle out on the right. He'd mistimed hopelessly and the former first-team player didn't even break his stride, but as James stood up he slipped a piece of glass from the pocket of his shorts and drew the sharp edge up his leg.

He was too chicken to press down hard and the first attempt didn't even break the skin, but the second try cut into the tight skin around his calf muscle and produced a dribble of blood.

'Owww,' James yelled, as he looked around for Bruce.

Bruce had been waiting for James to go down and was on the scene in seconds, offering him a hand up.

Bruce inspected the wound and tutted. 'That's barely a nick, you tart. If you show Sasha that he'll laugh his arse off.'

'Bugger *off*,' James said indignantly. 'There's plenty of blood there.'

'Gimme the glass,' Bruce said, as he looked around.

Fortunately play continued in a disorganised scrum around the distant goalmouth and the only spectators – Sasha and the coach – had lost interest in this pathetic excuse for a training session.

'I know what you're like,' James said, as he palmed the glass over to Bruce. '*Don't* go mad.'

Bruce bent forward as if he was concerned about James' injury, then sneakily pressed the jagged edge into the tiny cut before ripping it out in a downward motion.

'What the . . .' James said, clutching his agonised leg. He would have yelled out, but he had to cover up because the injury was supposed to have happened when he'd gone down half a minute earlier.

'That looks much better,' Bruce said, as a torrent of blood poured down James' leg into his crumpled football sock.

'What have you done?' James gasped, as Bruce gave him a lift out of the mud. 'I'm bleeding to death.'

'Don't exaggerate,' Bruce grinned, before he ran to the bench.

'What's up, champ?' Sasha said disinterestedly, as he looked up and saw Bruce with James hobbling behind him.

'My cousin cut his leg,' Bruce explained, holding out the bloody chunk of glass. 'Have we got any first-aid stuff around?'

By this time James was close enough for Sasha to see the state of his leg.

'I'll get the first-aid kit out of the van,' the manager said, much to the alarm of James and Bruce.

'Forget that,' Sasha said, as he leaned forward and inspected James' leg. 'You can't clean up all that blood without running water. Go over to my place and my missus will fix it up: she was a nurse, she'll know what to do.'

34. FOIL

'That worked OK,' Bruce smiled, as he helped James to limp across the empty car park.

'You're a git,' James moaned. 'You know I've got a low pain threshold.'

'That's just a posh way of saying you're soft.'

By the time they reached the main gate, James had walked off some of the pain and didn't need Bruce's arm around his back. As they passed on to the street, Bruce ducked behind a tree and grabbed a small backpack Chloe had dumped there half an hour earlier. It contained everything he'd need, hidden beneath a layer of dirty sports kit: a tiny PDA with a built-in voice recorder and camera, a couple of compact listening devices and a stun gun just in case things went wrong.

They rang the bell and were surprised when sixteen-year-old Lois Thompson opened the door. She looked like she'd been chilling in front of the TV, dressed in grey sweat pants with a ripped knee and a giant Luton Town football shirt that must have belonged to her dad.

'Hey,' Bruce said. 'James slashed his leg, is your mum home?'

'Did my dad send you over?' Lois tutted. 'He knows she goes to Weight Watchers on Monday night.'

'Oh,' Bruce said, exchanging an awkward glance with James as Lois examined James' leg.

'Looks nasty,' she said. 'I can take a look if you like. I used to be in the St John's Ambulance when I was a kid.'

'Would you mind?' James nodded. 'It's a long walk home.'

'Try not to drip blood anywhere.' Lois let them into the hallway. 'It's brand new carpet and my mum would freak.'

'Thanks,' James said, pulling off his football boots.

'Leave 'em on the mat,' Lois smiled. 'The first-aid stuff is in the big bathroom up on the first landing. Can you manage the stairs?'

'I can hold the banister and hop,' James grinned.

Lois looked at Bruce, unsure why he'd taken off his boots. 'Aren't you going back to the game?'

'Oh . . .' Bruce said.

'There's not much going on,' James said, covering hurriedly. 'Can't he wait for me here? I might need help coming back down the stairs or whatever.'

'I guess,' Lois said. 'It's Bruce, isn't it?'

Bruce nodded.

'I tell you what Bruce, you both look half frozen. Why don't you go in the kitchen and make some tea? There's all kinds of biscuits in there too.'

Bruce had been knocked off his stride when Lois answered the door, but he now realised that the search would be easier with only one person in the house and being left alone downstairs was perfect.

As Bruce cut into the Thompsons' expensively fitted

kitchen, James wound his football shirt around his leg to stop the blood dripping and began walking upstairs.

'First on the left,' Lois said.

She reached in behind James and pulled on a light cord, revealing a space that was as big as James' room on campus. There was a large corner bath, a stack of lifestyle magazines beside the toilet, a separate shower cubicle and a wicker lounge chair in front of a circular window.

'Sit down,' Lois said, as she threw a bath towel over the bottom half of the lounger to keep the mud off. 'I'll sponge off the worst of it, then you can have a soak in the bath and I'll bandage it up when you're clean.'

'Cool,' James nodded, sitting down with his grubby legs stretched out in front of him.

'Raise your leg up, so I can see the cut,' Lois said, as she leaned over the bath and turned on the taps.

'You've got a nice house,' James grinned.

'Parents are a pain though,' Lois smiled, as she knelt on one knee and began peeling off his football sock. 'You must get heaps more freedom living in the Zoo.'

*

It was a large house and Bruce had to be completely sure that Lois was the only person home. After scrubbing his hands under the mixer tap, he filled the kettle, then grabbed the backpack and headed out into the hallway.

He moved stealthily in his socked feet. His first step was to open the door that went into the basement. He peered down the slatted wooden steps and was pleased to see all the lights out and no sign of life.

Next, he raced down the ground-floor hallway, checking

that the living- and dining-rooms were empty before opening the door to Sasha's study. The room was a fair size, done out in matching Ikea office furniture. The longest wall was all shelves, crammed with books: mostly the histories of football clubs and biographies of players. Two partially melted trophies rescued from the Mad Dogs clubhouse stood atop the filing cabinet.

Bruce unzipped the PDA from the backpack and used it to phone Chloe.

'I'm in the study now,' Bruce whispered. 'James is upstairs being cleaned up by Lois. Are you in place?'

'I'm in the car directly across the street,' Chloe said. 'If anyone comes in or out you'll be the first to know.'

'First impressions aren't good,' Bruce said. 'It all looks like football stuff.'

'Sasha's had the cops on his back for yonks,' Chloe said. 'He's too smart to leave anything obvious in his own home. Remember what we discussed: be thorough and keep your eyes peeled for small clues.'

'Will do,' Bruce said, as he ended the call and flipped open the leather appointments diary in the middle of Sasha's desk.

It was mundane stuff: hospital appointments for a bad knee, a meeting about the insurance on the clubhouse, taking the car in for a service. But as Bruce flipped it shut he noticed Sasha had used the inside front page to write down several phone numbers and he used the PDA to snap a couple of photographs.

Next he moved on to the desk drawers. Amidst the pens, clips and elastic bands were a couple of CD-ROMs, but there was no computer in the room and Bruce didn't have the equipment on hand to copy them. The next drawer was stacked with old photos, whilst the large file drawer at the bottom appeared to be a makeshift liqueur cabinet, stacked with partially drunk bottles of vodka and brandy.

It was only as Bruce pulled the drawer open to its fullest that he spotted a pair of old Nokia phones squeezed between duty-free sized bottles of Jack Daniels and Cuervo Gold. The handsets looked cheap. Maybe they were just phones that Sasha no longer used, but the way they were propped deliberately between the bottles made him wonder.

Whilst home phones, internet connections and contract mobiles are easy for police to listen in on, pay-as-you-go mobiles, bought and topped up with cash, are completely anonymous. What's more, they're cheap enough for criminals to use for a few weeks and throw away before the police get wind of them.

Excited by the phones, Bruce laid each one on the desk and switched it on. As the grey and black LCDs went through the start-up screens, he was relieved that neither handset was set up for a PIN number. As soon as the phones detected the network, Bruce dialled *#06# and the phone's unique handset ID flashed up on screen. He flipped the PDA into voice-record mode and carefully read out the numbers before placing the handsets back exactly as he'd found them.

Bruce looked around the room and decided that his next move would be a rummage through the filing cabinet and then a flick through the bookshelves, just in case anything had been tucked inside.

*

Upstairs, Lois slid her hand across James' thigh as she stared at the clean rectangle of flesh around his cut.

'It's not all that deep,' she murmured. 'We've got some binding plasters that will hold the two halves of the cut together. It should heal up fine.'

Lois backed off and swished her hand through the clear bath water. 'Feels about right to me,' she said. 'I haven't put in soap or anything because it might sting if it gets inside the cut.'

'You wouldn't want that,' James smiled. 'I'm a total baby.'

'You don't look like a baby,' Lois noted admiringly, as James stepped towards the bath. 'Do you work out?'

'I lift some weights,' James nodded. 'Nothing major.'

There was an awkward pause. He had to pull down his shorts and boxers before climbing into the water, but Lois stood less than a metre away and she clearly wasn't going anywhere.

'Don't be shy on my account,' Lois smirked. 'I've seen plenty of blokes in the nude.'

James didn't want to seem like a prude, but he didn't like the idea of being naked in front of Sasha's daughter. His solution was to turn towards the bath and drop his shorts quickly so that she only got a flash of his bum. Mercifully, Lois had backed up to the bathroom door by the time he'd settled into the hot water. He figured she'd be out of the room by the time he'd soaped his arms; but instead of leaving she slid the bolt across and pulled Sasha's Luton Town shirt over her head, unveiling a bright orange sports bra as she approached the bath.

'What do you reckon?' Lois grinned, as she unhitched the bra.

'Stop!' James spluttered. 'No offence, Lois, but if your dad found out about this he'd kill me . . . Slowly.'

'It'll be OK,' Lois said reassuringly. 'Mum won't be back for ages and if Dad comes in he'll go straight down the basement to play cards.'

'But,' James said anxiously. Lois was sexy and completely up for it, but the image of what her powerfully built father had done to the councillor was fixed in his head.

'You only just moved into town and I heard from Wheels that you didn't have a girlfriend,' Lois said, as she pulled down her sweat pants. James was stunned by the lack of underwear as she opened the bathroom cabinet and spun a foil-wrapped condom across the room. It hit his arm before landing in the bathwater.

'What's that for?' James asked stupidly. He could hardly breathe and half expected to wake up and find it was all a dream.

'I don't know where you've been,' Lois said, as she stepped into the water and kissed James on the neck. 'And your mate's wandering around downstairs, so if you want some action you'd better hurry up.'

35. SIMEON

James felt numb as he walked down the front steps of Sasha's house. He hadn't wanted to put his muddy kit back on after the bath, so Lois dug out one of Sasha's old tracksuits and a pair of trainers. Both were a couple of sizes too big, but that was the least of his worries.

The fact that he'd just lost his virginity felt like a three-hundred-kilo gorilla on his back. And to make matters worse, Lois had suggestively mentioned that he could *bring the clothes back any time he liked*.

'You're acting weird,' Bruce noted, as they walked away from the Thompsons' house towards the bus stop. 'Is everything OK?'

'Course,' James said, shrugging half-heartedly and keen to change the subject. 'How did you get on with the search?'

'Not bad. You were up there with Lois for *ages*, so I had a chance to go through everything. I got the numbers for a couple of pay-as-you-go phones. I snapped some interesting business cards and I even managed a quick rummage through the cupboards in the living-room. I don't think I've unearthed anything spectacular, but it might get us somewhere.'

'The phones sound good,' James said, though he found it hard to concentrate. His heartbeat was all over the place and there was a two-thousand-voice choir in his head screaming *you just had sex!*

'Are you *sure* you're OK?' Bruce asked again. 'You look pale and you're all clammy.'

James wished Bruce would stop talking and let him get his head straight. 'I guess it's the cut on my leg,' he said irritably. 'You dug that glass in too deep.'

'You know what's weird though?' Bruce asked, raising one eyebrow slightly.

'What?'

'You know Lois asked me to make a cup of tea?'

James nodded.

'Well after I'd searched Sasha's study, I made a quick cuppa and when you didn't come down I started taking it up the stairs.'

'You *what?*' James gasped.

'It was really strange,' Bruce smirked. 'When I got up near the bathroom I could hear water splashing everywhere. You were making this kind of low groaning noise, then afterwards I could have *sworn* that I heard Lois saying that you *weren't bad for a first timer.*'

James realised he'd been rumbled. 'She was all over me, Bruce,' he blurted. 'You've *got* to keep this quiet.'

'Do you reckon?' Bruce laughed. 'Sasha would hook you up by your scrotum and Dana . . . Well, let's just say she wouldn't be too happy if she found out.'

James had grown to hate his reputation for cheating on girls and he really cared about Dana.

272

'It *wasn't* my fault,' James shouted. 'Lois locked the bathroom door and then practically jumped on top of me.'

Bruce wasn't listening. 'You're *such* a jammy dog. She's got a good body. Was it as amazing as everyone says it is?'

James got a kick out of the fact that he'd leapt into the adult realm, while Bruce was forced to remain curious. 'It was OK,' he shrugged. 'I mean, it's definitely nice to have done it. But Lois kept bossing me around, which wasn't exactly how I imagined it . . .'

'The dominant female,' Bruce giggled, 'very kinky. Kerry's gonna burst when I tell her.'

'For god's sake,' James said. 'You can't tell *anyone*. You've got to swear, Bruce. And I'm only fifteen and a half, so I could get expelled if the staff find out.'

But by this time Bruce was laughing so hard that he could barely stand up. 'Sasha's daughter!' he howled. 'You dirty little goat.'

James was starting to get annoyed. 'Will you shut up? It's dark and there could be anyone walking around here.'

'Sorry,' Bruce grinned, as he wiped tears on to the sleeve of his tracksuit top. 'Don't worry, I'm your mate and was only joking about telling Kerry, but . . .'

Bruce couldn't finish the sentence. He was laughing so hard that he had to clutch his stomach to stop his sides hurting.

*

The boys had arranged to meet Chloe at a bus stop about a kilometre from Sasha's house. From there they made the short drive to her hotel near the town centre. It was gone eleven when they arrived, but the gang lifestyle revolved around late nights and long lie-ins, so neither boy was tired.

'You look like you've been laughing,' Chloe said as the boys stepped into her room.

For a moment James thought Bruce was going to crack up again, but after a little snort he managed to get a grip on himself.

'Care to share?' Chloe asked.

'Oh, it was nothing,' Bruce lied. 'Just this old lady with one of those fancy poodles with all the hair done up in pompoms. They always make me laugh.'

Chloe looked baffled. 'It never ceases to amaze me the stuff teenage boys think is funny,' she said. 'I've got the laptop logged into the police computer. You said you had phone numbers or something?'

Bruce guffawed as he sat at the small hotel desk and pulled the PDA out of the little backpack. 'The main thing is that I've got a couple of pay-as-you-go phone numbers,' he said. 'Do you want me to run them?'

'Sure,' Chloe nodded. 'If you know how to use the system.'

Bruce opened the PDA and played back the voice recordings he'd made of the numbers and handset IDs. Technically, you were supposed to get a judge's approval to access mobile phone records, but in reality the intelligence services had instant access to call records from all of the major networks. If they found anything interesting, they could always get permission afterwards.

As a long list of phone numbers appeared on the laptop screen, Bruce was delighted to see that both mobiles had been heavily used right up until earlier that evening.

'Print everything off,' Chloe said. 'I don't have analysis

software here, so we'll have to go through it by hand.'

Over the course of the mission, James, Michael, Bruce and Gabrielle had collected the phone numbers of gang members whenever they could. The big men like Sasha and Major Dee covered their tracks by regularly switching phones, but most of their deputies stuck to one handset. Despite this, there were still more than a hundred numbers on the list.

Once three months of Sasha's calls had dropped into the tray of the laser printer, Chloe divided the twenty sheets into three piles and split them evenly with the boys. They each grabbed a pen and began marking off numbers.

'07839 is Savvas' home number,' Bruce said. '25614 is one of Wheels' phones.'

Chloe and James skimmed through their papers, writing the name of the person Sasha called beside each instance of the number being dialled. Within ten minutes, they'd marked off most of the numbers and eliminated a few others – such as the garage that was fixing Sasha's car – by using a reverse searchable version of the telephone directory.

'I've still got one number that comes up every day or so,' James said, as he lay on Chloe's hotel bed. 'It's a mobile ending 42399.'

Chloe nodded as she ran her finger down the list of Mad Dogs phone numbers. 'I've got it on my sheet too. It's an unregistered mobile, but it's not on the list.'

'Yes it is,' Bruce said, waving his copy of the number list at Chloe. '42399, Simeon Bentine.'

'Where?' Chloe asked, as she slid her nail down the page for the third time. 'I can't see it.'

Bruce had made a discovery and seemed pretty full of

himself. 'I'm not using the list me and James got,' he explained. 'This is Michael and Gabrielle's list.'

'Get out of town,' James grinned, as he snatched the paper from Bruce to confirm that the phone numbers matched. 'You're right . . . So who the hell is Simeon Bentine?'

'No idea, but Michael should know where he fits in,' Chloe said, as she picked up her mobile from her bedside cabinet and gave him a call. 'Hey, is it safe to speak?'

'Chloe,' Michael said fondly. 'It's safe. I'm in a cab heading off to some house party.'

'Sounds like fun,' Chloe said. 'Listen, I'm here at the hotel with James and Bruce. We've got a call log from an unregistered mobile phone found in Sasha Thompson's house. It looks as if he's been spending a lot of time speaking to a man called Simeon Bentine. Ever heard of him?'

Michael sounded shocked. 'You said Simeon? E-O-N?'

'That's what I said. Who is he?'

'He's Major Dee's money man. I've only met him a couple of times. He's in his fifties, not much in common with the other Slasher Boys. Dresses in a pinstripe suit, drives a dark blue Mercedes E-class, respectable. You know, not blinged up or anything.'

'So you'd be pretty surprised to hear that this guy is on the phone to Sasha Thompson almost every day?' Chloe asked.

'This is *huge*, Chloe,' Michael said excitedly. 'This is the mother we've been waiting for. Simeon is the money man, which means he always knows when Major Dee is doing a big deal because he has to put the cash into position.'

'Major Dee's drug consignments have a history of being robbed by the Mad Dogs,' Chloe noted.

'Exactly,' Michael said. 'And it could easily have been Simeon who started up this whole war by telling Sasha where Dee kept his stash of cocaine.'

'Thanks for your help,' Chloe smiled. 'This sounds big. I'll call you back as soon as I know more.'

'Good news?' Bruce asked as Chloe put her phone down.

'As good as it gets,' Chloe said. 'I might even have hugged you if you weren't still wearing half of the Mad Dogs FC training pitch.'

'So it looks as if Simeon Bentine is Sasha's mole inside the Slasher Boys,' James said. 'What are we gonna do about it?'

Chloe shrugged. 'I'll speak with Maureen and Zara. We'll need a while to think it through, but this is something we can use to our advantage for sure.'

36. FRONT

It was gone 1 a.m. when James got home, but he lay awake, feeling on edge and asking himself the same questions over and over: *Could he trust Bruce not to spill the beans on campus? Could Sasha possibly find out? And Dana . . .* You don't always realise that you're taking someone for granted until you risk losing them.

James had never told Dana that he loved her, but realised now that he did. She was hilariously funny and he adored the way she ambled about in scruffy clothes, not caring what people thought about her. Dana managed to be sexy without spending hours plastering make-up over her face and the fact it was all so effortless somehow made it better.

But the weird thing about being fifteen – or maybe just the weird thing about being male – was that at the same time as James felt terrible about cheating on his girlfriend, he couldn't help wondering if he'd ever get another chance with Lois. She wasn't the most amazing person in the world, but she had a great body and he quite fancied trying out sex again when he wasn't numb with shock.

In the end, James abandoned sleep. He pulled a tiny crack

in the curtain on his side of the room and opened a cheesy paperback biography of a motorcycle champion that had been stuck on the front cover of his latest motorbike magazine. James was no connoisseur of literature, but it took him all of five pages to work out that it was a pile of crap and he was back to thinking about Lois in the bath when his mobile rang.

It was 5:57 when he saw *Wheels* flashing on the display. 'Hey mate,' James said.

The ring had woken Bruce, who sat up rubbing his eyes.

James practically swallowed his tongue when he didn't hear Wheels' voice.

'All right,' Sasha said. 'Feelin' fit?'

'Yeah,' James gulped. He kept hearing *I just shagged your daughter* in his head.

'Sorry about the ungodly hour, James, but I just had a call from a mate of mine; we're heading over to the Rudge Estate to take care of that bit of business we've been planning.'

'Right,' James nodded.

'I wasn't gonna bring you in on this bit, but I've got a couple of my lads dealing with some other business and this has to happen within the next few hours. Besides, I've really come to appreciate your loyalty, coming out for training when others have turned their backs.'

As soon as Sasha mentioned *loyalty*, James worried if he somehow knew what he'd been up to with Lois. 'Thanks,' he said weakly.

'It's not gonna be a picnic, but if you're up for it, I can get a car along for you and your cousin in fifteen minutes. I'll give you a grand a piece and I'm a fair man, so I'll cut you in if we do well.'

'I guess,' James said, still nervous about Lois. 'I mean . . . *Sure*. We'll get suited and booted.'

'Wheels reckons you've both got body armour and a couple of titchy handguns. Is that true?'

'Yeah,' James said.

'Where'd you get hold of them?' Sasha asked curiously.

'Guy we did a couple of jobs for in Scotland. He couldn't pay us, but he had a ton of dodgy weapons and some Kevlar suits ripped off from an army base.'

'What about ammunition?'

'A clip,' James said. 'Same for Bruce I think.'

'Right,' Sasha said. 'Wear your armour and bring the guns, but I might have to upgrade your firepower. I want you down on the doorstep when I arrive or I'll be pissed off.'

'No worries, Sasha,' James said.

He realised how tense he'd been as he put his phone down and saw its shape marked out in his palm where he'd been clutching it tight.

Bruce was sitting on the edge of his bed, trying to catch the conversation. 'Are we on for something?' he asked eagerly.

James shrugged and rubbed his fingers through his sweaty hair. 'He says it's going down at the hard front, but don't you think it's just a bit weird that he happens to call me tonight?'

Bruce grinned. 'What, because of your little bath-time adventure?'

'Well, what else?' James snapped.

'I heard him ask you about guns and body armour,' Bruce pointed out. 'You're being paranoid. This room isn't secure; if he wanted your gonads on a platter he would have burst in and grabbed you right out of bed.'

'Guess you're right,' James said uncertainly, as he walked to his locker and started grabbing some clothes. 'But he specifically mentioned loyalty . . .'

James decided on a baggy polo shirt that would stretch over his body armour as well as his nanotube reinforced jacket.

'Sounds like he's expecting serious gunplay,' Bruce said, as he stood beside James grabbing stuff out of the next locker. 'You'd better wear the leg armour too.'

'I *hate* that stuff,' James said.

He'd never worn the lightweight leg armour, which covered his bum and the upper section of his legs with a series of cream-coloured Kevlar plates that made him look like an Imperial Stormtrooper out of a *Star Wars* movie.

Leg armour is much less common than the chest protection that every serious villain wears nowadays; but it wasn't out of place because serious young criminals and wannabe drug dealers regard a thousand quid's worth of body armour as a status symbol to go along with their flash watch, mobile phone and the weapon they tuck inside their designer jeans.

'I know it makes your arse itch,' Bruce said, as he pulled his armour up his legs and began tightening a series of Velcro straps, 'but there's plenty of places where I don't want to get shot and this covers several of 'em.'

James felt almost obscenely butch as he led Bruce out of the room with the armour bulking out his clothes, a gun strapped to his leg and a knife tucked inside his Timberland boot. He'd worn similar levels of equipment on training exercises, but never on the streets.

'We'd better let Chloe know what's occurring,' Bruce said, dialling her number as they ambled down the stairs, ahead of schedule but with less than four hours' sleep to their names.

There was a new staff member on the Zoo reception desk and she was still green enough to try enforcing the rule that you had to sign the book if you came in or out between midnight and 7 a.m.

'There you go,' James said, handing back the Biro and clipboard as Bruce headed through a door with its shattered glass panels boarded up. The sun was coming up and the sky was a mix of purple and orange.

'What did Chloe say?' James asked.

'Not much,' Bruce shrugged. 'She said to be careful and if it gets dangerous we save our arses first and worry about our cover later. Oh, and she's been on the blower with the liaison at the police station. Apparently the councillor Sasha stomped has got a dozen broken bones including a fractured skull, but he's not telling anyone how it happened.'

'Poor guy didn't have a hope,' James said, shaking his head. 'Sasha's a complete animal.'

'I've heard that his daughter's a bit of a tiger too,' Bruce smirked.

*

After all the fuss to dress and get downstairs quickly, their ride was a quarter of an hour late and the wait was made uncomfortable by a cop car slowing down to check them out.

'Sasha's gone on ahead,' Wheels said, as he pulled up in his Astra, which was now sprayed black. 'Get in the back: there's gloves, masks and guns for each of you in the gym bag. I'll show you how to use them when we get to the flat.'

James and Bruce climbed in the car and Wheels pulled away almost before they slammed the doors. Bruce opened the drawstring on an orange Nike gym bag, revealing two Glock 9 machine pistols. Glocks were amongst the most powerful handguns available. They were rarely seen out of the hands of Special Forces and close protection officers, and were virtually unheard of amongst British criminals.

The two agents exchanged worried looks. The Glocks could fire twenty rounds in a few seconds; and in a kill-or-be-killed situation, the boys might not have any choice about pulling the trigger.

'Fully automatic, really nice guns,' Wheels said. 'But ammo's rarer than pink dog turds in this town, so you'd better not fire them without good reason.'

'So what's going down?' James asked. 'Sasha didn't tell us much on the phone.'

'I don't know all the details myself,' Wheels said. 'Sasha's a master of planning this kind of thing and I pretty much go along with what he says. The only thing I know is that there's a meeting set up and a major drug deal is going down involving the Slasher Boys.'

'Cool,' James said.

He'd been surveying the flat for close to three weeks and he knew that most of the dealers who lived and worked in the hard front looked West Indian, but this was the first time he'd heard confirmation that they were linked to Major Dee's crew.

*

Sasha, Savvas and a black dude were waiting at the flat. James grinned when he recognised Kelvin Holmes standing in the middle of the living-room. Kelvin had recruited James into Keith Moore's organisation three years earlier. The mission had resulted in Kelvin getting a three-year prison sentence, but fortunately he had no clue that James was responsible.

'Blast from the past!' Kelvin said affectionately when he saw James. 'You've got big! I hear you've been up north.'

Kelvin was scarily muscular, but he looked pretty lame in navy slacks and a short-sleeve shirt with a Royal Mail logo over the breast pocket.

'You're working for the Post Office now?' James asked.

'One day only,' Kelvin grinned, as he pointed towards a large amazon.co.uk parcel resting against the wall. 'Special delivery.'

37. POST

It was 7:40 a.m. when Kelvin approached the hard front, with the Amazon parcel under his arm and a mail bag slung over his back. Savvas and Wheels crouched in a stairwell less than ten metres away, with silenced handguns in holsters under their jackets. James and Bruce were behind them, leather gloves over their hands and black balaclavas ready to pull over their faces before they moved in. Sasha was in the next block watching through the surveillance cameras. As the boss of the Mad Dogs, he left most of the dirty work to his younger deputies.

Salty beads streaked down Kelvin's forehead as he stood at the reinforced door. He could hear a couple speaking inside as he jammed his thumb on the doorbell for a second time.

'Parcel,' Kelvin shouted. 'I know you're there but I ain't got all day.'

A couple of bolts slid off and the door opened a few centimetres, still secured by a heavy chain. The instant it moved, Savvas and his three companions jumped out of the stairwell and began moving along the balcony towards the flat.

The woman behind the door was in a state, with a duvet wrapped around her shoulders and a yellow muck weeping from an infected eyeball.

'Hey,' the woman yawned, as Kelvin passed a clipboard and Biro through the doorway. Then she screamed back down the hallway: 'More of your poxy books, Tyler. How come it's not your arse I see moving out of bed?'

As the woman scrawled her name in a white box, Kelvin slipped a 60,000-volt cattle prod out of his back pocket and jammed it into her belly. She flew away from the door, convulsing as she collapsed backwards into a rack of coats hanging on the wall.

Outside, Wheels pulled down his balaclava and ran forwards holding a giant pair of bolt croppers. Kelvin pushed his trainer against the door to make the chain tight and Wheels cut it.

Kelvin didn't have body armour or a gun and the woman had seen his face, so he backed off and let the other four take care of business. A woman shouted as Savvas and Wheels charged into the living-room waving their guns. As planned, James raced on down the hallway and burst into the main bedroom, while Bruce pinned the woman to the hallway floor, locking her arms behind her back with disposable cuffs and forcing a rubber gag into her mouth.

A smell hit James as the bedroom door came open: a mixture of urine and old sweat that made him glad he hadn't eaten breakfast. After weeks of surveillance, James was certain that they'd seen everyone come and go enough times to know exactly who was inside, but he was staggered to find a small boy staring out from between the wall and a chest of drawers. He looked about five, but he had a dummy in his mouth and clearly hadn't seen bathwater in weeks.

James was so appalled by the sad little figure that he lost concentration, allowing the man in the bed to reach under the mattress and grab a knife. But James ripped the Glock out of its holster and held it in the air.

'Put that down before I blow your head off,' James said strictly.

He looked back when he heard a row breaking out in the hallway directly behind him. One of the dealers had tried making a sprint out of the second bedroom, but he'd clattered into Bruce, who'd taken him down with a palm thrust hard into his solar plexus.

'Get everyone tied and bring 'em in here,' Savvas shouted from the living-room. 'Then we'll search for the gear.'

'Put this in your mouth and pull the strap behind your head,' James ordered, as he grabbed a rubber gag out of his pocket and threw it on to the bed.

The man did what he was told.

'Now your wrists,' James said, putting the gun to the man's head as he looped plastic cuffs over his hands and pulled them tight.

All this time the filthy little lad stared dumbly. 'All right mate?' James said, trying to be as reassuring as a masked man holding a gun can be. 'Don't be scared. We're not gonna hurt you.'

The living-room smelled funky, though nothing like as bad as the bedroom. There were dirty cups piled everywhere, the ashtrays were stacked and there were about a hundred

Playstation games and DVDs in a mound near the TV, most of them out of their boxes.

It was a small space and it got even smaller with three gagged men on the sofa, two gagged women on the floor and the little boy standing in the corner with his bony legs crossed.

James and Bruce stood guard in the living-room while Savvas and Wheels tore the other rooms apart searching for drugs and money.

'Why don't you get some toys to play with,' James said gently, concerned that traumatising a five-year-old with a gun would be yet another item on the long list of things that would keep him out of heaven.

But the boy didn't move. James noticed a couple of plastic cars jammed under the edge of the sofa and he kicked them across the carpet. After a couple of seconds the boy kicked them back. He seemed starved of attention and after the car had been kicked back and forth a couple of times, the little lad smiled and came over towards James.

'Can I hold your gun?' he asked.

James looked down at the matted hair and tried not to gag as he breathed the lad's smell. There were welts on the back of his arms where he'd been whipped. The sight made James boil.

'It's only for grown-ups,' James said, as he reached down his pocket. 'But I've got some chocolate éclairs.'

James was going to pull out one sweet, but when he saw the little boy's face light up he gave him the whole packet. The lad scrambled back into his corner and crammed two toffees in his mouth.

'Take it easy,' James said. 'You'll choke.'

But the boy took the warning as a threat and he crouched down nervously, clutching the sweets to his chest and primed for an explosion of tears.

'Check this out, kids,' Wheels boomed, as he struggled into the room with a large backpack. He unzipped it and pulled back the flap, unveiling bags filled with powdered cocaine and honeycomb-like bricks of crack.

Bruce's eyes were bulging. 'How much is that lot worth?'

Wheels shrugged. 'Ain't had time to weigh it, but it's gotta be at least seventy grand.'

Savvas looked at his watch as he strode into the room. 'Looks like we're all secured. Is everyone behaving themselves in here?'

'No problems,' James said.

'Hey, you've got some sweets,' Savvas said, smiling at the boy in the corner. 'What's your name?'

But the lad was too shy to answer. Savvas shook his head in disgust as he stepped towards the two women.

'Which one of you junkie bitches is his mother?' he asked angrily.

Neither woman could speak with the gags in their mouth, and neither nodded. So Savvas picked the one on the left at random. He grabbed her by the chin and bashed her head against the wall.

'Give him a bath,' Savvas said, as he stepped back shaking his head in disgust. 'How can you let him walk around in that state?' Then he looked over at Bruce and pulled a tenner out of his pocket. 'We're gonna have to wait here a couple of hours. I've put the kettle on, but I'm not eating anything out of that filthy kitchen. Would you nip down to the café across the street and get the bacon sarnies in?'

*

To avoid suspicion, Savvas untied one of the dealers and let him continue the daily routine of taking orders and passing small packets of drugs through the letterbox when the doorbell rang.

James' little friend seemed half starved. After finishing off his chocolates, the boy ate an entire bacon-and-fried-egg sandwich and shrieked happily as he kicked a small football up and down the hallway with his masked friends. But things got tense as ten o'clock drew near.

Major Dee's Jamaican connections gave him an unrivalled ability to move large quantities of cocaine from South America to Britain, using the Caribbean as a stop-off point. As well as selling through the Slasher Boys and other West Indian gangs in the south east, Dee also supplied drugs to major dealers in the north of the country, in particular to a Salford-based gang that controlled door security and the drug supply inside pubs and clubs all over Manchester.

Instead of stealing the drugs and running, Sasha's ambitious plan was to rob the Slasher Boys' drugs and the Salford crew's money. Both groups were predominantly black, which meant Kelvin would have to answer the door or the Salford crew would know something was wrong.

But that was far from their only problem. Sasha knew the time and place that the deal was going down, but he didn't know how many men the Salford crew would bring. Seizing the drugs had been easy because the dealers were at home and half asleep. But the northerners were coming to do a hundred-grand drug deal, which meant they'd be right on edge.

But Sasha was a pro. He'd been robbing drug dealers for more than twenty years and he knew his stuff. As well as Kelvin, Savvas, Wheels, James and Bruce inside the hard front, he had two men poised in a flat three doors down, a youngster down in the road who was supposed to slash the northerners' tyres when they arrived and a man stationed on the roof of the next block with an assault rifle and optical scope. The whole team was linked with walkie-talkies and Sasha himself would run the show from the flat across the street where James and Bruce had mounted the surveillance.

The wait became painful. James had a layer of sweat between his skin and his body armour and it itched like crazy. His watch seemed to be going in slow motion as ten o'clock came and went.

They'd put the boy in the back bedroom out of harm's way, but he wanted to carry on playing and he cried until Wheels banged on the door and threatened to whack him.

At 10:07 the youngster down at street level put a message over the walkie-talkies. There were six black men in two cars. Five of them stepped out, while one waited in the driver's seat of a BMW.

'Martin, I want both cars immobilised as soon as they're out of sight,' Sasha replied.

James had never spoken to Martin, but he was only seventeen and he sounded out of his depth. 'I can't, boss,' the kid said. 'There's a guy sitting behind the wheel.'

'You've got a gun,' Sasha said bluntly. 'Use it.'

A shiver went up James' back when he heard the order over the radio. This had always been serious business, but

Sasha giving the order to put a bullet through someone's head made it a hundred times worse. His voice was flat – like a man ordering a latte rather than an execution – and CHERUB's ethics committee wasn't going to like it one bit.

'Boss, are you sure?' the kid asked. 'There's people around and you told me I was only gonna slash the tyres—'

'Do what you're told,' Sasha shouted. 'If I have to come down there and sort the cars out I'm gonna be sticking bullets through two skulls, not one. Now what's their status?'

'Five men heading upstairs,' Martin said shakily. 'Two have got big bags – the money, I guess.'

'You reckon, Sherlock?' Sasha sneered. 'Units inside the house, are you ready?'

Savvas stood less than a metre from James as he spoke into his radio. 'Good to go, boss.'

'Units at number sixteen, I want you out on that balcony blocking off the staircase as soon as the Salford boys go inside,' Sasha said.

A fresh voice came out of Savvas' radio. 'Roger that, boss. We're all set.'

It was only two floors up, but it seemed like the walk from the car park took the Salford crew for ever.

'They're out on the balcony,' Sasha said. 'Keep this channel clear unless it's urgent. Good luck everyone.'

The doorbell rang and Kelvin walked slowly towards the front door as Savvas pointed his gun at the hostages. 'I've got two hundred rounds a minute out of this baby, so if I hear so much as a sharp intake of breath I'll waste all five of you.'

Out in the hallway Kelvin opened the front door to the five northerners.

'You must be Pete,' Kelvin said. 'Come right in, it's in the kitchen.'

The leader of the Salford boys wore sunglasses and had a full beard. 'Who are you?' he spat, talking fast and going for his gun. 'Where's Tyler? Nobody told me about a change of personnel.'

Kelvin raised his hands anxiously. 'Peace, brothers,' he said, as he stepped backwards. 'The major just called me over here to do this thing. I don't know about who goes where, or who you supposed to be seeing.'

'Show me the shit,' the bearded guy said as he stepped into the hallway, but he was highly suspicious and he pointed at the two men holding the bags of money. 'Wait out there and one of you call Major Dee and ask what the *hell* is going down.'

James and Savvas could hear everything from behind the living-room door. Kelvin didn't have a gun and would be a dead man the second the Salford boys got their call through to Major Dee. The plan was to wait until the northerners and the money were in the kitchen where they'd be easily contained, but Savvas realised it was never going to get that far and raised his walkie-talkie up to his lips.

'All teams move,' he said.

Wheels was the first one out of the living-room door, whilst Bruce came out of the bedroom on the opposite side of the hallway. As the Salford boys reached for their guns, Kelvin spun around and made a lunge towards the relative safety of the kitchen.

Meanwhile, two more of Sasha's men had burst from a flat along the balcony and ran towards the three Salford men in the doorway. James and the hostages jolted with fright as gunfire echoed along the concrete balcony.

As Kelvin scrambled into the kitchen, the man with the beard took aim at his back; but Bruce shoulder-charged and knocked him to the ground.

'The money's moving away,' Sasha screamed over the walkie-talkie. 'The guys with the bags are running back towards the stairwell. That driver *better* be dead, Martin.'

'It's cool, boss,' Martin said proudly.

'Cut them off at the bottom of the stairs, kid,' Sasha ordered. 'I'm coming down to back you up.'

While all this was going on James waited in the living-room guarding the hostages. He dived to one side as a ricochet shattered the barred window. The chunks of flying glass had enough momentum to tear down the curtain rail, flooding the gloomy space with sunshine.

Out in the hallway Kelvin had wrapped a muscular arm around the bearded man's neck and was giving him a beating.

The three Salford boys who'd been in the doorway were retreating under heavy fire from the men out of the flat two doors along, but that still left Bruce in a tight hallway with Pete – the bearded man's second-in-command – less than two metres away.

Pete was pulling his gun and Bruce realised he couldn't beat him on the draw. As a shot tore down the hallway, Bruce dived low, expecting to get hit. But the bullet sheared through the door at the end of the hallway and Bruce found himself with his arms locked around a set of chunky thighs.

Bruce was extraordinarily strong for his size. He grabbed Pete's shooting arm and pushed his hand upwards so that his second shot tore through the ceiling, then twisted him into a thumb lock, making the gun drop out of his hand.

Worried by the sounds of struggle, James raced out into the hallway to check that Bruce was OK. He saw Bruce drive Pete backwards out of the front door and pin him against the railings outside. Bruce had to back up to make enough space to swing a punch and finish his opponent off, but as he let go he noticed that one of the Salford boys with the bags of money had doubled back and was sprinting along the narrow balcony towards him.

Less than three metres from Bruce and running at full pelt, James couldn't see any outcome apart from Bruce getting knocked down. As James snatched his gun from its holster and almost tripped over Wheels – who'd been knocked down during the struggle – Bruce swung around. His elbow caught Pete in the side of the head, knocking him sideways, then he turned his back on the man running towards him and leaned forward.

As the dude crashed into him, Bruce let him roll over his back before springing up and tossing his assailant high into the air. If they'd been on the ground he would have slammed down on his back, but instead he went head first into the banister atop the metal railing.

The blue sports bag rattled a boarded-up window and hit the balcony, but the man who'd been holding it found his fingers clutching wrought-iron posts as his legs slipped over the edge, ten metres above ground.

Sasha's voice came out of Bruce's radio as he took a final knock-out swing at Pete.

'I'm eyeballing two cop cars,' Sasha said as James picked

up the bag of money. 'Grab what we've got and ship out.'

Savvas emerged through the front door, followed by Kelvin – who'd donned a mask – and Wheels, who had the backpack stuffed with drugs on his back. As they made a dash for the stairs down to the ground, the dangling man lost his fight to haul himself up the railings and crashed two storeys to the ground.

When they emerged into the courtyard at the bottom he was spread-eagled on the concrete, groaning for help. James did a three-sixty and saw that one of the Salford boys had been shot in the leg as he ran off and now lay unconscious between two parked cars. He also noticed blood spattered up the inside of a BMW windscreen. There was no sign of Sasha, Martin or the two men who'd been in the shoot-out on the balcony.

'Nightmare,' Wheels said, as he handed the pack full of drugs to Bruce, then ripped a plipper out of his pocket and climbed into the driver's seat of a Honda Accord. The siren of an approaching cop car sounded like it was less than a street away.

Savvas squeezed up on the back seat with James and Bruce then slammed his door. They hadn't stopped to open the boot and the drugs and money were piled up on their laps.

Wheels scraped the Micra in the next bay as he reversed out at speed. James looked over his shoulder and saw the nose of a cop car pull into the street as they tore off.

38. PARTNERS

Ideally the Mad Dogs would have kept the Salford Boys contained inside the flat. The dealers could hardly have dialled 999 to report that their drugs had been robbed and the cops would never even have known that a robbery had taken place.

But the operation had spilled on to the street and half a dozen Rudge Estate residents had called the cops. There was a dead man in a BMW and two more Salford Boys in a mangled state on the pavement. The cops would also find the flat upstairs with the five hostages tied up in the living-room.

So whilst Sasha was glad to have nabbed a backpack stuffed with drugs and a hundred grand in cash, he knew the cops would be sniffing around. None of the dealers would talk, but the cops put a lot more effort into a murder than a robbery and the forensic team would pull the hard front to pieces.

To cover their tracks, Sasha wanted everything burned. Everyone abandoned their gloves and masks inside the Honda, and once he'd dropped everyone off, Wheels took it straight to a breakers' yard. Within an hour of the raid, the interior was burned out and the metal shell had been squeezed into a tiny cube. Once he got home, Wheels would clean up the guns and drive them sixty kilometres to an industrial unit where Sasha stored equipment used in robberies.

Kelvin was the only gang member who'd gone unmasked and ungloved inside the hard front and this made him vulnerable. He'd been in prison, so the cops would have a sample of his DNA and they'd pull him in for questioning if they detected it. But Sasha looked after his own and Kelvin would be protected with an alibi.

Kelvin could easily claim that his DNA was in the flat because he'd been there to visit a friend and Sasha would fix things so that he could say he was doing a cleaning job at a local betting shop at the time the robbery was taking place. The betting shop was owned by one of Sasha's cousins and they'd fake the surveillance videos inside the shop with the proper date stamp and everything. The cops probably wouldn't believe it, but a jury would almost certainly give him the benefit of the doubt.

As a final precaution, James, Bruce and everyone else involved in the raid was ordered to put their outer clothes and shoes into bin liners as soon as they got home. The bags either had to be burned or dumped in a communal bin at least three kilometres from where they lived. Obviously James and Bruce didn't want to lose their clothes – including their nanotube-reinforced tops – so they gave them to Chloe to take back to campus.

*

By noon James was exhausted. All the running around in body armour had made him stink, but he ached too much to care and lay face-down on his bed trying to catch up on his sleep.

Bruce had managed some sleep the night before, and couldn't resist tickling the sole of James' foot as he came back from the shower with a towel around his waist.

'Leave off,' James moaned.

'That was *such* a buzz,' Bruce enthused. 'When I threw that guy over my back! Did you see how he looked when he was trying to hold on? It was like—'

Bruce made a face, but James didn't bother pulling his head off his pillow to look. 'You know, sometimes I wonder if you're entirely right in the head?' James said. 'A fight in the dojo is one thing, but you seriously messed that bloke up.'

'Why are you being such a misery?' Bruce asked, as he rolled deodorant under his arms.

James finally turned to look at his friend. 'Bruce, do all the girls on campus think I'm an arsehole because I cheated on Kerry?'

'They talk about you,' Bruce grinned. 'Sometimes they slag you off, sometimes they say you're cute. What matters is that they talk about you.'

James was baffled. 'What *are* you on about?'

'Haven't you ever noticed that girls only talk about guys they fancy?' Bruce explained. 'They might be bitching or slagging you off, but they only talk about guys they like.'

'I'd never thought of that,' James nodded.

'It's guys like me who have to worry,' Bruce said, as he pulled on a pair of jeans. 'I'm skinny, I'm ordinary-looking and I don't get sixth-form girls jumping on me in bathtubs. So don't go moaning to me about *do the girls on campus like me* because you've probably had more girlfriends already than I'm gonna get in my whole life.'

'You just need more confidence,' James said, taking pity on his friend. 'And you've got Kerry now. I mean, I don't get on with her these days, but she's still hot.'

'I'm still a bit amazed that she's my girlfriend,' Bruce admitted.

'Anyway,' James said. 'I'm thinking about me and Kerry, and my cheating on her was like a wedge between us. I could never really look her in the eye, because there were all these lies in the background. I don't want it to be like that with Dana.'

Bruce's eyebrows shot up. 'You can't tell her that you boffed Lois! She'll kill you.'

James shrugged. 'I think I have to.'

'But what if she dumps you?'

'Well *hopefully* she won't,' James shrugged. 'I mean, Dana's different to Kerry. I think she'll be OK if I explain exactly how it happened. She might even appreciate me being honest.'

Bruce laughed. 'If you're lucky, she won't dump you, but I wouldn't bank on her *appreciating* it.'

There was a gentle knock, followed by Michael's head coming around the door. 'Hey,' he said, 'mind if I come in for a second?'

James and Bruce weren't supposed to associate with Michael, but as the mission had gone on they'd become slightly more relaxed. And as they all lived at the Zoo it wasn't unnatural that a casual friendship should exist between them.

'Have you spoken to Gabrielle lately?' James asked, as he rolled on to his back.

'Just this morning, she's doing great,' Michael said, wafting his hand in front of his nose as he looked at James. 'So is not washing some kind of new fashion statement for you white boys?'

James tutted. 'I'll take a shower in a minute.'

'And who are you calling *white boys*?' Bruce demanded. 'You're spending too much time with your Jamaican friends.'

'At least I didn't call you honkies. But you're right, I'm gonna have to watch myself when I get back to campus. I said that Gabrielle was *my bitch* in front of Maureen and Chloe the other day.'

'So is this a social visit or what?' Bruce asked.

'Chloe's heard all about your little shoot-out this morning, but she's not happy 'cos you haven't briefed her yet and I think I let it slip that you'd both been back for over an hour.'

'What's her problem?' James moaned. 'We've got phones, she could have rung us.'

'She didn't want to call until she was certain it was safe for you to talk.'

'Oh well,' James said as he sat up. 'Bruce can call her while I'm in the shower.'

'Great, let *me* get yelled at,' Bruce said.

'It's good news about Simeon Bentine,' Michael said. 'Have you heard the latest?'

James shook his head. 'Not since last night.'

'They've analysed the pattern of calls and it seems that

Sasha and Simeon are talking to each other at least once a day. They're going to record the calls for a couple of days, then they're going to pull Simeon in and threaten to drop him in it with Major Dee if he doesn't play ball.'

James thought for a second. 'What about our cover?'

'Chloe thinks we'll be fine,' Michael said. 'There's several different ways that the cops might have tracked the calls, and while Sasha's been changing his phone regularly, Simeon's had the same one for over six months. It's even registered in his own name.'

James shook his head. 'Unbelievable!'

'Yeah, but it's about time we had some luck on this mission,' Bruce said.

*

While Mad Dogs FC had all but disappeared, Sasha continued to meet his crew regularly in his basement. James and Bruce were invited and Junior came along too. With his pocket money suspended and Sasha not letting him earn, the basement was the only place where Junior could afford to socialise.

By nine the three boys had played pool and downed a few cans of beer. The poker game was lively, but the atmosphere was jovial because a lot of people had made money that morning and Sasha wasn't at the table. He'd been holding a series of meetings upstairs in his office and James and Bruce were amongst the last to be called up.

'Boys,' Sasha smiled, as they pulled open the door. 'Savvas tells me that you two did a blinding job. Did you do like I said and dump the clothes and everything?'

'Of course,' James said.

'And you,' Sasha said, pointing at Bruce. 'That dude you threw over the balcony broke a shoulder, an arm and both legs. My mate at the hospital reckons it's a miracle he wasn't paralysed.'

James couldn't fail to be impressed by Sasha's contacts. The Mad Dogs might not have been the biggest gang in town, but they had friends in all the right places.

'I said a grand apiece, but we made out big so I'm putting your shares up to fifteen hundred. Now that's a lot of money for kids your age. I don't want you getting flash, because the cops have always got an eye on the Zoo.'

'Don't worry,' James assured him. 'We'll buy some clothes to replace what we threw out, but we'll spend the rest gradually.'

'Have you got somewhere to stash it?' Sasha asked.

James nodded. 'The lockers at the Zoo are crap, but I've got a spot behind the skirting board where I keep what's left from the hotel robbery.'

'If you're sure,' Sasha said, as he reached into a briefcase and pulled six slim bundles of £500 in twenty-pound notes. 'That's all good money,' he added. 'Totally untraceable. Now go off and enjoy yourselves.'

'We're always up for anything,' James said. 'Just let us know.'

'I'll do that,' Sasha smiled. 'There's always money to be made for a couple of smart lads like you.'

As they headed out along the hallway, Lois yelled James' name from the living-room. The entrance was an archway, and she sat on the couch with her legs tucked under her bum and a box of chocolates in her lap.

'How's your leg doing?' she asked.

'Seems to be healing up nicely,' James said, feeling awkward. 'Thanks for your help.'

There was no way to acknowledge what had happened the night before with Bruce standing next to him and Sasha down the hall.

'That's good,' Lois said icily. 'But don't bother coming back with my dad's clothes. He's got plenty of others.'

Lois' tone and her body language made it clear that it wasn't just the clothes she didn't want to come back.

'Tossed away like rotten fruit,' Bruce gloated, as they headed back towards the basement. 'That's gotta hurt!'

In a way James was relieved. Having Lois after him was bad for the mission and his personal safety. But on a human level, he'd been rejected and it hurt. He didn't know if it was something he'd done, or maybe Lois always treated men like that. Either way, she was older and more experienced, and while James didn't regret what had happened, he felt like a little kid who'd been invited to the big boys' party, only to have everyone laugh at him.

Feeling sore as he headed down into the smoke-filled basement, James couldn't resist turning his anger into spite by grabbing the money out of his tracksuit top and waving it in front of Junior, who was slumped in the corner waiting for his turn at the pool table. He'd downed at least four beers and looked wasted.

'Check my wad out,' James grinned.

Junior's mouth dropped. 'This is *so* bogus,' he snarled. 'I introduced Sasha to you less than a month ago and now you're both loaded.'

'It's fifteen hundred,' James teased, as he tried to pinch Junior's cheek. But Junior batted his arm away and stood up.

'I'm sick of being treated like a baby,' he spat. 'Sasha's an arsehole.'

Junior said it loud enough that people could hear, although everyone knew he'd never have dared if Sasha had been in the room.

'You wanna watch that mouth, Junior,' Savvas said seriously. 'Your name's not gonna protect you if you wind Sasha up.'

James felt bad about teasing Junior and he pulled £100 out of his pocket and tried putting it in Junior's hand. It was the worst thing he could have done.

'I don't want your charity,' Junior growled, before turning to Savvas. 'And I don't want to get lectured by a sodding Paki either.'

A great wave of ooohs shot around the room as Savvas squared up to Junior. Savvas wasn't huge, but he was a grown man and Junior was only fifteen.

'What did you call me?' Savvas yelled. 'Would you like me to scrub the floor with your face?'

'Well it'd make a change from your mum doing it,' Junior yelled back.

The only reason Junior didn't get a slap at this point was because Savvas didn't know if Sasha would stand for it. Bruce squeezed between them, and it said something about the reputation he'd already gained that Junior and Savvas backed off, despite the fact that Bruce was easily the youngest person in the room.

'Cool it,' James said, grabbing Junior's arm. 'Let's take a walk.'

'I just want to earn like everybody else,' Junior shouted, as James led him up the wooden staircase.

'Maybe we could talk to Sasha,' James said, looking towards the office.

But Junior was in no mood to talk to anyone. 'I'm outta here,' he said, as he headed down the hallway and grabbed the front door.

If James had been focused entirely on the mission, he would have headed back downstairs to the basement. But he was annoyed at himself for teasing Junior about the money and he followed him down the front steps.

'I didn't mean to wind you up,' James said. 'I was an idiot.'

'It's not you, it's *them*,' Junior said, close to tears as he stormed towards the football pitches across the street. 'I'm sick of being Keith Moore's son and you know what? Screw the lot of them. I've been around crooks all my life and I'm not an idiot. If they won't let me get my hands on some cash, I'll go out and earn myself.'

'Like how?' James asked. 'You're on parole, mate. You've only gotta make one slip and you're buggered . . .'

'I know places,' Junior said. 'We could be like Wheels. Ducking and diving, mugging some rich dirtbag here, robbing a fancy car there.'

By this time they'd reached the gates of the park, but it was dark and they were locked.

'Who said anything about *we*?' James said pointedly.

'Why not, James?' Junior said, as he rested his feet on the bottom of the gate and squeezed his head between the bars. 'I know you're earning off Sasha, but look at today. You robbed two hundred grand. Sasha makes a hundred and fifty and you made what, five grand?'

'Fifteen hundred,' James said.

'He's having a laugh,' Junior grimaced. 'You and me together could make *real* money.'

James liked Junior and it was the kind of harebrained scheme he would have gone for in his pre-CHERUB days. But his mission was to bring down the Slasher Boys and Mad Dogs, not encourage Junior to set up a rival crew.

'Maybe in a few months,' James said, knowing full well that he wouldn't be around by then. 'I mean, me and Bruce are earning decent money from Sasha. We can save up and then set our own crew up when we've got the cash to do it properly.'

'I guess,' Junior said. 'But I'm not earning in the meantime.'

James thought about offering Junior money again, but he was clearly sensitive about taking charity and James had a nasty feeling that he'd blow it on cocaine if he did.

'I wish I was older,' Junior said, as he jiggled his arms, rattling the gate. 'Being fifteen is so crap. I wanna go to a bar or a club. I want money and drugs and girls with *massive* tits.'

James started to laugh.

'I tell you what,' Junior said. 'If I can plan a job – not some chicken-feed half-arsed job but a proper raid like Sasha does – would you be my partner?'

'Sasha wouldn't like it,' James said, shaking his head.

'Come *on*, James,' Junior begged. 'We'd be great partners.'

James was tired and doubted that Junior would remember the conversation by morning.

'Whatever,' James shrugged. 'Partners.'

Junior broke into a huge grin and put out his hand. 'Gimme some skin.'

And the two boys slapped their hands together before rounding off with a beer-fuelled hug.

39. GRILLED

Pulling a suspect is a tricky business. If you bust them at home or at work someone is going to know that it happened and then a whole bunch of other people – including criminals and bent police officers – are going to see them getting dragged into the police station. If Simeon Bentine was arrested and questioned in the normal manner, Major Dee and Sasha Thompson would probably learn all about it.

To get around this, Chloe spent the whole of Wednesday following Simeon to see how he lived his life. Interrogation wasn't Chloe's speciality, so she asked her old boss John Jones to come down from CHERUB campus and help out the following day. She'd told her liaison with the Bedfordshire police what was going to happen, but there are strict rules about arresting, cautioning and threatening suspects and Chloe was going to break almost all of them.

To make life even trickier, Simeon worked out of a dilapidated office above a shop less than two hundred metres from the Green Pepper café; so there were always going to be Slasher Boys in the neighbourhood.

The brass plaque beside his front door said that Simeon

was an accountant, but Chloe had checked him out and found no evidence that he'd earned any of the initials engraved after his name.

John and Chloe watched from inside a workman's café as Simeon arrived for work, just after 9 a.m. He placed a blue disabled badge in his windscreen, before unlocking a door sandwiched between two shop fronts and bounding up a narrow staircase. Once the pair saw the light flicker through the blind in his office window, they headed out of the café and cut between the rush-hour traffic. They didn't give Simeon time to settle in. They wanted him on edge.

By the time the two mission controllers reached the cracked lino at the top of the stairs, Simeon was standing in the reception where his secretary worked, placing a paper filter into a coffee machine.

'Good morning,' Simeon said warmly as they stepped through his frosted glass door. 'I'm afraid I'm not open to the public. If you'd like financial advice you can make an appointment with my secretary, she's due in at any moment.'

'Linda won't be here today.' Chloe smiled.

'I believe she's having some difficulties with her car this morning,' John Jones said as he slid a bolt across the door.

'What are you people?' Simeon asked apprehensively. He'd been playing a dangerous game with two gang bosses and clearly feared the worst.

'Perhaps we can take this through to your office,' Chloe said gently.

'Are you cops?' It wasn't that Simeon relished getting busted, but at least cops wouldn't blow his brains out.

'In your office,' John said firmly, pulling back his

overcoat to show that he had a gun. 'Sit down and we'll talk matters over.'

John's demeanour and Chloe being female was enough for Simeon to decide that they were cops. 'I could have you for this,' he said, wagging his finger as he sat down. 'There's proper procedure.'

'There certainly is,' John said, as he reached across the desk and pulled Simeon's phone off the hook. 'But you can't make a complaint if you don't know who we are.'

'The security services are always interested in the drug business,' Chloe said, as she flashed a fake MI5 ID. 'Drug smugglers and terrorists are almost interchangeable when you get to the top level.'

'But a man should only have one master,' John added.

Chloe smiled. 'And a man with two should at least have the common sense to switch his mobile phone once in a while.'

'If you have information, arrest me,' Simeon boomed, sweeping his hand through the air. 'Otherwise get outta my face.'

'We *could* arrest you,' John said. 'But you're not that big a fish.'

'We're more interested in what *might* happen if recordings of conversations between yourself and Sasha Thompson slipped into the hands of Major Dee,' Chloe said. 'What was it you said yesterday? *Don't worry Sasha old friend, I'll be sending some juicy business your way soon.*'

John nodded. 'And the amount of paperwork we have to fill in if we bust anybody these days, it would be so much easier to have Major Dee deal with matters . . .'

Simeon ran nervous fingers through his greying stubble. 'Will you pay me for information?'

John and Chloe both laughed. 'We think you're making enough already,' John said.

'We're looking at the big picture here,' Chloe said. 'You're leaking information so that Sasha Thompson can rip off Major Dee. If you can tell us exactly where it's going to take place, the cops can set up surveillance and tape the whole show.'

Simeon shrugged. 'You don't need me for that if you're listening to my phone calls already.'

'It's a one-shot deal,' Chloe explained. 'We want to know every detail; not just what goes between you and Sasha over the telephone. If we get it right we'll have strong evidence of Major Dee, Sasha Thompson and all of their little helpers handling drugs and guns.'

'And what happens to me?' Simeon said. 'They'd kill me, in prison or out. I'd need full immunity and a free ride out of the country.'

'You're not getting immunity,' John said. 'But we'll turn a blind eye long enough for you to move your assets out of the country and ship out to Jamaica, or wherever else you think you'll be safe. I know that's not perfect, but it's better than an appointment with Major Dee's cordless drill.'

Simeon sucked air between his teeth. 'It could be difficult . . .' he said. 'Very tough to get Sasha and the Major together at one time. They're both cautious men.'

'The Mad Dogs are a small crew,' Chloe said. 'Sasha coordinates all of the big robberies personally.'

Simeon steepled his fingers and nodded. 'There is one way, but . . .'

'But what?' John asked.

'Major Dee rarely handles major deals himself. But he's desperate to stop the Mad Dogs stealing from him. If the Major was tipped off about being robbed by the Mad Dogs, he'd be in on the ambush for sure.'

John whistled. 'So you tip Sasha off about a drug deal, you also find a way to tip Major Dee off about being robbed, and the cops will be on hand to film the entire show.'

'It's quite a plan, Simeon,' Chloe said. 'Maybe you could balance a ball on the end of your nose at the same time.'

'I'm fifty-three years old,' Simeon replied. 'I don't want to go to prison and I don't want Major Dee to kill me. I'm not stupid. People at your level only approach people like me when the game is already rigged. I'll work with you, but I have a solicitor in London. I want paperwork drawn up guaranteeing me safe passage out of the country, signed by whoever my solicitor wants it signed by to make it legal.'

'Sounds fair,' Chloe said. 'But what's our timescale for you setting this up? Are we talking weeks, months, or what?'

'Major Dee has two or three large shipments of cocaine coming out of Jamaica every week,' Simeon explained. 'But Sasha needs time to plan carefully and I suppose the police would need time to set up surveillance too?'

'Absolutely,' Chloe nodded.

'Then perhaps ten days. There's regular shipment that comes in by container. I've never mentioned it to Sasha because it's one of Major Dee's mainstays.'

Chloe looked baffled, but John understood.

'You earn plenty out of Major Dee,' John clarified. 'You only want Sasha to skim off some cream, not to destroy the whole Slasher Boys organisation.'

'Precisely,' Simeon nodded. 'I have a friend who can give me exact information on the delivery of cocaine by this afternoon. I can tell Sasha about the delivery immediately, but letting Major Dee know that he is likely to be robbed is more complex. I'll have to put some thought into exactly how we achieve that.'

'Obviously we can help you out,' Chloe said. 'But now you're working for us you'll have to stay in touch and we'll need to know where you are at all times.'

Simeon stood up and reached casually across the desk to shake hands. 'If you're fair with me you'll have no problem,' he said.

40. SPOILED

James hadn't seen Junior since their hug on Tuesday night. He called up during a rare appearance at school and James agreed to meet him by the gates as he left. It was a bright afternoon and the boys pouring out of the tatty school building were all in shirt sleeves.

'I called yesterday to see if you were OK, but your phone was off or something,' James said.

'It's my mum,' Junior explained. 'Woke me up at seven yesterday morning and told me to put on a shirt and tie. She'd stitched me up with an interview at yet another private school. It was right in the middle of nowhere, with all these kids playing rugby and countryside all around it. God it was a toilet . . .'

'You're not going are you?' James said anxiously. 'I'm on the waiting list at this school. If you leave, I might have to start getting educated again.'

'Don't worry,' Junior grinned. 'I didn't want my ma getting upset, so I played along during the interview and stuff, but this idiot deputy headmaster kept going on about the cadet force and how they liked to *mould young boys like me*, as if I was Blu Tack or something. Then he started talking about the Inter-House Cup, which was like *why do I give a shit?* The thing was, I never actually thought they'd accept me, but this place must have been in serious need of pupils because they offered to take me for a trial period.'

'Oh crap!' James gasped.

'I totally freaked,' Junior continued. 'I mean, I didn't mind playing along when I didn't think they'd take me, but once I realised that I was like *millimetres* from going back to boarding school I went nuts. I started making really loud chicken noises and there were some little kids outside the window and I leaned up to the glass and yelled *do any of you fags want to buy cocaine?*'

James laughed uneasily. 'You're a nutter.' He was worried about the way Junior was going off the rails.

'It got me out of the school, but it wasn't really funny 'cos my mum was bawling her eyes out,' Junior said. 'I mean, I know she cares about me, James, but I wish she'd leave me alone. I'm never gonna be the little lawyer that she wants me to be. I ended up promising that I was going to knuckle down at school and try getting my GCSEs.'

'So she was OK after that?'

'She was better, but she's not a Muppet. Just because I'm in school today doesn't mean that I'll be in school tomorrow . . . And you know what I was talking about the other night?'

'What?' James said, though he knew and he'd been dreading it.

'I've got a job,' Junior said. 'There's a kid in my tutor group called Alom. His parents run some chicken-shit travel agency in town. They've got a *bureau de change* in there as well and there's always cash in the safe because they do money transfers. You know, like people sending money home to their relatives abroad and that?'

'And what do *you* know about cracking safes?' James asked cynically.

'Not a sausage, but I do know how to stick a gun to someone's temple and say, *Open the safe or I'm gonna decorate the wall with your brains.*'

As Junior said this he unzipped his school pack, revealing a gun. James eyed the rough metal seams, and noticed that the handle was made out of shiny plastic instead of wood.

'That's *so* fake,' James said. 'It looks like an Airfix kit.'

'It's a blank firing replica,' Junior said. 'But it's been drilled out to fire real ammunition.'

Britain has some of the tightest gun controls in the world. These crudely converted weapons were common, but James wasn't impressed.

'I wouldn't touch one of those,' he warned. 'You pull the trigger and it's as likely to explode in your hand as fire a bullet.'

'But the dude's not gonna *know* that when I stick it in his face, is he? And besides, you've got that little gun. That's a quality piece.'

'When are you gonna do it?' James asked, as they walked past a huge crowd of kids at a bus stop.

'I cased the joint last night. They open early and shut late.'

James shook his head. 'Junior, you don't case a joint in *one* night. Me and Bruce spent three weeks looking at that hard front before Sasha moved on it.'

'It's one old Indian dude,' Junior said, sounding narked. 'He carries the key to the safe with a big bunch of other keys on his belt. We get up early tomorrow morning. We grab him just as he opens, he pulls out the money and we're out with five grand in under five minutes.'

'Sorry mate, but I don't like it,' James said.

'What!' Junior gasped. 'This is a *sweet* job, James. I've had my eye on it for a while.'

'Sasha won't—'

Junior cut him off. 'Don't mention that man's name, OK? Maybe *you're* raking it in, but I've got six quid and an HMV voucher my mum gave me for Easter; and that's no exaggeration.'

James decided to play for time. 'I'm not saying no, but remember what I said about getting some money together and setting up our own crew properly? I can lend you a few hundred to tide you over until then.'

'I'm sick of hand-outs,' Junior yelled. 'All my life I've been Keith Moore's son, or I've had my mum on my back, or Sasha looking out for me. I want my own action. I can rob the travel agent tomorrow. Then I'll use the money to buy some coke and grass and I can sell it around at school. The sixth formers snort and smoke like there's no tomorrow, but they're too scared to approach a dealer on the street so they'll always pay over the odds. Give it a month and we could have twenty or thirty grand, fit girls on our arms and all the white powder we can stick up our noses.'

James shrugged. 'It just isn't the right time for me, Junior.'

'You know what your problem is?' Junior sneered. 'You're chicken.'

James tutted. 'Yeah I'm chicken. I just helped take down a hard front for Sasha. That's how chicken I am.'

'There you go again,' Junior shouted. 'Sasha, Sasha, Sasha. Stick with him then, arsehole. I planned the travel agent as a one-man job anyway, so I'm going in tomorrow whether you and your boyfriend like it or not.'

'Junior, calm down,' James said, as he tried to grab Junior's arm. 'There's kids everywhere.'

But Junior shoved James away. 'Get your hands *off* me. You're treating me like a baby, same as everyone else.'

'Come on, mate,' James said.

Junior's push almost knocked him into a Year-Eight kid walking behind them.

By the time James had regained his footing and told the kid he was sorry, Junior was storming down the road. James knew there was no point going after him.

*

Bruce was lying on his bed at the Zoo when Chloe called.

'The meeting went really well,' she said. 'Simeon's going to set up a deal for next Wednesday. The ethics committee aren't gonna be happy when they hear about the hard front, so this is going to be our only shot at taking down Major Dee and Sasha before we're all hauled back to campus.'

'At least we've got a chance,' Bruce said hopefully.

'Simeon *is* making all the right noises, but he's hardly what I'd call trustworthy and we'll have to keep our eyes on him. I want you and James to stick as close to Sasha as you can. He seems pleased with you boys, so hopefully he'll drop some hints at the planning stage. The police have also been doing surveillance on Sasha, but so far they've got nothing except blurry photos and I wouldn't hold out much hope of things improving.'

'It's a small crew,' Bruce said. 'So even if we're not involved in the planning, Sasha's bound to want us involved in the robbery.'

'Hopefully so,' Chloe said. 'I'm going to ask Michael to do exactly the same for Major Dee's side of the operation. I'm liaising with Chief Inspector Rush on the anti-gang taskforce, but he's concerned that his unit isn't a hundred per cent leak free, so he's getting experts in from another force to run the surveillance operation. The local coppers won't be told what's going on until shortly before they have to move in and make arrests.'

'I'll make sure James is in the loop,' Bruce said.

'Where's he disappeared to?'

'He went to meet Junior,' Bruce said, as he glanced at the watch resting on his bedside table. 'I thought they'd go into town or something, but James called to say that he was coming back here, so I expect we'll head over to Sasha's later on.'

'OK, keep in touch,' Chloe said.

Bruce put his phone down and headed off to the toilet for a pee. James was in the bedroom when he got back and he wasn't happy.

'Junior's *such* a moron,' James yelled furiously, as he pulled his top off and flung it at his bed.

'What's he done?'

'He's got a crappy converted pistol and he's planning to rob some travel agent first thing tomorrow morning. I did everything I could to talk him out of it, but he won't listen.'

Bruce shrugged. 'He's a spoilt brat. What did you expect?'

James looked surprised. 'I thought you said he was OK.'

'Sure, he's a good laugh. But he's wasted all the time and it's pretty clear to anyone with a couple of brain cells that his career path is of the behind-bars variety.'

James made a throttling gesture with his hands. 'I'd love to slap some sense into him.'

'What did Chloe say when you told her?' Bruce asked.

'Nothing. I haven't told her.'

'Right, of course,' Bruce nodded, 'she would have been engaged 'cos she's been on the phone to me.'

'I haven't *tried* to tell her, Bruce. I don't plan to either.'

'What?' Bruce said, raising his eyebrows. 'If it's just a stick-up they can make it look like the cops happened to be walking by so that our cover doesn't get blown.'

'But I don't want Junior to get sent down,' James said, sitting on the edge of his bed and grinding his palms against his cheeks. 'I know he's a basket case, but I happen to like the guy and I don't want to be responsible.'

'And what if he loses his rag and shoots someone in the head?' Bruce asked. 'Do you want that one on your conscience?'

'I . . .' James mumbled, contorting his arms and hating the fact that he was in the wrong. 'This is all my fault. It was me winding him up about the money that made him storm out of Sasha's gaff the other night.'

'Give over, James,' Bruce said. 'You didn't help, but he was heading for trouble before you got anywhere near him.'

'I really like Junior. He's not, like, just someone on a mission.'

Bruce smiled. 'You care because he's *you*, James.'

'What are you on about?'

'Before you came to CHERUB your mum was a crook, just like Junior's dad. You were spoiled and you'd been in trouble with the police, like Junior. You're both bright but lazy. You've both got a quick temper. Junior is exactly what you would have become if you hadn't joined CHERUB and been knocked into shape.'

James could see some truth in this, but he wasn't going to admit that Bruce was right. 'That's so dumb,' he sneered. 'Why can't I just like the guy?'

'James, at least if he gets picked up tomorrow he's still only fifteen. It's armed robbery and he's already on parole so they'll hammer him, but he'll only get five or six years because he's not an adult. By the time he gets out he'll be close to getting his trust-fund money and hopefully he'll settle down.'

'This is *such* crap,' James moaned, screwing up his face as he reached into his tracksuit bottoms and grabbed his mobile to call Chloe. 'I can't believe I've got to grass him up . . .'

41. JUNIOR

Junior got up at 7:30 a.m. and felt queasy as he showered in his en-suite bathroom. He put on his uniform because he wanted his mum to think that he was going to school, but he packed trainers, gloves and a blue Adidas tracksuit on top of the gun in his school bag.

Part of Junior wanted to back out, but that's what everyone would expect and he was determined to prove he was his own man. Plus, he'd always dreamed of having his own crew and he reckoned James would come around to his way of thinking once he'd made some money.

Junior's twin, April, sat at the dining table downstairs in her blue jumper and white school tights. She had her science books spread out and seemed to have brain ache as she stared at her chemistry textbook.

'It's a miracle,' April grinned, glancing at her watch as her brother stepped into the kitchen. 'Did you wet the bed or something?'

'Nah,' Junior shrugged. 'I thought I might get in early and kick a ball around with the lads before class.'

In fact, the combo of a stretch in young offenders and

major-league truancy meant that Junior hardly knew anyone at his school; but April didn't know that.

'I really hope you keep your promise to Mum this time,' April said. 'You're no genius, but you're not thick either. I know you're behind with your GCSE work, but if you're serious about going back to school, I could help you to catch up over the summer holidays. Or maybe Mum could pay for a tutor . . .'

'Yeah maybe,' Junior said, dreading the thought of a summer tutor as he pushed a couple of white slices into the toaster. 'What are you swotting for?'

'Chemistry mock,' April said.

'I wish you were more of a laugh like in the old days,' Junior said. 'Before Dad went to prison we went to youth club together and had all the same mates and everything. Now you hang with boffins.'

April laughed. 'My mates are the normal ones, Junior. They go to school, they do their homework and have a laugh at the weekend. No snorting coke, no robbery and nobody getting locked up for six months . . .'

'Stiffs,' Junior snorted. Then he mocked his sister's voice: *'Yeah, and Sharon only got sixty-two per cent in her French and it served her right 'cos she totally sucks up to Miss LeFromage. I really hope Matt's at the party on Saturday because he makes my knickers wet every time he walks in the room. OOOOOOOH!'*

April tutted. 'Can't you shut up? I'm revising.'

'It's only a mock.'

April looked up from her books and eyed her brother closely. 'What's going on, Junior?'

He feigned innocence. 'What makes you think I'm up to anything?'

'Twin telepathy,' April said. 'You're fidgeting, your head's all sweaty and you've started on me for no reason. Tell us where you're going.'

'Nowhere . . . well, except school.'

'You should stop hanging around with that idiot James Beckett,' April said. 'He's bad news.'

'He's a mate,' Junior shrugged.

'He's a *complete* tosser.'

'You're only saying that because you had a big thing for him and he dumped you.'

April shook her head. 'That was three years ago. I had a crush, but I was twelve and now I'm totally over it. Can't you settle down? Don't you think that you've put Mum through enough already?'

Junior's toast popped up and he sauntered off to butter it without answering the question.

'I've gotta catch my bus,' April said, checking her watch as she gathered her books into her backpack. 'I wish you'd sort yourself out. You drive me up the pole, but you're still my twin and I care about you.'

'I care about you too,' Junior said, as he bit the first corner off his toast. 'Don't worry about me, I'll see you tonight.'

Junior watched as April went out the garden door and crunched across the gravel to the street. The twins were past the age where they needed help getting ready for school, and unless Julie Moore had an early tennis lesson she usually stayed in bed until they were out of the way.

After he'd finished his toast, Junior walked into the hall

and checked that his mum was watching GMTV upstairs before cutting into the living-room. He didn't want to risk bumping into his sister at the bus stop, so he called the mini-cab office at the end of the road and arranged to be picked up on the corner in ten minutes' time. Then he ripped off his school tie and started changing into his tracksuit and trainers.

*

Indian Sun was a thriving business in a side street a couple of hundred metres from Luton's main shopping area. The lettering in the windows offered package tours to Goa from £499, but the shop mainly served the area's large Asian population, with everything from cheap calling cards to money transfers and airline tickets.

Junior thought Indian Sun was a good target because of two things he'd learned from the Mad Dogs. Firstly, places that exchange and transfer money usually have larger sums of cash on hand than banks, but are often family businesses with much lower levels of security. Secondly, for a variety of religious and cultural reasons people from Asian backgrounds are less likely to use credit cards and often purchase large items with cash. This trait means businesses with lots of Asian customers are targeted by armed robbers.

Junior didn't want his driver to identify him after the robbery, so he got the cab to drop him a couple of kilometres from Indian Sun. He walked the rest of the way, heading down the high street in sunglasses and a baseball cap, keeping his head down to avoid being picked up by security cameras. It was still before nine and all the shops had their shutters down.

He was shaking as he turned into the side street, surprised that it was quite lively. Four women with too much make-up on stood huddled in the staff entrance of a department store. The newsagents had a stream of customers, as did the Bagel Basket directly opposite Indian Sun.

The travel agency was also open, its metal sign with a list of exchange rates standing on the pavement, but only one of its three white shutters had been opened. A shudder ripped through Junior as soon as he eyed the target. He patted his hand against his body for a reassuring feel of the gun strapped to his side.

Junior's mind was going at warp speed and he kept thinking about April and his mum as he pulled on a pair of leather gloves; but he was confident about pulling the raid off. Sasha had always protected Junior from actually being involved in robberies committed by the Mad Dogs, but he'd heard Wheels and the rest of the crew talking about crimes they'd committed and their constant bickering over the best ways of doing stuff.

While opinions differed on the details, everyone agreed the basic: case the joint, use overwhelming force, be quick, don't leave forensic evidence, wear bland clothes, cover your face so that you don't get picked up on CCTV cameras and mix it up so that the police can never predict what you'll do next.

There are no certainties when people go around with guns and almost everyone's luck runs out, but when crooks stick to the rules, their chances of getting caught on any individual robbery are slim.

An electric chime startled Junior as he stepped through

the agency door. As expected, the shop had been unlocked by Praful Patel, an elderly man who'd set up Indian Sun more than twenty years earlier. The giant bunch of keys was hooked to his belt loop with a spring-loaded clip.

The only trouble was, there were two tough-looking dudes sitting across the desk from him. The stocky men looked like they hailed from the Balkans and the dried-out mud on their boots suggested that they were builders. A small bunch of ten- and twenty-pound notes sat on the desk and Praful Patel was patiently filling out a three-part counterfoil with the brightly coloured logo of a wire transfer agency at the top.

'The fee is five pounds plus two per cent,' Praful explained, as he carefully tore the bottom sheet off the form. 'Your wife must give the password to collect the money at the other end.'

The men looked thuggish, and with their wages piled up on the desk, Junior reckoned it best to let them go before pulling the gun. Waiting was tricky because there was always a chance someone else might walk in, but he felt that his only option was to head for the rack of brochures and pretend to browse.

It felt longer, but within two minutes the men were on their way out of the door, moving briskly to their cash-in-hand labouring jobs at a hotel under construction behind the department store.

'Can I help you, young man?' Praful said, acutely aware that people Junior's age don't have much call for travel agents.

'Open the safe,' Junior ordered, backing up to the door and sliding the latch across as he whipped out the gun.

Praful raised his hands warily. 'I don't keep large sums here,' he warned. 'I've been robbed too often.'

Junior unzipped his school bag and dumped it on the floor. 'I didn't ask for your bloody life story,' he snarled, as he swept the cash on the desk into his bag. 'Open the safe and give me what you've got.'

The elderly man had back trouble and groaned as he went down on one knee to put the key into the door of the safe. Junior was disappointed as it swung open: there was a whole bunch of aeroplane tickets in envelopes and the cash drawer from a till containing about £100 in British currency and small bundles of euros, US dollars and rupees.

Junior had been expecting more. 'Where do you keep the rest?' he asked bitterly.

'There is no rest,' Praful said, as he picked out the money and placed it in the bag.

'Bullcrap. I've seen people come in here and change five hundred pounds at a time.'

'Two-hour service,' Praful said, pointing at a sign on the wall that said: *For security reasons, we now require two hours' notice for all currency exchanges of more than £150. Please call ahead!*

'Give me a bloody break,' Junior moaned. 'Where's the rest of the money?'

'Off premises,' Praful said. 'This is the third robbery. The last two times I lost many thousands of pounds. Now I can't get insurance.'

Junior tried to figure how the system might work. The money was probably stored at Praful's home, or perhaps the safe was a red herring and the money was stored elsewhere on the premises.

Junior reckoned there might be a way of getting it, but he'd heard Wheels and the Mad Dogs say that hanging around a crime scene was the most dangerous thing you could do. And maybe he hadn't made the thousands of pounds he'd hoped for, but he reckoned that the bundles of foreign currency would be into four figures when he exchanged them, which was enough to make the next couple of months bearable.

Junior grabbed his school bag off the carpet tiles and pushed the gun back inside his tracksuit as he stepped out of the door. He was appalled to see a silver BMW police cruiser parked directly across the narrow street, with two cops inside munching on breakfast bagels.

Junior choked as he heard Praful locking the shop door to stop him going back inside. As he began to walk, an alarm went off inside Indian Sun. He sped up, hoping that the cops wouldn't link him to the bell, but the cop on the driver's side yelled out and he started to run.

It was only a hundred metres to the pedestrianised high street, but the removable bollard that gave access to delivery vans was down and the cruiser went after him. Junior ran flat out past a couple of shops, looking for an alleyway, as a PA announcement ripped out of the tannoy on top of the car.

'Stop running and raise your hands. Repeat, stop running and raise your hands.'

Junior couldn't see the cops backing off unless he aimed the gun at them. He noticed a small seating area up ahead and sent a crowd of pigeons fluttering as he charged between two rows of benches, then ducked behind a tall concrete planter.

'Back off,' he shouted, waving the gun in the air as a police motorcycle rolled out of a side street behind him and one of the officers stepped out of the car.

'Put the gun down, son,' the cop said. 'You'll only make things worse for yourself.'

As Junior pointed the gun at the cop, the motorbike growled towards him.

'Stay *back*,' Junior shouted.

He thought about shooting the motorcyclist and running on, but got distracted by another cruiser pulling into the street behind the first. It came up on the opposite side of the benches at speed and braked to a halt less than thirty metres away.

Two cops jumped out of the back and took cover. Both men wore armoured helmets and flak jackets.

'Put the gun down,' the driver of the armed response unit shouted over his tannoy, as he cruised forward at walking pace with the two armed officers creeping behind the vehicle.

Junior shook as the gun wavered hopelessly above his head. He had enough sense to know he wasn't going to outrun two cars and a motorbike. He considered taking a shot, but couldn't help thinking that the police marksmen were more likely to shoot him than he was to shoot them with his converted piece of junk.

That left two options: put the gun down and get busted or turn the gun on himself. And suicide seemed fleetingly attractive as he imagined his mum's reaction to him getting busted again and the way Sasha's crew would piss themselves laughing when they found out he'd been caught. Maybe the reason they'd all treated him like a baby was because that's exactly what he was . . .

'Put it down son,' the cop who'd stepped out of the first car said. 'You're not old enough to die.'

And maybe it was just a line he'd been taught at police training college, but something in the voice was sincere enough to calm Junior down. He lowered his arm before throwing the gun into the bushes and standing up slowly with his hands above his head.

'Come on then, you slags,' Junior said, as he fought off tears. 'Put me back where I belong.'

42. RUSH

Chief Inspector Mark Rush was in charge of the anti-gang taskforce. He was the only officer within the Bedfordshire force who knew about the CHERUB operation and had met regularly with Chloe and Maureen since the mission began four months earlier. He'd watched the CHERUB agents on surveillance operations and been involved in Michael's arrest and questioning after the death of Owen Campbell-Moore, but he'd never spoken to any of the teenagers directly.

Now that the mission was coming to its close, Inspector Rush asked to meet the agents – including Gabrielle – so that he could say thanks and brief them on the final take-down. Chloe agreed, but to minimise the chances of everyone being seen together, she set up the meeting in the private function room of an Italian restaurant on the outskirts of London, half an hour from Luton.

Five days had passed since Junior got busted and James was still beating himself up about it. He was also missing Dana and weighed down with guilt about sleeping with Lois. His worst moment had been in Sasha's basement the evening after Junior got nabbed, with the entire Mad Dogs crew re-enacting Junior's *I'm not a baby* speech and laughing about his rotten luck. Still, the plush restaurant cheered James up and the chubby Chief Inspector arrived bearing gifts.

'Haven't got kids,' he explained, as he pulled four envelopes out of his bomber jacket. 'I've got no idea what you'd like so I copped out and got gift vouchers. You can get games, books or whatever.'

James smiled as he opened his envelope and joined in the round of thanks as the inspector sat down and opened a menu.

'Did you get here all right?' Chloe asked.

'No probs,' the inspector said. He looked at Gabrielle. 'How are you feeling now? I lost a couple of nights' sleep over you.'

'Not bad,' Gabrielle smiled. 'I had a hospital appointment yesterday. The doctor seemed happy with the way everything's healing. I've been doing some brisk walking on campus to help get my strength back, but I still get sore if I try anything too vigorous.'

'Have you got any good scars?' Bruce asked.

'More than you,' Gabrielle shot back. 'I'm visiting a cosmetic surgeon who's gonna see if there's anything they can do to cover the scars. Like, skin grafts or something.'

'I reckon they should leave them alone,' Michael said, as he smiled at his girlfriend. 'They're part of you now.'

'Give us a look then,' Bruce said.

Gabrielle stood and gathered up her waist-hugging T-shirt, revealing the three pink scars across her belly, each one crisscrossed with faint stitch marks. Then she twirled to show the puncture mark in her back.

'I thought you only got stabbed twice,' James said, confused.

'They had to make extra incisions when they tied all of her tubes back together,' Michael said. He took Gabrielle's hand and kissed her neck as she sat down. 'You're the most beautiful girl in the world,' he said softly.

'I've got a massive scar on my leg,' Bruce said, as he started pulling up the leg of his tracksuit bottoms.

'Put it away,' Chloe said firmly. 'We're here for a relaxing meal and a briefing on tomorrow's operation. I don't want to see any more scars.'

'That's good,' Inspector Rush grinned. ' 'Cos the only one I've got is on my bum.'

The inspector was trying too hard to ingratiate himself with the kids and his joke went flat, but the waitress came in to break the awkward silence. James eyed her tight black trousers as she took orders and gathered up menus.

'So, Inspector,' Chloe said as the waitress stepped out, 'perhaps you can give us a run-down on what's happening tomorrow.'

'I'm in my civvies so call me Mark,' the inspector asked. 'In essence, the plan is straightforward. Simeon Bentine has revealed that Major Dee gets a regular shipment of cocaine hidden inside drums of cooking oil that are shipped from the USA by container.'

'I thought Dee's contacts were in Jamaica,' James said.

'They are,' Chloe explained. 'We're not sure exactly how the smuggling operation works. But customs are hot on shipments from the Caribbean, whereas canned goods from the USA are much less likely to be searched. The cocaine is probably brought on board the container ship in a small boat mid-Atlantic. Then they throw the real drums of cooking oil over the side and replace them with drums partially filled with cocaine.'

'From a technical point of view it's pretty clever,' Maureen added. 'The tins are airtight so there's no way anything can be picked up by sniffer dogs or electronic systems. A container filled with metal cans is also very difficult to image electronically and the only way for customs to inspect what's inside a drum is to break the seal, which will spoil the produce.'

'It's the kind of racket that you'll only ever stop by getting inside information,' the inspector said. 'So even if we fail to nab our major suspects tomorrow, we'll still seriously degrade their ability to bring cocaine into this country.

'Officers from the Leicestershire force have already installed surveillance equipment in the warehouse where the deal is going down. But they had to tread carefully because Sasha Thompson and his boys have also been staking the joint out.'

'That's good though,' Michael said. 'It means they're definitely planning to show.'

The inspector continued. 'All being well, Simeon reckons the container will land at Dover around midnight tonight. It'll be picked up on a truck and driven to the warehouse, for a meeting between the smugglers and Major Dee's crew. The container ports get congested, so they could arrive at the warehouse any time between nine and eleven tomorrow morning.'

'Are the smugglers Slasher Boys?' James asked.

'They're not part of Major Dee's crew, but they have links with his associates in Jamaica.'

'Simeon says it's cash on delivery,' Maureen noted, 'so they're certainly not *that* close.'

'Once the container's delivered, it will take ten to fifteen minutes to unload the drums containing the drugs,' the inspector said. 'The drums that are removed will be replaced with real drums of cooking oil and the truck driver will take the container on to its destination.'

'And that's when Sasha Thompson makes his move,' Bruce said.

'Exactly,' the inspector nodded. 'Sasha doesn't have the time or manpower to go through the whole container trying to find the drugs; but he's going to want to get his hands on the drugs *and* the money. That means the Mad Dogs have to make their move in the short window after the drugs have been separated from the container cargo, but before the smugglers drive off with their money.

'But of course, as Simeon has also tipped Major Dee off about the robbery, this is going to be the point where all hell breaks loose. We're talking about two highly armed gangs going into an all-out battle. I'm guessing a dozen men on the Mad Dogs' side – all with guns – and probably double that number of Slasher Boys.'

'Total carnage,' Bruce gloated, clearly relishing the prospect.

But Chloe wasn't smiling. 'I don't like that attitude, Bruce. More than twenty people have died; Gabrielle was almost one of them. You four have got to make sure you're *not* inside that warehouse when the shooting starts.'

'We're going to have sixty-two firearms officers on the

scene including several we've seconded from London,' the inspector said. 'But it's too risky to send officers into the warehouse against more than thirty criminals armed with automatic and semi-automatic weapons. If we can safely make arrests at the scene we will, but we don't want to end up with a siege on our hands, so we'll be using a soft cordon.

'Some suspects will get out of the warehouse and be tracked by helicopter surveillance and vehicle pursuit teams. We have addresses for most gang members and we'll be swooping on any that make it home. Our target is to arrest *every* Mad Dog and Slasher Boy that comes within a kilometre of that warehouse, without any officers getting hurt.

'We've set up two special operations rooms to charge and question members from both gangs. I've also got two major-crime-scene forensic units from the smoke who are going to seal the area tight and pick up every footprint, fingerprint and DNA speck in and around that warehouse. I want Major Dee and Sasha Thompson behind bars and their respective gangs completely crushed.'

'Sounds good,' Gabrielle smiled.

'So where do we fit in?' James asked.

'Information,' Inspector Rush said. 'We obviously don't want you getting hurt, but you three boys are the only reliable people we have inside the gangs.'

'*If* we're inside,' Bruce said. 'Sasha's hardly spoken to me and James in the last week. I've asked if he's going to put more work our way and he keeps brushing us off.'

'He's probably been busy organising the robbery,' Chloe said. 'The Mad Dogs are a small crew; I don't see how they can ignore you two after you did so well with the hard front.'

'I'm definitely OK,' Michael said. 'Major Dee's already told me we're going out to nail Sasha tomorrow. He wants me on the roof of the warehouse keeping look-out. I can either hunker down, or sneak off before it turns nasty.'

'Make sure you do,' Maureen said.

'Assuming that we do get invited to the party, what kind of information are you looking for?' James asked.

'I need you boys to tell me how many people Sasha's bringing, how many cars, what weapons they're using. The Mad Dogs usually communicate with walkie-talkies. If you can tell us what frequency they're transmitting on, we can earwig everything they do and record it to use as evidence.'

'I'll see what I can do,' James said.

'But it won't be easy,' Bruce added. 'I mean, we might be able to send a few sneaky text messages or a quick call from a bathroom, but we can't be having ten-minute phone conversations about everything that's going on.'

'Dialling and connection makes phones slow,' Chloe said. 'I've got some miniature transceivers coming down from campus. They're disguised as sticking plasters. They're voice-activated, so you just stick one on your wrist and it picks up your voice if you push down and speak within ten centimetres of the pad. They're low power, so the signal range is only about a kilometre, but Maureen and I will be close to the warehouse.'

'It'll look dodgy if me and James have both suddenly got plasters though,' Bruce noted.

'It's not a problem,' Gabrielle said. 'I've used them on another mission. You can stick them on clothes, like inside your lapel or the cuff of a shirt. Only thing is, they're much stickier than real plasters so don't put them anywhere hairy or you'll know all about it when you rip them off.'

*

Wheels called James up as Chloe drove them back from the restaurant.

'Where are you?' Wheels asked.

'London,' James lied, giving the first excuse for being out of town that came into his head and then scrambling to justify it. 'Me and Bruce got fed up hanging around the Zoo and decided to splash some of the cash we made in the West End.'

'Shit,' Wheels said. 'Can you get back here? Sasha's got some business for you tomorrow.'

'Excellent,' James said. 'What are we talking about?'

'He's keeping it close,' Wheels said. 'But he's been working his guts out. He's got Savvas working on three vans and he's called in the Kruger brothers. You wouldn't know them because they're semi-retired, but they've just flown in which can only mean something *massive* is going down.'

'Any idea how much we're talking about?'

'Five grand apiece for you and Bruce, more if it goes well. But we need you back here ASAP. Sasha wants you both to have passport photos taken.'

'What for?'

'No idea, James. Sasha's giving us all different jobs and keeping everything under his hat. Right now I'm heading over to pick up a fast motor. You'd better get the first train back to Luton. Both of you get your pictures taken in the photo booth and I'll send someone over to pick them up.

You should be able to get a train from Kings Cross and be there by half two.'

'Sounds OK. What—' But the other end of his call had gone dead. James pocketed his phone and turned to Chloe. 'You'll have to drop us at a station somewhere, so it looks like we're coming back from London.'

Bruce tutted. 'We're only a few miles out of town, you knob. Why did you say London?'

'Because he put me on the spot,' James said irritably. 'And he wants our photos taken. How weird is that?'

Chloe rolled out her bottom lip. 'Sounds odd. You must be going in under disguise, wearing ID badges or something.'

'And Wheels mentioned a name I haven't heard before: the Kruger brothers. Does it mean anything to you? Oh, and he said Savvas was preparing three vans and Wheels was picking up a fast motor. In my book, that means he's going to be sending in more men than we were expecting.'

'That's good,' Bruce said. 'More crooks to catch.'

Chloe nodded. 'Headache for Inspector Rush though. We'd better tell him he needs more manpower.'

43. POPS

The Zoo was never lively at 7:30 in the morning. James, Bruce and Michael were heading to the same place at the same time, so it was hardly surprising that they ended up at adjacent tables in the dining-room. They couldn't act too close in public, but they exchanged a few taut words before Michael headed upstairs to don his protective clothing.

James was tense and only managed half of his Cocoa Pops and a small banana. On the other hand, Bruce had wolfed down scrambled egg, kippers and three slices of bread.

'You never get nervous,' James said, as the two boys headed through the lounge and out of the front door.

'I've trained myself to focus,' Bruce replied. 'Breathing, concentration and the fact that nothing gets me going like the prospect of a monumental punch-up.'

James managed to smile, but as they headed down the street he couldn't help wondering if Bruce's love of violence didn't indicate something not quite right in his head.

The weather had turned warm and Sasha told the boys they'd have an opportunity to change before the raid, so they carried their body armour and guns inside backpacks.

'Nice motor,' Bruce grinned, when he saw Wheels waiting for them in the driver's seat of a BMW M5. 'Bit fancier than the Astra.'

The front passenger seat was taken up by a man with a face like thousand-year-old limestone. James and Bruce squeezed into the back alongside his equally fearsome-looking mate.

'James, Bruce, these are the Kruger brothers,' Wheels said. 'Tony and Tim, this is James and Bruce.'

'Morning,' James said, as he slammed the car door.

Chloe had run the Krugers on the police computer and pulled up a long list of suspected armed robberies, but no convictions apart from a couple of stretches in youth custody back in the 1980s. It seemed strange that two brothers whose careers had been based around carefully planned robberies were coming to help Sasha take down Major Dee, but James reckoned it made sense when he saw them up close: out of all the hard men he'd ever met, these two were the ones James would have wanted on his side in a rumble.

'Sasha speaks highly of you boys,' Tim Kruger said, as he reached across the back seat to shake hands.

His voice was gravel and he clamped James' hand so tight that it felt like he was going to crush bone, but Bruce took his turn as a challenge and squeezed back. James was in the middle with the two arms stretched across his lap and Bruce's bony wrist apparently being crushed by a fist the size of a ham. After ten tense seconds the handshake broke and Tim Kruger exploded in a volcanic laugh which sent shockwaves through James' body.

'Tough little bugger this one,' Tim roared approvingly.

'Not much meat but there's a grip like a vice on him.'

They drove on for fifteen minutes, passing through the Thornton Estate where James had lived on his first mission in the area. He felt a slight kick of nostalgia as they skimmed past shabby houses and football pitches that evoked memories of long forgotten kickabouts, but they drove on through the back of the estate into an area of industrial units that bordered on to the high-fenced compound around Luton airport.

A 737 passed over seconds after leaving the runway, making a roar that shook the entire car. After a few more seconds, Wheels turned off the road into the car park surrounding a branch of Sofa World. It still had *Closing Down* and *Last Day 75% Off Everything* banners draped on the exterior.

He slowed to a crawl as he cut across the empty parking bays and under a half opened metal shutter, which was immediately pulled down by two members of Sasha's crew dressed in yellow overalls.

James and Bruce were baffled as they entered the cavernous space, which still had a scattering of tatty shop fittings and was marked out with aisles and carpeted areas for displaying soft furniture.

Half a dozen Mad Dogs sat on stained and broken sofas that even the final day's *Discount Madness* hadn't shifted, drinking tea and waiting for something to kick off. Two black Mercedes vans and the cab of an articulated truck were parked on the carpet. The vans were freshly painted with the logo of an airport catering company stencilled on the side, while the truck looked like something out of a sci-fi movie, with a thick sheet of Plexiglas bolted over the windscreen and a battering ram made from two huge H-bar girders welded to the front.

James was last out of the car and he couldn't help thinking that something was wrong. The Krugers, the passport photographs and the fact that the airport was miles from where Major Dee was doing his drug deal had already made James wonder if things were going according to plan, but the set-up inside Sofa World sent him into a full-on panic.

'You've all made it,' Sasha said happily, as he ran out of an office and – clearly knowing better than to try a handshake – gave Tim and Tony Kruger friendly thumps on the shoulder. 'It's all come together so well, the gods must be smiling on us.'

'Is Savvas back from the other place?' Wheels asked.

Sasha nodded. 'He's wired up enough sticks of gelignite to blow the joint sky high,' he grinned. 'Major Dee isn't gonna have a clue.'

'What about the money?'

'I just got the call,' Sasha said. 'The money's on board and the plane should be taking off from Schipol any minute now.'

'Ahem,' Bruce said, clearing his throat. 'Me and James are putting our butts on the line the same as everyone else. Is anyone gonna tell us what's going on?'

*

Over the other side of town, Major Dee had a spring in his step and the scent of Sasha Thompson's blood. He had six men inside the small warehouse to do the drug deal. Thirty more were discreetely parked in the surrounding streets, along with specially invited guests from a London-based crew Sasha had ripped off the previous year and some men from Salford, whose wounds were fresher.

Doubting that the Mad Dogs could muster more than twenty men, Major Dee had adopted a simple strategy. After securing his supply of drugs from the smugglers, he'd let the Mad Dogs enter the warehouse and try to steal them. But when they tried to leave, they'd find the building surrounded by an armed posse outnumbering them by at least three to one. It would be a slaughter.

Michael arrived at a meeting point in a side street ten minutes from the industrial estate where the deal would take place, then walked to the warehouse and moved quickly up a fifteen-metre access ladder built on to the back. The roof was made from corrugated metal that clanked underfoot. It felt warm on his hands as he laid in front of a ventilation shaft.

He pulled a Philips screwdriver out of his pocket and used it to undo a holding bracket at one end of a moss-covered slat. Once it grated free, he pushed his head through the gap and stared at the warehouse below. Major Dee didn't use walkie-talkies, so his final step was to sit up and make sure his mobile had a signal.

Michael called Major Dee to say he was in place, then sent Gabrielle an *I LOVE U* text as he looked up at the bright morning sun. It only took her a few seconds to text back:

KEEP SAFE LUV U2

*

James had all of his protective gear under a tracksuit Sasha had brought for him. They'd taken everyone's mobiles because cops can use them to trace your location, but he still had the transceiver disguised as a sticking plaster stuck on his neck.

'Are you gonna be in there all day?' James yelled, as he thumped on the door of the staff toilet near the entrance to Sofa World.

'Takes as long as it takes,' Savvas said. 'And you're not gonna want to come in here after I've finished.'

'But I'm busting,' James moaned.

'Go out around the back and pee against the wall.'

'Are we allowed out?'

'Just tell Riggsy that I said it was an emergency.'

Riggsy was one of the older Mad Dogs. He was a serious poker player who hated it when the youngsters got rowdy in Sasha's basement.

'Where'd you think you're going?' he asked, cutting James off has he headed for a fire door.

'Savvas said it was OK,' James said. 'He's been in the bog for about twenty minutes.'

Riggsy found this hilarious and he yelled at the men sitting on the sofas: 'Here, the boy says Savvas is back on the shitter again!'

Everyone cracked up, but James was baffled and Riggsy had to explain.

'Savvas always gets the squirts when he's nervous about a big operation. Now go out and have your piss, but make it quick because we're on the move the second Sasha gives the word.'

James headed through the fire door and out on to a narrow section of concrete. There was only a wire fence between himself and the busy car park of the DIY store next door, so he jogged to the rear of the building and stood facing the wall.

'Chloe,' he whispered, as he pressed a thumb on the transceiver.

The receiver was designed so that it never blurted out a message at an inappropriate moment. The tiny speaker only worked when he pressed the plaster down with his thumb.

'Chloe,' James repeated, as he pulled down the front of his tracksuit bottoms and tried to extract his penis from inside his body armour. He didn't really need to go, but he had to make a puddle or the others might get suspicious.

'James? James, I can barely hear,' Chloe answered, before the signal disintegrated into a mass of digital noise. 'Where are you? I got stuck in traffic and then we lost both of your mobile signals.'

'Sofa World, out near the airport,' he whispered. 'Listen, I've only got a few seconds. We're in *deep* doo-doo. Sasha's flipped this whole thing on its head. Apparently untold valuable cargo goes through Luton airport every day and the Krugers have been after robbing it for years. Sasha knows all about the warehouse and we're going into the airport while the cops have their hands full on the other side of town.

'He's got some massive battering ram and I've been given plane tickets and a false passport. That's what the photos were for. I don't know all the details, but we're robbing cash from a flight that left Holland about forty minutes ago . . . Oh, and Wheels mentioned Major Dee and sticks of gelignite in the same breath. I reckon they're planning to blow up the warehouse. You'd better get Michael out of there.'

James stopped talking, partly because he was short of breath, and partly because he had to scramble backwards as a gust of wind blew his pee towards his trouser leg.

'Shit,' he gasped, as he shook himself off and looked at a big wet streak down his tracksuit. It was embarrassing, but it wasn't the most important thing in his life at that moment. He kept his thumb pressed down on the plaster, but Chloe didn't respond.

'Chloe,' he hissed. 'Chloe, did you hear *any* of what I just said?'

There was no response. A second later Wheels came around the corner.

'It's time, James,' he yelled. 'I've got to drive you to the airport.'

44. RIPPLE

The container truck reversed into the warehouse at 9:37 a.m. The driver was alone and didn't appear to be armed, which was no surprise because Simeon had said that the handover was routine.

Michael peered through the roof into the bare concrete space as the container doors swung open. The driver worked alongside three of the Slasher Boys, climbing into the container and rolling each heavy drum of cooking oil down a plywood sheet on to an old mattress at the bottom.

Each drum was slowed by one of the Slasher Boys and manhandled on to a mechanical scale. The smugglers had mixed drums containing cocaine amongst drums full of oil and the only way to tell them apart was by a slight difference in weight.

Once a drum with cocaine inside was identified, the final pair of men worked to extract it from the oil. One peeled back the aluminium lid, while another – wearing an elbow-length surgical glove – plunged his hand deep into the gluey liquid and retrieved a vacuum-packed brick of cocaine.

He then cut away an outer layer of plastic which dribbled

with strings of yellow oil, before throwing the clean brick beneath into the boot of an Alfa Romeo. Once the twelfth packet of cocaine had been recovered, the men began rolling the hefty drums back up the ramp. They also replaced the ones that had been opened, so that the end customer would be greeted by a full container and have no idea that his weekly shipment of cooking oil formed part of a cocaine smuggling route.

Michael thought the operation uncharacteristically slick considering that it was run by someone as disorganised as Major Dee. His stomach was turning somersaults as the container banged shut and he took his head out of the vent and looked around, expecting to see Mad Dogs at any second.

But he was startled to see youths cutting through overgrown weeds on an adjacent patch of land. Most of them were teenagers holding bats and guns, and although he didn't have time to count, Michael guessed there were at least fifty of them.

He grabbed his phone out of his top and wondered whether to call Maureen or Major Dee first; but his calls were being monitored in the mission control room on campus, so he went for Major Dee.

'How does it look from up there?' Dee asked, sounding full of himself.

'Big problem,' Michael gasped. 'There's a massive gang of boys coming towards the warehouse. Fifty at least.'

Major Dee sounded disbelieving. 'The Mad Dogs don't have fifty men.'

'It's *not* the Mad Dogs,' Michael said. 'They look like Runts. Sasha must have tipped them off.'

'Fifty,' Dee shouted anxiously. 'Hang it up, I've gotta get the boys moving.'

Michael rolled on to his stomach as the phone went dead. He crawled to the edge of the gently sloping roof and watched the Runts closing in. Then he noticed a change in the light behind him. At first it seemed like a glint from the sun, but within a second there was a blast of heat and the building started to tremble.

*

Wheels was a beautiful driver. Effortlessly fast and totally confident, he weaved through cabs and baffled tourists to reach the drop-off area at the front of Luton airport's main terminal.

'Sorry I couldn't let you boys know about this sooner,' Sasha said, as he led James and Bruce through a set of automatic doors and into the terminal. 'We've waited years for a chance to rob this airport and I had to keep my cards close. We almost did it a couple of years back when the Queen opened the new hospital, but there wasn't a flight with the right sort of cargo.'

'You've got people inside the airport?' James asked.

'Loads,' Sasha nodded. 'It's the biggest employer in town. Half of my crew has friends or relatives who work here. You don't even need to worry about getting your face on the security cameras, 'cos we've had some leads pulled.'

They had reached the security desk for domestic flights. Their boarding passes had been downloaded and printed out before Sasha left home and there were only a dozen people ahead in the queue to get coats and bags X-rayed.

As they crept forward, James worried that his body armour

would set off the electronic barrier, even though Savvas had checked him over with a handheld metal detector back at Sofa World. But James could never stand in a security line without worrying about something. He began inspecting his fake passport.

The picture taken at Luton station the previous afternoon was goofy, but he was impressed by the standard of the printing and watermarking and decided that the passport was probably a blank stolen out of a passport office or consulate.

The security officer merely scanned the barcodes on their boarding passes and didn't even look at the passports before pointing them towards the walk-through metal detector. James had seen that the flight listed on his boarding pass was leaving from Gate Eleven and was confused when Sasha started in the other direction.

'The tickets are just to get us through security,' Sasha explained. 'We're heading for the cargo terminal.'

They had to walk past seven gates, ending up at a doorway adjacent to the first-class lounge marked *Private Aviation Only*.

The counter in front of it was unmanned. Sasha produced a security pass and slotted it into a lock. After a green light and a buzz, the door came open and the trio jogged down a short ramp towards a staircase and a set of automatic doors where passengers would usually board a bus to reach an aeroplane parked away from the terminal.

Up to this point Sasha had appeared to be on top of things, but panic came into his eyes as he looked around.

'What's up?' James asked.

'There's supposed to be some stuff waiting for us.'

'Got it,' Bruce said, as he wheeled a catering trolly out from under the staircase.

Sasha pulled up the shutter on the trolley's side and smiled with relief as he saw a duffle bag and three sets of overalls.

'Put these on,' Sasha said, beginning to kick off his shoes as he passed sets of beige overalls with *LUTON SECURITY* written on the back. 'Careful with your fingerprints.'

James was already sweltering with the body armour under his tracksuit and he felt ridiculous as he pulled on yet another layer of clothing. Meantime Sasha had taken caps and sunglasses out of the bag.

'Keep 'em on in case we bump into someone,' Sasha explained, as he pulled the brim down over his eyes. 'You two look young, and I don't want anyone to eyeball me because when something gets robbed around here my mugshot is always the first one the cops pull out of the box.'

To make life even hotter, Sasha pulled out sets of gardening gloves before handing each boy a gun.

'Glocks, same ones you used on the hard front the other day,' he explained. 'The airport cops have got machine guns, so *don't* start shooting unless you have to because you'll know all about it when the anti-terrorist squad shoot back. The good news is that less than a dozen cops work this entire airport and right now their backup is trying to pick up Major Dee on the other side of town.'

The doors leading on to the sunny tarmac opened automatically and Sasha stepped out and looked around. Three yellow and white airport buses were parked less than fifty metres away and they began jogging towards them.

Time seemed to ache as the roof shuddered beneath Michael. The explosives had made a huge metal blister in the side of the warehouse. As flames licked through gaps between roof plates, the building flexed, making its corrugated sections groan like a metal sea.

Michael held on for as long as he could, but even though his body armour gave some protection the metal was getting hot. Down below, two Slasher Boys and the truck driver had scrambled out through a fire door, only to find Runts vaulting a low wall and steaming towards them with weapons drawn. Major Dee had ordered the deaths of eight Runts who'd been involved in the murder of Owen Campbell-Moore, so Michael wasn't expecting the youngsters to show any mercy when they got hold of Dee's men.

He heard a couple of gunshots as a chasm opened between the two roof sections directly behind him. It seemed only a matter of time before the whole roof collapsed. Michael had to climb down, even if it meant facing the onslaught of Runts.

As he ran to the edge, the opposite end of the roof began to sag, turning the centre into a huge chimney pouring out black smoke. He stepped on to the top rung of the access ladder, the wind pushing dense smoke into his face.

His eyes stung as he moved down. More Runts were pouring over the wall, but they'd been split into two groups when a stream of cars and mini-buses filled with Slasher Boys pulled up in the street outside.

Within seconds there were guns blazing in all directions. Mercifully, the panic this caused set a lot of the Runts running for cover and Michael slid down the last half of the ladder without being spotted.

As soon as his feet hit the ground, he ripped out his handgun and took off the safety, then ran as fast as he could. The gun battle on the opposite side of the building had become ridiculous and Michael's heart banged as a police helicopter swooped over, parting the clouds of smoke.

Shocked by the level of violence, Inspector Rush had changed tactics, abandoning the soft cordon and ordering his officers to seal the area and prevent the mayhem spreading into a nearby shopping precinct.

Michael's eyes and lungs burned from the smoke, but he picked up speed and vaulted a wall into the street behind the warehouse. There were two police cars parked at one end and he knew he'd get cuffed and clobbered if they nabbed him. The other direction looked more promising and he sped on for fifty metres.

When he reached a corner he saw a wrecked car. The passengers had escaped, but the driver was slumped over the steering wheel, unconscious. He looked like a Runt and he was no more than fifteen years old.

Michael thought about trying to give first aid, but the helicopter swooped again and its presence made him acutely aware of the danger. He charged on, diving into a narrow side street as a carload of Runts screamed past. He thought he was OK, but when he looked back he was horrified to see the car reverse and turn after him.

Michael ran on past two warehouses with the car closing in. There was a grass square beyond and he sped through the gate, dodged a woman walking a golden retriever and began sprinting across neatly mown grass. The car couldn't follow, but two Runts got out of the back.

By the time they'd reached the park gates, Michael was close to a primary school on the opposite side of the square. He glanced through the hedges along the park's edge and saw that the car had taken a left turn to cut him off as he exited.

His only safe route was through the school. He scrambled up the chain-link fence bordering the playground. The windows of a classroom filled with Year Twos was less than five metres away, but none of the kids looked his way until a gunshot ripped off somewhere on the other side of the wall.

By the time Michael had dropped into a goalmouth painted on concrete, twenty-five sets of little eyeballs stared at him. One of the chasing Runts had started to climb the fence, while another ran around the school's perimeter looking for the entrance.

Michael would never have a better chance to go on the offensive. As soon as the Runt dropped off the fence he charged. The Runt had a knife in his hand, but as he swung forward it thumped harmlessly into Michael's body armour.

Michael twisted the knife from the youth's hand and went into automatic. It would have been easy to kill him with the gun, but that's always a final option. He had time to incapacitate the Runt before his mate found the school gate, so he twisted his wrist into a lock, kept twisting until the Runt's arm snapped and ripped the Runt's shoulder out of its socket with a final jerk.

Inside the classroom the teacher was frantically

shepherding her young pupils into the far corner of the room, but for every six-year-old who couldn't look, another had their face against the window refusing to look away. Several screamed when Michael stepped back, giving them a clear view of the Runt's bloody face.

Michael could handle one Runt, but there was also a chance of the two lads in the car joining the hunt. If they'd only had knives he might have fancied his chances of fighting it out three against one, but some Runts had guns and there were too many little kids around to take risks.

He decided it was best to hide and ran towards a red door at the back of the school building. As he burst through, a teacher's assistant saw his gun and squealed.

'I'm not gonna hurt you,' Michael yelled, in a voice that was far from reassuring. 'Keep the kids out of the way and make sure someone's called the police.'

Michael looked around and realised that he was in a school library, with a life-size cut-out of Alex Rider staring at him from the opposite side of the room. There was only one exit behind him and a good view out across the playground. It seemed like the perfect position to hold out until the cops arrived.

But everything changed when he saw an Asian lad sprint across the playground, gun in hand. Stocky, with giant gold rings, Michael had never seen him before, but knew the face from a surveillance photograph.

He opened a crack in the library door and aimed his gun at the youth who'd tried to kill Gabrielle.

45. BUS

The airport was marked out with yellow lanes and a strict twenty-mile-per-hour limit. Sasha sat at the wheel of the bus, Bruce on the long bench behind and James stood with one hand on a green pole and the other holding out the photocopied directions.

'Next left,' James said, as they cruised behind the wings of a small Airbus.

Sasha hadn't got the knack of steering the bus and was alarmed to find himself heading towards a tight gap beneath a terminal walkway. He slowed to a crawl and looked worried as the roof cleared a height restriction sign by centimetres.

They emerged from the short tunnel into bright sunlight blanketing the cargo terminal. Sasha followed the yellow path in front of four parked jets painted in the livery of an international courier company, and then swung out across open tarmac, heading for a solitary 737 cargo plane.

Two men were unloading the plane using an automated conveyor, with aluminium freight cubes rolling down a belt on to the back of a flat-bed truck. As the bus closed in, James recognised the hulking outlines of the Kruger brothers.

'You're late,' Tim Kruger shouted, switching off the conveyor as James and Bruce stepped down from the bus. He leaned in and looked at Sasha, who'd stayed behind the wheel. 'The cargo men are unconscious in the terminal and the cage is set to blow.'

James and Bruce were handed rubber gas masks as Tony pulled a remote detonator out of his pocket. 'Fingers in your ears,' he said, giving the boys less than two seconds to comply before he pressed the button.

A white flash burst from the open door of the fuselage ten metres above them. The sound echoed across the tarmac and made the plane roll back half a metre on its giant tyres. As smoke billowed from the doorway, the Kruger brothers grabbed a set of access steps and wheeled them towards it.

Tim looked towards James and Bruce. 'You'll see eight bricks inside the cage. Grab 'em and throw 'em down the steps.'

Sasha claimed that James and Bruce were doing this part of the operation because they were young and fast, but as he raced up the steps James couldn't help feeling that it was because no other bugger wanted to do it.

A lot of the smoke had cleared by the time the boys reached the doorway. Nothing seemed to have caught fire, but it was still tough to see. James peered into the cockpit and saw that the blast had destroyed most of the instrumentation and set off enough warning alarms to make it sound like an amusement park.

With their gas masks filtering the smoke, Bruce stepped the other way and grabbed a reinforced door. The Krugers were explosives experts and the blast had made neat holes in the gate of the high security cargo area, commonly known as the cage.

Bruce stepped into a dark space less than three metres deep, and flipped on the lamp fitted to his mask. The blast had buckled the aluminium shelves at the back of the cage, causing its contents to spill into a pile on the floor. He swept aside a mass of envelopes and small boxes that probably contained precious stones or jewellery and bent at the knees to grab the first brick.

Thirty centimetres wide, twenty deep and twenty high, each plastic-wrapped brick contained two hundred and sixty thousand dollars belonging to the United States government. The shipment had left America for Amsterdam the night before and was bound for Iraq, where the money would be used to pay the security forces.

Bruce passed the brick out of the door to James, who backed up to the outer door before hurling it down the staircase into the arms of Tony Kruger. It took less than forty seconds to extract two million vacuum-packed dollars and load them on to the bus.

As the boys ran down the steps, they spotted an airport fire engine racing towards the scene. It could only be a matter of seconds before the airport police were on their backs too.

James jumped on to the bus behind Bruce and the Kruger brothers, and Sasha floored the accelerator without bothering to shut the doors. Their exit was on the opposite side of the airport, but whilst Sasha wanted a quick getaway he discovered that the hydraulic brakes locked on every time he reached twenty-five miles an hour.

'There's a bloody speed limiter,' Sasha yelled, as he turned around the nose of the plane and began heading back towards the passenger end of the terminal.

Tim Kruger watched in shock as the speed limiter locked on for the third time.

'Makes sense,' James said quietly, as he sat on a padded bench next to Bruce. 'You wouldn't want your minimum-wage airport bus driver putting his foot down and careering into a fifty-million-pound jet.'

Twenty miles an hour felt agonisingly slow as they drove along the path in front of the terminal, passing the shadowy outlines of a dozen passenger jets.

But there was still no sign of airport police as Tim Kruger radioed through to the rest of the team: 'We're passing Gate Three and should be at the exit in just over a minute.'

'Roger that,' Savvas answered. 'I'm heading in.'

'There's the cops,' Bruce yelled, as he looked behind and saw two airport police cars roaring across the tarmac with their sirens blazing.

They were closing fast as Sasha took a final slow turn around the end of the passenger terminal. The vehicle access point where fuel tankers and catering trucks entered the airport was directly ahead of them, complete with heavy barriers and a security booth with an armed guard inside.

James only glimpsed it before he saw the truck with the battering ram welded to the front barrelling towards the gate at more than fifty miles an hour. The huge ram tore into the security booth, ripping the entire structure out of the ground. As the truck ploughed on, it hit a kerb so fast that the front wheels flew off the ground. It shattered the exit barriers and closed on the side of the terminal building.

'He's ballsed it up,' Tony Kruger gasped.

Savvas was supposed to brake hard and turn once he was through the gates. But your brakes don't work when your wheels are off the ground.

A wall of sparks exploded around the front edge of the battering ram as the truck touched down, throwing the helmeted Savvas across the cab. The truck smashed into the terminal building, tearing a massive hole and exposing ventilation shafts and a service corridor.

'Jesus,' Bruce gasped, as dust billowed and masonry chinked to the ground. 'That must have knocked him out.'

Sasha stopped the bus and the two black Mercedes vans roared through the tangle of concrete and wire where the security barriers had been. James and Bruce grabbed a brick of money and ran towards them.

At the same time, Savvas fought to open his stricken truck, but the collision had buckled the door and he was forced to climb through the window. The two airport police cars had stopped fifty metres behind the bus and the Kruger brothers ripped out machine guns and fired warning shots into the air.

'Stay *back*,' Tony warned.

Bruce started making a second run with two bricks of money. James was about to grab the last one when Sasha pointed him towards the truck.

'Go help Savvas. He's stuck.'

Savvas was losing his struggle to get out of the truck. A jet of water sprayed out of the rubble inside the terminal as James jumped on to the steps leading up to the cab. He grabbed Savvas by his overall, but Savvas' shoulders were wedged and his breathing was laboured.

As James tried to undo the chin strap on Savvas' helmet, a blast of automatic gunfire gave him the fright of his life. He slipped off the steps and put his trainer down awkwardly, turning his ankle and collapsing on to his heavily padded behind.

James glanced around warily. There was no sign of Bruce or the Kruger brothers and the gunfire seemed to have come from behind the remains of the security booth. The officer inside had dived out before it was destroyed, and now used the debris as cover as she shot at the wheels of the black vans less than ten metres from her position.

The getaway drivers had no option but to reverse through the mangled gates at speed. As James stood up it seemed everyone else had made it into the vans and his only company was the half conscious Savvas.

He thought about running for it, but with someone shooting from behind the booth and the two police cars sure to close in now that the Krugers weren't covering his back, surrender seemed like the only sane option. Then he eyed Sasha lying flat in the doorway of the bus.

*

Michael was a good marksman. He'd practised extensively with his compact pistol and the Runt who'd stabbed Gabrielle was crossing the playground less than ten metres away. It was an easy shot.

Cherubs are taught only to shoot when they're in immediate danger and the Runt didn't even know he was being targeted. But Michael's training was mangled by his love for Gabrielle. He wanted the person who'd almost extinguished her life to suffer and his rage was almost overpowering.

Can I get away with it? Probably. Could I live with myself? Definitely. Wouldn't killing him make me just as bad as him? Could I really kill another human being?

Much as he hated the Runt, Michael was surprised to discover that he didn't have the heart to kill in cold blood. He lowered his aim and thought about shooting the Runt up the arse or in the leg, but wherever a bullet enters you can be dead inside three minutes if it hits an artery.

A slamming door made Michael look back and he heard running in the corridor behind him. His first thought was of the two Runts who'd been inside the car. But he could hear voices: a near hysterical woman and an older man trying to calm her down. The cops had given top priority to a call from a primary school.

'This is the police, can you hear me?'

Michael took a quick glance back out of the window and saw that the Runt had stopped moving. He'd lost Michael and had no idea what to do next.

'I can hear,' Michael shouted back.

'I want you to put your gun down and slide it across to the far side of the room,' the cop said calmly. 'I need to be able to see your weapon when I open the door.'

Michael considered bursting out of the triangular door and going after the Runt, but firearms teams work in pairs and the most likely outcome would be a bullet in his own back. Even with body armour and nanotubes, he didn't fancy it.

'Quickly,' the cop shouted.

'I'm putting the gun down now,' Michael shouted back.

He clicked on the safety and removed the clip, then threw both against the far wall of the room. One of the cops must have been peering through the door at the back because he charged in instantly, pointing his handgun at Michael as Alex Rider and a display of Horrible Histories clattered to the floor.

'Hands on your head, on your head!'

Michael did what he was told as another officer stormed into the room.

'Get up, face the window.'

While the officer slammed Michael against a bookshelf and locked handcuffs behind his back, the Runt spotted a police uniform inside the library and began sprinting towards the school gate.

'OK, mister,' the officer said, as he jerked Michael away from the window and shoved him forward so that his colleague could pat him down. 'You're under arrest. You have the right to remain silent, but anything that you do say can be taken down and used in evidence against you.'

'He's wearing full body armour,' the other cop said incredulously, as he pulled a hunting knife and a cellphone out of Michael's trouser pocket. 'Carrying a firearm, assault with a deadly weapon. You're looking at five years and you can't be more than sixteen years old . . .'

'Get out to the car,' the first cop growled, as Michael wondered if Gabrielle would have wanted him to pull the trigger.

46. CASH

Sasha kept low as he sprinted out of the bus with a $260,000 brick under his arm. James was scared of getting shot and wondered if he should fake an injury and leave Sasha's capture to the police. But Sasha knew the airport well and James didn't like the idea of him getting away.

James straddled the rubble and followed Sasha down a breeze-block corridor as a recorded female voice repeatedly told them that there was a security alert and to evacuate the terminal by the nearest exit.

After thirty steps the pair found themselves in a stockroom piled with yesterday's newspapers and boxes of crisps. Sasha put his head around the door at the opposite end and stared into a deserted shop.

'Looks clear,' he whispered.

They crouched low as they walked between two racks of magazines and peeked on to the airport concourse. When they'd arrived it had been jammed. Now the open space was dead except for the tannoy announcement and the squeaking boots of an armed officer patrolling the polished floor.

'Is it safe?' James asked.

But Sasha had moved away. He reached behind the counter and grabbed a large carrier bag.

'Open it,' he said, as he passed the bag to James.

James held the bag, enabling Sasha to drop the brick of cash inside.

'How do we get out of here?' James asked, as he eyed the cop's machine gun.

Sasha pointed out of the open shop front and to the left as he pulled a knife from inside his trousers.

'Passengers evacuate into the bus terminal, which is fifty metres that way,' he explained in a whisper. 'We'll make sure Robocop's looking the other way when we step out, but once we get outside there's going to be a couple of thousand people hanging around waiting to be let back in.'

James felt queasy with fear as Sasha stuck his knife inside the carrier bag and sliced the plastic wrapping away from the money. He briefly considered shooting Sasha in the leg, but before he got a chance Sasha thrust a stack of hundred-dollar bills into his hands.

'What's this?' James asked.

'Crowd control,' Sasha said mysteriously.

*

The stolen cash would have easily fitted into a single van, but Sasha's plan called for two because the police would be stretched thin and two vans would maximise their chances of getting away with at least half of the money.

Bruce had a ten-minute ride in the back of a van, with Tim Kruger, eight hundred thousand dollars and a slow puncture in the left rear. They ended up in an overgrown courtyard on the edge of the Thornton Estate.

Wheels waited in the powerful BMW, with the boot open. Two bricks of cash were loaded inside, while Tim Kruger stuffed the two that belonged to him and his brother into a Samsonite wheelie bag. He pulled it across the pavement and lifted it in the back of a Renault parked across the street.

As Wheels followed the Renault's exhaust plume, Riggsy – who'd been driving the van – fetched a can of petrol from the cab and began splashing it around.

'You look like a lost dog, Brucey boy,' he smiled.

'Where's the other van?' Bruce asked anxiously. 'Did you see what happened to James and Sasha?'

'Different meeting point,' Riggsy explained.

'But I'm sure they got left behind,' Bruce said. 'I ran for the van and jumped in and I saw Tony Kruger jump in the other one—'

Riggsy didn't like teenagers and sounded annoyed. 'Keep calm, kid. Get out of those bloody overalls and toss 'em in the van before I burn it.'

Bruce was so worried about James that he'd forgotten he still had *LUTON SECURITY* written across his back.

'When things go bad you've got to keep your head,' Riggsy said, as Bruce hurriedly peeled his overall down his arms. 'Go back to the Zoo, think up a bloody good alibi and keep your head down. Whatever you do, don't try and contact Sasha before he contacts you. I can drop you at the bus station if you like.'

As Riggsy spoke he pulled a lighter out of his pocket and gave Bruce a *hurry up with the overalls* look. Bruce looked in the back of the van and realised that it was a goldmine of forensic evidence: fingerprints and DNA from half the Mad Dogs crew, as well as several sets of overalls. The mission was going to be over either way, and it was just him and Riggsy left on the scene.

'Dammit,' Bruce moaned. 'Give us a hand. I can't get these overalls over my boots.'

'Stop pissing around,' Riggsy snapped. 'Why didn't you slip your shoes off first?'

Riggsy moved in to give the overalls a tug, but when he bent forward Bruce kicked him in the side of the head with his right boot. As Riggsy slumped flat on his face, Bruce stepped effortlessly out of the overall and crouched down to make sure that he was unconcious.

He took a good look around before pressing the transmitter on his neck.

'Chloe?' he said.

'Loud and clear, Bruce.'

'Have you heard from James?'

'I'm listening to the police radio,' Chloe said. 'I think he's inside the airport with Sasha.'

'Thank god,' Bruce gasped. 'I thought he might have been shot.'

'Well he's not out of the woods yet.'

'Listen,' Bruce said. 'I'm out on the edge of the Thornton Estate. The street's called Euphonium. I've just taken out one of Sasha's crew and there's a van here. It's full of evidence but it's been doused in petrol. Can you get some cops out here?'

'I'll try.'

'I'm gonna grab Riggsy's car keys and get out of here, but

when he comes round he's probably gonna remember that I knocked him out.'

'Gotcha,' Chloe said. 'I'll call Inspector Rush and tell him that it's high priority. I'll make sure Riggsy doesn't contact any of the other Mad Dogs until you and James are safely out of the picture.'

*

Sasha waited for the cop to turn his back before sprinting out on to the concourse, with James tight behind. They'd reached the fire exit before the armed officer knew what was occurring and Sasha hit the glass door so hard that he knocked an unarmed security guard to the ground. Much to James' relief, several yellow-bibbed airport staff stood in the doorway, making it too risky for the marksman to fire a shot.

As James broke into fresh air and sunlight he saw that the bus terminal and surrounding car parks were jammed with passengers who'd been evacuated when the truck crashed into the side of the building.

Under normal circumstances a breach of security would have brought out the entire local police force to seal off the airport; but all their spare manpower was on the other side of town dealing with the Runts and Slasher Boys. Sasha knew that he had fewer than a dozen airport police to deal with and reckoned that his escape was only a matter of getting lost in the crowd.

'Free money,' Sasha shouted, as he crossed the road outside the terminal.

He grabbed a handful of hundred-dollar bills out of the carrier bag and threw them upwards. They'd been vacuum-packed, so the money spun high into the air before the wind separated it.

Sasha repeated the exercise as they jogged on through the packed bus terminal. By the time the third pile of money began fluttering down people had caught on. There were a few shouts of *oh my god* and *it's real* and people started scratching around the floor. When Sasha threw a fourth, larger pile over his shoulder and towards the airport entrance, a crowd of over a hundred surged forward to pick it up.

Several armed officers had now reached the exit, but they had no chance of catching Sasha and James as more than a hundred people fought over the fluttering dollars.

'I always wanted to do this,' Sasha said, as he launched a final volley of money.

Within two minutes James and Sasha were in a giant parking lot several hundred metres clear of the terminal. There was no sign of pursuit and they'd slowed to a brisk walk. The only people nearby were evacuees who'd returned to sit in their parked cars.

'We need to lose the overalls,' Sasha said, before pulling his two-way radio out of his pocket. 'I'm in the east side car park; can someone get a car out here to pick us up?'

As Sasha spoke James noticed a female cop dive out from behind a panel van just ahead of them. It was the same woman who'd shot at them from behind the security booth. She'd made an educated guess that Sasha would try vanishing into the crowd and instead of pursuing him through the terminal she'd run around the outside of the building and sprinted ahead.

'Hands up,' she shouted firmly, as she aimed her machine

gun at Sasha's chest. He was wearing body armour, but from this kind of range there was no guarantee it would save him.

James wasn't in the mood for any more trouble and threw down his gun, but Sasha kept moving towards her.

'You shoot me and you'll be under investigation for months,' Sasha grinned, as he dropped the carrier bag of money. 'There's still more than a hundred grand in there. If I left it here for you, nobody would ever know.'

'Final warning,' the officer shouted.

By this time Sasha was less than three metres from the female officer. James glanced back and saw another cop and an airport security guard running between the cars towards them.

'One more step,' the officer said, but she realised that Sasha had no intention of stopping and pulled the trigger.

'Christ,' Sasha said, sounding oddly composed as the bullet knocked him backwards. Although his body armour had been punctured it had taken most of the force out of the shot and the metal case had lodged itself between two ribs.

'Well isn't it your lucky day,' the officer said, as she stood over Sasha with the gun aimed at his face.

47. STATION

The police ended up arresting thirty-six Slasher Boys and eighteen Runts. Fourteen more youths and two police officers had been hospitalised and whilst five had gunshot wounds, serious stab wounds or burns, only one person had died.

While Sasha was taken to hospital under police guard, James found himself stripped to his boxers and locked in a police cell. The surrounding cells were packed with Runts and Slasher Boys, banging on the walls and screaming threats at each another.

Every so often the cops would come and take someone for questioning. With two officers in the hospital and more sent home injured, the ones who remained on duty didn't stand for nonsense. Anyone who mouthed off got a slap or a baton in the guts and prisoners who stood by the flaps in their doors claiming to be hungry or thirsty were told either to shut up or to drink water out of the toilet.

'We cleaned 'em just last year,' a female officer cackled. 'So lap it up, boys!'

Baiting the cops was the one thing that united the rival gangs. Her words inspired a defiant chorus of *get your tits out*, which only ended when the loudest Runt's cell was opened by three officers with riot shields. James heard his screams as they pinned him back against the wall and let the female officer demonstrate inappropriate use of an extendable baton.

After more than ten hours without food and nothing but a teensy carton of orange squash to drink, James jumped up when his cell door came open.

'Your mum must be shagging the Chief Constable,' the officer said sarcastically, as he threw a stiff paper overall and a set of flip-flops at James. 'You're getting bailed.'

'What about my clothes?'

'All personal effects have been taken for forensic examination. As you can imagine there's a bit of a backlog today; so I wouldn't bank on seeing any of 'em this side of Christmas.'

James pulled the overall up his limbs and fastened the zipper along the front. The flip-flops slapped against his heels as the officer led him down a hallway to the Charge Sergeant's office.

'Sign here and here,' the officer said, as he slammed a clipboard down on his desk.

James was knackered and came precariously close to writing James Adams instead of James Beckett; not that anyone would ever have noticed.

'Don't come back,' the officer who'd taken him from the cells said, as he shoved James towards a door.

James had no phone, money or even proper outdoor clothes so he was a bit worried until he spotted Chloe at the end of the corridor.

'You OK?' she smiled, as she handed him a bottle of water and a large fruit and nut bar.

'You beauty,' James grinned, as he tore the bar open and crammed six chunks into his mouth. 'I'm *totally* starving.'

'Come on,' Chloe said, as James ripped the top off the water and downed half of it in one go. 'I've got Maureen and the others out back in the car park.'

'Where are we going?' James asked quietly, as they walked up a flight of steps. 'Campus?'

'Straight away,' Chloe nodded. 'Bruce knocked out Riggsy to preserve evidence. We've doped him up so that he won't remember much when he comes around, but there's few Mad Dogs wandering the streets and I'd rather you boys didn't bump into them.'

Chloe had a Toyota people carrier parked in the darkness amidst police vans and cars. Maureen was in the driver's seat, Bruce in the middle row and Michael was in the back wearing a disposable overall like James'.

'Looks like I was the only one smart enough not to get nicked,' Bruce giggled, as James sat beside him.

James turned around to ask Michael if he was OK.

'Cops treated me like dirt, but I'll live.'

'Michael says the fighting around the warehouse was mental,' Bruce grinned, as Maureen drove the big Toyota out of the parking space.

'What happened about Major Dee?' James asked.

'Not a thing,' Chole said. 'As far as we can tell he pegged it as soon as he saw the Runts coming. The police followed the car he was in and pulled him over, but they got nothing. Not even a Stanley knife or a spliff in the glove box.'

'That's a bit crap,' James tutted. 'What about the surveillance? Weren't some of Dee's lieutenants seen in the warehouse setting up the drug deal?'

Bruce shook his head. 'You mean the talcum powder deal.'

'*What?*' James gasped.

Chloe nodded, as the Toyota turned a sharp corner. 'After a good deal of fighting the cops did manage to surround the warehouse,' she explained. 'The explosion destroyed a lot of evidence, but the car boot was down when it went off and the bags of drugs were protected from the blast. Only problem was, they'd already been switched.'

'Do you think Sasha robbed them?' James asked.

'We're pretty certain that Simeon Bentine was behind it, either with or without the Mad Dogs,' Chloe said. 'The cops went to Simeon's office and he's vanished into thin air.'

James tried to figure all of this out in his head. 'So we got Sasha. Savvas is in the hospital and Bruce got the van before it was burned out, which should give us enough evidence to nail Riggsy and the rest of the Mad Dogs.'

'That's about right,' Chloe said.

'No sign of the Kruger brothers or any of the money yet though,' Bruce noted. 'Wheels and the others who got away won't be showing their faces any time soon.'

'But they're all either locked up or on the run,' James said. 'Which isn't a *bad* result.'

'But it's a long way shy of our original plan to get all of the senior Mad Dogs and Slasher Boys in one little warehouse and surround them with cops,' Michael said.

'It's a shame,' Chloe yawned. 'We didn't touch Major Dee

and we can't press drugs charges against anyone because there weren't any drugs.'

Maureen shook her head. 'And in that sort of chaos it's going to be hard to prove which weapon belonged to who. They'll all claim to have picked up someone else's weapon to use in self defence because their life was in danger and nobody will testify. The lawyers will have their work cut out getting convictions.'

'And the gang war rolls on,' Bruce said dramatically. 'Only the Slasher Boys are the real psychos and without the Mad Dogs keeping them in check there's going to be absolute carnage.'

'The Runts have got a lot of manpower though,' Michael said. 'If someone took charge, they'd be a match for the Slasher Boys.'

'They're bound to get more organised,' Bruce said. 'There must be one Runt with a few brain cells.'

James stared out the window at the passing streetlamps and sounded annoyed. 'So basically we just spent two months trying to stop a gang war, but all we've done is made it worse.'

'Not necessarily,' Chloe said, feeling like it was her duty to cheer up the three tired agents. 'We gathered a lot of intelligence, all of which the anti-gang taskforce will use in their ongoing battle. Just because we're going back to campus before everyone is in prison doesn't mean that the mission is a failure.'

'It's still crap though,' Bruce said. 'We came so close.'

'Oooh, burgers,' James said, as they whizzed past a couple of fast-food joints. 'Can we stop? Apart from that chocolate, I haven't eaten since breakfast.'

'I hate that greasy shit,' Michael complained. 'It turns my guts.'

'Right now I'm so hungry I'd settle for a dead rat on a stick,' James said.

Maureen looked across at her boss. 'There's a roundabout up ahead, Chloe. I can turn back if anyone wants something to eat.'

'No,' Chloe said definitively. 'Wait until we're out of Luton. I want to get as far out of this godforsaken hole as I can.'

'And never come back,' Bruce added.

48. SIN

It was eleven o'clock when James arrived back on campus and closer to midnight by the time he'd ditched his paper suit and cleaned up. Dana was asleep, but he was desperate to see her.

'Hey,' James said softly, as he sat on Dana's bed and reached across to dab her on the chin. She always slept in the far corner of her double bed, with her face buried and a shoulder touching the wall.

James got a rush as she opened her eyes and gave an involuntary smile. She shuffled across the bed and gave him a toothpasty kiss.

'How did everything go today?'

'Not great,' James said wearily. 'I ended up robbing an airport, our informant seems to have stitched us up and made off with half a million quid's worth of cocaine and the cops didn't arrest half the people we were expecting to.'

'I saw the robbery on the news,' Dana yawned as she sat up. 'It goes like that sometimes, mate. In fact, in my case I think it's gone like that a bit too often.'

'Listen,' James said. 'I've got something to tell you. Kind of a confession.'

Dana cracked a giant smile. 'Who was she? Not April Moore again?'

James was taken aback by the casual response. 'It wasn't April but, I mean . . . How can you put it like that?'

'I know what you're like,' Dana explained. 'Your eyes are out on stalks every time something goes by in a short skirt and I'm a realist: you were gonna get up to something on a mission sooner or later.'

'But that's not *really* me,' James said. 'Well . . . I *was* like that when I was with Kerry. But I cheated on her loads of times and it ended up that there were all these lies between us; and Lauren blackmailing me and people making comments behind my back. It got so that I could hardly look Kerry in the eye. I hated all the lying and I was never going to cheat on you.'

Dana looked confused. 'But you did anyway?'

James wrung his hands together. 'Well here's the thing. I was kind of . . . Well . . . I sort of *accidently* had sex with this guy's daughter.'

Dana's mouth dropped before she burst out laughing. 'Accidentally,' she hooted. 'What, you were strolling along minding your own business when you tripped over and landed on a naked girl?'

James was completely thrown. He'd expected tears and violence.

'It wasn't like that,' James said. 'I was having a bath. She threw off her clothes and climbed in with me. She was pretty sexy and . . . I mean, let's face it, no guy is gonna turn that away.'

'OK, you've confessed,' Dana said icily. 'What now?'

Now that she'd stopped smiling, James could see the hurt in her eyes. 'I don't know,' he said. 'I was stupid and I swear it'll never happen again. You can do anything you like to me. I mean, if you feel like hitting me you can hit me. Or I'll buy you dinner, or write one of your essays – anything. Just *please* give me another chance.'

'Does anyone else know?' Dana asked.

'Bruce overheard, but he's sworn to secrecy.'

'So you didn't rush up here to tell me before I found out some other way?'

James shook his head as he stepped off the bed and held his arms out wide. 'Take a swing,' he said. 'Break my arm, kick me in the nuts; I totally deserve it.'

'No,' Dana said thoughtfully. 'You only want me to hurt you to appease your guilt. You want me to do a Kerry, and go mental and throw stuff at you and punch you and call you every name under the sun. Then you think we'll kiss and make up and go on exactly like before. Well I'm sorry, but I'm not giving you the satisfaction.'

James felt his heart sink. 'You're dumping me?'

'Did you hear me say that?'

'I don't know *what* you're saying,' James said, holding his hands to his head. 'You're acting all weird. Can you at least tell me how you feel, or something?'

Dana scratched her nose. 'I don't know . . . Hurt, confused. I can't just forgive you, but I'm impressed that you were honest when you didn't have to be. You wouldn't risk it unless you actually cared about me.'

'I hated all the lies between me and Kerry,' James

explained. 'I don't want it to be like that with you.'

Dana rubbed a spot on the bed. 'I could do with a cuddle.'

James had a tear welling up as he sat down and pulled Dana tight. 'I'm really sorry,' he said. 'I missed you while I was away and I was so scared that you'd ditch me.'

Dana whispered as her cool fingers slid under James' T-shirt. 'You're fifteen, I'm sixteen, pretty soon we're going to be doing more than kissing on this bed . . .'

'How about now?' James grinned.

Dana gathered the fat on James' back and dug in her thumbnail. 'I *wouldn't* push your luck right now.'

'I'm a pig,' James admitted, holding up his hands as Dana pushed him away. 'Sorry.'

'Here's the thing,' Dana said seriously. 'If this girl goes around jumping into baths with people she hardly knows, I'd say she's probably slept with quite a few. She might have given you more than you bargained for.'

James shook his head. 'I'm OK, she gave me a condom.'

'Well it's better than nothing,' Dana said. 'But condoms aren't a hundred-per-cent effective and they don't do anything to prevent crabs or lice. You'd better make an appointment and get yourself checked out.'

'Dana, come off it. I mean, she's our age and we only did it once—'

'You only *need* to do it once.'

'But I'm under sixteen,' James protested. 'If I go over to the medical unit I'll get busted.'

'It's confidential,' Dana said.

James groaned. 'Fine, I'll make an appointment in the morning.'

'Good,' Dana said. 'But I'll be going with you to make sure you don't chicken out.'

'Why would I chicken out? I've had blood tests before.'

'I'm not talking about the blood test,' Dana smirked. 'Remember that video we watched in class? The big long cotton bud that they have to stick up your pee hole to take a swab?'

'You what!' James spluttered.

'You probably didn't see it,' Dana continued. 'Every boy in the room had their eyes shut for some reason . . .'

'That looked *really* painful,' James winced.

'It's up to you, dearest,' Dana said. 'But we've almost got carried away a couple of times and I'm not taking stupid risks, so you can have the test, *or* you can get yourself a new girlfriend.'

'I guess,' James nodded sheepishly. 'It's only pain, right? And I probably ought to anyway.'

'It's just a pity they don't let people watch,' Dana smiled. 'I'd be able to make a mint selling tickets.'

EPILOGUE

Following his arrest, SASHA THOMPSON spent eleven days in hospital recovering from his gunshot wound. The body armour almost certainly saved his life. He later faced criminal charges for armed robbery, possession of firearms, stealing a motor vehicle, incitement to riot and criminal damage, and was sentenced to fourteen years in prison.

DAVID KEMP (AKA WHEELS) was captured whilst trying to board a ferry to France with a suitcase containing $250,000. He was charged with conspiracy to commit armed robbery, vehicle theft and using a false passport, and sentenced to four years in custody. He will serve the first part of his sentence in a young offenders' institution.

SAVVAS THEOKELSIS suffered brain damage, caused by a lack of oxygen as he lay trapped in the door of the truck. The Crown Prosecution Service tried to bring charges, but a judge ruled that he was unfit to stand trial.

Savvas now has severly reduced mental capacity and is looked after by his mother and younger sister. They have launched a bid for financial compensation, claiming that police officers kept Savvas in an airport holding cell for four hours before he got proper medical attention.

KELVIN HOLMES was questioned in connection with the robbery of the hard front. Despite fingerprint and DNA evidence, all the charges were dropped when the dealers he'd held hostage refused to give evidence. Fearing reprisals from the Slasher Boys, Kelvin left the Luton area and is now believed to be living in South London.

Nine other members of the defunct Mad Dogs crew received prison sentences of between three and twelve years for offences relating to the airport robbery. ALAN 'RIGGSY' RIGGS received a nine-year sentence.

Police are still seeking four suspects, including the brothers TIM and TONY KRUGER, along with more than one million dollars belonging to the United States government.

The Crown Court threw the book at JUNIOR MOORE. He was charged with armed robbery, possession of a firearm, possession of cocaine, resisting arrest and violating parole. He got a seven-year sentence, the maximum that can be handed to someone under the age of sixteen.

The sentencing judge asked that Junior be given a priority placement on a treatment scheme for youngsters with drug and alcohol problems. Unfortunately, funding for these schemes is limited and priority is given to youngsters serving shorter sentences.

DeSHAWN ANDREWS (AKA MAJOR DEE) was questioned in the aftermath of the warehouse riot, but released without charge. Over the following months he masterminded an increasingly bloody gang war between the Slasher Boys and Runts. One casualty of the war was the Green Pepper café, which was gutted in an arson attack.

In mid 2007 several of Major Dee's closest associates were arrested in connection with the murder of AARON REID and two other teenage boys. Fearing prosecution, Dee fled the country and is believed to have returned to his native Jamaica. He is currently wanted for questioning in connection with eleven murders.

SIMEON BENTINE is now believed to have masterminded the operation to steal the cocaine from the drums of cooking oil, under the noses of the police, Mad Dogs and Slasher Boys. He successfully sold on the cocaine and escaped Britain, but associates of Major Dee eventually caught up with him. His mutilated body was recovered by the Jamaican police.

NORMAN LARGE and his adopted daughter HAYLEY now live seventy kilometres from CHERUB campus. Norman has worked as a security guard and a shop assistant. His application to train as a prison officer was turned down due to his heart problems.

After his savage beating at the hands of Sasha Thompson, ill health forced CHRIS JONES to resign both from his council seat and from his day job as a science teacher. He continues to have difficulty with his vision and is partly paralysed down his left side.

CHIEF INSPECTOR MARK RUSH remains in charge of the Bedfordshire anti-gang taskforce. Despite the failure of the grand scheme to capture the Mad Dogs and Slasher Boys in one swoop, Rush regarded the demise of the Mad Dogs as an important step forward in the battle against gang violence.

An investigation into how Sasha Thompson learned of the police raid on the warehouse uncovered links between the Mad Dogs and two administrative staff within the anti-gang taskforce. Both were dismissed after a disciplinary hearing, but there was not enough evidence to bring criminal charges.

The CHERUB ethics committee wrote a lengthy report on the anti-gang mission. Although they praised the four young agents for their commitment and bravery, CHLOE BLAKE and MAUREEN EVANS were criticised for underestimating the dangers involved.

After leaving CHERUB campus, KYLE BLUEMAN spent seven weeks living with Meryl Spencer. He set off on a round-the-world holiday with his old friend Rod Nilsson. When he returns he will begin studying law at Cambridge University.

Zara Asker has forgiven Kyle for the incident with Norman Large and agreed that he can visit his old friends during the holidays and earn some money helping out around campus.

DANA SMITH made the clinic appointment for JAMES ADAMS. The examination was more embarassing than painful and the results were all clear.

LAUREN ADAMS is unhappy about being suspended from missions but gets on with most of the young red-shirts she has to look after each evening. However, there are a couple who she'd quite happily crack around the head.

GABRIELLE O'BRIEN's fitness continues to improve. She is now jogging regularly and has begun non-contact combat training in the dojo. Her relationship with MICHAEL HENDRY remains as close as ever.

Chairwoman Zara Asker was impressed with the quick thinking BRUCE NORRIS showed to preserve the evidence inside the van and with the rest of his performance throughout the anti-gang mission. He was awarded the black CHERUB T-shirt.

CHERUB: The Recruit

So you've read *CHERUB: Mad Dogs*. But how did James Adams end up at CHERUB in the first place?

CHERUB: The Recruit tells James' story from the day his mother dies. Read about his transformation from a couch potato into a skilled CHERUB agent.

Meet Lauren, Kyle, Kerry and the rest of the cherubs for the first time, and learn how James foiled the biggest terrorist massacre in British history.

CHERUB: The Recruit available now from Robert Muchamore and Hodder Children's Books.

CHERUB: Class A

Keith Moore is Europe's biggest cocaine dealer. The police have been trying to get enough evidence to nail him for more than twenty years.

Now, four CHERUB agents are joining the hunt. Can a group of kids successfully infiltrate Keith Moore's organisation, when dozens of attempts by undercover police officers have failed?

James Adams has to start at the bottom, making deliveries for small-time drug dealers and getting to know the dangerous underworld they inhabit. He needs to make a big splash if he's going to win the confidence of the man at the top.

CHERUB: Maximum Security

Over the years, CHERUB has put plenty of criminals behind bars. Now, for the first time ever, they've got to break one out . . .

Under American law, kids convicted of serious crimes can be tried and sentenced as adults. Two hundred and eighty of these child criminals live in the sunbaked desert prison known as Arizona Max.

In one of the most daring CHERUB missions ever, James Adams has to go undercover inside Arizona Max, befriend an inmate and then bust him out.

CHERUB: The Killing

When a small-time crook suddenly has big money on his hands, it's only natural that the police want to know where it came from.

James' latest CHERUB mission looks routine: make friends with the bad guy's children, infiltrate his home and dig up some leads for the cops to investigate.

But the plot James begins to unravel isn't what anyone expected. And it seems like the only person who might know the truth is a reclusive eighteen-year-old boy.

There's just one problem. The boy fell from a rooftop and died more than a year earlier.

CHERUB: Divine Madness

When a team of CHERUB agents uncover a link between eco-terrorist group Help Earth and a wealthy religious cult known as The Survivors, James Adams is sent to Australia on an infiltration mission.

It's his toughest job so far. The Survivors' outback headquarters are completely isolated. It's a thousand kilometres to the nearest town and the cult's brainwashing techniques mean James is under massive pressure to conform.

This time he's not just fighting terrorists. He's got to battle to keep control of his own mind.

CHERUB: Man vs Beast

Every day thousands of animals die in laboratory experiments. Some say these experiments provide essential scientific knowledge, while others will do anything to prevent them.

CHERUB agents James and Lauren Adams are stuck in the middle.

CHERUB: The Fall

When an MI5 operation goes disastrously wrong, James needs all of his skills to get out of Russia alive.

Meanwhile, Lauren is on her first solo mission, trying to uncover a brutal human trafficking operation.

And when James does get home, he finds that his nightmare is just beginning . . .

CHERUB: The Sleepwalker

An airliner explodes over the Atlantic leaving 345 people dead. Crash investigators suspect terrorism, but they're getting nowhere.

A distressed twelve-year-old calls a police hotline and blames his father for the explosion. It could be a breakthrough, but there's no hard evidence and the boy has a history of violence and emotional problems.

Lauren Adams and Jake Parker are sent to investigate, but they hate each other's guts. Meanwhile, James is getting into trouble back on campus . . .

CHERUB: The General

The world's largest urban warfare training compound stands in the desert near Las Vegas. Forty British commandos are being hunted by an entire American battalion.

But their commander has an ace up his sleeve: he plans to smuggle in ten CHERUB agents, and fight the best war game ever.

CHERUB: Brigands M.C.

Every CHERUB agent comes from somewhere. Dante Scott still has nightmares about the death of his family, brutally killed by a biker gang.

When Dante joins James Adams on a mission to infiltrate the Brigands Motorcycle Club, he's ready to use everything he's learned to get revenge on the people who killed his family . . .

Look out for *CHERUB: Shadow Wave*, coming soon from Robert Muchamore and Hodder Children's Books.

And don't miss the rest of the CHERUB series: *The Recruit, Class A, Maximum Security, The Killing, Divine Madness, Man vs Beast, The Fall, Mad Dogs, The Sleepwalker, The General* and *Brigands M.C.*